PRAISE FOR

CHOSEN BY BLOOD

"A gripping tale! In *Chosen by Blood*, Virna DePaul creates the perfect blend of danger, intrigue, and romance. You won't be able to put this book down."

—Brenda Novak, *New York Times* and
USA Today bestselling author

"DePaul's debut novel, *Chosen by Blood*, snap, crackles, and pops with action, adventure, and a heart-pounding romance. She builds an intriguing world populated by fascinating characters. You won't want to miss this one!"

—Karin Tabke, author of *Blood Law*

"Sexy, suspenseful, and very, very smart. I couldn't put it down." —Eileen Rendahl, national bestselling author

CHOSEN BY BLOOD

Virna DePaul

BERKLEY SENSATION, NEW YORK

THE BERKLEY PUBLISHING GROUP
Published by the Penguin Group
Penguin Group (USA) Inc.
375 Hudson Street, New York, New York 10014, USA
Penguin Group (Canada), 90 Eglinton Avenue East, Suite 700, Toronto, Ontario M4P 2Y3, Canada
(a division of Pearson Penguin Canada Inc.)
Penguin Books Ltd., 80 Strand, London WC2R 0RL, England
Penguin Group Ireland, 25 St. Stephen's Green, Dublin 2, Ireland (a division of Penguin Books Ltd.)
Penguin Group (Australia), 250 Camberwell Road, Camberwell, Victoria 3124, Australia
(a division of Pearson Australia Group Pty. Ltd.)
Penguin Books India Pvt. Ltd., 11 Community Centre, Panchsheel Park, New Delhi—110 017, India
Penguin Group (NZ), 67 Apollo Drive, Rosedale, Auckland 0632, New Zealand
(a division of Pearson New Zealand Ltd.)
Penguin Books (South Africa) (Pty.) Ltd., 24 Sturdee Avenue, Rosebank, Johannesburg 2196,
South Africa

Penguin Books Ltd., Registered Offices: 80 Strand, London WC2R 0RL, England

CHOSEN BY BLOOD

A Berkley Sensation Book / published by arrangement with the author

PRINTING HISTORY
Berkley Sensation mass-market edition / May 2011

Copyright © 2011 by Virna DePaul.
Cover art by Tony Mauro.
Cover design by Rita Frangie.
Interior text design by Tiffany Estreicher.

ISBN: 978-0-425-24154-7

BERKLEY® SENSATION
Berkley Sensation Books are published by The Berkley Publishing Group,
a division of Penguin Group (USA) Inc.,
375 Hudson Street, New York, New York 10014.
BERKLEY® SENSATION and the "B" design are trademarks of Penguin Group (USA) Inc.

PRINTED IN THE UNITED STATES OF AMERICA

10 9 8 7 6 5 4 3 2 1

To Craig, Joshua, Ethan, and Zachary,
You have been and always will be my true happy
ending, as well as my beginning and middle, too.
I love you, always and forever.

ACKNOWLEDGMENTS

There's a saying that to be a writer, you might as well open a vein and bleed on the page—that's how personal and often painful the process can be. Such is life. Sometimes, however, no matter how short an acquaintance, a seemingly minor connection can have a major, positive impact on a person's dream. In the best of circumstances, lasting relationships are formed and strengthened.

To everyone who helped me achieve *this* dream (you know who you are), thank you. We struggle together, celebrate together, and even prop each other up and carry one another out of the darkness and into the sun. I think it's made me a better writer and human being.

In particular, I want to thank:

My awesome agent, Holly Root, and my wonderful editor, Leis Pederson, for loving my stories, taking a chance, and making my work shine;

The copy editors, art department, and all the other behind-the-scenes people at the Berkley Publishing Group who helped get this book ready and in stores;

Susan Hatler, for being a wonderful critique partner, as well as a friend willing to e-mail, call, Skype, and fly across several states to stay in touch;

Brenda Novak and The Scarlets, for helping me get started;

Nia and Len Fishler, who, from the moment I saw them together, radiated "recognition";

Lori Wilde, Nina Bruhns, Mary Buckham, Dianna Love,

and the other RWA instructors and writers I've met, for teaching me and cheering me on;

Margo Lipschultz, Matrice Hussey, Kim Whalen, Karin Tabke, Hilary Sares, Lori Foster, Brenda Novak, Larissa Ione, and Eileen Rendahl, for believing in me and spending time/effort on my behalf;

The F5 (Rachelle, Jeannie, Tiffany, and Julia) for walking "the darkness" alongside me and shining bright;

Vanessa Kier, Cyndi Faria, Karin Tabke, Poppy Reiffen, Tawny Weber, Tina Folsom, and Grace Chow, for being my comrades-in-arms, and helping me be a better writer while making the journey a blast;

My friends in BDRWA, SFARWA, SVRWA, Sac Valley Rose, and Calgary RWA for your support; ditto for those at savvyauthors.com and online elsewhere;

My very large family (DePaul; Meyers; my sister, Carol; brothers; nephews; nieces; aunts; cousins; in-laws; and variations thereof) for giving me a safe place in a crazy world to become who I'm meant to be, even if it sometimes confounds you. I love you all;

Cora and Vince DePaul (aka Mom and Dad), for sacrificing more than I wanted you to so your kids could be happy; and

My boys, Craig, Joshua, Ethan, and Zachary, for loving me no matter what.

They will be pulled from the darkness only to be placed in another kind. First, the dark red of blood unites them, a wall of strength against the tide. Then, the blackness of despair weakens them, ripping them apart. Six only shall remain, linked arm in arm. Love and hate. Pleasure and pain. Life and death. Greed and compassion. Blindness and clarity. Strength and weakness. Felt by all but then rejected, until the choice is made.

Only one shall survive.

—FROM THE MAGE'S ANCIENT TEXTS

Dear Readers,

Please sign up for my newsletter at www.virna depaul.com to access free bonus material about the Para-Ops team, including a short story on Wraith's "awakening."

Thank you for your support!
Virna DePaul

PROLOGUE

One downside to being a vampire's best friend was knowing she could read your mind.

Not that Noella ever would, at least not without good reason, but still . . . Something about the way Noella looked at her tonight put Felicia on edge. There was a certain knowledge in her eyes that hinted at questions to come. Questions that Felicia had to avoid at all costs.

Now, as the two of them strolled the perimeter of the grand ballroom's dance floor, Felicia turned to her friend. "Every vamp in the nation must be here," she marveled. "Maybe every vamp in the world."

Noella St. Claire Devereaux laughed and hooked her arm through Felicia's. "Just about. Those well enough to travel, anyway." As they continued to walk, she peered at Felicia from beneath her eyelashes.

"What?" Felicia groaned good-naturedly.

Noella patted her hand. "You've certainly made an effort to greet them all. All except a certain dharmire, that is. Has Knox upset you?"

Felicia stumbled slightly. Inwardly cringing, she stopped walking and forced herself to smile. "Of course not. He's been busy playing host, that's all. With magnificent results. It's been a wonderful party," she said truthfully. The food had been delicious, the grounds beautifully appointed, and the guests charming; the fact that Felicia was miserable was beside the point. "The perfect way to celebrate your ninth wedding anniversary."

After a slight pause during which Felicia held her breath, Noella said, "Acknowledging I've been married that long makes me feel old. It also reminds me how long it's been since I last saw you. You really must try to visit more often, Felicia."

"The Bureau's struggling right now. Federal crime is at an all-time high with the recent insurgents. Every agent is working overtime."

"I don't care. I miss you." Noella pouted. "Don't make me sic Knox on you."

Flushing despite herself, Felicia covered with a mock shudder. "Okay, okay. I'll visit more often. Believe me, I know how ruthless you can be when you want something."

"Dear Goddess, Felicia, whatever do you mean?"

Felicia snorted, both at Noella's innocent act and her invocation of the Earth Goddess Essenia. Many Otherborns had changed religion over the years, but most of them, especially vamps, still worshipped the Goddess. She was thought to be only one of several deities, but she was the most revered because of her allegedly steadfast devotion to all living creatures. "Dear Goddess nothing. Your ability to take down the clan's most sought-after bachelor is rivaled only by your ability to wrap your husband around your finger. Annette Bening could have taken lessons from you when she was courting Warren Beatty."

For a moment, a furrow marred Noella's perfect skin and her mouth twisted ruefully. "Take him down, huh? Sure, it was a piece of cake. It just took a hundred years or so for him to give up his odd notions about soul mates, and I'd already waited almost two decades before even trying to convince him to. He was over three hundred years old when we finally married. That's practically unheard of for a vamp's first marriage, full vampire or not."

"Who knew Knox would play so hard to get?" Felicia said the words lightly, almost tauntingly, knowing that Noella would take the bait and rise to Knox's defense. "He should thank the Goddess Essenia every day that you didn't turn your sights on someone else."

"He wasn't playing hard to get, Felicia. He just views marriage more seriously than most vamps. When Knox loves, he loves fiercely. He couldn't imagine marrying more than once, so he wanted to be sure. Sure he married the woman he could love for eternity."

For eternity, Felicia mentally echoed. Because he needed to marry another immortal. She took Noella's hand. "And he did." Felicia swallowed hard and forced out the words. "You are his soul mate, Noella."

Raising one hand, Noella cupped her cheek. "Sweet Felicia," she whispered, her dark eyes flaring brightly before going blank. "I've never believed in soul mates. Most vampires don't. Knox's romanticism comes from his father's line. I've envied it at times, but I've also cursed it." She shook her head as Felicia's eyes widened. "Please. Don't misunderstand. Knox has made me very happy, and I think the children and I have brought him happiness as well."

"Of course you have," Felicia interjected. "You—"

"But," Noella said firmly, "I know he's never felt truly complete, either. He married me out of duty and, yes, even affection, but I've never been the soul mate he wanted."

Felicia took a shaky breath and struggled for the right words to reassure her friend. Finally, she said, "A person can have more than one soul mate, Noella. Maybe it's just taken Knox time to . . ."

Noella spotted something over Felicia's shoulder. Grinning broadly, she released Felicia, raised her arm, and waved. "Speak of the devil. Knox!"

Felicia had already started to panic with Noella's talk of soul mates, but now that panic magnified tenfold. "I need to get this." Felicia gestured to the sleek communicator hooked to her evening bag.

"But I didn't hear—"

Swiftly moving away from her friend, Felicia called, "I'll catch up with you in a bit. Go dance with your husband."

Moving toward the ballroom's double French doors, Felicia vaguely heard the band start another song. It was a haunting melody, romantic and slow. She couldn't quite place it, but it made her heart ache all the same.

At the doors, she turned just in time to see Knox take Noella in his arms. Her friend was feminine and petite. She looked a little pale and tired, and she was definitely getting thinner, but she was still the perfect foil to Knox's decadent good looks, even down to their matching silver hair. In the corner, Knox's mother, Bianca, and his brother, Zeph, watched the dance, too, matching smiles on their pale, gaunt faces. Felicia couldn't help wincing at the evidence of their decline.

Damn that filthy vaccine, she thought. The U.S. government had made it available to almost every human over eight years ago, before the start of its Second Civil War; almost everyone had taken it, thus changing their blood so it no longer provided vamps the nourishment they needed. Even now, when peace had been declared and the Others were being integrated into society, there was no way to reverse its effects. That meant vamps continued to starve. And suffer.

At least vamp children, Felicia consoled herself, had no need to drink blood until they transitioned at puberty. Noella and Knox's twins, Joelle and Thomas, were flourishing. And thankfully, as a dharmire, Knox had been relatively unaffected. Although he required blood, he didn't need as much of it because of his human DNA, a benefit he'd hopefully pass on to his children. She knew how guilty he felt because of his continuing strength, but his clan was lucky to have—

The music stopped.

Suddenly, Knox looked up and their eyes met. The pull toward him was so immediate that Felicia actually took several steps forward. But then Noella's gaze shifted toward her, making her freeze.

It was definitely time for her to leave.

Unlike Noella, Felicia believed in soul mates. In the notion that certain individuals were two halves of the same whole, one soul divided in two and never completely fulfilled without the other. She was also open to the notion of multiple soul mates, just as she was to the concept of multiple lives. Unfortunately, however, she strongly believed in the sanctity of marriage and that an individual was entitled to claim only one soul mate at a time.

Knox had claimed Felicia's best friend before they'd ever met.

She whirled, only to run right into a broad chest. With a gasp, she took a step back. Bony fingers squeezed her arms in a punishing grip. It was Dante Prime, Zeph's father and, she'd been told, the most recent addition to the Vamp Council.

Felicia couldn't stand him, and the feeling was mutual. That was how she knew Prime's, "Lovely party, isn't it, Felicia?" was meant to draw blood. She, however, simply raised her chin and said, "Yes, it's beautiful."

When she tried to pull away, his grip tightened. "Aren't you going to congratulate me on my appointment to the Council, Felicia?"

Angry, she tore herself out of his grasp, not caring how it might look to others. "Congratulations, Prime. I'm sure Knox will appreciate your advisement on the occasional matter."

As she'd expected, he took immediate insult to her statement. "Advisement?" he sneered. "How dare you? The Council is the equivalent of the humans' judicial and legislative branches. Composed of our most respected elders—"

"Whose decisions can, ultimately, be vetoed by the executive branch, namely Knox or his mother." She feigned confusion. "Or am I wrong? After all, while the Council can pass laws, Knox can strike them at any time. That sounds advisory to me."

"Why you . . ."

Prime's face suffused with blood, but Felicia shook her head. "Don't bother showing me out, Prime."

Leaving him fuming, she strode onto the patio.

Leaning against a stone column, she willed her pulse to calm. She wasn't distraught over the run-in with Prime, she realized, but still feeling the aftereffects of seeing Noella and Knox dance. Each clamoring beat of her heart seemed to call out: No, no, no. No, I want him. No, it's not fair she saw him first. No, it's not fair she can give him what he needs and I never can.

Closing her eyes, she clenched her fists, furious at her weakness.

Taking several determined breaths, she checked her pager, but the Bureau was leaving her alone for once. She forced herself to walk the lush beauty of the Devereaux gardens. High above her, the top of the Dome blended with the night sky, seeming to disappear so all she saw was the twinkling of a thousand stars. Come daylight, it would shield vamps from the harmful rays of the sun. The Dome that Knox had designed and helped build was in many ways reflective of himself—a blend of modern convenience and old-world charm, separate from the rest of the world even as it thrived within it, a bubble where trusted Others and humans alike were allowed to gather in peace and friendship, but only on his terms and when he felt it was safe.

It was a brilliant blend of organic and artificial materials, aesthetically pleasing and functional, from the panels that let in fresh air to the generators that regulated the temperature and amount of light allowed inside.

"Noella wanted me to check on you."

Gasping, she spun around. Even under the artificial lights that lined the garden path, Knox's eyes flickered with heat and vibrancy. While he always dressed well, the black tuxedo emphasized the long, muscular lines of his body. It also highlighted his less-refined features—the sharp angles of his warrior face, flawless but for the small scar above his upper lip à la Harrison Ford. He'd gotten the scar when he was eight, Noella had told her, before he'd had the ability to heal himself. When she imagined licking the scar and the flesh between her thighs clenched, Felicia tried telling herself it was only because she'd always been a Ford fan.

Funny how denial became so much easier with time. She cleared her throat and forced a polite smile. "Why didn't she—"

"Materialize here herself? You *have* been gone a long time, haven't you, Felicia?"

He took her right hand and held it. Just held it. Biting her lip, she told herself to pull away but instead curled her fingers into his. "Is she that ill?"

Knox hesitated. "She's weak due to the limited supply of pure blood, yes, but that's not why she can't teleport. She didn't want to tell you, but she lost that power long ago. After the babies and then the miscarriages—"

Disbelief had her pulling away. "That affects teleportation?" She'd never heard that. All she knew about a vamp's ability to teleport was that it was limited to places he or she had been before. If she'd known Noella couldn't travel so easily, she would have come to see her more often.

Or would she? She'd been avoiding her friend for a reason—the one standing right in front of her.

"Sometimes. In full vampires at least. It's why Noella rarely leaves the Dome. Without the power to transport, our females are even more vulnerable. Add to that a limited food supply . . ."

She briefly closed her eyes, picturing the emaciated frames of the many vampires inside. Damn it, she would not feel guilty. She might be a federal agent, but she hadn't condoned the FBI's actions in formulating the vamp vaccine. Nonetheless, unreasonable guilt prompted her to take his hand again. "The Bureau's working to reverse that. It has been ever since peace was declared."

He smoothed his thumb across her palm and she felt the caress on her nipples. Between her legs. On the nub that was swelling and aching for his touch. With a knowing smile, his touch firmed, making her bite her lip to keep from screaming. "And will it continue to do so," he crooned, "when we're all dead? For the sake of science?"

"Don't say that," she whispered, terror beating out lust. "You're immortal."

"We're only strong immortals when we're able to feed. Right now, many of us are simply existing; eventually our enemies will come after us." Knox's mouth twisted sardonically. "But no one ever said war was pretty. Even after the fighting ends, there are casualties."

"Yes. Life is full of casualties," she said softly. "And even with all the new races we've discovered, even with our common belief in a creator and an afterlife, we've no guarantee there's anything better waiting for us there. Not that any of you are willing to admit anyway . . ."

"Unfortunately, Otherborns don't have a direct connection to the Goddess any more than humans have to their Gods. Only those granted entry into the Otherworld have claimed to see her, but maybe someday . . ." He frowned then shrugged, as if wanting to recall his words.

Felicia understood why. "Yes, maybe someday you'll see her for yourself. While you're still alive, I mean. Again, lucky for you you're immortal. Increases your chances, right?" Her last sentence was meant to be teasing, but her repeated references to his immortality only made her feel foolish. And sad. She tugged at her hand but he refused to let it go. "I have to go," she pleaded, hating her weakness.

"Dance with me." Desire pulsed in the air and his command

radiated hunger, one that beckoned to her and made her dizzy with the need to give in.

Disoriented, she licked her lips. "What?"

"You're going to run again. We won't see you for years. So dance with me."

"No. I don't want—"

He pulled her into his arms, cutting off her words. Their chests and hips pressed together, and almost immediately he began a simple waltz, leading her so she was floating in his arms. The faint scent of mint rose between them and she leaned closer, barely able to stop herself from burying her face in the crook of his neck.

That same haunting melody was playing, and she wondered—

"It's Chopin. Waltz number five."

She gave herself a few seconds to enjoy it. The feel of his arms. His hair tickling her face. It was when she imagined them dancing at their own anniversary celebration that she pulled away.

A few seconds were apparently enough to have her thinking of forever. Don't let him touch you again, she thought. Don't let him destroy the wall you've used to protect your heart all these years.

She'd just started to turn when he touched her arm. "Noella knows how we feel and wants to give us ease."

She froze. "Ease?"

"She knows why I married her, Felicia. She's not angry."

Violently, she jerked away and rounded on him. "No? How about hurt?"

He said nothing for several seconds. "Noella's been free to make her own choices when it comes to bedmates. And she has."

Eyes wide, she gasped. She knew the vamp society had different thoughts on marriage and fidelity, and most married vamps often participated in at least one "mating-pair." Felicia looked toward the ballroom and pictured her friend as she'd been in Knox's arms. She'd looked so happy. So fulfilled. And she'd never said anything to Felicia about—

"I know you don't understand. You're not that type of woman."

Felicia pressed her lips together. What kind of woman was that? The kind to enjoy the pleasure of more than one lover? Or the kind to put the clan's need for increased numbers ahead of love?

Either way, he was right. At least, she hoped so. It just proved how very different they were.

Because while Felicia believed in doing one's duty, Knox took duty to a whole different level.

She knew he loved Noella, but even if he hadn't, even if, for example, he'd fallen in love with a human, his soul mate, *before* his wedding—Felicia's heart constricted at the thought—she suspected he would have married a full vampire like Noella anyway. In doing so, he could proliferate the vampire bloodline, but also distance himself from his own humanity.

But was that all Knox was willing to do? Did he, like Noella, feel a mating-pair was his duty, as well? And if so, just how many pairs were they talking about? Unable to stop herself, she asked, "Have you . . ."

His expression darkened, but he nodded. "In the past, yes. Noella wanted another baby and she was too weak to carry another one to term herself. She was—"

"You have other children?" she interrupted, sounding horrified.

"Of course not," he snapped. "If I had another child, you'd know about it. There were no offspring, and I haven't been with another female in years. But now?" Once more, he moved toward her. "Why shouldn't I—why shouldn't *we*—if she's willing . . ."

"Willing to what?" she exploded, warding him off with a raised hand. "Share you with me? Let us pleasure each other until she's strong enough to give you more children?"

"She loves us both, Felicia."

"And I love her. All the more reason I'd never do something to hurt her. Ever."

"Never say never," he gritted, his eyes blazing furiously. "This isn't about me wanting to fuck just for the sake of fucking. You feel it, too, Felicia. You've always felt it. When we met, it wasn't an introduction, it was recognition. My soul and yours. We belong together."

"If that were true, it wouldn't hurt so much to be around you. You're married—"

"To a female I love, but am not in love with. To a female who knows the difference and does not require my fidelity." In obvious frustration, he shook his head. "Life is more complicated than a human with limited years can ever realize. We're talking about the survival of a whole race. The vamp vaccine is destroying us, especially those with full blood. For some reason, dharmires inherit the strengths without needing the pure human blood that full vampires do. Vampire females have always been more rare, but now males of strength are of limited numbers, too. I can't just ignore that."

For a split second, she felt swayed by his words. By his logic. It was why she'd vowed to lie if Noella ever questioned Felicia about her feelings—fear that Noella would offer something she couldn't refuse. Her heart jumped, urging her to open her arms to him, but she forced herself to remain still. She understood the vamp clan's need to increase its population. She understood why Knox believed he needed to be part of that. But that was his choice, just as it had been his choice to marry Noella and, she supposed, to stay married to her.

She visibly jerked at the thought. Vamps didn't believe in divorce. Even thinking the word in relation to Knox and Noella made her feel guilty. And foolish.

She had a choice, as well, and she prayed she was making the right one. She forced herself to whisper, "I'm not asking you to ignore anything."

"You are," he charged fiercely, "every time you continue to

deny us because I can't pledge you eternal fidelity, any more than I can my wife."

Wife. Wife. The word played in her head, reminding her of who she was and what she expected from herself and others. "There is no us," she said sadly.

"I refuse to accept that."

"You desire me now, but you're right—I have limited years on Earth. I need to live those years honoring what I believe. I don't believe in—in what you're asking me for. Besides," she reasoned desperately, "I'm just a passing fancy. When I'm gone, you'll be glad—"

"No." He growled and pulled her into his arms. She saw the terror that flashed in his eyes. "No." Before she could stop him, his mouth took hers. And it was exactly as she'd feared it would be.

Devastating.

His mouth took but it also gave. It plundered even as it cherished. His tongue rubbed hers, then retreated, mimicking a different dance and causing the music to swell even louder, until it obliterated everything but the moment.

It was heaven. The kind of heaven one only dreams about, especially when her life has been filled with fear and uncertainty and pain. The kind of heaven that a mortal can't have.

She wrenched away and backed up, wiping her hand against her lips.

He was breathing roughly, his expression almost desperate. "You can't run from this forever, Felicia."

Shaking her head, she kept moving. "I won't have to." She tried to smile even though her lips trembled. "When I'm long gone, you'll get to see the peace that time brings. A peace I can only imagine. You and Noella and your family will share that together."

His muttered oath was thick with emotion—denial, regret, determination—but she spun around and ran as fast as she could toward the common area. She moved past several guests, noting that in addition to the sprinkling of humans, there were several werebeasts and werecats present. A mage entertained some children, sparking fireworks that exploded their brilliant colors across the Dome sky, illuminating all the residences protected within it.

She spotted one of the horse-drawn carriages that would take her to the departure area. Knox's car was parked in his garage, but cars were only driven within the Vamp Dome when they were leaving or returning from outside. Sadly, however, most full vampires, who made up 90 percent of the clan's population, were too sick to leave the Dome now.

More than ever, the Dome was fulfilling its intended purpose—protecting those Knox loved. It didn't just shield vamps from the sun or defend them from those who wished them harm. It now provided vampires a safe haven from prying eyes and gave them something even if their bodies wouldn't—dignity. Protecting the clan was the only reason that the Dome had been created. But maybe someday, Felicia thought . . . She turned back to take a final glance at Knox's home and the gardens where she knew he stood.

Someday the rest of the world would go where Knox was trying to lead them.

Someday today would lead to better things.

ONE

Kyle Mahone, director of the FBI's Special Ops Tactical Division, quietly hung up his phone instead of slamming it down the way he wanted to. He'd expected Dex Hunt to be suspicious of the Bureau's job offer. What Other wouldn't be? The rest had certainly proceeded with caution, asking one question after another.

The werebeast, however, had done something the others hadn't.

He'd laughed his ass off.

Swiveling in his chair, Mahone looked out his window, clenching his fists until his knuckles were white. He'd gotten where he was by being smart, working hard, and maintaining his cool. But something about the werebeast's taunting had hit home.

Infuriating. Smart-assed. Cocky SOB. The epithets didn't come close to describing Hunt. Still, he was the best marksman in the nation, human or Other. He was also skilled in the martial art of Karakai, a combination of Karate and crazy-ass gymnastics the Others had come up with. That made Hunt lethal from a distance and in close quarters. Add the fact he could shift into something that would make Freddy Krueger look cuddly and Hunt would be invaluable to the success of Team Red, the FBI's first special ops team to recruit both humans and Others. In addition to Hunt, Mahone had already offered spots to a human, a human psychic, a mage, and last but not least, a wraith.

Wraith, as in ghost. The dearly departed.

A no-longer-living, d-e-a-d person who swore like a trucker, adored ABBA, wore four-inch stilettos, and unlike the other handful of wraiths that were known to exist, refused to take a real name. Instead, she'd sworn to answer only to "Wraith" until she discovered her true identity. Her surly attitude wasn't ideal, but she was a survivor to the extreme—incapable of being killed by any known methods. She also happened to be an expert in ammunitions and explosives.

Twenty years ago, Mahone would have checked himself into an insane asylum before admitting he believed in any of the Others, let alone a wraith. Now the future of the world seemed to rest in their hands.

Wearily, Mahone rubbed his hands over his face. According to the crazy dream he'd had two weeks ago, the fate of the world, or rather the fate of its inhabitants, actually rested more in *his* hands than anyone else's—on his ability to choose the right combination of six individuals, humans and Otherborn, to serve on a *new* type of special ops team—a Para-Ops team.

Talk about pressure.

If it had been up to him, a Para-Ops team would have been formed years before, as soon as the President and all the Otherborn leaders had signed the Humanity Treaty. Instead, the U.S. government had left things up to local law enforcement agencies, which, while usually well intentioned, were simply unable to deal with the lingering prejudice and suspicion that naturally followed half a decade of civil war. Another five years had passed since peace was declared, yet the nation and its citizens were still recovering. Some days, Mahone doubted they'd ever find peace again. For that to occur, he knew the United States people needed help—a team dedicated to ensuring the rights of humans and Others alike, both domestically and internationally.

The dream had obviously been a manifestation of his growing unease and frustration with the President's unwillingness to step up to the plate. But in the end, the dream had also given Mahone the cajones to force the President's hand. Either give him the green light to form the FBI's first Para-Ops team comprised of humans and Others, or accept Mahone's resignation.

Now he had no one to blame but himself if the team turned out to be a disaster. Unfortunately, the call with Hunt wasn't exactly promising and he still had one more offer to make— the position of team leader to a dharmire. And not just any dharmire, but Knox Devereaux, the son of a vampire Queen and an infamous French revolutionist human, Jacques Devereaux.

This morning, Mahone had e-mailed Knox, his message concise: *Teleport to headquarters as soon as possible. Nora will buzz you in.*

Knox's reply had been even more concise. *Three.* For Knox, that was code for, "I'll be there at three o'clock, you bastard, just long enough to make you squirm."

Mahone checked the clock. Less than an hour away. Which meant Mahone needed to focus. It would be foolish to face Knox while he was still distracted by crazy dreams or a smart-ass were. Once again, he replayed the conversation with Hunt, trying to determine the point that annoyance had shifted into more.

Yes, he'd laughed at Mahone's offer, but the werebeast's laughter had barely died down before he'd gone for Mahone's throat. "A team to help both humans and Others, huh? Tell me, Mahone, how many Others do you call friend? How many do you drink a beer with when you're watching a game?"

Mahone's answer had been in his silence, just as Hunt

had obviously expected. Even so, he'd persisted, giving Hunt both the parameters of the team's purpose, as well as a brief description of its first mission. When he was done, Hunt hadn't been laughing, but he hadn't jumped to accept Mahone's invitation, either.

No, he'd said he'd think about it.

Mahone snorted and shook his head.

Think about it. As if they weren't discussing one of the most elite teams in the world. As if riding a motorcycle to nowhere and back was half as important as things like justice or survival, or hell, even revenge.

But it was all bullshit.

Hunt didn't just want revenge, he craved it. What Mahone had proposed would give it to him in spades, complete with a "get out of jail free" card.

The werebeast could think about it all he wanted; in the end, he'd accept just as the others would.

Feeling marginally more settled, Mahone flipped Hunt's file shut and secured it. He swiped his hands over his face. When a spark of memory hit him, however, he froze.

How many Others do you call friend?

The question, virtually identical to the one posed by Hunt, drifted through his mind in a decidedly more feminine voice. Mahone frowned as he connected the voice to his dream.

How many Others do you call friend? The question played over and over, until he finally managed to form an image of the creature that had asked it of him in the dream. A creature he instinctively cringed away from remembering.

But he couldn't help remembering it, either.

Closing his eyes, he recalled how, in his dream, he'd dozed off at his desk. The sky had been dark. The building deserted. Then he'd been blinded by a flash of light and the sudden appearance of a creature at the light's center. A creature he'd never seen before nor ever wanted to see again.

She had hair that was comprised of colors both familiar and

unfamiliar, floating around her in undulating waves, each strand a living, breathing entity.

A face that, instead of eyes, a nose, and a mouth, had hollow, cavernous sockets, bottomless and dark, terrifying and hypnotic, yet so beautiful it had made his own life force try to push itself out of his body to get to her.

A body that, underneath her diaphanous, flowing gown was neither female nor male, but both and so much more than he could understand.

After that first shocked look, he'd turned away from her and that's when she'd asked him, "How many Others do you call friend?" When he'd answered, "None," too scared even to think of lying, she'd told him her intentions and lamented the failure of an ancient prophesy. She'd listened when he'd told her about his idea for Team Red. And then she'd told him to form the team, explaining in shocking detail what would happen if the team failed to serve its purpose. If Mahone failed to deliver what he promised.

When he'd asked her who she was—*what* she was—she'd merely said "a divinity." In other words, she was a goddess. And a pissed-off one at that.

Thank *his* God it had been a dream.

Mahone opened his eyes, disgusted at the feel of sweat trickling down his temple. With a shaky hand, he grabbed a glass of water and chugged it down. Then he heard a voice, no longer in his memory but as if the speaker was standing directly beside him.

It wasn't a dream, Mahone. Thanking your God won't make it so.

You have one year to prove the team can do what you said. One year and not a second more.

Whirling around to scan his empty office, Mahone dropped his glass and the traces of water within it poured out, staining the remaining files on his desk.

He knew instantly he'd been kidding himself. He hadn't

dreamed the creature's visit any more than he'd dreamed the War. Instead, the living nightmare that had become his life was merely intensifying.

Falling back in his chair, he stared blankly at the water pooled on his desk, then slowly cleaned up the mess, stacking his files with precision before straightening his tie and smoothing out his jacket.

Minutes later, two raps on his door made him jump and curse. He knew immediately who was standing outside. He took a deep breath. Then another. The last thing he wanted was more drama, but he simply called, "Enter."

Simultaneously, he prayed, hoping that even though it hadn't been his God who'd visited him two weeks ago, and even though he hadn't prayed to Him in a very long time, God was still there and willing to hear him.

Special Agent Felicia Locke knew the minute she saw the willowy dharmire that there was going to be trouble.

She'd chosen the bar because it was as far from Pennsylvania Avenue and the J. Edgar Hoover Building as one could get and still be in Washington, D.C. With its spray-painted façade, dim lights, and ramshackle assortment of tables and chairs, the Black Hole was also light-years away from what a typical federal agent would consider reputable, let alone palatable. In its favor was the fact it served the best brandy in the state, strong and undiluted. That and some privacy was all Felicia wanted. She'd just locked her car and was walking toward the bar's back entrance when a dharmire, who couldn't have been more than sixteen years old, stumbled around the corner of the building and into view.

Felicia immediately recognized the female as half-Other; although she had a vampire's silver hair and black eyes, her skin was sun-toasted, just a shade lighter than a graham cracker. She clung to the arm of a stocky man with no neck, squinty eyes, and slicked-back hair. The man pushed her against the side of the building and covered her slim body with his own.

Felicia's prediction of trouble formed not because the man was ugly, but because he was unkempt and, considering the foul things he was saying, obviously uncouth.

She'd never met a vamp who'd willingly suffer the company of someone so appallingly unrefined. It would be like asking one to wear jeans or, God forbid, drive a beat-up old truck down a public highway. As a rule, vamps didn't do casual or tacky.

Even so, she tried telling herself that maybe the girl just looked young. There was no accounting for poor taste, after all. But the closer she got, the more apparent it became that the dharmire was under the influence. Her silver pupils were dilated and glassy, and she appeared to cling to the man out of necessity rather than affection.

The man shifted to the side just as Felicia walked within ten feet of them. She saw the fine gold chain and pendant around the dharmire's neck—a smaller, more feminine version of the one Knox wore and an exact replica of the one Noella had worn all her life. The same pendant Felicia's best friend had been wearing on the day she'd died, a gaping hole in her chest where her heart had once been.

Felicia came to an abrupt stop and blinked her eyes several times to make sure she wasn't imagining it. But no, it was real and it was a real bitch of a sign. Noella had died exactly one year ago today and it couldn't be coincidence that, before Felicia even had a chance to get rip-roaring drunk while avoiding Knox at the same time, a female appeared who was from Noella's clan—*Knox's* clan—and in obvious need of help.

Thoughts of Knox assailed her. Had Kyle Mahone gotten in touch with him? She'd been fully briefed on the Bureau's plan to add a new team to the FBI's elite, super-SWAT group referred to as the HRT, Hope Restored Team. She knew that team was the crucial step toward stabilizing relations between humans and the Otherborn races they'd once fought. And despite her preference to stay as separated from Knox as possible, she knew he was the right choice to lead it. Most civilians craved peace now, but it was a constant, often bloody battle given the insurgents, humans and Others alike, that resisted.

On the other hand, Felicia thought, still staring at the man and the dharmire . . . There would always be individuals who just naturally preyed on those weaker than themselves.

Okay, okay. Message received.

No rest for the wicked.

Despite how shaken Mahone still felt, he didn't flinch when Special Agent Leonard Walker threw open his door and stalked into his office. Instead, he leaned back in his chair, crossed his arms over his chest, and waited calmly for the explosion.

He didn't have long to wait.

Even so, compared to an ethereal creature with the power to enter his mind and, oh yeah, the apparent ability to destroy the earth, Walker was hardly a threat.

The man planted himself in front of Mahone's desk, thrusting his face forward as if to compensate for his lack of height. "This is some kind of joke, right?"

It was obviously a hypothetical question. No sooner had Walker asked it than he thumped his fist on Mahone's desk.

"Ten years ago we were hunting these fuckers down, and now we're supposed to fight next to them?"

"Not too long ago," Mahone reminded him, "I wouldn't have been able to sit at the front of the bus with you, Walker. Now you answer to me. Times change."

Walker narrowed his eyes, making Mahone stiffen. Most of the time, Walker was an okay agent; what he excelled at was training exceptional ones. Walker had all the right moves, but only in theory. When it came to applying them in the field, where subtlety or quick thinking was required, Walker became set in his ways. He trained with all the special ops teams, but he wasn't going to train Team Red.

"Don't give me that ACLU, politically correct, we're-all-equal bullshit, Mahone. Regardless of the color of our skin, you and me, we share the same DNA." Walker jerked his thumb toward the office window. "These—these freaks are—are . . ."

Mahone cocked a brow, amused at the blustery man's red-faced loss for words but equally pissed at his lack of restraint. He allowed a hint of steel to edge his voice. "Don't let the fact that we graduated the Academy together make you forget your rank, Walker. Stay civil. And shut my door. Now."

Licking his lips, Walker searched Mahone's face, then quietly shut the door.

"Freaks or not," Mahone said a moment later, "the Others we've selected are half-human and they have special skills that no amount of training can duplicate."

"Our men are the best—"

"No question about that. But being fully human means they have limitations. The Others aren't aliens that just landed on Earth a decade ago. They're citizens. They live among us openly now. Hell, some of their ancestors roamed Earth before we did." He laughed at the irony. "We just didn't know it."

"'Cause they didn't want us to know. 'Cause they needed victims—"

"Victims like Manson's? Ng's? Dahmer's?" Mahone snorted. "Find me a species that hasn't been tainted by bad blood and I'll hand in my resignation right now."

"I'm not going to let you do this."

Mahone's brows lifted at the blatant threat in Walker's voice. Mouthy was one thing. Insubordinate something altogether different. "You might want to reconsider how you—" Mahone began, his voice low.

A commanding knock on the door interrupted him.

Walker spun around as Mahone got slowly to his feet.

Knox Devereaux was early.

Mahone couldn't say how he knew the half-vampire/half-human was standing outside. He just did. Mahone refused to attribute his racing pulse to fear, but it pissed him off anyway.

Mahone had known Knox for over ten years. The dharmire wasn't as overtly hostile as Hunt, but in some ways, his calm, formal mannerisms were twice as unsettling. Probably because anyone with an ounce of intuition could sense the passion boiling just beneath his controlled façade. Mahone had picked Devereaux to lead Team Red because his strategic skill, leadership ability, and calm under pressure couldn't be beat. Yet he knew there was so much more to the vamp. Mahone had seen for himself how dangerous the dharmire could be when his control gave way to blood lust, or straight-out lust—always for one particular woman.

Several more knocks shook the door.

Mahone's gaze found Walker's. "Team Red's a done deal," he snapped, hoping the decision wouldn't turn out to be the biggest mistake of his life. "And if you threaten me again, you'll wonder if we share the same DNA, after all." In a louder voice, he called, "Enter."

The door opened and Knox Devereaux stepped inside. He was, as always, impeccably dressed. Tall and grim-faced, his dark pants, expensive black duster jacket, and polished boots made him look like a *GQ* outlaw.

Yes, indeed, Mahone thought. The times had changed.

The right to life, liberty, and the pursuit of happiness no longer applied just to humans.

Wraiths had the right to vote. A court had just ruled that a mage's right to practice magic was akin to one's right to worship. And vamps, both full vampires and dharmires alike, couldn't be denied health coverage based on "malnourishment" being a preexisting condition.

The Others were demanding their due and making their presence known.

Soon, they'd be protecting some of the same individuals they'd fought just years before.

God bless the U.S. of A.

And just to be safe, the Goddess Essenia bless them all.

He'd done his best. By assembling Team Red, he'd either save the world or damn it. If Team Red failed, they wouldn't know the full ramifications of doing so.

Mahone, on the other hand, would take the knowledge straight to Hell.

Maybe, just maybe, Knox Devereaux could help make sure that didn't happen.

TWO

Walking into Mahone's office, Knox instantly sized up the two men in front of him. Mahone was the only one of importance. The other man—loose jowled with thinning hair and a soft middle straining the buttons of his suit jacket—had "bigot" spelled all over his pinched, disapproving face, but Knox couldn't have cared less. Everything about him—from his hostility to his poor dress—radiated grunt. A bigoted grunt wasn't worth his time. But even so, Knox thought evilly, he couldn't just ignore the man.

That would be rude.

"Am I interrupting?" Knox murmured, his solicitous tone failing to disguise his lack of concern any more than his wrap-around Ray-Bans disguised what he was. The men couldn't see his silver pupils and coal black irises, but Knox's unusual height, deceptively lanky frame, and "prematurely" silver mane would have given him away even if he hadn't been wearing the chain and medallion with his clan's insignia—three inverted triangles, linked together, two on top and one beneath. The two represented a vamp's fangs, while all three symbolized his clan's most enduring principles: strength, honor, and constancy.

Knox had always worn the medallion with pride, long before these humans had learned its meaning. It had helped him endure the years of hiding. Helped ease the sting of cowardice he felt each time he stood alongside his mother, telling his people they had to hide what they were.

Now?

He smiled, deliberately flashing the bigot a good view of his incisors. Without even trying to use his mind-reading powers, Knox knew his name was Leonard Walker.

With a low curse, Walker skirted past him, taking great care to navigate around Knox as if the slightest brush of their clothing would contaminate him. He barely breathed the words, but Knox heard them loud and clear.

"Filthy bastard."

Knox considered letting the man walk past, but frankly, he didn't want to. Within seconds, he had him by the throat. He tsked and leaned in close, close enough that he could smell the man's fear radiating off him. Knox closed his eyes and acknowledged that while he was far from enraged—he felt mildly angry, annoyed really—his actions felt good, like stretching muscles he too often kept bound.

Walker gasped Mahone's name, the sound snapping Knox's eyes open. A quick glance confirmed the director had taken his seat again, a look of mild interest on his face. Knox turned back to the man, lifting him higher until his feet barely touched the ground. "Maybe you don't know my parents were married, Mr. Walker, but I take umbrage at you calling me filthy. Like all vamps, I'm quite particular about my hygiene. Filth isn't something we abide if at all possible."

Any remaining color drained from Walker's face. Knox released him, removed a linen cloth from his jacket pocket, and wiped his hands with insulting deliberation. Walker followed the movements, swallowed, then glared at his boss. "I'll remember this, Mahone," he wheezed.

"Good. Now get the hell out of here."

Walker slammed the door shut behind him while Knox pocketed his handkerchief.

"I'm sure the asshole deserved that, but you know mind-reading is off limits," Mahone said.

Knox stiffened. As if he could forget. As his clan's primary leader during his mother's weakening, Knox had signed the Humanity Treaty and agreed to the UN's corresponding resolution, which was designed to prevent further bloodshed if and when the Others outside the United States chose to reveal themselves fully. Both documents limited a vamp's ability to mind-read or wield the power of persuasion unless "absolutely necessary." He'd signed them because it had been in his clan's best interest. And no matter what someone like Walker thought, vamps were creatures of honor. Knox lived by the rules he set, just like everyone else.

Narrowing his eyes behind his sunglasses, Knox planted his palms on the director's desk, and leaned in close. That this man—this *human*—would dare doubt Knox's integrity after what *he'd* done to Knox's mother was beyond insulting. "And you know," he said softly, "that some information just telegraphs, whether I'm in someone's mind or not. Plus, I've got eyes and ears, and he didn't bother hiding his disdain."

Mahone didn't blink. "There are many who feel the same way."

Straightening, Knox tilted his head and flexed a brow. "Shocking. You mean there are humans that don't like blood-sucking immortals? I suppose my first clue should have been when one shoved a wooden stake into my mother's chest. Didn't kill her, of course, but it sure did piss her off."

That had been over a hundred years ago, when fears of the occult, Charles Darwin, and aliens were challenging man's faith in God and a human-centered universe.

Mahone hesitated. "How *is* your mother?"

Knox almost smiled. Whether the human ever rectified his past mistakes or not, Knox wasn't going to make it any easier for him. "As well as any female who knows her clan is dying and that her government still possesses the means to finish the job."

"The vaccine doesn't kill vamps," Mahone snapped.

"No. It just contaminates what we need to stay alive."

"Your kind don't die—"

"Don't even try," Knox warned. Given the state of his clan, half of them might as well be dead. Since the distribution of that damn vaccine, the vamp clan had been able to find a few immaculates, human donors with clean blood, but they were extremely rare. The rest of the time, his clan drank the blood of animals. That was more acceptable for the clan's limited number of dharmires, whose need for pure blood was diminished, but even they still felt its loss. Knox was nowhere near his optimum strength; he hadn't been for a long time. As for the full vampires in his clan? At best, they were listless. At worst, delirious, bordering on insane.

Not even Mahone knew how bad things had gotten.

"So why am I here?"

Mahone leaned back in his chair and studied Knox intently. "You're here because you want something I might be able to give you."

Knox cocked a brow and smirked at the human his mother had once called "friend." "And what's that?"

"A chance to save your clan."

Felicia took several steps closer to the human and the dharmire. The male finally spotted her and snapped, "What you looking at?"

Felicia pretended to flinch and drop her keys, making him laugh. Stooping down, she watched as the man once more pressed up against the girl and whispered something that made the dharmire giggle. The giggle, however, had an edge of hysteria to it. When the man groped her breast, Felicia couldn't take it any longer. Straightening, she addressed only the female. "Excuse me, miss, but you need to come with me."

"Back off, bitch."

Almost wearily, Felicia smiled tightly. "That's 'Special Agent Bitch' to you, sir. This female's underage and obviously under the influence, which means—"

"She's twenty-five," the man jeered.

Yeah, and Hugh Hefner keeps inviting me to the Playboy Mansion, Felicia thought. "Perhaps you didn't hear me when I said I was a special agent. As in, I'm with the FBI."

The man laughed with obvious disdain. "I heard you." He tauntingly tongued the dharmire's ear, flicking it obscenely even as Felicia's eyes narrowed. The dharmire looked completely out of it. "Did you hear me when I told you to back off? Bitch."

A warning buzzed in Felicia's ear. Even with today's turbulent climate, there weren't many citizens who'd so casually disparage a federal officer. Instinctively, she reached inside her jacket for her weapon. Before she could close her fingers around the butt of the gun, however, someone grabbed her from behind, clamping her arms to her side and cutting off her air.

"Hey, Toby," the man restraining her said, "thanks for keeping her busy while I—"

Felicia slammed the back of her head into her assailant's face and then, spreading her fingers wide, dug them into the vulnerable skin near his groin. With a surprised shriek, the man's arms loosened slightly, enabling Felicia to twist around. With a vicious chop to his neck, she took him down. Smoothly, she spun, pulled her weapon, then pointed it at "Toby," who had just taken a step toward her.

"Uh-uh," Felicia said softly.

He froze.

Crouching, never taking her eyes off Toby, she pat-searched the man on the ground. He was still out cold and would be for a while. Holding up his ID, she memorized his name before returning his wallet to his pocket. Then she rose and smiled tightly. "So, Toby, who is she and where did you find her?" she asked, jerking her head at the dharmire, who was now swaying and blinking owlishly at them.

"She's my girlfriend . . ." he began even as he reached inside his jacket.

Felicia shot a round into Toby's shoulder. He fell back against the wall with a muffled shout. His legs buckled and he slid to the ground. Staring first at the spreading blood on his shoulder, then at Felicia, he exclaimed, "You fucking shot me!"

"You reached inside your jacket," she calmly responded.

"Not for a weapon, you crazy bitch!"

"What then? A Hallmark card?"

He didn't answer.

"Yeah, that's what I thought." Stepping closer, she reached inside his jacket, pulled out a cheap .22 caliber pistol, and tucked it inside her rear waistband, shifting so that Aaron Turner, the man on the ground, could never reach it should he wake. Her eyes flickered disdainfully to Toby's groin and, she was certain, the other diminutive accessory he was packing. "Why am I not surprised? Now, I'll ask you one more time and then I'm going to aim lower. Who is she?"

"I don't know . . ." He screeched when Felicia lowered her sights on his crotch. "No wait! Her name's Mara. I picked her up at the Greyhound Station around the corner. I invited her for a drink."

"Uh-huh. And what'd you pump her up with first?"

"Just—just some ecstasy."

Shit. Drugs didn't affect vamps as badly as they did mages, but a vamp who took one dose of ecstasy would likely be twice as affected as a human. Twice as helpless. "Did you rape her?"

"What? Of course not." The man whimpered when Felicia took a step closer. "I didn't, I swear."

Gently taking the dharmire by the arm while keeping the gun steady, Felicia guided her to her side. "I hope you're not lying. If you are, you'll have to deal with something far scarier than me. This girl is part of the Devereaux clan."

The man paled even more and sweat covered his face in a glossy film. "D—Devereaux?" he whispered. "You mean she belongs to that—to that vamp who fought in the War? The one who—who . . ." He swallowed hard, obviously too scared to continue.

"So you have heard of him. Good. Then I don't have to say anything more, now do I?"

Stepping carefully around Turner, Felicia tugged the girl toward her car. She'd just opened the passenger door when Toby's whine reached her.

"I didn't know she was his."

Felicia paused. She looked down at the young girl beside her and smiled ruefully. "Then that was your first mistake. Because they're all his."

Felicia tucked the dharmire into her Honda Civic and clicked the seat belt into place. The girl closed her eyes, but a few tears escaped anyway. "You know Knox?" she whispered.

"Yeah. I know him." Felicia got behind the wheel and watched Toby stumble into the bar. Swiftly, she used her cell phone to call the local FBI office and gave the field agent on duty her location, as well as the names and descriptions of Toby and his friend. The Black Hole's perimeter was video monitored per federal regulations, so she also instructed the field agent to seize the digital files. When she hung up, Mara opened her eyes and sighed.

"Good," she murmured. "I was afraid he was going to get away."

"On my watch?" Felicia said lightly. "Nah." The girl was obviously more cognizant than she'd let on. She'd likely been playing possum, waiting for a chance to escape. Smart.

"He's going to be pissed at me."

Instinctively, Felicia knew the girl referred to Knox, not Toby or Aaron. "Probably," Felicia agreed. Felicia started the car and pulled out of the parking lot. She stopped for a red light about five blocks away. While she was waiting for it to turn green, the dharmire—Mara—sniffed.

"I just wanted to see what he sees. Goddess, it's not fair that he gets to travel and we don't. We fought for freedom but we're still prisoners."

"You didn't take a bus here, did you?"

She shook her head. "I teleported. I'd been to the Greyhound Station before, a couple of years ago with my parents. I've always wanted to come back, but Knox talked me out of it. Now that I can teleport on my own . . ." Mara shrugged.

Felicia smoothed a hand over the girl's silky hair. Moonlight and morning dew, she thought, just like Noella's. "He's trying to protect you. From people like that man."

"I know. I hate that he's always right."

The girl's head lolled as she seemed to fall asleep. Felicia continued to stroke her hair. She swallowed tightly as she thought of Knox; as always, desire and affection were what she felt first, followed swiftly by guilt. She'd never be able to have one without the other.

"Not always," Felicia whispered. "But enough to be damn annoying."

When the light turned green, she drove through the intersection, then pulled over to text her boss. Kyle was likely with Knox at this very moment. After they talked, Knox would want to see Dr. Barker's lab notes himself. Then he'd teleport back to the Dome. Who knew? Maybe Mara would be home before Knox found out she was missing.

Felicia gave Mahone a rundown on what had happened, including the fact she'd fired her weapon. Even with the videotapes, the paperwork would be a pain and she imagined going back, making good on her threat to shoot Mara's "friend" in the balls. But her priority was getting Mara safely home. Whether she chose to tell Knox all the details was her decision. Felicia certainly wasn't going to narc her out.

Not when she was so committed to avoiding Knox herself.

* * *

Several hours had passed since Mahone had rocked Knox's world. In that time, Knox had read all the files Mahone had given him. Now, he stared at the man he grudgingly respected but certainly didn't trust.

Regardless of whether Mahone was telling the truth, Knox had no choice but to agree to his offer. He'd do anything to save his dying clan, and that included leading a team of half-Otherborn. The team's first mission?

Recover the antidote for the synthetic virus that rendered human blood incapable of nourishing vamps. The very virus the FBI had created and distributed just before the beginning of the War.

Talk about ironic.

The real kicker was that the existence of the antidote was presumed, but not confirmed. With more questions than answers, Mahone's so-called Team Red would have its work cut out for them.

Even so, for the first time in a long time, Knox felt hope.

It was a hope he tried to temper, as well as disguise with genuine skepticism. "What guarantee do I have that this antidote really exists?"

"None. You already knew our scientists, like yours, were searching for an antidote. Now you know exactly what I do. The project leader, Dr. Neil Barker, was murdered two weeks ago. A week before his death, Dr. Barker thought they were close. He'd developed a formula that appeared to reverse the effects of the vamp vaccine after it was injected into lab rats and cadavers, or mixed with human blood samples. Before he could be sure, he wanted to move to the next step—testing the formula on a live human being."

"Why?"

"In part to determine its viability—they'd come close before, only to have the antidotal effects fade within a few days—and in part to track whether it had any dangerous side effects, both for humans and for the vamps who would be feeding from them."

"Did you give him permission?"

"I wanted more data on the residual effects exhibited by his existing test subjects. Dr. Barker didn't say so, but I sensed he was holding back. Whether it was impatience or something else, I felt he was making the switch to human testing too quickly. After he was murdered, his autopsy revealed his blood was clean of the vamp vaccine. The other five scientists on his team are clean as well. The most logical presumption is that they were all injected. Obviously the antidote worked and none of them seem to be the worse for wear because of it. Now none of them are talking. We have no proof of any wrongdoing on their part, so why would they? They all stand to be millionaires once they sell the formula to the highest bidder."

"If your scientists gave up that vaccine, something more important than money is at stake. If it were just that, given the methods I'm sure you're using to make them talk, one of them would have caved by now."

Mahone met his gaze steadily, revealing neither agreement nor guilt.

Knox pushed his fingers through his hair and began to pace, then froze. Anyone who knew him well knew he paced when he was troubled. Sometimes it was easy to slip into old patterns and let his guard down around Mahone, especially when it seemed Mahone was doing him a great favor by telling him about the antidote. He had to remember that Mahone's loyalty was and always would be to the U.S. of A., and that what looked like a favor was always going to come with strings. "Since you're obviously not thinking clearly, how about I run through the possibilities?"

Mahone flushed when Knox's less-than-subtle jab hit home. "Fine."

"Even if Barker decided to test the antidote on humans before he could be sure of the side effects, why would he risk all the scientists? Have you considered that the vaccine reversed itself? Maybe because of something the scientists were exposed to as a group?"

"Bureau employees are tested regularly, often by Dr. Barker himself. Again, it's a way to track the viability of the vaccine in the human population. Just recently, results showed the effects of the vaccine are holding. If there was any chance of the vaccine reversing itself, we'd know about it."

"But are you absolutely positive all of them were inoculated to begin with? It would be easy for Dr. Barker to forge blood work results—"

"Why would he? Dr. Barker worked for the Bureau before I came on. He helped develop the vaccine, for God's sake." Mahone leaned back in his chair and crossed his arms over his chest. "He took it, just like all Bureau employees were required to. He made sure his scientists not only took it but agreed with the cause before they began working on the antidote."

"What about guards? All human, I presume."

"You presume wrong."

Knox's brow lifted. "Others?"

"A few. Just because we haven't had Others on any of our teams before now doesn't mean we haven't been trying to integrate them. Most of them are in administration, but we've had a vamp, even a mage and a werecat, on our security detail."

"A vamp from my clan?" Knox challenged, knowing it wasn't the case. If one of his clan had been working for Mahone, he'd have known about it.

"No. We've pulled from a few of our international stations. Others we felt wouldn't be tainted by wartime experiences."

Knox smirked. "You mean Others who still live in the shadows. Who still abide by the 'don't ask, don't tell' principle. Smart of you, though a little hypocritical, considering it was your people that found us and persuaded us to 'out' ourselves in the first place."

"It didn't work out the way any of us had hoped. So what other possibilities are you thinking, other than the scientists being cured without their knowledge?"

Wanting to confront Mahone on his "didn't work out" understatement, Knox nonetheless let the remark go. "Failing spontaneous reversal, the most likely scenario is the antidote was administered to Dr. Barker and the five other scientists. But did they take the antidote voluntarily or did one of them, or even someone else, force it upon them all? If so, why aren't at least some of them talking?"

And how, Knox thought, could he be sure they weren't? He studied Mahone, then decided the phrase "absolute necessity" applied at the moment. Swiftly and skillfully, he reached out, prodding Mahone's thoughts, specifically focusing on whether Mahone was telling the truth about the antidote and the scientists.

What he discovered made his knees weak.

Mahone was telling the truth.

Mahone believed the antidote existed. He believed it had been forcibly taken from Dr. Barker and he wanted Team Red to get it back, not only to ingratiate himself to Knox, but to save Knox's clan, including the vampire he loved.

Bianca Devereaux, Knox's mother.

Knox pulled back and stared at Mahone. It appeared he could trust the human after all, at least with this. However, that didn't mean Mahone's superiors didn't have a different agenda or that they were telling him the whole truth concerning the scientists.

"Greed comes in many forms, Mahone. If the scientists are culpable, how can we know they sold the antidote as opposed to destroyed it? Maybe they simply wanted to prevent vamps from getting our hands on the cure."

Mahone snorted. "One hidden extremist in the group, maybe. But as you just pointed out, all five? No. Either they're all guilty of selling the antidote or . . ." Mahone frowned.

"Or they're all innocent," Knox murmured. "You know that's a possibility," Knox urged, tapping the background files Mahone had given him earlier. "Each of them was handpicked and cleared for high-security work. All of them had an established history with the Bureau, some of them having worked on projects that would make finding an antidote child's play by comparison. If they'd wanted to get rich by selling government secrets, they've had that opportunity many times in the past."

Something like unease flickered across Mahone's face.

"Let me read their minds," Knox pressed. "I can—"

"I've already suggested that. Unfortunately, as you've just pointed out, getting into their minds would give you access to a hell of a lot more than their guilt or innocence in this matter. The President feels a little uneasy about that."

"Where are the scientists?"

"Someplace secure. Someplace I don't even know about." He raised his brows at Knox's silence. "If you'd like to read my mind again, you'll see I'm telling the truth about that, too."

"Am I supposed to feel guilty? Don't worry," Knox countered. "I didn't probe too deep. As far as a vamp's mother is concerned, there are some things a son just doesn't want to see."

Mahone scowled darkly, but Knox kept on talking. "What else is on the table?" he asked.

Mahone's eyes rounded with feigned disbelief. "You mean the antidote itself isn't enough? Is this the same selfless vamp leader I've heard so much about, willing to prove his loyalty to his clan at all costs despite the human DNA that sullies him?"

Gritting his teeth, Knox ignored the bait Mahone was throwing out. He couldn't, however, dismiss the guilt and uncertainty that prodded him. Mahone's comment wasn't only an insult, it was one tinged with knowledge—of Knox's father and his execution, and of Knox's feelings for Felicia and what kept them apart. Still, did Mahone know what Knox was contemplating next?

As Knox had predicted, his recent trip to France hadn't done a thing to lessen his desire for Felicia. In fact, it had strengthened his determination to have her. At the same time, however, he couldn't deny that the Vamp Council's recommendation for a new mate was a good one.

He'd grieved Noella's death tremendously but he couldn't deny it had given him a brief feeling of freedom—freedom to be with Felicia. It hadn't lasted long. No matter Mahone's disdain, Knox *was* duty bound to consider his clan's best interests and marrying a human was not in it.

Unlike Noella, Michelle Burgeon wasn't of royal lineage, but her family had tremendous influence where foreign vamps were concerned. Marrying her would unite Knox's clan and those abroad, creating a bridge of solidarity that could only benefit them all. As much as he had to accept that, however, his trip had served other purposes. First, he'd had to make sure that Michelle would be a loving mother to his children. Second, he'd had to be clear with her about Felicia.

He'd do his duty, yes, but this time, however, he wasn't willing to give up everything for his clan. Not when he could care for them and have Felicia, too.

Michelle had freely agreed to marry him knowing that he loved Felicia and would only stray from her for purposes of getting Michelle with child. Still, Knox hadn't promised her anything. He couldn't agree to marry Michelle or any vampire until he'd had more time with Felicia. More time to convince her that their love could transcend race and human morality. More time to convince her they belonged together no matter what his duty demanded of him.

He still wasn't sure how he was going to do that, but Mahone could give him the opportunity to try.

With a start, he realized that Mahone was staring at him. Swiftly, he said, "Duty is one thing, Mahone, but I'm not discounting the fact that the antidote you're dangling in front of me might not even exist. Even if it does, it may not be safe for humans or vamps to take. Then what good will it do me? I'm going to need more than a potential cure to do what you're asking."

"Fair enough," Mahone retorted. "How about a half-million dollars then?"

"How about a million?" Knox countered.

"That would require additional authorization. Is that what you're asking for?"

"To start with."

"Don't get too greedy now. We want you on the team, but we certainly don't need you."

"I think you do. Otherwise I wouldn't be here."

"That still doesn't—" A series of tinny beeps interrupted him. Mahone frowned and retrieved his phone from his pocket. "Excuse me." He stared at his phone screen. Frowned. Looked up at Knox. "Are you familiar with a dharmire named Mara?"

Knox jerked in surprise. "Mara Jacobs. Why?"

"Because she's in D.C. Not too long ago, she ran into some trouble." Mahone quickly held up a hand. "She's fine. She's with Felicia."

Knox took a deep breath, willing his taut muscles to relax. "Felicia?"

"She says the vamp will be back at the Dome before morning."

"Tell Felicia to bring her to me."

Mahone smiled. "Her message said to tell you she's not going to."

Annoyance came first. Then Knox smiled, too.

"Oh, and one other thing," Mahone said, his widening grin obviously forming at Knox's expense.

"What?" Knox asked cautiously.

"She said to cut the girl some slack and remember you were sixteen once." Mahone laughed and shook his head. "Damn, the woman's got balls. You gotta love her, huh?" Almost immediately, Mahone winced.

Knox nodded. "Yes. Gotta love her. Which, by the way, brings us back to our conversation."

Understanding sparked in Mahone's eyes. "So you'll lead the team?"

"I'll lead the team," Knox confirmed. "For the antidote. For one million dollars. And for Felicia. None of which are negotiable."

THREE

VAMP DOME
PORTLAND, OREGON

The next day, Knox hesitated outside his mother's bedroom door just as a feminine laugh drifted through the smoothly polished wood. A wave of relief coursed through him, so intense he actually had to flatten one palm against the door to steady himself. He and the children had been in France for only a few days. When they'd returned, his mother had been too ill for visitors, so he'd left to meet with Mahone before he'd had a chance to see her.

It appeared his mother was feeling better. Perhaps she'd been given an infusion of pure blood or perhaps she'd simply fought off the weakness herself. Whatever had happened, Bianca Devereaux was laughing for the first time in a very long time.

Knox closed his eyes. Three hundred years ago, his mother had been vibrant and healthy, with long silver hair that sparkled more than the most precious of jewels and pale skin reminiscent of rose-infused cream. She'd looked exactly like the Queen she was—elegant, ethereal, almost too beautiful to be real—a royal vampiress whose pure blood was reflected in her regal posture, tall, slim lines, and symmetrical features. Back then, Knox had been too young to recognize the innate sensuality that had drawn men to her like flies, but she'd been fierce in her affection, in the way she'd taught him right from wrong, and in her devotion to her clan. She'd been strong, so much stronger than most female vampires once they had children, Noella included. That had started to change after Knox's father had died.

Or to be more precise, his mother had changed, right after Knox's human father had been executed for treason by order of the High Vamp Council. Given the circumstances, the vampire Queen's attempts to overrule the Council's order had been ignored.

Straightening, Knox tapped on his mother's door. When it opened, he almost winced. He'd let himself dream because of one soft laugh. Looking at her now, there was no denying his mother barely resembled the strong vampiress she'd been at the beginning of the French Revolution.

It wasn't simply that she'd physically aged when, as an immortal, she should have looked exactly as she had when Knox had been born. It wasn't even the fact that grief had creased a perpetual furrow between her brows or that the hair that had once been smooth and shiny was now dull and clipped close to her head.

No, his mother's decline was most evident in her grayish pallor and the sunken hollows of her cheeks. Beneath her nightdress, her limbs were frail, sleek muscle having long given way to sagging skin and protruding bone. Her eyes glimmered so feverishly that for a moment he feared for her sanity, but then she raised a trembling hand to his cheek. "Son. I'm glad you're home."

Knox quickly clasped his mother's hand, kissed it, then cradled it against his face. As relieved as he'd been to hear her laugh, he was twice as relieved to hear her voice, soft and steady, cognizant of who he was.

With a small smile, she dropped her hand and motioned him

inside the luxurious sitting room that adjoined her bedroom. Sinking onto a chaise covered in a creamy damask silk, she patted the cushion beside her. When he sat, he saw the photos and memorabilia scattered on the small coffee table. He wondered what had produced the laugh he'd heard. Wrapping her hands around one of his arms, she nestled her head on his shoulder. "So how are my grandchildren faring? Did Michelle and her family spoil them rotten?"

"You mean you don't know already?" Knox teased, already aware his mother would never take liberties, even if she could, by reading his mind without permission. Long ago, the vamps in his clan had discovered a way to prevent other vamps from exercising their powers over one another; it wasn't so much suspicion that had motivated the invention as much as a common need to feel secure in one's own skin. Walking around thinking that anyone could read your mind or make you do things against your will didn't exactly promote feelings of security. In that way, Knox understood why most humans feared them.

To his surprise, his mother's eyes flickered with pain and skittered away at his joke, but not before Knox saw the truth in them. He sucked in a breath. "You can't . . ."

Once more meeting his gaze, she shook her head, confirming that in just a few days, she'd indeed lost her power to read minds. "How . . ."

"A friend offered her permission for me to try and—and I couldn't."

Pity came first. "Mother, I'm sorry." Although she'd long ago lost the ability to teleport, reading minds was one of the first skills a vamp developed. That she'd lost that power must be humiliating. Gently, he squeezed her hand.

Anger swiftly followed. "Damn them," Knox growled. When his mother moved away, he stood and paced in front of her while raking his hands through his hair. "Damn them all for creating that filthy vaccine."

"They were scared, Knox. They didn't know—"

"They knew," he roared, immediately feeling ashamed when she winced. Bending on one knee in front of her, he took her hands in his. "They knew, Mother," he said quietly. "Their whole purpose in creating the vaccine was to eliminate our food supply, which would naturally eliminate us—our strength, and thus any threat we posed."

"They did what they thought they needed to do to protect themselves. Kyle—the FBI—has committed significant resources to finding a cure."

"That doesn't mean they'll succeed." Knox sighed and straightened. He'd have to tell her about the antidote and his agreement with Mahone at some point, but he had to take care. He didn't want to raise her hopes for a cure—both for herself and Zeph, as well as the clan she loved—until he knew more. "Mother, yesterday I met with—" His words came to an abrupt stop when he saw the caramels on the cherry side table. He stiffened, walked toward the table, and picked up the small box.

Felicia had been here.

In disbelief, he turned to his mother, who raised her chin defiantly.

"She came the day after you left for France," she said softly.

Picking up one of the candies, Knox shook his head. She'd been in this very room, yet he hadn't sensed her. Hadn't smelled her. Perhaps his own powers were dwindling faster than he'd thought. "How did she get inside the Dome without my approval?"

His mother lifted an imperious brow. "You may rule it, Knox, but only with my permission. I am still the Queen of this clan. I'm allowed to have visitors."

"You're allowed to, yes," Knox gritted. "I'm quite aware that it's only because of my strength that I rule."

"You rule because you carry royal blood. Because you are my eldest heir, a descendent of the first vampires to walk the earth. You rule because of your inner strength as well as your physical strength."

"But it's the physical strength that makes the clan tolerate my rule, even if that strength is a result of sharing the blood of a traitor."

His mother gasped, but at which part of his statement he wasn't sure. Holding up a hand to forestall her protest, Knox carefully replaced the box, but pocketed the single piece of candy. "But that doesn't explain why you'd keep news of her visit from me."

"You were gone."

"Which is the only reason she came."

His mother's gaze remained steady on his, but only for a few seconds. She looked away. "She asked me not to tell you."

His lips flattened. His anger was swift and automatic. Before he could stop himself, he said, "And of course, your loyalty lies with her, a human, rather than with me?"

His mother's eyes rounded with hurt before they narrowed. She pointed toward her door. Both of them pretended not to see her arm shaking with the effort to hold it up. "Don't forget you're half-human, too. And if you're going to accuse me of disloyalty, you can—"

"I'm sorry," Knox interrupted, gritting his teeth in frustration. "I didn't mean—I wasn't referring to the past or to—to *him*. But I don't understand why you wouldn't tell me. I could have been here before she left."

The anger in his mother's face softened. "And that's why I didn't tell you. She deserves a fighting chance against you."

Stunned, he stepped back. "You make it sound like I want to hurt her," Knox growled.

"What you are, what she can never be, will hurt her." A distant look swept over her as she stared at something on the coffee table. Reaching out, she picked up a dried rose carefully preserved between two small squares of glass. "Trust me on this," she said softly. "I know."

"Don't compare Felicia to him," he warned.

"Why not? Your father was human, Knox."

"Meaning?"

"Meaning, you're hoping to marry Michelle Burgeon and have Felicia, too."

"It's the way of vampires. We don't swear an oath of fidelity upon marrying."

"But it's not the way of humans. It's not Felicia's way. Your father—although it was hard for him—he was able to share me for a time with Zeph's father. Felicia isn't willing to do the same. Why do you think things will end any better for you than they did for me? Why won't you accept that a relationship with Felicia will hurt you, and thus hurt the clan?"

"There's no reason we can't be together," Knox insisted stubbornly. "She's stubborn. She's idealistic. But she's not a traitor."

For an instant, his mother's eyes flashed red, startling him. "Neither was your father," she said fiercely, "no matter what the Council thought."

"It's what everyone thought," Knox pointed out. "Quite rightly, since he confessed."

As fast as his mother's temper ignited, it left just as quickly. She actually cowered away from him, making him curse. "I'm sorry," he said stiffly, "but I believed him. I still do."

"I know," she whispered, her voice clipped now. She set the rose down and folded her hands in her lap. "And I'm sure he forgave you anyway."

Knox sighed wearily. How often had they had this argument? How often had his mother protested his father's innocence despite all the damning evidence to the contrary? "I don't want to argue with you, Mother."

"Then let's not. Argue, that is." She closed her eyes and tilted her head back on the chaise. Several seconds ticked by and Knox wondered if she'd fallen asleep.

"Mother . . ."

Wearily, she raised her head. Then she patted the cushion again and forced herself to smile. "Tell me about your visit and then you can tell me what evil plan you've cooked up for Felicia."

Wary now, Knox cocked a brow and sat beside her. "What makes you think there's an evil plan? I only want to do my duty and have Felicia, too."

His mother—his elegant, refined, royal mother—actually snorted. "I don't have to read your mind to read you, Knox. I've known it was only a matter of time before you went after Felicia with full force. You are, after all, your father's son, capable of deep and committed love. I only regret that so much responsibility has been placed upon you. Not only the need to rule in my stead, but the belief you must have yet more children with a vampire in order to prove your allegiance to the clan."

Knox frowned. "My need to mate with a vampire is fact, not belief. Our numbers are dwindling—"

"And stopping that must fall on you? Even given your other responsibilities?"

"I—If I can help, I must. Felicia will come to accept that."

"And she might suffer even more as a result."

Knox struggled against another twinge of guilt. Of course he didn't want Felicia to suffer. But what else could he do? Even when he'd been married to a vampire he'd thought he could fall in love with, Knox hadn't been able to stop wanting Felicia. He needed her. And now that Noella was gone, he was going to have her. Like it or not, he, like his mother, had fallen in love with a human.

But, he told himself, there the similarity would end.

Knox would cherish and protect Felicia as long as she lived, but Knox wouldn't marry her the way his mother had married his father. Nor would he allow his love for her to endanger his clan or take precedence over his duty as its leader. He was a member of an immortal race, one that had never been hampered with conservative notions about sex. To vamps, marriages built on fidelity—even love, for that matter—were a luxury. He couldn't afford to cater to Felicia's softer sensibilities. He was no longer married, but he still had a duty to ensure that his clan proliferated, now more than ever. Understandably, it was for those reasons that Felicia continued to deny him. Fair or not, he was willing to do everything short of coercion or force to change her mind. He was counting on his deal with Mahone to up the ante.

Knox stood. "If you'll excuse me, Mother, I have an important appointment that starts shortly. I need to—"

"What will you do when you're forced to choose between your love and your duty?"

Refusing to believe such a possibility existed, Knox shook his head. "There's no reason I'll have to choose—"

"What *if*, Knox?"

"Felicia isn't a traitor. She would never betray any of us. But," he emphasized, "if at any point she poses a threat to this clan, I'll do what I have to do to protect it."

"Does that include killing her?"

He didn't flinch. "Yes," he said, meaning it, although the only reason he even contemplated such an absurd thought was because his faith in Felicia was unwavering.

Still, as he stared at the first rose his father had given his mother, Knox tried to imagine being put in the position his mother was suggesting.

Could he kill Felicia if it meant saving his clan? Maybe. But even though he'd spent the last decade with only snatches of time with her, none of them more intimate than a brief dance and one stolen kiss, thoughts of her had kept him going during the worst moments of the War. It was as if the mere knowledge of her existence, coupled with his determination to be with her one day, was as important to him as breathing. If he killed her, he'd be giving himself a death sentence.

He would die without her.

"Please tell the children I'd enjoy seeing them today."

Knox shook himself from thoughts of betrayal and killing, and kissed his mother's cheek. "I will, Mother, just as soon as I see them."

* * *

An hour later, Knox watched Mara Jacobs's parents lead the young dharmire out of his office. If he'd known the identity of the human who'd shot her full of drugs, he'd have hunted him down and killed him. Fortunately or not, he didn't, but at least Felicia had pumped a bullet into the bastard. That was some small consolation.

"You were a little harsh with her, don't you think?"

Stiffening, Knox turned toward his younger brother, Zeph, who was in the same stance he'd adopted since Mara had first entered the room. Arms crossed over his chest, he leaned against a bookshelf, glowering at him.

"You'd rather I'd held back and risk her doing something foolish again?"

"She's young. Curious. She doesn't like being confined to this Dome any more than the rest of us."

"'This Dome' provides us protection. I'm fortunate that with a simple application of sunblock, dharmires can withstand the sun. This Dome enables full vampires to be active during the day. It's not a prison, it's a haven. And Mara will have plenty of time to explore when she's older and more knowledgeable about how things are."

"And how are things, besides screwed up? This Dome isn't keeping us from growing weaker with every day that passes . . ." Several harsh coughs racked Zeph's body, clearly taking their toll. He closed his eyes for several seconds, and the dark circles beneath them had Knox's pulse hammering out of control.

"You should be resting," he snapped. The product of Bianca's only mating-union, something commonly expected of vamp females—single, married, or widowed—due to the vamp clan's low attrition rate, Zeph was just ten years younger than Knox. Because he was a full vampire, however, the effects of the vamp vaccine had hit him hard, while Knox's dharmire status had mostly protected him thus far. Compared to the elders in their clan, like his mother, Zeph's youth had delayed the effects of malnourishment somewhat. However, the speed of his decline in the past month wasn't encouraging.

Zeph slowly opened his eyes. "All I ever do is rest. I'm tired of resting. I'm tired period."

"Meaning what?"

His brother said nothing.

Knox growled, "Damn it, Zeph—"

"Oh, relax," Zeph grumbled. "I'm not going to try and kill myself or anything stupid like that. If Mother can bear it, then so can I."

Although he was relieved his brother didn't have thoughts of suicide in mind, helpless fury made Knox's limbs tremble. Once more, he thought how twisted Fate was. His mother and half brother were full vampires, with the blood of their powerful ancestors running through their veins, and yet Knox, who only carried half that blood, was virtually immune to the weakness that was slowly destroying them. "Have you visited her today? I know she'd love to see you."

"Not today. Truthfully, I've been avoiding her. We've been butting heads and I don't want to contribute to her feeling any worse than she does. Although I'm beginning to think she's feeling more like herself. Arrogant and stubborn, just like you."

Knox snorted. "As opposed to you being what? Your father isn't exactly the most humble vamp I've ever met." That was putting it mildly. Dante Prime was an arrogant vamp whose arrogance had simply magnified after Bianca had chosen him for a mating-pair. The fact that he'd cared more for the honor of being chosen than for Bianca herself or the son they'd produced had been more than obvious to everyone—including Zeph.

That was why, when his brother smiled, there was a trace of bitterness to it. "Good point and one my father would be quite pleased to hear. As a member of the Vamp Council, the last thing my father wants is to appear humble. The Council's diminished capacity is humiliating enough as far as he's concerned."

"What do you mean, diminished capacity?" Knox said with a frown. "The Council serves an important role in our society. It always has."

"The Council advised against a treaty with the humans, you ignored them. They can pass laws, but you can strike them. So be honest, Knox, the Council's role is more advisory than anything else."

Knox studied his brother. He'd heard rumors of unrest and plans to up the Council's authority. To impose more limits on the vamp ruler's ability to override its decisions. Up to now, however, they'd only been rumors. "Advisors they may be, but my mother and I hold them in great esteem. We respect their opinions, even though we may not ultimately agree with them. Do you—or your father—have a problem with that, Zeph? Is there something I should know?"

For a tense moment, Zeph merely stared at him. Then he shrugged. "The only problem my father and I have is with each other, but that's nothing new, now is it?"

Knox hesitated, studying his brother closely. Then, sensing no malice from him, Knox said, "Your father is a difficult man, Zeph, but he cares for you, just as he cares for our clan. You and I may not always agree with his methods, but he's never given me reason to doubt his loyalty. If he's unhappy with his position on the Council—"

"I told you he's not. And can we please not talk about my parental issues? I'm feeling sick enough as it is."

Knox sighed but let the matter drop. "Fine. If you don't want to talk about your parental issues, can we talk about mine? Because, well, Mother and I have been going round about several issues, as well."

With rounded eyes, his brother raised a hand to his chest. "No. You? Mr.-Duty-and-Honor-Above-All-Else? What could she possibly find at fault with you? Other than your hard-on for a human, of course."

"Don't go there, Zeph," Knox said, his voice flat. He couldn't stand for anyone disrespecting Felicia with such talk, even his own brother, and reducing his feelings for Felicia to a bodily reaction was disrespectful to them both. "While I may seem a bit rigid when it comes to duty"—Knox gritted his teeth at Zeph's combo snort and eye roll—"it's because I've had to work twice as hard as the rest of you to earn the clan's trust and respect. I'm well aware that if it weren't for Mother's failing health and my continuing strength, I would never have been allowed to lead."

"True. It wasn't as if the clan took your heroism, superior strategic skills, and your ability to kick ass into account." Zeph scowled. "Get over it, Knox. You more than earned the clan's trust during the War."

"And lost much of it just as easily when I signed the Treaty with the humans. Your father never fails to remind me of that, Zeph, and he's made his opinion of Felicia quite clear."

"Ahhh, that's right. He thinks you're better off with someone else. So how'd it go? The first meet-and-greet with your intended fiancée. I can't believe I haven't asked yet." Zeph turned away, his shoulders rigid with what Knox suspected was the effort to keep himself upright. "What did you think of the beautiful Michelle Burgeon?"

"She's beautiful, certainly. And willing."

"Willing to take second place to Felicia?"

The sudden intensity in Zeph's voice made Knox hesitate. "I explained the situation and she agrees that a union between our families and the production of a child is sufficient cause to marry."

"Then congratulations. I hope Felicia has grown more open-minded in the past year." Zeph coughed several times and winced as he turned to face Knox. "You know, you may be right about my needing to rest."

"I'll help you—"

Zeph glared at him. "The day I need you to help me to bed is the day I hire someone to cut out my heart."

Knox froze. "Fine." He watched his brother's slow exit, then turned toward the east side of the residence. Remembering his mother's request, he headed toward the children's wing, which entailed taking a series of winding corridors. Along the way, he thought of Kyle Mahone and the woman who continued to affect his life despite her valiant efforts to stay as far away from him as possible.

Had Mahone told Felicia about Knox's demands?

If he had, how would he deal with her refusal?

Because Knox didn't doubt for a second that Felicia's initial response would be refusal.

He heard the children before he saw them. They were having their afternoon history lesson with Serena, their tutor. Stopping in the doorway, he watched the twins, who sat properly erect in their little wooden chairs but for their swinging feet. They took turns making faces at each other while trying to pretend they were listening to their teacher.

"Your French isn't any better than it was before you visited France, *chérie*. Tell me, Joelle, what were you doing the whole time in France that you didn't have time to study the language?"

Knox frowned at the critically phrased question. Joelle had been doing exactly what Knox had encouraged her to do. Playing with her cousins. Having fun. Running around the gated estate in a country where vamps still hid who they were and, for now it seemed, led better lives for their silence. At least, dharmires did. But Knox knew the "don't ask, don't tell" European policy he'd mentioned to Mahone couldn't be sustained for long. The vamp vaccine had been widely distributed overseas, forcing Europe's full vamps more and more into the shadows. That meant, whether they hid their true natures or not, they were practically on the verge of extinction. Moreover, although the rest of the world, when pressed, acknowledged the existence of Others within America's borders, it refused to recognize them within their own. Most countries had even enacted certain visa restrictions that would, in effect, if not in express language, limit the right of any recognizable Others to cross into their land.

Thomas came to his sister's rescue. "Madam Serena, I'm a little confused."

"About what, Thomas?"

"Mademoiselle Burgeon seemed to be very fond of Papa, but he'd never met her before. How can that be?"

A short pause, then Serena said, "Friendships can be formed across great distances, Thomas. You have a pen pal in France yourself, do you not?"

"Yesssss," Thomas drawled. "But when I met him, he didn't cling to me half the time. Not the way Mademoiselle Burgeon did with Papa."

Knox winced. Michelle had been extremely touchy the first few days, before she'd finally accepted Knox's love for Felicia was real and unwavering.

"Well, I'm sure—"

"Do you know what else confuses me?" Thomas interrupted, clearly having lost interest in Michelle.

Serena sighed. "What's that?"

"While in France, my cousin Bernard said Grandfather didn't die as a soldier in the French Revolution, but because he was a traitor."

Instinctively, Knox flinched.

"Thomas," Serena whispered, then shushed him. Knox imagined her looking fearfully toward the doorway, but he'd already ducked out of sight. His heart pounded as he listened.

"I told Bernard he was a liar, but he said Grandfather admitted it. Admitted that he told his friend, André Calmart, how to kill vamps."

"His name was Calmet and your cousin Bernard is a troublemaker," Serena hissed. "You need to forget that name."

"But why?" Joelle asked. "If Grandfather was friends with Calmet, he can't have been bad."

Knox closed his eyes as a voice from the past—his own voice—swirled around him. "My father isn't a traitor," he'd told Dante Prime, Zeph's father. "So what if Calmet writes of vampires. That doesn't mean Father told him anything."

In response, Prime had read Knox a passage from Calmet's

Dissertations sur les apparitions, des anges, des démons et des esprits, et sur les revenants et vampires de Hongrie, de Boheme, de Moravie et de Silésie, a book in which the Catholic Church officially acknowledged the existence of vampirism for the first time. In that passage, Calmet had provided details, including the fact a vamp couldn't turn a human without dying himself, and the one way to kill a vamp, by ripping out his heart and burning it. The only logical conclusion was that Calmet's friend, Jacques Devereaux, had revealed secrets he'd sworn to take to his grave. Calmet's book, Prime said, was the reason why the vampire mortality rate had skyrocketed during the French Revolution, leading to the deaths of over one-third of Knox's clan, a clan that hadn't been that large to begin with.

Still, Knox had refused to believe him. Even at twelve years of age, he'd remained unwavering in his belief that his beloved father would never willingly give humans the ability to kill vamps.

Until his father had confessed to doing just that.

"Stop pulling my hair, Thomas!"

Joelle's shriek brought Knox back to the present. Shaking his head, he cleared his throat, then entered the room.

"Papa," the twins cried simultaneously before launching themselves at him. "Where have you been?"

"Discussing business with your Uncle Zeph, who is lying down for a nap, so please don't disturb him, okay?"

Thomas laughed maniacally, causing Knox to narrow his eyes even as he suppressed the urge to laugh along with him. "Thomas," he warned.

With a sweet smile, Thomas patted Knox's hand. "No worries, Papa. I shall leave Uncle Zeph in peace." The "for now" in his promise was clear, but Knox didn't call him on it. Instead, he hugged them closer and thought fondly of Noella. "Grandmother is feeling better today and would love to see you." The children clapped their hands, thrilled with the idea of seeing their grandmother and, Knox was sure, getting a sweet treat—

most likely caramels. "I also wanted to tell you that I'm going to be away for a while. I have important business to attend to, but I'll be back when I can."

"Are you going to see Aunt Felicia?"

Knox frowned, but he couldn't accuse Joelle of reading his mind or anyone else's. Vamps didn't begin to develop their powers until after puberty hit. "Why do you ask?"

Joelle, the spitting image of Noella, shrugged. "You just got that look in your eye when you said 'important.'"

"You are certainly very observant," Knox said, flicking the end of her nose. He looked up at Serena, who didn't do a good job of hiding her disapproval. Because he'd interrupted their lesson? Or because of Felicia? Knox shrugged. If it was the first, she should know by now that when he wanted to see the kids, nothing else was more important. If it was the second? Serena had better make sure Knox never confirmed it was the second.

He smiled at Joelle and Thomas. "It so happens I am going to see Aunt Felicia. And I'm hoping that sometime soon, I'll be bringing her here to visit. Would you like that?"

The children squealed, and he talked with them for a while longer before he encouraged them to get back to their lessons and be good for Serena. As he left, Knox realized he hadn't qualified his statement about seeing Felicia. Obviously, he didn't doubt he *would* be seeing her.

Yes, she'd refuse the moment Mahone told her his demands. But Knox was counting on Mahone to persuade her otherwise. If he didn't, Knox would.

One way or another.

FBI HEADQUARTERS
WASHINGTON, D.C.

Three days after hearing about the antidote, Knox returned to Mahone's office.

Mahone gestured to the chair in front of his desk. "Thank you for coming. I'm hoping you're ready to accept the Bureau's offer?"

Lips flattening, Knox remained standing. "Assuming you've done what I've asked, then yes. But I am curious about one thing, Mahone. Something we failed to discuss the other day. Since vamps are the only race in danger of going extinct, exactly what are you using to entice the others?"

Steepling his fingers on the desk, Mahone's gaze didn't waver. "We've offered you due consideration in exchange for your serving the United States government. What we've offered the others is irrelevant."

"Hope for my clan and the protection of my children are not what I view as consideration; they are absolute necessities. Plus, if I'm going to be leading these Others, then what motivates them is damn well my business. More so even than what would have motivated your scientists to sell the antidote they created in the first place."

"Money isn't too difficult a concept to grasp," Mahone drawled.

"And as I told you before, it's not just money, Mahone. Not if all five of the remaining scientists are involved. I need to read their minds. I need to know who and what we're dealing with."

Knox threw out the assertion for kicks. He didn't really expect Mahone to agree. To his surprise, Mahone hesitated.

"Mahone?" Knox prompted, his tone suggesting that Mahone was a recalcitrant child trying to keep a secret.

Mahone glared at Knox. "I told you it wasn't about me. The President was concerned about you accessing more information than you should."

Not missing Mahone's phrasing, Knox stepped closer. "And now?" Knox asked softly.

"And now that we have reason to believe North Korea bought and obtained the antidote, the President is reconsidering."

Knox raised his brows, his blood tingling with a rush of

adrenaline. Since his initial meeting with Mahone, Knox had made lists summarizing the information he knew, as well as every potential theory he could come up with. As far as a possible buyer was concerned, North Korea was certainly on his list of potential governments that would benefit by the antidote. Whenever possible, it promoted itself as an Others supporter, which was laughable really, given North Korea's fanatic pursuit of homogeny in all things.

If they obtained the antidote and provided it to vamps, secretly or not, they would gain a powerful ally. While Knox didn't believe anyone in his clan would be so weak, there were other clans—clans smaller in numbers, clans that were fractured and dissatisfied with the terms of the Humanity Treaty—that might.

"The vamp guard you were telling me about the other day, is he guarding the scientists now?"

Mahone leaned back in his chair, his suspicion readily apparent. "Why do you ask?"

"Because I'm wondering what you know about him. Would he be susceptible to bribery if North Korea were to contact him?"

"How open-minded of you to voice suspicion of a vamp. Or is that because I told you he isn't from your clan?"

Knox refused to answer and Mahone shrugged. "Kristoff Lafleur has worked with the FBI for almost twenty-five years. We just didn't know for most of that time that he was a vampire. He's proven his dedication time and again, and I have no concerns that he's involved in this. On the other hand, we intercepted a transmission yesterday between North Korea and one of its allies, in which a high-ranking military leader referred to their recent success in obtaining a 'cure.'"

Not missing the way Mahone had brushed off his concerns about Lafleur, Knox nevertheless felt a surge of excitement that the word "cure" had indeed been linked with the North Korean government. It was weak evidence, but evidence nonetheless. They'd need more, however, before launching an offensive attack. "I'm assuming your people will continue surveillance while Team Red is gathered?"

"That's right." Mahone shrugged. "And who knows? I'm betting you'll get your chance at the scientists, too." For a moment, Mahone looked troubled, but then he smiled mockingly. "But only after you've officially agreed to join the Bureau. That way, even if you manage to discover the antidote's chemical composition, I'll still have your word that you'll lead this team."

"What about my word that I won't siphon out other top-secret information? Don't you want that?"

Mahone smiled slightly. "National secrets aren't what you want, Devereaux. I know that, even if the President needs some convincing."

That was good to know, of course, but no real surprise. Mahone knew Knox's needs were few—take care of those who belonged to him and make sure that a certain stubborn human finally accepted that she fell within that category. "You never answered before. Can I assume you've made the proper arrangements to get me what I want?" Knox asked.

Before Mahone could respond, his phone rang. He glanced at the clock before answering.

"This is Mahone." He paused, then gave a slight nod. "Send her in." He hung up. "Speaking of what you want," Mahone murmured softly.

Every muscle in Knox's body tensed. "She's here?"

"Yes."

Breathing became slightly easier as relief hit him. "So she agreed."

"Not exactly. I haven't had a chance—"

Knox immediately closed his eyes. A heavy disappointment warred with annoyance that Mahone hadn't even approached Felicia with Knox's demands. "She doesn't know," he confirmed flatly.

"Not yet. After rescuing that dharmire, she left town for a few days."

Knox growled. "I don't give a—"

A firm knock interrupted them. Muscles pumped as if for battle, Knox stood there. He didn't turn, not even when Mahone called for his visitor to come in.

"I came as soon as I—"

It didn't matter that he was in Mahone's office, that Mahone was watching him, or that he and Mahone had just been discussing something as important as his clan.

He hadn't been in the same room with her in years, but his body's reaction to her presence was the same as it always was: instantaneous.

Her scent hit him like a sledgehammer and was followed by a wave of longing so intense it almost felled him. His skin prickled and his fangs ached as he fought to keep them sheathed. He couldn't stop the hardening of his dick, however, or the urge he had to grab her and transport her to the Dome. To his bed. To someplace where duty and time dissolved, and he could just be with her.

She didn't gasp or take a breath. Her words simply stopped. Something rare crystallized inside him.

Had she gotten over him? Had she found someone else?

Another emotion—pure, undiluted rage—filled him at the thought of her with another. It made everything else, every other emotion he'd ever felt, seem innocuous. Made him want to rip off his clothes—the luxurious symbols of civility that he normally loved—and make her see him as he truly was—primal, lethal, and fucking ready to prove to her that she was his, once and for all.

Instead, he took a deep breath and willed himself to calm. He opened his mind. Just a hair. Just enough to sense the desire buried beneath her resolve. Enough to dismiss that foreign emotion of fear and tamp down his rage.

When he was assured of his control, Knox slowly turned and faced the human female he'd wanted to bite from the moment he'd seen her. She was dressed conservatively in a white oxford shirt and navy blue pants, her auburn hair pulled back into a tight ponytail. Taller than most females, she was neither delicate nor bulky. While most would consider her average in looks and sex appeal, Knox saw what most didn't.

He saw the strength in her supple body.

He saw her courage, her compassion, and her integrity.

And at that moment, he saw the fiery sensuality that flared in her eyes before she banked it and stared at him with a practiced look of mild curiosity.

Felicia had always tried to hide her attraction to him, but she'd always failed. Nevertheless, he'd abided by her wishes and kept his distance.

But not anymore.

Not-the-fuck-anymore.

He didn't speak the words, but given the way her eyes widened, she'd guessed at his thoughts.

Knox dipped his head in a courtly bow. "Hello, Felicia. Imagine running into you here."

FOUR

"Didn't you see the sign? We don't serve your kind here."

Dex took another slow drink of his beer before spinning around on his bar stool. Leaning back, thighs spread wide, he stared at the guy in front of him.

He was a were, too, which didn't make an iota of difference.

Dex's "kind" didn't fit in anywhere, not even with his own race. Not even with *either* of his races.

Instead of responding, however, he drained the beer bottle. Lazily, Dex wiped his mouth and set the bottle down on the bar before signaling to the bartender, a pretty blond mage who'd been flirting with him earlier but now looked scared shitless.

"I'll take one more."

The blonde hesitated, but jerked into action when Dex glowered at her. She set a fresh bottle in front of him, then quickly backed away.

He grabbed the bottle and raised it to his mouth.

"I told you—"

The ass-were growled as he tried to snatch Dex's bottle.

In one fluid motion, Dex slammed the bottle into the bastard's face while grabbing the guy's nuts in a punishing grip. He twisted for good measure. The guy howled pitifully as glass shattered, breaking his nose and slicing his skin. Dex just pressed harder, barely feeling the bite of glass on his own palm.

When the crowd edged closer, several growls confirmed the presence of more werewolves, as well as their readiness to shift into wolf form so they could rip Dex's throat out. Dex spun the werewolf into a choke hold at the same time he pulled his blade. He pressed the buck knife to the werewolf's throat. Then, to make his point, he sliced off the guy's ear.

The werewolf's pained shriek made everyone freeze.

A flash of color in his periphery caught his eye but the scent was familiar. Sweet. Still innocent, if innocence was still possible in this world. There was a light touch on his shoulder. "The police are on their way. I'm sorry," the blond bartender added. "I need this job."

"My beer."

She jerked her hand away. "Oh, yeah. Sure." She retrieved a bottle, cap on, and held it out. Then she shook her head. "You've got a bike, right?"

"Outside."

Protecting his back, Dex moved toward the door, still dragging the now-passive werewolf with a choke hold. His eye caught the sign near the restroom, the one he'd missed before. NO PETS ALLOWED.

Dex clenched his teeth. It didn't matter that he was part were. As a half-Otherborn, a werebeast rather than a werewolf, he was considered a yapping dog. A whipped pet. A fucking joke.

The blonde, who'd been trailing him, followed his gaze and winced. Again, her expression was genuinely apologetic. The faint sound of sirens drifted toward them.

"Get the door," Dex instructed.

She pushed open the door and then closed it after the three of them stepped outside. Dex shoved the bleeding were to the ground, making sure he'd block the door long enough to give him time to leave. As always, his bike was close by in case he needed to make a quick escape. He took the beer from the girl, shoved it into his saddlebag, and climbed on. He revved the motor.

"How'd you know?" she yelled as he backed up.

Dex knew immediately she was referring to his drink order. He'd paid her up front. Three beers plus a tip. "Just a lucky guess," he yelled back.

"You gonna take that job?"

Recalling the call he'd gotten several days ago, Dex smiled, the expression so rare for him that it actually felt foreign. Director Kyle Mahone had practically choked the offer out, causing Dex to laugh long and hard. Unfortunately, he'd been able to think of little else since. Today, when the mage had asked him what was "up," Dex had flippantly replied he was considering a new job. "Depends," he said now. The sirens were getting louder, but he waited for her question.

"Depends on what?"

"Whether they're afraid of the big, bad wolf."

"You want them to be afraid?"

He ignored the slight reproof in her gaze. Innocent, he thought again. But she'd get over that really quick, he was sure. "If they're afraid enough, they won't even try to keep me on a tight leash. They'll just leave me the fuck alone and let me do what I do best."

"What's that?"

"Survive to live another day."

As he roared off, Dex internally amended his last statement.

He'd survive to make sure justice was served.

Served in the slowest, most painful way possible.

FIVE

Felicia shouldn't have been surprised to see Knox.

She'd smelled him—that unique combination of soap and fresh mint, clean and elegant—before ever entering the office. She'd brushed it off as her imagination—a rookie mistake. She should have known better than to dismiss her intuition, especially where Knox was concerned.

She'd dreamed of him for years. While her dreams couldn't be classified as clean or fresh or elegant, they usually ended with her lying limply on top of him, shivering with pleasure and breathing in that heavenly smell.

Still, Kyle should have warned her—

Dragging her gaze away from her reflection in Knox's glasses, she glared at Kyle. The rat just shrugged his shoulders. She turned back to Knox. "Somehow, I don't think our 'running' into each other is an accident. Am I wrong?"

"No."

If her heart hadn't been racing as quickly as her blood was heating, she might have smiled. Vamps, even dharmires, had few weaknesses, but their inability to lie was one of them. As it was, she simply waved for him to continue.

Instead, he took off his sunglasses.

This time, she couldn't hold back her gasp.

His gaze, twin stars radiating more heat than the sun, pinned her as effectively as if he'd covered her body with his. She'd just started to picture it—hard flesh pressing on soft, lean muscles rubbing against sensitive curves, sharp fangs sinking into her and drawing pleasure throughout her body—when his raspy voice jerked her out of her self-induced trance.

"We'll get there."

It was a smoky promise, spoken so confidently that it pissed her off almost as much as it scared her.

"No. We won't. And stop reading my mind."

He smiled and leaned closer, his words for her alone. "I didn't have to read your mind, love. You're flushed and breathing hard, and I can see your tight little nipples even under that starchy shirt of your's. But I won't tell if you won't." As he straightened, the small glimpse she got of his fangs made her wet.

Wetter.

She knew if she looked down, his cock would be lengthening as well.

Eyes still on hers, he commanded, "Tell her."

Kyle's answer, although swift, was accompanied by a glare that told her Knox wasn't using his power of persuasion. "Knox has agreed to lead HRT Red."

Felicia didn't blink. She'd known Knox would accept the Bureau's offer.

After all, it was his best hope for saving his clan.

And saving his clan motivated everything Knox did.

"He has a few conditions," Kyle clarified.

She snorted. "Let me guess. Money. Lots of money." She said it with no disdain.

All vamps, vampires and dharmires alike, craved money because they were sensualists. They loved soft, rich fabrics, beautiful accommodations, and quiet, powerful, sexy cars. Knox drove a black Audi TT with buttery seats that had had her panting the one time she'd been in it. Vamps were also reputed to be incredible lovers. Incredible skill. Incredible stamina.

She'd heard Noella's ravings for years. But that had been before—

Guilt and grief combined, threatening to rip her apart. She forced her thoughts to the benign. Vamps. Wealth. Hedonism.

Yes, she supposed if she had to live for eternity drinking nothing but blood, she'd make up for it any way she could.

Hours of mind-blowing sex certainly was a good way to start.

Damn, she thought. You just can't stay away from that, can you?

"The money's not the problem," Kyle said.

"There's a problem?"

"That's up to you."

Automatically, her gaze jerked to Knox's. He stared back at her, his expression blank but his eyes managing to radiate . . . anticipation? Satisfaction?

Both, she decided. Which made no sense.

"Knox has asked for your participation."

Annoyance made her frown. "I told you before, I'm trained in hostage negotiation and security, not—"

"Not on the team. With his children. I believe you've met them."

"Yes." Knox's twins, a boy and girl, were ten now. Years away from showing their vamp traits. Joelle and Thomas occasionally e-mailed her, but she only let herself get so close. And it wasn't close at all. Not anymore.

"Knox has asked that you stay with them."

"Stay?" she echoed dumbly.

"Live with them. In the Dome. As extra security while he's on the team."

She looked back and forth between the two men. "You're joking."

"I assure you, my children are not a joke," Knox commented darkly.

"I never thought otherwise," she snapped. "But I have a life and a job and neither involves you. I'm afraid you'll just have to get someone else to babysit."

"Joelle said she expects you to bring more caramels."

At Knox's words, her quick inhalation of breath was almost painful. The memories pounded at her. Her visits with the children. The way she'd snuck them caramels. Until she'd had to stop going because it had just been too painful to be near Knox. And too tempting. Although she'd managed to see Bianca once or twice over the years, she'd deliberately stayed away from the others, fearful that it would be her breaking point. That she'd bend, just as she'd almost bent two years ago.

That's what horrified her the most. That she'd been that weak. That needy for him that she'd almost accepted what he and Noella had offered.

Never again. Sick to her stomach, she forced herself to look at Knox and speak without wavering. "The answer is no." Then, turning on her heel, she walked out of the office.

"Felicia . . ."

She ignored Kyle's call and blindly headed down the hall, not breathing again until she was in her office with her door closed and locked.

The dharmire didn't bother going after Felicia on foot. One second he was standing in front of Mahone, and the next he was gone. He hadn't even had to say "Beam me up, Scottie" first.

With Felicia's expression of betrayal still haunting him, Mahone collapsed in his chair. He sympathized with her more than she knew.

Over the years, she'd fought the good fight against Devereaux. If his wife hadn't been killed by a group of insurgents one year ago, she probably would have kept on fighting and won. Now, however, Mahone's money was on Devereaux. The vamp was not only smart, but willing to fight dirty to get what he wanted. To him, fighting dirty wasn't incompatible with keeping one's honor, not if the fight would benefit more than it would hurt. Devereaux had convinced himself that being with Felicia would benefit them both more than it would hurt them.

Just as Mahone had convinced himself that keeping the whole truth from Knox Devereaux was a temporary necessity. Hell, given the greater secret he was keeping from everyone else, it had been easy. The Goddess might disagree with his methods, but he really didn't give a rat's ass.

A corner of his mouth tipped up. Yeah, Mahone, he thought. You're a real badass when she's out of the room and out of your head, aren't you?

But hey, he'd do whatever it took to make this team a success, including getting the lay of the land before giving Team Red too much information.

While they weren't at war anymore, only so much trust could reasonably be expected between the Others and the Bureau, at least until time proved that trust warranted.

The success of Team Red's first mission was a critical step in that process.

Mahone shut his door, locked it, and established a secure line to the White House. In under a minute, he was connected to the President of the United States.

"Good afternoon, Director. I'm assuming all the offers have been tendered?"

"That's right, Mr. President. The wraith and Mr. O'Flare have accepted. The others have shown enough interest that I'm confident they will as well."

"Any surprises in terms of what they expect in return?"

"None, except Mr. O'Flare has asked for an IOU to use sometime in the future."

The President chuckled. "Smart move for a man who doesn't seem to have any specific needs at the moment. So he turned down the money?"

"Without even blinking."

"And Mr. Devereaux? Has he indicated why he's reluctant to take the lead?"

Mahone hesitated. "He's still not buying the theory that the scientists would sell out their country for money. He wants answers. Reassurance."

"I thought you provided the assurances when he read your mind."

"With respect to what he was looking for, it seems I did. But I think we should give him access to the scientists. Otherwise, we risk his unease turning into outright suspicion."

"So you're recommending we let him try to read their minds?"

"That's right."

"And you'll make sure the proper arrangements are made first?"

"Yes. There's every reason to believe we can control the situation. What comes of it isn't as important as the gesture."

Several seconds of silence ticked by before the President spoke again. "Do it. I want him on board and the team assembled. The sooner we get the antidote, the sooner the team can focus on the hot spots we've identified."

"And once they've proven themselves," Mahone answered, "we'll be able to come clean with the rest."

Mahone didn't phrase it as a question, but the President answered as if he had.

"Perhaps. Let's take things one step at a time, Director. Keep me posted."

"Yes, sir." Mahone hung up and raked a hand through his hair.

One step at a time, he repeated to himself.

As he packed up his stuff to head home, Mahone thought of Hunt's questions, posed days before. The ones that had so eerily echoed those of the Goddess who'd visited him.

"Tell me, Mahone, how many Others do you call friend?" he'd asked. "How many do you drink a beer with when you're watching a game?"

Hunt's hostile tone had bugged him, but the question itself really hadn't. No, he didn't have an Other for a friend, and certainly not one he drank a beer with after work. The truth was, though, Other status had nothing to do with it. Mahone didn't have a human friend he drank beer with, either.

For the first time in a long time, Mahone wished it weren't true. It was times like this that calling someone to get shit-faced drunk with sounded pretty damn good.

Teleportation.

Felicia had just locked her office door when the word popped into her head.

It was followed swiftly by two other thoughts. She was a fool, and Knox had been in her office before.

She'd just registered the luscious smell when Knox materialized in front of her. She backed away until she hit the door.

He didn't move. He didn't crowd her.

He didn't have to.

She felt him. All over.

"Running again?"

"Leave," she croaked as panic flared.

"Not this time."

The calm words infuriated her. "What game are you playing? I'm not at your beck and call. If you want to go off and play soldier—"

He kept his voice soft, but there was no denying the savage fury and desire that glittered in his eyes. "I don't play. I subdue. I rescue. I fuck. I kill if I have to."

It wasn't bravado or threat, simply fact. It was easy to forget that Knox, for all his elegance and charm and sophisticated clothing, was a warrior. One that would fight with his bare teeth and hands to protect his own.

Despite the chemical warfare used against the vamps, they'd held their own during the War. Knox's leadership had been a huge reason why the Otherborn clans had briefly joined to fight their common enemy—humans. Of course, most of those alliances had now fractured as each clan had once again focused on its own needs.

"They want you, Felicia."

"And what your children want, they always get?" She'd meant to sound flippant, but was afraid it came out wistful instead.

Stepping back, he seemed to deliberately bank the fire in his eyes. "If I can't have you, it's only fair they should."

"You didn't want me. Not enough."

The fire within him exploded, pulsing into the air and licking at her mercilessly. Shaking his head, nostrils flaring, his smile resembled a snarl. "Now that was an incredibly stupid thing to say."

"I didn't mean—"

Palms flattened on either side of her head, he caged her in with his arms. His eyes glowed, the irises expanding until she couldn't look away.

Why had she said that? All these years, she'd never doubted his physical yearning for her. The only reason they hadn't made love was because she'd refused him. Was that what she'd meant? That she'd wanted him to ignore her protests? To ignore the fact that he was married to her friend? And when Noella was gone, to ignore his unshakable sense of duty so he could leave procreating vampires to other vamps?

Yes, she realized. Some small part of her—some crazy, irrational, lust-crazed part of her—actually resented the fact that he'd done and continued to do the honorable thing, as if that somehow proved he couldn't have wanted her as much as he'd claimed.

Her thoughts were so horrifying that she finally managed to look away. She pushed at his chest, trying to put some space between them. He refused to allow it. "Look at me," he growled.

She shook her head, then gasped as she felt the slight tingling that preceded persuasion. "No," she whispered, even as part of her cried, Yes. Make me come to you. Don't give me any choice.

But then the tingling stopped. Breathing hard, he lowered his forehead and pressed it against hers. At the same time, he pressed his hips into her, grinding his iron-hard length into the vee of her legs. "You didn't mean what, Felicia? To challenge me? To dare me to do what you've wanted me to do? What I've been dying to do since I first saw you?"

Eyes widening, Felicia stopped pushing and instead gripped his sides underneath his coat. She wasn't aware how desperately she clung to him, or that her nails pinched into him, until he growled, "Yes, hang on to me. Pull me closer, baby."

And she *was* pulling him closer.

Oh God, she thought, biting her lip to stifle a whimper. The combination of his dark voice and the press of his body was exquisite, and she couldn't stop her hips from arching up toward him. Their clothes separated them, however, and she moaned out her frustration, wanting to feel his thick cock against her. Inside her. Filling her hand. Her body. Her mouth.

Noella had once told her how much Knox loved oral sex.

"No," she gasped, trying to fight off the desire that was coursing through her body like a drug.

"Yes," he snarled. He lowered his head and sipped at her neck with a gentle kiss, then raked his fangs against her ear. He shuddered, reminding her that when aroused, a vamp's fangs were almost as sensitive as his cock. At the thought, Felicia felt herself cream her panties again, the wetness that had never disappeared, forcing her body to prepare for his penetration.

Dizzy with need, she choked out, "When you first saw me, I was with your wife. My best friend. Noella. Do you remember her?"

He stiffened, but didn't raise his head. Blasts of heat hit her throat as he struggled to breathe. "Noella's dead."

She shook her head, not in denial since her friend's death couldn't be denied, but in hopelessness. Apparently, he felt it, too.

"Damn you." He straightened and backed off, just a bit, until their bodies no longer touched. "Why you?" he whispered. "Why is it I can only feel this way with you?"

His pained question pierced her like a dagger. She shoved him away and he let her.

Somehow, with her body still empty and aching for him, that inexplicably angered her even more.

"I guess it's your curse. But hey, you should have 'doing without me' down to a science by now. All you need to do is find a female with vampire blood and hope she lasts a little longer than the last one."

As soon as the words left her mouth, Felicia wished she could take them back.

It was a weird twist in the otherwise immortal vamp race that even as a female vamp gave life, she risked losing her own. Then the FBI had invented the vaccine, which had all but turned vamps into a dying race.

Loyalty to Noella had been a factor, but it was vampire frailty that had and always would keep them apart. His father's betrayal fueled Knox's loyalty to his vampire ancestry. It focused his duty to mate with a female of vampire blood and do his part in populating their clan. In despising his father's weakness, Knox also despised the part of himself that shared his father's blood. The human part. Whether he knew it or not, that meant some part of him would always despise *her*. Sometimes that hurt so bad she wanted to rail at the injustice of it all.

But as much as his nearness sometimes hurt her, her words shamed her. "I'm so sorry. That was a horrible thing . . ."

Her voice trailed off and she stared at Knox. He was looking at her unflinchingly, not with disappointment or recrimination as she'd expected. In fact, his expression had seemed to go deliberately blank—blank but for the faintest edge of guilt in their dark depths.

Unbidden, her eyes filled with tears. "You've already found her. Haven't you?"

He closed his eyes briefly and took a deep breath. "Felicia . . ." he murmured.

"Did you?" she demanded.

He nodded. "The Vamp Council has someone in mind, someone that can help unite our clan with those abroad."

The hurt was almost debilitating. "And this someone," she choked out. "She was the reason you and the children went to France?"

"Yes, but I've already explained everything to her, Felicia. Why we'd marry. That I'm in love with you. That the only times we'll be together are to—"

Felicia laughed. It started as a small chuckle, then progressed to a high-pitched giggle, and then to an almost hysterical guffaw. She fumbled behind her for the doorknob and thought of her friend.

Noella.

The beautiful, sweet-natured full-blooded vampire who'd married Knox and bore him two children. The one who'd died, knowing that Knox had wanted Felicia. And that Felicia had wanted him, as well. Whoever this female was, whoever the Council had picked out for Knox, was going to walk right into the same fate. If Felicia allowed it.

"Stop," Knox snapped. "Stop thinking of her. Them. This has nothing to do with Noella or Michelle."

"Michelle? That's a beautiful name—"

"This is about you and me and the hunger that won't go away, no matter how you try to deny it."

"It will go away," she cried. "It did. All you have to do is stay away from me."

He barked out an incredulous laugh. "I've stayed away from you long enough and that was my mistake. I let your romanticized notions about fidelity sway me, when what I should have done was fuck you. Hard. Fast. Every day until you admitted you were mine."

Shocked, her mouth opened and closed as she struggled to

respond. She'd seen him lose control before, but not like this. Or maybe it wasn't that he was out of control, she thought. Maybe he had simply made a decision and wasn't going to mince words letting her know that. The notion made her tremble with a hint of fear and a tidal wave of desire.

Walking up to her, he palmed her hips and lowered his head until his rough breaths stroked her ear. "And you are mine, Felicia. Every inch of you. Your tits. Your ass. Your mouth. And your sweet, hot core. I'm going to love every single inch of you." His teeth nipped at her again, harder than before, and his voice got even deeper. "When the time is right, I'm going to have you and I'm never going to let you go."

"Stop!" she cried, even as she imagined it, his body taking hers in every way possible. She ached for him just as she'd always ached. Hungered as she'd always hungered. Her body was so close to orgasm that she was shaking, but still she denied herself. No matter what he said, he wasn't hers. He couldn't be.

Pleadingly, she whispered, "Please don't do this to me, Knox. Please. Marry this female the Council has picked out. Marry her, have children with her, and leave me alone."

Her desperation must have gotten through to him because he suddenly jerked back. Eyes almost completely silver, he stared at her. "Felicia . . ."

She finally managed to get the door open and slipped outside.

Thankfully, he chose to let her go.

She'd barely been able to resist him. She honestly didn't know if she could do it again. From the moment she'd seen him, long before the kiss they'd shared two years ago, she'd wanted him. Wanted him enough to consider sharing him.

And sharing him would kill her.

It would take her love and slowly strangle it, leaving behind nothing but bitterness and regret, as well as the inescapable knowledge that she had allowed it to happen.

So no, she didn't know if she could resist him again. But resisting was all she'd ever done and all she could ever do.

SIX

Wraith barely reached Quantico without losing it. Even with the private jet and driver that Mahone had provided, she was jittery. Out of her element. She'd long ago left the reservation and the protection of her kind to walk among the living, but she'd confined her walking to a small area of Los Angeles that she was familiar with. Here, nothing was familiar. No one had touched her—Mahone had made sure of that—but her fear of even an accidental touch had made her so tense that the stares of those around her, human and Other alike, pierced her like arrows.

Of course, she didn't let anyone see that.

Popping her gum, Wraith walked behind her escort while readjusting her headphones and resuming the playlist on her iPod. The rousing chorus of "Dancing Queen" played softly, relaxing her without interfering with either her hearing or awareness. She might look unaware to others, even distracted, but Wraith knew exactly how many people they passed, what they were wearing, how they smelled, and whether they'd looked at her with disdain or simply avid curiosity. Most did both.

She shrugged. It was hard not to be curious about a woman with short, spiked, shockingly white hair à la Billy Idol, especially when her skin and lips had a slight blue tinge that she didn't bother to hide with makeup anymore. The fact that she wore complementary electric blue four-inch stilettos and tight black leather wouldn't help her meld into a crowd, either, but that wasn't what she wanted. She'd learned to use her appearance to keep people rattled. That way, she kept them from seeing how much rattling her own knees were doing.

"Please wait in here."

Nodding at the somber-faced man who'd silently escorted her inside the winding corridors of the FBI Academy's lesser-known sister facility, Wraith stepped into the room. She deliberately kept her gaze off the death mark pulsing on the man's chest, then took a deep breath when he closed the door, shutting her inside the large sterile conference room.

She'd smelled the man's illness as soon as she'd gotten into the car. The sickly stench had almost made her gag before she'd managed to control herself, so she took the opportunity to suck in as much clean air as she could.

It wasn't long before Mahone arrived.

"I trust everything went smoothly?"

"Not a fucking problem," she clipped, suppressing her smile at Mahone's instinctive wince. People, men in particular, were so predictable. Having breasts and a filthy mouth unnerved them every time.

"Devereaux is here and ready to meet the team. As you're the first one to arrive, I thought you might want to . . ."

She saw the moment Mahone stumbled.

She might want to what? Eat? Rest? He'd obviously forgotten wraiths did neither, but he recovered quickly.

"Read up on the other members." He held out a stack of files.

Wraith took them even though she'd done her own research on the team members. She pierced Mahone with a gaze he couldn't see behind her dark glasses.

"I'm assuming my file contains only the information we agreed upon?" Again, based on her research, she already suspected it did. She couldn't be certain, however, that Mahone hadn't supplemented the files he'd created on his computer, or that those files hadn't been shadow files designed to throw her off.

Trust no one; it was her motto for a reason.

Mahone nodded. "That's right."

"No mention about my vision?" she clarified. "Or the . . ." She swallowed audibly as dark memories pressed at her.

"That's right," Mahone said softly. "No mention of what happened to you. Just the necessities we agreed to. 'Hands off' being the primary one."

Still holding the files in one hand, Wraith threw her arms out and grinned. "Then let's get the fucking show on the road, shall we? Because the sooner we get the damn antidote, the sooner I get what I want."

What I need, she internally amended as she followed Mahone down yet another hall. First, information. Then the means to kill herself the way nature should have done in the first place.

SEVEN

A week to the day after Mahone had offered him a position on Team Red, Knox realized exactly how much faith Mahone had in his abilities.

Too much.

Mahone must have thought Knox was a miracle worker in addition to a masochist. Why else would he have introduced the three Others in front of him as his team members? The fifth member of the team, Dex Hunt, hadn't yet bothered to show, but Knox wasn't surprised or concerned by his tardiness. From the little he knew about him, the werebeast would arrive in his own good time, but he'd be there. Knox was more surprised by the three he'd just met.

The mage, Lucy Talbot, and the human, Caleb O'Flare, each sat in a chair. Both appeared relaxed. No one looking at them would guess at the blood they had on their hands or the blood they were willing to shed in order to get what they needed.

As for the wraith who was pacing the floor? She seemed too unstable to function on her own, let alone in a group during intense combat situations. She'd removed her sunglasses over ten minutes ago, but Knox still hadn't gotten used to her filmy eyes. They, more than anything else, announced how dead she was inside. And it had nothing to do with her lack of a pulse. This female had been through things that went beyond the horrors of war. Maybe beyond anything that Knox could imagine, which considering who he was and what he'd seen in his lifetime, was saying something.

Still, Lucy was the biggest surprise.

To cover her baldness the way most female mages did, Lucy was wearing a dark chestnut wig styled into a razor straight bob with bangs. Her face was lightly accented with makeup but she still looked younger than she had in the surveillance photos. Too young to have killed her first mark at sixteen. Too young to have studied with a Senior Mage learning the kind of magic that less than 5 percent of the mage population could master. The kind of magic most mages spoke of in whispers using words like "dark," and "unpredictable," and "abomination."

"This is ridiculous!" The wraith came to an abrupt stop and braced both hands on her hips. She snapped her gum. "So what if the piece-of-shit wolf isn't here yet? Let's get this show on the road."

Knox frowned and opened his mouth to reply, but Lucy beat him to it.

"What would be the point in that?" Lucy countered. "We'd just have to go through it all again when he got here. Why don't you take a seat and relax instead of trying to show us what a badass you are."

They all stared at the mage. She'd managed to make her jab without sounding remotely hostile. The wraith glared at her anyway, as if deciding the best way to take her down. O'Flare didn't even try to hide his amusement.

O'Flare was another one who'd take time to understand. He gave the impression that little bothered him. With shaggy blondish-brown hair and green eyes, he'd be almost pretty but for the strong, angular bone structure he'd inherited from his Native American mother. Plus, he was tall and broad-shouldered, with a long, muscular body that would look equally at home slouching in a chair or rappelling down a mountain. According to his bio, mountain climbing was a favorite hobby of his. The face would be useful for missions requiring the assistance of a swayable female, but Knox would have to trust the body to protect his life. And possibly save it. By all accounts, O'Flare had proven his skill as a medic time and again. Plus, his psychic powers had saved not just his own ass, but those of several soldiers in his previous platoons.

Knox sighed as the wraith took a step toward Lucy.

If he wasn't careful, she was going to draw blood and give O'Flare a chance to prove how good a medic he really was.

"Ease down, Wraith," he snapped. When she grudgingly took a step back, Knox looked at the others. "She's right. We are wasting time. Mr. Hunt will have to play catch-up. First order of business is a warning: I need to be certain each of you is committed to this cause. I warn you, if I find out otherwise, I won't hesitate to eliminate the threat you pose."

Wraith smirked, but other than that, she met his stare head-on. So did the others.

Satisfied, Knox nodded. "Good. Now, we're going to get to know each other a little better."

The wraith snorted, but this time the others wore matching expressions of rancor.

"Are we going to get in a circle and tell each other what our favorite color is?"

Knox didn't acknowledge O'Flare's joke. Once again, he reminded himself it was going to take time to earn their trust. They didn't realize it yet, but when Knox issued an order, even one couched in friendly terms, he expected it to be carried out, no questions asked. They'd learn that soon enough. "We've all been briefed on the particulars," he said, picking up a stack of files and tossing a folder to them one by one. "This is what we were all given, so of course we know everything about one another. Right?"

He nodded at the skeptical glances he received.

"Right. So who's going to reveal their deep dark secret first? The secret that's going to piss me off when it gives the enemy a hold over the rest of us." He looked at each of them. "No volunteers? Okay. Then why don't I go first?"

Instinctively, Knox hesitated. But again, if he was going to lead, he needed to lead by example. He'd been a wreck since seeing Felicia just over a week ago. Mentally, he snorted. More precisely, he'd been a wreck since he'd practically attacked her, grinding his dick against her while he'd threatened to take her, body and soul. He'd been out of control, furious at her statement that he hadn't wanted her enough to take her.

Just once, he'd wanted her to feel the full measure of his desire for her, so she'd never dare say such a stupid thing again.

In the process, he'd not only tortured himself, but her. She'd been on the verge of coming, yet pain and desperation had rolled from her in waves. Once more, he questioned whether he had the right to push for a relationship with her. She had valid concerns, after all, and he couldn't promise he'd never take another female. Not yet. Not before his clan's future was secure.

But he couldn't let himself think that way, he reminded himself. She wanted him. Hell, she needed him. Eventually, she'd come to terms with his need to produce other vamps. And he was going to do everything in his power to make sure that happened sooner than later.

Unfortunately, she was determined to make life difficult for him. Neither he nor Mahone had managed to convince her to stay at the Dome, where he'd been hoping to visit her and the children whenever there was downtime during his missions. It wasn't that she didn't care about the children's safety, she'd told Mahone, who'd obediently relayed her words to Knox. Rather, according to Mahone, "She asked what kind of idiot you took her for. She knows just how secure the Dome is, so any hopes you had of making her bend to your will through guilt were feeble at best. 'Feeble' is a direct quote, by the way. So where does that leave us?"

It had left them exactly where Mahone had expected.

Knox was still determined that Felicia would yield to him, but he was going to have to convince her without keeping tabs on her whereabouts and while earning his pay from the U.S. government.

Once more, Knox took in the three Others in front of him. Total honesty, he reminded himself, although his biology wouldn't allow him to lie even if he'd wanted to. Before he changed his mind, he confessed, "I've got two. The first? My father, a human, was executed for treason by order of the High Vamp Council. He confessed to revealing vamp secrets to a human during the French Revolution. As a result, hundreds of vampires were slaughtered."

"I'm sure growing up must have been a joy," Wraith muttered.

Knox shrugged. "Sometimes it was. Just know I owe it to my race to find this antidote. Any questions?"

"Why do you rule the clan?" Lucy asked.

Knox's stomach clenched but his gaze didn't waver. "I rule because of the vampire Queen's weakness and because of my own strength, for although the blood of a traitor runs through my veins, it's also that blood that makes me able to withstand the effects of the vamp vaccine." He paused a second, then continued, this time even more reluctantly. "My second secret? I'm in love with a human female."

Silence.

Finally, Lucy rolled her eyes. "That's horrible," she breathed.

Her blatant sarcasm almost made him smile. "Actually, it is. You see, she won't have me because, as you all know, the vamp race is dwindling in numbers. As its present leader, I feel duty bound to contribute to its repopulation."

"You mean she'd have to deal with you fucking female vamps in order to knock them up?" Wraith asked.

"Will you shut up," hissed O'Flare.

The wraith narrowed her eyes at him. "Why don't you try and make me?"

"She's right," Knox said loudly even as he clenched his fists. His first instinct had been to kill the wraith for her insult, but truth be told, she *had* been right. He just hadn't liked hearing it said so bluntly, which was no one's problem but his own. "She's right," he repeated. "But the point is, that's not included in your files or anyone else's that I know of. It should be. She should be. Because she's my weakness. If an enemy knew that, he'd use her to get to me. And that means he'd use her to get to you. Her refusal to be with me doesn't change that, it just means I can't protect her. And I don't want to hear another word about it unless it's a matter of personal security. Got it?"

No one said a thing, but he hadn't expected anything else. He pointed at Wraith. "You next."

She arched an arrogant brow. "Why me next?"

"Because as the walking dead, you're certain to have more baggage than the rest of us."

"That's ridicu—"

"He's right," O'Flare interrupted.

Wraith turned on him. "Mind your own fucking business."

"Anything that weakens the team is his business," Lucy said in that same rational tone she'd used since she'd arrived. "Denial being one of them."

"Listen, you bitch," Wraith spat, walking closer to the mage. Knox reached out to grab her arm, but she jerked around and hissed, "Don't you dare!"

Whoa. Right. No touching the wraith.

Knox held up both hands. "You will not attack another team member." He gave the slightest of smiles to lighten the tension. "Bad for morale."

"I'm not afraid of you hurting me. You touch me and I'll kill you. Then who's going to lead this team?" She cast a disdainful glance at the others. "I don't want the job and there's no other palatable option."

Lucy stood, finally looking pissed off, but O'Flare just burst out laughing.

Knox crossed his arms over his chest. "You think something's funny here? Then why don't you tell us your secret weakness?"

O'Flare shrugged and leaned back in his chair, stretching his long legs in front of him and cupping his hands behind his head. "My psychic powers aren't exactly reliable. They're spotty, but have come in handy a time or two. They usually come to me in dreams that I have to interpret. The ones that I've had warning me of danger generally focus on people who are close to me, either in proximity or emotion."

"Since I'm planning on keeping my distance, I guess you're useless to me. Somehow, I'm not surprised," Wraith said.

O'Flare smiled tightly. "You never know. You just may grow to like me. Want to know what my second weakness is? I'm irresistible to women."

"Oh, spare me, Romeo."

O'Flare ignored the wraith to look at Knox. "No, really. Take that little scene a second ago? When Mahone told me there were two females on the team, I warned him to expect trouble, and here the two girls are, fighting over me already. If someone had knocked down the door and come in shooting, we'd have been goners."

The wraith was a blur of movement and then she was straddling him, one hand yanking his hair back as the other shoved a small gun under his chin. "You, maybe," she purred. "This girl? She'd be walking away before anyone even thought to clean up the bodies."

Braced to grab her, Knox cursed at his carelessness. Just because another's touch could hurt her obviously didn't mean the wraith wouldn't suck up the pain to make a point. Then again, her bare skin only touched O'Flare's hair—the other parts pressed against him were clothed. Did that make a difference? It was something he should have known the answer to.

Sloppy, Knox. Damn sloppy.

He took a step toward her, but O'Flare's heated, furious gaze met his. "No," he snapped. Turning back to Wraith, O'Flare slowly raised one hand to her face. Although she didn't flinch, his hand stopped a hairsbreadth from her cheek. "Of course you wouldn't be one of the bodies, darling. You're already dead, after all. But walking away is the last thing you'd want for yourself, right?"

Wraith sucked in a breath and left his lap with decidedly less grace than she'd used to get there. "Fuck you!"

O'Flare smiled tightly. "Thanks for the offer, but I prefer females with a little heat to them. You're so cold, and I mean that literally, you'd freeze my dick off before it got inside you."

"Don't!" Lucy gasped, her eyes wide and filled with pity as she looked at Wraith.

Knox made a mental note: Another weakness identified. The mage hid a soft heart beneath her cool reasoning.

The wraith's head snapped toward Lucy. Then she smiled, her blue-hued lips curling evilly. "You think I deserve your pity? You think this—this human," she spat, "can hurt me?" She snorted and backed away.

O'Flare continued to stare quietly at the wraith. When she turned away, his eyes flickered with regret before going blank. The man's gaze locked on Knox's, then at a point over his shoulder. Knox stiffened.

"Jesus," growled a raspy voice behind him, the speaker's disgust more than obvious. "If this is what I've got to work with, kill me now."

Knox took a fortifying breath and turned around.

The werebeast had arrived.

Slightly less than six feet, Dex Hunt was still taller than most werebeasts. His sheer brawn, heavy muscles packed onto a rangy, broad frame, was more common in his full-blooded ancestors than in half-weres. Burnished skin, thick tawny hair, and light hazel eyes, however, placed him squarely in the half-were corner.

Their gazes locked. Despite his mocking words, Hunt stared Knox down, a clear challenge in his gaze. Maybe it was because Knox knew weres believed in only one alpha male per pack. Or maybe it was simply because he hated Hunt on sight. For whatever reason, Knox felt it happen.

Beneath his loose clothing, his muscles hardened and swelled. Knox grew taller, broader, not enough to rip his clothes but enough to make them strain their seams. He felt his fangs lengthen and knew from the sound of Lucy's gasp that his eyes had shifted from silver to a demonic, glowing scarlet. Control slithered away and a primal growl vibrated in his throat.

"No fucking way," O'Flare breathed.

Knox's mouth stretched into a tight smile. One by one, he looked at his crew. None of them, not even the wraith, would meet his eyes directly. They'd clearly never seen the transformation of royal vamp. Perhaps it was better they did so now.

Sometimes individuals performed best when they were too scared not to.

Knox returned his attention to Hunt, who not only met his stare head-on, but jerked his chin in challenge. "Might as well get it over with now," Hunt drawled.

Laughter, a sinister, chilling sound, tickled Knox's throat.

Oh yeah, he thought.

Things were going to get a whole lot more fun before the day was through.

Knox took three lightning-quick steps toward Hunt, then froze. His nostrils flared as he caught her scent. A second later, he saw the woman standing just behind Hunt.

What the fuck?

Felicia.

What was she doing—

Before he could complete the thought, a heavy weight slammed into his chest, knocking the air out of him and propelling him off his feet. He didn't stop until his body slammed into a wall on the other side of the room. Knox hit the ground. Stunned, but immediately moving into a crouch, he blinked as dust and plaster rained down on him, momentarily obstructing his vision. When it cleared, he saw Felicia wrestling with the werebeast. And then he saw the werebeast shove her down.

With an enraged shout, Knox teleported so fast he caught her before impact. He lowered her, gently but swiftly, then almost instantly wrapped his fingers around Dex Hunt's throat.

Imagining that Hunt's throat was an aluminum can, Knox squeezed.

Only one thought remained.

Kill the bastard who'd touched Felicia.

Felicia scrambled to her feet and tried to latch on to Knox's arm. Before she could, he dragged the werebeast, who was already wheezing for air, across the room and threw him like a shot put into the same wall he'd slammed against moments before. Already weakened, the wall literally crumbled as Hunt's body hit it, plaster and Sheetrock caving in so that it cradled Hunt between its studs like a hammock defying gravity. The werebeast was struggling to get free, teeth bared and growling, when Knox grasped him by his jacket lapels and tossed him to the ground.

Looming over the were, Knox pressed his foot into Hunt's neck and asked, "If you're hoping to shift before I kill you, *dog*, you better do so now."

Shaking off her paralysis, Felicia rushed forward. "Knox!"

He jerked his head up, pinning her with those ruby red eyes and pointing a finger at her for emphasis. "Don't. Move."

The order, combined with his fierce appearance, had its desired effect. She literally froze again, unable to believe her eyes. She knew how royal vamps transformed when they were pushed beyond their limits. She'd read about it. She'd never seen it before, though, and the sight of Knox—bigger, buffer, and badder—was mind-boggling. When Hunt groaned, recapturing Knox's interest, Felicia lunged toward them. "He's part of the team."

"He pushed you," Knox fired back.

"Only because I was about to beat the shit out of him."

A snort came from somewhere near the ground. Hunt, who

seemingly had managed to catch his breath despite the foot pressed to his throat, wiped the back of his hand across his mouth and studied the blood staining his flesh. "Let's not get carried away, Red. I just didn't want a hysterical female to get in my way while I shoved this vamp's face in the ground."

"Shut up—" Felicia snapped, but it was too late.

Knox gripped the were's thick, wavy hair in one hand and literally lifted him off his feet. "Are you talking about this vamp, perhaps? Because you—"

Knox grunted when Hunt's legs kicked out, scissoring so that they struck him in the face before wrapping around his neck in a vicious vise. Although Knox released Hunt's hair, the werebeast simply pulled himself around, as if Knox were an apparatus, and landed a blow to Knox's abs.

Staggering back several steps, Knox grunted.

"If you're gonna teleport away before I kill you, vamp, you better do so now," the werebeast taunted.

Knox laughed. The feral sound of it sent a shiver down Felicia's spine.

Not in fear, but in desire.

And that was wrong on so many levels.

"You should have shifted when you had the chance." Arching his fist like a pendulum, Knox rammed it with brutal accuracy into Hunt's crotch. Immediately, the were's legs loosened and Knox gripped them, using them to fling his opponent across the floor like a rock skipping over water.

"Ouch," a male voice said from behind Felicia. Whipping around, she glared at the shockingly handsome human who could only be Caleb O'Flare.

"Do something!" she shouted. "They're going to kill each other."

O'Flare shrugged. "Better each other than me."

"Damn it!" Felicia pulled her weapon and fired it near the two males, who were now locked in a wrestling move that eerily reminded her of the waltz she'd danced with Knox so long ago. Neither one of them so much as flinched.

Felicia looked toward the other females in the room. The wraith was leaning against a wall, pretending great interest in her cuticles. The mage, however, nodded when she caught Felicia's eye. "Okay, okay," she muttered. The petite female took a deep breath, closed her eyes, and raised her arms above her head, palms together. Slowly, she lowered her arms until her hands were pressed prayer-style against her lips.

"Fuck!"

Felicia turned at the hoarse yell. Knox's fangs were deep in Hunt's arm. With his other arm, Hunt pounded his fist into Knox's face several times, bloodying it but failing to dislodge him. Swiftly, Hunt reached behind him and whipped out a buck knife with a four-inch blade.

"Hurry!" Felicia yelled at the mage.

The mage's eyelids snapped open, revealing only the whites of her eyes, as if her eyeballs had rolled to the back of her head. Fine tremors shook her body, but there was no other movement.

Neither Knox nor Hunt yelled out again, but their heaving breaths and grunts increased in volume and speed. The hand in which Hunt gripped the knife shook as he struggled to push it forward and into Knox's chest. Some invisible force was clearly holding him back, and relief made Felicia dizzy. "Keep going," she encouraged the mage. "It's working."

"Don't distract me," she snapped.

Felicia pressed her lips together. As she watched, Knox and Hunt slowly began to separate. Knox's fangs slipped free from the were's arm, blood dripping from the tips. When several feet separated them, Felicia moved forward, intending to plant herself between them so they couldn't go at each other again without going through her.

She was almost there when the mage gasped. "Look out," she said, but it sounded strained and barely audible.

In a blur of movement, Knox had Hunt pinned to the floor, the were's blade now turned against him and pressed to his throat.

"Damn it!"

Felicia's gaze jumped swiftly toward O'Flare, who was now kneeling beside the mage. Lucy was sprawled on the floor. Weakly, she lifted her head and explained, "Trying to move a living object . . . hard anyway . . . he's too strong."

Felicia cursed when the mage fell back to the floor. "She's okay?"

O'Flare nodded curtly. "I think so."

"Good." She turned back to the fight, prepared to jump on Knox if she had to. What she saw stunned her yet again. Although he still pinned the werebeast down, Knox was literally shrinking, his overblown muscles relaxing until he no longer resembled a vamp on steroids. The red in his eyes faded until they were once more normal, but that didn't extinguish the anger that radiated from him like a furnace.

It did, however, enable Felicia to breathe just a little easier. In this case, shrinkage was good. It meant Knox wasn't enraged to the point where he couldn't control himself any longer.

"Apologize for pushing her," Knox spat.

Hunt narrowed his eyes, gritting his teeth when Knox sank the tip of the blade into his throat, making him bleed.

"Knox!" Felicia gasped. "No."

He didn't even glance at her. "Say it or I'll shove the whole thing through."

"I could shift before you did it," Hunt muttered.

"Maybe, but then you really would have to run away. With your tail between your legs. Is that what you want?"

Several tension-filled seconds passed before Hunt shifted his gaze to Felicia. In a remarkably steady—maybe even remotely pleasant—tone, Hunt said, "I apologize for shoving you."

Knox grunted, but was apparently not yet satisfied. "Now accede to my leadership."

"Fuck you," Hunt growled, but the curse held little heat. In fact, unless Felicia was mistaken, she thought she sensed amusement in the were's expression, as well as a hint of grudging respect.

"Say it," Knox gritted.

"Fine," Hunt finally said. "I accede to your leadership. Can you let me the fuck up now or are we going to waste more of the day?"

After a brief hesitation, Knox withdrew the knife and stood. He didn't offer a hand to help Hunt up, but when the were stood, Knox held out the buck knife, handle first. Hunt took the knife and replaced it in the sheath at his back.

The two males turned toward Felicia and the three others. She was still taking in their expressions—O'Flare looked amused, Wraith pissed off, and the mage slightly sulky—when Knox stepped up to Felicia. Taking her arm in a gentle but firm grip, he led her out of the room and into the hallway. He backed her into one of the walls and caged her in with his arms, much like he had in her office just days before.

This close, she couldn't avoid the sight of his bleeding and battered face that even now was rapidly healing. By the time he spoke, all evidence of the fight with Hunt was gone. Once again looking like the ubercontrolled, refined vamp she was used to, he smiled grimly. Lifting one hand, he caressed her throat, pressing his thumb against the spot that she could feel fluttering with her racing pulse. "Now that that's settled," he said softly, "why don't you tell me what you're doing here?"

Felicia swallowed, knowing that her answer was just going to enrage him again. She forced herself to say it anyway, the vivid memory of his transformation and fight with Hunt reminding her why she'd accepted a position on the team in the first place.

Accusations of racism aside, she and Knox had more than simple DNA separating them. Their values, their interests, their very way of life were worlds—no, galaxies—apart. After the debacle in her office, she'd finally accepted it. Truly accepted it.

Knox wouldn't force her.

She, and only she, was what would keep them apart.

Just as it was she who would help bring this team together.

"Felicia," he warned when her silence obviously went on too long.

She tilted her chin and stared into his beautiful eyes. "Haven't you guessed?" she murmured. "Team Red has been assigned two humans. One a human psychic and the other one . . . not." She shrugged and smiled. "I'm the not."

EIGHT

"You lied to me."

"I didn't lie." Mahone held up his hands when Knox whipped around, the wrath of Hell in his eyes. "I didn't. You demanded she stay at the Dome with your kids. She refused. You decided you'd lead Team Red anyway and deal with her on your own. Well, you'll certainly have that chance now."

"She was targeted for the team from the very beginning, not just after she refused my demands."

"She was targeted, yes, but she hadn't accepted the assignment. In fact, she'd refused it, several times, claiming she didn't have enough skill to bring to the team. She changed her mind after the two of you hightailed it out of my office. I had assumed you'd managed to persuade her somehow, but didn't want to take credit for her change of heart."

"Damn you," Knox yelled. He slammed a fist into the conference room wall, barely feeling anything even though he left behind a good-sized hole. "I'd never use the power of persuasion on an innocent female, let alone Felicia."

"And I never said otherwise," Mahone said mildly. "We

both know your power of persuasion isn't simply a matter of mind control."

"I can't serve on a team that she's a part of. Not this team. Not this mission."

Mahone shrugged. "Then our agreement is null and void. Because now that Felicia has agreed to join the team, the President won't allow her to be removed. He was adamant that humans be proportionately represented on Team Red, and right now there are no other humans willing to take the job."

"She said herself she isn't trained for these types of missions. She's a hostage negotiator, for God's sake—"

"She's a trained field agent. She spent her early years growing up with a variety of Others, thanks to her parents, and that includes vamps. Lucy's expertise is communication, as in high-frequency radio versus radar. But being a hostage negotiator means Felicia is an expert with words and relationships. Think of her as part mediator, part damage control. I'd be an idiot, and so would you, to believe your team members are going to embrace you or each other with open arms. But you might at least try setting the right example." Mahone smirked. "You may have completely healed, but Hunt looks like he walked through a freaking glass door."

Knox rolled his shoulders, telling himself he didn't feel exactly how he'd felt when his mother caught him pinching Zeph as a baby. "That was partly just some good-natured sparring—"

"Felicia's good at her job and she wouldn't appreciate you questioning her skill."

"This isn't about her skill or strength," he exclaimed, his frustration obvious.

"Then what is it about?" Mahone questioned. "You're not the only one who has something to gain by the retrieval of the antidote. Or don't you realize that by now?"

"Why don't you enlighten me? Because as far as I know, the antidote won't benefit humans—"

"Felicia's parents were brutally murdered before the War started. Before you ever met her."

"I already know that," Knox said. He'd never specifically talked with Felicia about it, but Noella had filled him in on every detail. Felicia was an only child. When she was a teen, her parents had been agents in one of the FBI's original Strange Phenom Units, which investigated unexplained photography, debris, and crop circles. Instead of finding evidence of alien life, however, George and Rhonda Locke had discovered a small community of vamps—one led by the then thriving Queen. Knox had been living in France at the time, enjoying his freedom before he was to marry his intended bride, Noella St. Claire. He'd returned home early when things between Others and humans had started to become volatile. By then, he'd heard all about Noella's friend, Felicia.

Eventually, he met her. Always, he desired her.

Two years before war was declared, someone set fire to her parents' house. Neither one of them survived and the arsonists were never caught. One year later, he married Noella. And one year after that, war was declared.

"After Felicia's parents died," Mahone continued as if Knox had never spoken, "and despite the weird shit that you two had going on while your wife was alive, Felicia bonded with your family. With your children. With your mother. With you. Your family became hers. After Noella's murder, who did she have? No one—and don't interrupt me," Mahone snapped when Knox opened his mouth, "because *I* don't count and she doesn't think she can have you. Personally, I agree with her."

Knox instinctively wanted to refute Mahone's words. He didn't. Felicia was his. His mate. His woman. His soul. He didn't need to convince anyone of that but her. But first he needed to keep her safe, which meant off Team Red. "Her loneliness doesn't justify her presence on the team. And—"

"Stop being so dense," Mahone snapped. "She's alone, but she's not without feelings or compassion or loyalty. She's willing to work with you, the one person she'd give anything to avoid, because she wants to save the exact same people you do. Are you really going to take that away from her?"

Knox stared at Mahone as he ingested his words. He hadn't stopped to think of it that way, but of course it was true. He'd been too focused on his own anger to see it. His anger at being duped by Mahone. Anger because he believed Felicia had been placed on the team because Mahone didn't trust Knox to do his job. Anger because he knew Felicia's participation in their first mission could jeopardize any relationship he eventually—*maybe*—was able to start with her.

And finally, anger that he hadn't figured out Felicia's reasons for wanting to join the team himself.

In addition to Mahone and Knox's mother, there were others who questioned Knox's determination to have Felicia. More than one elder on the clan's Vamp Council had spoken to Knox about the female human he lusted after, as well as his duty to marry another vamp. "Fuck her all you want," Dante Prime had encouraged with no concept of how much danger he was in at the time. "We trust you, Knox. You have led us well during our Queen's illness. Unlike your father, you've proven your human blood won't affect your loyalty to the clan."

Knox had walked away from Prime, his jaw clenched, his fingers flexing, his brain struggling to remind him that Prime, like the rest of the Council, had always been prone to the same weaknesses as any other vamp, including fear of change. Given the horrors they'd suffered during and after the War, that would be especially true now. Nonetheless, the Vamp Council had reluctantly consented to Knox joining Team Red—as if their consent would have made a bit of difference, Knox thought crossly—because of the lure of a cure.

Still, if Team Red's first mission failed—if Felicia was on the team when it failed—would Prime find a way to blame her? Would he accuse her of acting with the FBI to dupe him? Would he accuse Knox of jeopardizing the mission for a piece of human ass, thus forcing Knox to prove once again where his loyalty lay?

Right now, those possibilities were probably the biggest reasons Knox didn't want Felicia on the team.

"Knox!"

Knox jerked at Mahone's shout. He blinked at the human male, frowning when he saw the man's distress. "What's wrong?"

"What the hell did you do? Go into some kind of trance?"

"I was . . . Never mind that," Knox clipped out. "What's going on?"

With one last perplexed look, Mahone gestured to the phone on the table. "I told you about the call I got from the President earlier this morning. He's agreed to let you see the scientists. That is, if you still feel it would be helpful to read their minds."

Knox cocked a brow, surprised in spite of himself. President Cameron Morrison had never struck him as the type of man to take uncontrolled risks, and if letting a vamp read the minds of the nation's most elite scientists wasn't one such risk, Knox didn't know what was. "I don't think its helpfulness is really in question, do you? Will the whole team be going?"

"Just you. And we're going to have to jump through a number of hoops first, including moving them from their current location. After you see them, they'll be moved again."

"Smart," Knox mocked. "That way I can't teleport in to grab whatever secrets I miss the first time."

"That's right," Mahone said in all seriousness.

"Of course, if I did happen to discover where they've been moved, I can always read their minds from a distance."

Mahone snorted. "Play someone else, Knox. Or are you telling me you've discovered a way to do long-distance mind reading?"

When Knox said nothing, Mahone's left eye twitched. "Have you?" he finally asked.

"Have I what?" Knox queried innocently.

"Discovered a way to read minds from farther than fifty feet?"

Knox grinned. "I didn't realize we were trading secrets, Mahone. Before I answer, why don't you tell me something first?"

With a wave of his hand, Mahone indicated that Knox should ask away.

Knox leaned closer to the man, bending slightly so he could stare into his eyes. "How did it feel, paying the scientist who invented the vamp vaccine, knowing that the female vampire you were in love with would slowly waste away because of it?"

It was almost a full day after telling him she was on the team that Felicia saw Knox. Mahone had come and gone, and Knox had called a team conference. With Lucy and O'Flare sitting and Wraith once again pacing, Felicia noted with some amusement that Knox was valiantly trying to ignore her. He was pretty much succeeding until Hunt walked in and made a point of taking the empty seat next to her instead of one of the five others that had been closer to him. At that point, Felicia saw Knox's eyes practically turn green and had to smother a smile with her hand.

Even now, her body's response to his presence shocked her. The ache in her heart, however, far exceeded any that her body produced; it was comforting to see that Knox's feelings for her surpassed pure physical desire, even if the prevalent feeling was jealousy.

"I have business I need to take care of tomorrow, possibly even the day after that. Before I leave," Knox said, "I want to run you all through some exercises and drills, so I can evaluate firsthand your different strengths and weaknesses."

"Don't get your stopwatch out too soon," Hunt said. "I didn't sign on for boot camp."

Felicia arched a brow and turned toward the were. "What's the matter, Hunt?" she asked lightly. "Afraid I'm going to make you look bad?"

Hunt's eyes rounded just a hair before he looked her up and down with an appreciative glance. "Not possible, Red, but on second thought, I'd love to see you try. In fact, I'll even give you a head start, so long as you promise to wear some shorty-shorts while you're running."

"Everyone is going to do the drills," Knox gritted out, "or you can pack your bags. In case it didn't come through earlier, I'm in charge of the team and that means I need to see you in action—in training and on the streets."

"Since I haven't been tossed out yet," Felicia drawled, "I'm assuming I'll be taking part in all this?"

Knox glowered at her. "I told Mahone my concerns that you don't have the right training for this position, but he assured me I was wrong. In fact," Knox said sweetly, a considering look in his eyes, "one of the things Mahone mentioned you're quite skilled at, Felicia, is verbal judo. How about I give you the floor and you tell us what that is?"

Hunt's snort was not in the least bit unexpected, nor was the fact that everyone else ignored him. With his arms crossed over his chest, Knox stared at Felicia, clearly challenging her. She understood perfectly what he was doing and it pissed her off. Since Mahone wasn't cooperating, he was trying to embarrass her in front of the team by picking a particularly controversial topic for her to discuss. If the team rejected her, he assumed she'd run off to lick her wounds. He obviously didn't know her as well as he thought he did. Standing, she strolled up to him, noting that he moved aside to keep a respectable distance between them.

It threw her. For all his current manipulations, Knox had never avoided her physically before; suddenly she wondered just how pissed he was. With all eyes on her, however, she shook it off.

She looked steadily at each of them. "The whole premise of verbal judo, just like the physical kind, is conscious, deliberate control of your words and actions in order to achieve a desired result. In a high-stress situation, sometimes the worst thing you can do is respond with your first impulse."

"Usually my first impulse is to shoot first and ask questions later. It's worked well for me up to now," Wraith said.

"I'm sure that's true," Felicia said. "Given our background, survival instinct plays a big role in why we're all here today. I'm not disputing that sometimes force must be met with force. But you're no longer working by yourself or in the midst of an infantry. This is a very intimate, specialized team and every move one makes is going to impact each of us. It could also make the difference between mission success and failure. Each of you needs to decide whether you're devoted to the team's mission goal or your own safety—because at times those two things may be incompatible."

Hunt shook his head. "Get over yourself, Red. We're not here for the greater good, we're here because we want something and the government's got us by the balls."

"I don't buy that, Hunt. If all you were doing was looking out for yourself, you wouldn't risk your life on a mission to retrieve an antidote that has no direct benefit to you. Whether you admit it or not, you're all here because you want to see change."

"I want to see change, that's true," Lucy interrupted. Felicia turned to the mage while suppressing a sigh of relief. If she'd had to lock eyes with Hunt for a second longer, she wasn't sure if she could have stopped herself from blinking, and that's exactly what he'd wanted her to do. She knew Hunt wanted change, but she also wasn't entirely sure how compliant he'd be to get it.

"The more tools we have, the better," Lucy continued. "So explain how verbal judo could help in a specific situation."

"Verbal judo is a technique used by hostage negotiators and law enforcement when facing off with a suspect. The trick is to avoid bloodshed by using tactical peace phrases. Anytime you can prevent escalation of a potentially dangerous situation, you should do so. It's a call you'll all have to make, maybe not on this mission, but eventually. For example, Wraith, what if a suspect pulls a gun on you but you know he's the only one who has the information you need?"

The left side of Wraith's mouth tipped up. "I know exactly where to shoot someone to inflict the most damage without killing him."

"So he's wounded and pissed off, determined to take his secrets to the grave. Now what?"

"Then the dharmire here reads his mind or the mage uses enchantment to make him talk. Isn't that why we're going through this whole group effort?"

"But what if Knox isn't around? Or what if you're out-gunned and you need to talk yourself to safety? Your everyday speech is enchanting, but dropping the F-bomb every other word might not work when a bad guy has his sights on you."

"My F-bombs aside," Wraith sneered, "he wouldn't get his sights on me in the first place. This is a ridiculous waste of time." Wraith popped the gum in her mouth and headed for the door. "Tell Mahone if he wants me on the team, it's going to be me, and not some doll he can program—"

"Wraith—" Knox began.

"Look, Wraith," Felicia interrupted in a firm but calm voice. Wraith stopped a few feet from the door. "The reason I joined the FBI was because of my parents, but the job is what ended up killing them. We're not friends, but while this might seem like a joke to you, I'm concerned about the safety of every member of this team. This is just one way to get you to think differently. Is there anything I can say to get you to listen with an open mind? Because Mahone had enough faith in you to think so."

Felicia watched Wraith's shoulders rise as she took a deep breath. Slowly, she turned and met Felicia's gaze. "Fine," she said. "Just get on with it, would you? I'm getting bored." Wraith walked to an empty chair and sat down.

Propping her hands on her hips, Felicia asked, "Any questions?"

Wraith straightened and scowled. "What—"

Hunt clapped his hands in a slow, staccato beat.

"Well done, Red. Your little display showed us how a direct attack results in hostility and how your verbal tap dance diffused it. In this case, it worked, but I'm not planning on getting rid of my knife anytime soon."

"Still, I think I made my point," Felicia said. "We can discuss the most common phrases and techniques another time." With a piercing glance at Knox, she walked past Wraith to her chair.

"Bitch," Wraith muttered.

"From you, I'll take that as a compliment," Felicia said.

Felicia didn't miss the way the wraith had to fight to keep from smiling. When she looked up, however, Knox's expression was hard and implacable.

"Everyone change into your workout clothes and meet outside in ten minutes," he said. "If any of you are capable of walking after our drills, we'll be going on a little field trip."

"What kind of field trip?" O'Flare asked.

Knox's smile was slight but packed with enough satisfaction to make Felicia's eyes narrow. "Think of it as a visit to the zoo, only the animals won't be in cages and instead of 'Do Not Feed' or 'No Flash Photography' signs, the prevalent theme is 'Every Man'—or in most of your cases—'Every Otherborn for Himself.'"

"Sounds like most of the places I stopped at on my ride here," Hunt said.

"Then you won't be surprised by the water trough that's outside," Knox responded. "The one that's labeled, 'Drown with Weres.'"

"Clever. You think of that all on your own?" Hunt asked. "Because weres, as a general rule, are excellent swimmers."

Knox shrugged. "I would be, too, if water was what prevented me from shifting into my immortal form."

"People aren't really that stupid, are they?" Lucy asked. "That they'd wave a red flag for all weres to see?"

"Patience, Lucy, and you'll be able to answer that question for yourself."

The answer to Lucy's question was that people really were that stupid. At around 9:30 p.m., five hours after Knox called them into the conference room, the six of them, aching and bruised from the workout Knox had put them through but all determined to hide it, stood before the rusted-out trough with the were epithet scrawled on front. The remote roadside bar behind it, a drab concrete building with a huge steel door, was located just outside the border of Virginia, in Kentucky. Although music was blaring from inside, the dominant noise was cheering studded with shouts and the occasional sound of breaking glass.

Hunt looked at the trough with disgust. "Damn rednecks might as well slap swastikas on it and burn a wooden cross while they're at it."

"Oh, they've got those inside, too," Knox confirmed. "Don't worry, though. Despite the area's . . . suspicion . . . of weres in the past, you won't have to shave your soul patch or deny your parentage tonight. On fight night, anyone with the right amount of cash is guaranteed entry."

"Interesting, but forgive me if I don't do a happy dance and shift when we get inside."

Felicia couldn't believe Knox intended for any of them, let alone Hunt, to go inside. Looking at the number of motorcycles parked outside and the way bloody bodies were being tossed out of the bar's front door every three minutes, Felicia grabbed Knox's arm.

"Problem?" he asked, cocking a brow.

"Actually, yes," she said through clenched teeth. "Putting us through our paces is one thing, but leading us into a slaughter is something different. We all completed your little drills. We're not here to pick fights or wind up in the emergency room. Just what are you trying to prove?"

"I'm not trying to prove anything except some people are built for combat and some are not. As you said before, you're the not."

She whipped her hand away, not even trying to suppress her expression of outrage and disbelief. "What do you think I've been doing as a special agent for the past ten years? Pruning roses and making homemade truffles?"

"Completing drills and shooting on a range aren't the same

as street fighting. Talking down a kidnapper with a hostage isn't the same as dealing with a sociopath bent on world domination." Knox turned to the others. "You should all go into this with your eyes wide open. In my opinion, anyone who gets thrown out that door instead of walking out of it doesn't belong on this team."

An explosion of cheers erupted inside just before another body was tossed out.

"What *is* this place?" Lucy asked.

"My guess is it's where people come to beat the shit out of each other for sport," O'Flare answered, his eyes shining with what almost looked like anticipation. Seeing that, Felicia's lips pursed. What was it with males and extreme sports that made them, even someone as laid-back as O'Flare normally was, want to beat their chests and prove they were the biggest, baddest boy on the playground?

"That's right," Knox confirmed. "An ultimate fighting ring without the television cameras or the obnoxious costumes. The rules are simple: Show up, sign in, and get it on. In other words," he said with a deliberate look at Felicia, "there are no rules."

"Gee," Wraith sneered, "thanks for that clarification. She wouldn't have gotten it otherwise."

Surprised by the wraith's support, Felicia crossed her arms over her chest. "In other words, it's the equivalent of human cockfighting." She stared at Knox in disbelief. "You couldn't have picked a better way to denigrate everything I told them earlier, could you? The whole time I was talking about verbal persuasion, you were planning this, weren't you? So what? Are we all climbing into the ring together or one at a time?"

"Neither," Knox said. "We're here to apprehend one of the fighters. A mage named Simon Randolph, who's killed the last seven of his opponents, both humans and Others. You'll know him by his signature tattoo, a bull tattooed on his bald skull. In addition to the fighting-related murders, he's wanted in connection with a bombing of the London metro last year, one that killed approximately twelve American tourists. He also happens to have been college roommates with one Kristoff Lafleur, a vamp who does security detail for the FBI. Lafleur was one of the guards watching over Dr. Barker's lab when Barker was murdered and the antidote stolen."

"Did Mahone authorize this?"

"Why? Are you gonna call him and tattletale on my ass?" Knox taunted.

Firming her lips, Felicia pushed past him and strode toward the door. "No, I'm gonna kick your ass, and then you're gonna kiss mine. In your dreams," she spat. She was about ten feet from the door when he grabbed her arm and wrenched her around.

"You're not going in there half-cocked and without backup." Knox looked like he wanted to spit nails, he was so angry, but she was sure he wasn't feeling half as angry as she; she felt like a dormant volcano about to blow.

"What's wrong, Knox?" she jeered. "Didn't you say the theme here was 'Every Otherborn for Himself'?"

"I didn't think you'd actually go inside," Knox admitted. "I figured you'd give us hell and walk off, leaving the apprehension to us."

"You actually thought I'd turn tail and run?" She jerked her arm out of his grip. "You really don't know me at all, do you?"

Knox cursed as he watched Felicia open the door to the bar and step inside. Maybe she was right. Maybe he really didn't know her. Despite knowing she was an agent, despite knowing she was one of the bravest women he knew, Knox would never have expected her to walk into that bar. On the other hand, he never would have guessed that the move, coupled with how flushed her face had been and how her eyes had flashed with the fire inside her, would make him so damn hard he could barely stop himself from cupping his aching balls to soothe them.

Over his shoulder, he snapped, "Cover her while I get Randolph. If it gets too rough, pull her out. I don't care if she fights you. If she gets hurt, I'm going to hold each of you responsible."

But no more than himself, Knox thought furiously, striding into the bar and pushing through the crowd. He spotted her instantly. Already perched on a bar stool, she handed the bartender a bill. She'd taken off her zip-up sweatshirt and wore only her jeans and a thin black muscle tee that hugged her breasts and left her toned arms bare. In disbelief, he watched her unwind her ponytail, shake out her hair, then smile at the bartender as he handed her a beer. Tilting her head closer to him, she listened to the bartender before laughing. Her sideways glance telegraphed her awareness of Knox and the fact she was enjoying her little show.

"When you were baring your soul yesterday, you failed to mention another reason the human doesn't want anything to do with you—you're a chauvinist."

Standing to Knox's right, Wraith seemed oblivious to the number of stares she was attracting or to the path she'd cleared in the crowd. Although several males kept their distance, their murmurs of curiosity and restless movements indicated they wouldn't stay back for long. "I'm not a chauvinist," Knox denied, noting that a particularly muscular feline eyed Wraith like she was a piece of candy. "Vamp females rule with equal authority in my clan. They enjoy all the rights of males. They serve in the military and local police."

"But somehow the rules change when it's a female you're fucking?"

Knox glared at Wraith, grinding his teeth together so loud they ached. "I'm not fucking Felicia," he snapped.

"And at this rate, you never will," Wraith taunted. "O'Flare and Hunt are signaling you."

Knox turned and caught sight of O'Flare, who stood a few feet to Felicia's right and jerked his head toward the tables lining the modified boxing ring at the center of the room. Several individuals were obviously waiting for their turn; Randolph, bare-chested but for a pair of skintight black trunks, his tattoo shining in the spotlights that had been placed in each corner of the bar, was at the front of the line. From the bloody mess the two current contenders were making of the ring, it looked like a new round would be starting soon.

Turning once more to the bar, Knox frowned when he saw Felicia's bar stool was empty. Spinning rapidly, he searched the room just as the announcer called the end of the fight. The loser was carried by the back of his neck and pants, and unceremoniously tossed outside. "The next fighter," the announcer declared, "is one who's defeated every single one of his opponents. His opponent tonight—"

Still unable to locate Felicia, Knox cursed, turned, and focused on the announcer, pinning him with a persuasive spell.

Without skipping a beat, the announcer stated, "Actually, his opponent tonight isn't up to the challenge, so we're calling out for volunteers from the audience."

"What?" The incredulous shout came from the man who'd just been climbing into the ring to join Randolph. He resembled a sumo wrestler, but one decked out from head to toe in Harley-Davidson leather and chains. "Who the fuck said I'm not up to the challenge? I'm gonna kick your ass—" The man lunged for the announcer, who calmly sidestepped him, allowing a pair of bodyguards to wrestle the biker to the mat.

Simon Randolph, shaking his head with disgust, watched while the bodyguards escorted his former contender outside.

"Do we have any volunteers?"

Cursing that he'd lost sight of Felicia, Knox opened his mouth to say, "Here." Before he could, he heard Felicia's voice call out, "I can kick the mage's ass."

Knox closed his eyes as the crowd erupted, many straining to see Felicia, who wasted no time in climbing into the ring. Lucy was right behind her.

"Me, too," Lucy announced, her slight body now topless but for the lacy bra she wore, calling attention to the fact that she wasn't as young as she looked.

Hunt appeared by Knox's side, breathing hard. "I had

Red cornered, but the mage totally snowed me. Pretended to enchant her so she could escort her to the door. I was right behind them when Lucy whipped off her top. Shocked me so much I—"

Flustered despite himself, Knox lost control of his persuasion hold. The announcer looked the females up and down, and sneered. "Nice try, ladies, but we don't allow pussy in the ring. If Simon here wanted to fight a tag team of girls he'd—" The announcer let out a shriek as he was suddenly propelled forward and slammed face-first into the mat. While the dazed man struggled to stand, Felicia high-fived Lucy, letting the crowd know one of them, but not which one, had initiated the mental shove. As the announcer pushed himself up on one knee, Felicia backed into one corner and half crouched, gathering the power in her legs. In a flash, she rushed the announcer, stepped on his knee, and swung her other leg, bent at the knee, around the man's neck. Swiftly, she raised her free leg across his chest then extended her body back so they both fell to the mat. She squeezed her legs tightly around the man's throat and within seconds the announcer lost consciousness. Releasing the man's head so it thumped back against the mat, Felicia rose and gave Lucy another high five.

"You have got to be kidding me," Hunt murmured. "Bet you didn't know she could do that."

Knox started forward, nearly ripping Hunt's head off when the were slapped a hand on his shoulder, restraining him.

"Calm down and look at Randolph," Hunt snapped.

"The bastard looks like he's ready to eat them alive," Knox countered. "Now get your fucking hand off me before I bite it off."

"You wanted her to prove she could handle being on the team and she's doing that. You stop her now and she'll never forgive you."

Knox stared into the were's eyes, knowing he was right. With a growl, he knocked off the hand on his shoulder. "Considering your performance yesterday, you've still got something to prove yourself. If she bleeds one drop of blood, I'm going in. You grab the mage."

Hunt nodded.

Randolph was circling Felicia and Lucy, who were now standing back-to-back in the center of the ring. No one in the cheering crowd seemed to care that the announcer was still lying in a heap beside them. Randolph lunged at Felicia, grabbed her arm, and tried to pull her toward him. Swiftly, Felicia extended her leg and kicked him in the balls. He was obviously wearing a cup because he didn't flinch. Instead, he backhanded her, sending her staggering back. Knox's muscles bunched and he couldn't contain the fury that had his eyes flashing red. It would be so easy to kill the mage, he thought, his fangs growing with the need to rip the male's throat out, right after he cut off the hand that had hit Felicia. At the same time, Knox saw Felicia regain her bearings and pride surged within him. Breathing hard and remembering Hunt's words, he forced himself to stand back.

Meanwhile, Lucy lifted her hands above her head. Simultaneously, Randolph's body levitated into the air, his face toward the ceiling. Slowly at first but then gaining speed, his body spun in midair. The propeller move was cut short, however, when Lucy suddenly grabbed her head and fell to her knees as if in great pain.

Randolph's body dropped, but he gracefully tucked and rolled, landing on his feet in front of Lucy. With a swift roundhouse kick, he knocked Lucy backward.

From behind him, Felicia let out a battle cry. Reaching out with her left arm, she locked it around the mage's throat, compressing his windpipe with her elbow while clasping her hands at the sides of his head. Stepping in front of his leg with one foot, she twisted to the side and used a reverse neck throw to hurl him on the ground. Recovering quickly, Randolph swept Felicia's legs out from under her. Knox could tell the fall knocked the breath out of her. "Enough of this shit," Knox said. "Where are Wraith and O'Flare?"

"Nine o'clock," Hunt said, not taking his eyes off the action in the ring.

"Shit," Knox muttered when he saw Wraith backed into a corner and hissing at the three men who'd penned her in. O'Flare stepped up behind the men and knocked two of their heads together. Wraith used the other man's distraction to punch him in the face. "O'Flare," Knox shouted. "Move out."

With a grim expression, O'Flare nodded. To Knox's shock, he reached out, grabbed Wraith's arm, and began pulling her through the crowd toward the door. "Hunt, I'm going in—"

But Hunt was already slipping into the ring. Felicia and Lucy had backed Randolph into the ropes. It was apparent he was straining to break Lucy's mental lockdown on his arms, which were pinned to his sides, even as Felicia punched him repeatedly in the face. The male's head lolled, making the tattoo on his head wave eerily as it swayed back and forth.

Hunt stepped up behind Lucy and said something in her ear. The mage nodded and shouted to Felicia, who backed away. Suddenly free, Randolph swayed and shook his head to clear it. The hisses from the crowd were clearly directed toward him. A look of murderous rage on his face, Randolph mentally slammed both Lucy and Felicia back several steps. Each one of them clasped their throats; Knox could see them gasping for air.

Knox was in the ring immediately. In slow motion, he saw Hunt slip behind Randolph and tuck his head into the mage's back, just beneath his shoulder. He wrapped his arms around the mage's waist and, locking his hands tight and bracing his weight on the balls of his feet, did a smooth body bend with an extremely short bridge, snapping the mage off his feet and slamming him headfirst into the mat. The mage's neck should have shattered beneath his own body weight, but it didn't. Both his arms, however, didn't fare as well. Reaching down, Knox dragged the man to his feet, then hyperextended both arms behind him until he felt bone snap. Randolph howled and immediately lost consciousness. Knox shoved the male at Hunt. "Bring him outside."

Breathing hard, he walked up to Felicia, who was gasping. She straightened when she saw him. She wasn't bleeding, but her face was bruised and swollen. A quick glance confirmed Lucy sported what would certainly be a black eye come morning. "You proved your point. We're leaving. Now," Knox growled.

Felicia turned to Lucy. Flinging one arm around the mage's shoulders, she led the shorter woman out of the ring and toward the entrance.

They all walked out the door on their own. As they did, Knox couldn't help smiling. Already, the team had proven that the phrase "Every Otherborn for Himself" wouldn't be applying to them.

NINE

It took a full day of preparation before the scientists were ready for Knox's visit. Eventually, however, Mahone and several guards were leading him to them. Mahone walked behind Knox, who was blindfolded, his hands in front of him, his wrists linked by a pair of steel cuffs. An abundance of caution, the guards had said. Mahone had rolled his eyes, in no mood for stupidity. Knox, however, had been amused.

He still was. That was fully apparent from the small smile on his face.

Of course, it could be that the son of a bitch was replaying the events of last night, including the shock on Mahone's face when he'd responded to the call that Knox had detained Simon Randolph, a fugitive the FBI had been trying to track down for months. When Mahone had asked where he'd found the mage, who was curiously dressed in nothing but spandex, Knox had simply smiled and said, "Felicia and Lucy kicked his mangy ass."

This morning, when he'd picked up Knox, Felicia and Lucy had sported matching bruises and satisfied smiles. No matter how much he threatened, Felicia wouldn't disclose what had happened.

That's when Mahone knew for sure she was in love with the dharmire.

As they walked the designated route through one hallway after another, Mahone rubbed the back of his neck, then pressed his fingers against his temple. The dharmire's final question to him yesterday echoed more loudly with every step he took. Mahone assured himself his thoughts weren't because Bianca's son had asked the barbed question so expertly. It probably wouldn't surprise anyone, including Knox, to learn that the question—and the answer—had been implanted into Mahone's head years before.

Nine years to be exact.

Mahone had met Bianca Devereaux six months before the War began, just when vamps had been trying to integrate themselves into modern society. As was to be expected, many of America's human population had panicked. His job had been to try and convince the vamp Queen to accede quietly to the FBI's requests, the top three being: (1) The vamps agree to live in a confined area; (2) they agree to wear electronic monitoring bracelets, similar to what in-home-custody defendants wore; and (3) they agree to wear some kind of identifying brand so that, when they were "mingling" with the human public, they were easily identifiable. Needless to say, Mahone's requests were met with Bianca Devereaux's utter disdain.

To his shock, however, the vamp Queen had returned the lust that had immediately sparked within him upon seeing her. What followed had been some of the most mind-blowing sexual experiences of Mahone's life.

Weeks before war had been declared, both he and Bianca had quietly agreed to end things. Almost a year later, Dr. Barker had come to Mahone and declared his success. He'd figured out a way to protect humans from the vicious bloodsuckers that threatened them. To inoculate human blood, he'd said, so that the primary substance that seemed to promote regeneration in the vamps was suppressed. With no nutritional benefit from the blood, Barker had continued, there would be no reason for the vamps to take it. It didn't mean that the vamps wouldn't kill humans just for the sheer pleasure of it, but, Barker had said philosophically, at least humans would have some reassurance so they could sleep a little better at night.

Barker hadn't understood why Mahone, instead of patting him on the back and congratulating him, had sunk into his chair and dropped his face into his hands. And truth be told, the devastation he'd felt then had been nothing compared to what he'd felt when he'd actually seen what doing without pure human blood would do to a full vamp.

Of course, he hadn't been foolish enough to think it wouldn't affect them. But the vampire race was a strong and hearty one. Plus, he'd known vamps sometimes drank the blood of animals. Because Mahone drew the line at injecting sheep or cows to protect them from vamps, he'd figured the vamps would survive just fine, even if they didn't thrive. After all, his goal wasn't to kill vamps, he told himself, but to protect humans.

A few years later, when he'd seen Bianca for the first time since the beginning of the War, she hadn't looked ill exactly, but she'd definitely been thin. Pale. Drained. Once again, he'd reassured himself that he'd done the right thing.

He no longer could. He hadn't seen Bianca again, and Felicia had refused to tell him anything about her health. The look in her eyes when she'd refused, however, had been telling enough.

It matched the look in Knox's eyes whenever he spoke of his mother.

Confusion. Pity. Horror. And most of all fear. Fear that a cure wouldn't be found in time.

The question had haunted him from then on. Exactly what happened to an immortal who was consistently starved?

Mahone hadn't stopped until he'd discovered the answer

himself. He'd seen the bodies. The emaciated vamps who'd been photographed in order to document the success of Barker's research, just before they'd been executed.

By now, Mahone knew Bianca probably looked beyond ill and closer to dead.

Imagining her decline flooded him with a sudden understanding for the Goddess's intentions. If humans—if *he*—could knowingly allow the vampire he loved to suffer so much for the sake of nationalism, perhaps she was right. Perhaps none of them deserved to go on living.

Mahone stumbled. Throwing out an arm, he caught himself against the wall and struggled not to empty his stomach. Knox stopped walking a few seconds before the guards did.

"Sir?" The guard looked from Knox back to Mahone, as if the vamp was the reason Mahone was so distressed.

Mahone shook his head. "Keep going."

They all began to walk again. Without missing a beat, Knox spoke softly, so softly that the guards wouldn't be able to hear him. "You want to know something funny? My mother has never doubted you love her. In a way, I think she finds your loyalty to God and country quite admirable. But then again, she's always been a bit impressionable where human males are concerned."

Mahone gritted his teeth to hold back any response. And really, what could he say anyway? Retorting with something vicious, such as "like father, like son," would be not only beneath him, and potentially dangerous, but unfair, as well.

Finally, they arrived. The guards stopped outside a set of closed doors. There were eight in total. Behind each door waited one of the scientists who had served on Dr. Barker's team. "We're here," Mahone said, although it was obvious Knox already knew that.

With a casual move, something that looked no more forceful than a twitch, Knox broke the chain manacling his wrists together. Lazily, he stretched his arms above his head. With a flick of one hand, he removed his blindfold and tossed it impudently to one of the guards. Then he yawned. "Thank God. All this subterfuge was beginning to make me sleepy."

The young guard who'd caught the bandanna scrunched up his face in confusion. "I thought vamps didn't sleep."

Knox laughed, nearly doubling over. Making a huge show of wiping tears from his eyes, he looked at Mahone. "Your men need to brush up on their Otherborn trivia, Mahone. Oh wait. Why don't we test you first? Do vamps sleep, Mahone? Or let me be more specific. Would a full vampire female sleep after a long night of fucking with a human who cares more about his job than—"

Mahone didn't think about the consequences of his actions. He simply hauled off and punched Knox Devereaux in the face. He infused the move with everything he'd been feeling— anger, frustration, and yes, fear. Fear that he was making a mistake. That he would fail.

The vamp's face whipped around at the blow, then slowly turned to once again face him. His eyes flashed silver, but there was no sign of the red that could accompany a killing heat—or intense passion. Breathing hard, refusing to look away, Mahone struggled not to remember the way Bianca's eyes had flashed red when he was inside her, and how the sight had always driven him over the edge. Every single time.

Knox drew his tongue along his bottom lip, sweeping up the small drops of blood that oozed from a cut. Vaguely, Mahone wondered if he'd split his lip on his fangs and if that was an occupational hazard of being a vamp. Funny, but he'd never heard anyone mention that, though perhaps that was because it was obvious.

"I'll let that one pass, *Uncle Kyle*," Knox drawled, "because I deserved it. But next time? Be prepared to rock and roll."

"I can't believe your mother raised such a self-righteous prick for a son."

Knox laughed. "And I can't believe she actually fell in love with a human male who'd let his job endanger her."

"She—" Mahone's words strangled in his throat. Of course he'd suspected, but to hear Bianca's son confirm so casually that she'd loved him was enough to bring Mahone to his knees. At least, figuratively.

Knox raised a brow. "Surprised?"

Mahone pressed his lips together. "No. But then again, I'm a coldhearted fool, willing to endanger a female I love to protect my people. Sound familiar, Knox?"

The dharmire stiffened and his nostrils flared. "It's not the same thing. I might act to avoid a direct threat, but what you did went beyond that. You poisoned a whole race's means of survival, when you had no idea the effect it would have."

"You're right," Mahone said quietly. "And I'll live with that until the day I die. Unless, of course, you can find the antidote to right my wrongs. If you do, what will you do then, Knox? What will you do when you no longer have the well-being of your clan as a reason to push Felicia away?"

"You're crazy," Knox snorted. "I'm doing everything but pushing her away."

"Is that right? So then I assume your answer is you'll marry her?"

When Knox didn't respond, Mahone laughed. "That's what I thought. Now, go on. Go ahead and read some minds. Make sure none of these men and women know where the antidote is or how it's made. We can argue about the benefits of being in denial another day."

Knox stepped up to the first door that Malone had pointed to. Abruptly, he stopped and turned back to Mahone. "Not marrying her doesn't mean I don't love her or that I wouldn't die for her, just as easily as I'd die for my children."

Mahone nodded, weariness suddenly making his chest feel heavy. "I know exactly what you mean."

Knox stared at Mahone for so long he actually shuffled his feet. "Not that it hurt you," he snapped in self-preservation, "but I'm sorry I hit you. Even if what you said was insulting, I need to maintain control."

The left side of Knox's mouth tipped up. He touched the tip of his tongue to one of his fangs as if it bothered him. "Apology accepted. And don't underestimate yourself, Mahone. You've still got quite a right hook there."

Mahone's jaw dropped open but Knox didn't see it. He'd turned and, with his game face on, entered the room to talk to the first scientist.

Knox stared at the slender, pale-haired woman whose moniker—"Dr. Maureen Lipinski"—had been issued by the Bureau upon her employment. Mahone had made it clear that the scientists' true identities were off limits, but Knox's first thought was that this one didn't look like a "Maureen." "Kate" perhaps. Or "Grace." Something classic.

She had a natural beauty, unenhanced by makeup or flashy clothes. Even her hair was simple, pulled back in a bun while still managing to appear stylish.

Lipinski was sitting calmly in the middle of a well-furnished room that even had a small refrigerator and sink against one wall. Knox approached her carefully and took the seat across from her. "Dr. Lipinski?"

She smiled thinly, then nodded. "That's right, Mr. Devereaux. Mahone told me you wanted to talk about Dr. Barker and the vamp antidote our team was working on. Honestly, I think it's a waste of time given we've been interrogated well over fifty hours, but you're welcome to ask anything you like."

"You seem very calm—very cooperative—for someone who's been through a difficult time these past few weeks."

Lipinski's smile stiffened. "Dr. Barker's death was certainly the start of a difficult time, yes. As to what's come afterward?" Lipinski shrugged. "We all knew the risk when we signed on to this project. Of course, those risks were the equivalent of side effect warnings on aspirin bottles, but they were there."

"So you don't mind being detained? Asked questions? Interrogated?" he asked in disbelief.

"I didn't say that."

Knox paused for her to elaborate, but she didn't.

"You were friends with Dr. Barker?" he ventured.

Lipinski's expression softened slightly. "I'd worked with him several times in the past. For long periods of time. He was a brilliant man. A compassionate one."

"So compassionate that he would inject himself and all of you with an untested antidote, regardless of the risk involved?"

"That's Mahone's speculation based on what I have to admit is damning evidence."

"But you don't agree with his conclusion?"

"I didn't say that, either. Frankly, I don't know enough to agree or not. I've seen the tests indicating my blood is clean of the vamp vaccine. I have no idea how that happened. Objectively, it makes sense that Dr. Barker clandestinely administered the antidote to us because he didn't want to wait for human testing to be approved. But at the same time, as someone who knew Dr. Barker and mourns his death, that scenario doesn't make sense."

"In my opinion, the events of the past decade make little sense."

"I agree. That's why I've spent the past year trying to rectify some of my government's wrongs. That's why I understand why you're here and what it is you're going to do."

Knox's brows lifted in surprise. "You know?"

Lipinski sighed. "I didn't need a genius IQ to figure it out, Mr. Devereaux. But having one didn't hurt, either."

"Do the others know?"

Lipinski shrugged. "I have no idea. We haven't been allowed to see each other since Dr. Barker's death. I'm hoping that will change once we're cleared of any wrongdoing and we can get back to work."

"That's your biggest concern? Getting back to work?"

"Of course. We were working on many different formulas, but the administration and results of those formulas were handled by Dr. Barker. For security purposes, only he knew the exact chemical composition of the final antidote. With time, however, we'll be able to isolate that formula, test it ourselves, and modify it if we need to."

"So this is all worth it to you?" Knox gestured to the room around him. "Isolating yourself? Living like this? To create a drug that may or may not help individuals you've never met?"

"A surprising question from someone who built his clan a dome so they would survive."

"We'd survive no matter what," Knox said softly, even as he acknowledged her point. "The Dome simply makes survival more palatable."

"Exactly," Lipinski said. "I believe a few significant sacrifices are sometimes necessary in order to make one's life meaningful."

Knox hesitated. The fact that he now respected this woman made what Knox was about to do even less desirable. Yet it had to be done. "I'll be careful. It won't hurt. May I?"

Lipinski nodded. "Go ahead."

She closed her eyes and took a deep breath.

Cautiously, Knox reached out to touch her mind.

Only, he touched nothing.

He reached out again, with more deliberation.

Again, nothing.

Knox was stunned. He'd never tried to read someone's mind before and failed. Why was it happening now? He saw no jewelry around Lipinski's neck. Nothing on her ears or fingers. Had the scientists developed another drug? One that blocked vamp powers?

At his continued silence, Lipinski opened her eyes, her surprise apparent.

"I didn't feel anything. Is it done?"

Troubled, Knox simply nodded, unwilling to give anything away. "Yes," he said testingly.

Lipinski breathed a sigh of relief. "Good. That's good. Now maybe Mahone will let us get back to work."

TEN

Felicia was riffling through the refrigerator in the dining hall when she sensed someone was watching her. Straightening, she casually took a bite out of an apple and swallowed before she turned around.

She held the apple out questioningly. "Hungry?" She took another bite, deliberately taking her time and making as much noise as possible.

Hunt smiled—well, wolfishly was the only way to describe it. "Not for an apple."

In spite of herself, she choked and felt herself blush.

"Need water?"

She shook her head and cleared her throat. "Nope. I'm fine."

"You certainly are."

That made her laugh out loud. She shook her head, wiping at her watering eyes with her fingertips. "Good one."

Looking anything but insulted, Hunt shrugged. "What can I say? It's been a long time since I've met someone worth flirting with."

Felicia made a big show of looking around her, then pointed

at her chest. "Are you talking about me? Because I know you're not attracted to me."

Both Hunt's brows popped into his hairline. "Is that a fact?"

"Yup." Felicia took another bite of her apple, chewing thoughtfully as she tilted her head and surveyed Hunt.

"Like what you see?" He'd probably been going for a dark, sexy tone, but the werebeast sounded more annoyed than anything else.

"You knew Knox was going to beat you, so why challenge him?"

Hunt straightened, a frown furrowing his brows. "I knew no such thing. If he hadn't used persuasion to disconnect from the mage—"

"He would have still kicked your ass. The only reason you got in as many punches as you did was because I was there, distracting him."

Stepping closer to her, Hunt didn't stop until his tight black T-shirt was two inches from the tips of her breasts. Felicia simply raised the apple to her mouth and sank her teeth in it.

Stepping back, Hunt shrugged. "Can't blame a were for trying." Crossing his arms over his chest, he leaned back against a stainless steel prep counter. "So where'd you learn the wrestling moves?"

"A girl's got to keep her secrets, doesn't she?"

He chuckled. "Depends why, I suppose. Some of those moves were Karakai, a uniquely Otherborn discipline. I'm wondering how you . . . Ah, right. Secrets," Hunt said when Felicia just smiled. Suddenly Hunt sobered. "You should have left Lucy out of it, though."

Felicia raised a brow. "Why? She's obviously tougher than she looks. She offered, I accepted. Job completed, Knox's expectations to the contrary. That is, we detained and questioned Randolph. It was a good lead for Knox to follow up on. The fact that Randolph knew nothing about Lafleur's work with the FBI wasn't Knox's fault."

"Sticking up for the vamp despite the fact he pissed you off yesterday, huh? You're definitely a loyal one. Anyone can see you've got it bad for him. You really should give it a go. Vamps, at least the females I've been with, generally do anything and everything in bed."

Something devilish urged Felicia to ask, "Even doggie style?"

The jab hit home.

Hunt frowned and reached for her. Quick as a snake, Felicia dropped the apple and grabbed Hunt's wrist, twisting it behind him and shoving him into the metal island. Cutlery and bowls rattled to the floor, but Felicia pulled the were's arm higher, wanting to hear him groan in pain.

Of course, he didn't.

"Easy there, Red. All you had to do was ask."

Felicia shoved him away from her. "You—"

"If you say bastard, I'm liable to puke," said Wraith as she walked into the room. "We're Others, for God's sake. If we can't come up with something more creative than that . . ."

Hunt straightened while Felicia picked up her apple and tossed it in the trash. "I'm not an Otherborn and neither are you," Felicia snapped.

"So what am I?"

"You're a dead human who can't remember who she is or why she's here."

Instead of snapping back with her usual hostility, Wraith shrugged. "True, but I'm still classified as an Other in the Treaty and the UN's resolution. That makes me—how should I put it?" She stretched her face into a farce of a grin, eyes wide and maniacal, lips straining to show every tooth in her mouth. She framed her face with her hands. "I know. Special," she crooned. Lowering her hands, she glowered. "Believe me, I wish I were dead because I'm certainly bored enough. When is your boyfriend coming back so we can get started?"

"He's not my boy—"

Caleb O'Flare, wearing nothing but a pair of loose boxers, stepped into the kitchen, yawning and scratching his chest. "Hey. Why wasn't I invited to the party?"

If possible, Wraith's features grew even tenser until she looked as if a soft breath would crack any semblance of control. "You're supposed to be psychic, aren't you? Figure it out."

After another jaw-popping yawn, O'Flare pushed his hair out of his eyes and traced a disdainful look down the wraith's form. "You wear your leather ensemble to bed, too?"

For a moment—just a fraction of a second—the wraith's eyes seemed to flinch. "How do you know I've been to bed? Maybe I've been out on the town, seeing how the population of Quantico, Virginia, likes to have fun."

"I'll tell you how they like to have fun," O'Flare said lazily. "The most important detail to remember? Corpses aren't involved unless they can keep at least one hole—their mouth—shut."

"Jesus, O'Flare," Felicia exclaimed. Even Hunt had lowered his gaze to the floor, as if he didn't want to be associated with that comment.

"What?" O'Flare frowned. "She started it."

"Fuck you," Wraith whispered before gliding away, her spine so straight it looked painful.

O'Flare watched her disappear through the doorway.

"Way to distract her from your hard-on, O'Flare."

At Hunt's words, Felicia's eyes widened and dropped to the front of O'Flare's boxers. Sure enough, the material was tented with what appeared to be a very long, very hard boner. How the hell had she missed that?

"Shut up, Hunt," O'Flare muttered. He stomped out of the kitchen, nearly running into Lucy Talbot.

Great, Felicia thought. Might as well deal with everyone tonight. "At least Knox isn't here," she muttered under her breath.

Famous last words.

No sooner had O'Flare put a light hand on Lucy's shoulder

to steady her than Knox appeared behind them. Felicia's breath caught the instant she saw him.

He'd avoided her yesterday, even as he'd run the team through intense physical exercises to assure himself of both their stamina and their fighting skills. Although she, like Lucy, didn't have the others' physical strength, she'd matched their stamina and mobility. At the firing range, her precision was beat only by Hunt and Wraith, who were classified as snipers. To Felicia, her ranking had been a momentous victory. It, like her performance in the bar with Randolph, proved not just that she deserved a spot on the team, but that she could function despite the overriding desire she felt anytime Knox came near her.

The same desire she felt now.

All she had to do was look at him and her pulse began a heavy throbbing beat between her thighs.

Knox's gaze swept the room, instantly landing on Felicia, then on Hunt, who stood the closest to her. When Knox's eyes sparked dangerously, Felicia instinctively took two steps away from Hunt.

Hunt's chuckle stopped her. "Don't worry," he whispered loudly, clearly wanting Knox to hear him. "He doesn't suspect a thing."

"Where's Wraith?" Knox demanded.

Everyone, including Lucy, who hadn't even witnessed the wraith's exit, stared at O'Flare. He shrugged. "Who knows? She only seems capable of saying two words in my presence, and usually they're not meant as an invitation."

"Everyone get dressed," Knox said, "and meet me in the lower conference room in one hour."

Felicia moved toward him as if pulled by an invisible string. If O'Flare and Lucy hadn't already been blocking her path, she might have actually reached out for him. "What's going on?"

Knox assessed her, his gaze so intense and probing that she felt vulnerable and exposed. Goose bumps dotted her arms and she was suddenly acutely aware of her bare breasts beneath her tank top. Her nipples had already tightened into small pebbles that probably stood out against the white cotton like headlights. She put a trembling hand on her forehead, wondering if her skin was actually as hot as it felt. Swallowing with difficulty, she forced herself to ask the question again.

Knox gave her the same answer. Nothing.

With a jerk of his chin, Knox said, "One hour."

He walked away, leaving her to glare at the spot where he'd been standing.

The silence in the room was taut and prolonged. O'Flare and Lucy stared at her with matching expressions of understanding. Hunt just stared at the floor, a small smile on his lips.

When the silence stretched on, Felicia held out her hands. "What?"

Lucy shrugged. "Nothing."

O'Flare laughed and threw a companionable arm around Lucy's shoulder. "Come on, Lucy, let's get ready before Knox decides to throw you in another fighting ring."

Lucy elbowed him as he led her away. "I beg your pardon, but . . ." Lucy's voice faded as the pair walked down the hallway.

"Don't worry," Hunt said as he walked past Felicia to follow the others out of the room. "I didn't have a great view, but I'd be willing to bet the vamp was sporting an even bigger boner for you than the one O'Flare had for the wraith. Maybe he'll show it to you later."

Shooting daggers at his back, Felicia actually struggled not to stick her tongue out at him. "I thought werebeasts were loners. You sure talk a lot for one."

Over his shoulder, Hunt said, "The whole 'I am an island' thing? It's still kind of new to me. Up until a month ago, I rode with a pack."

"Rat pack, you mean, don't you?"

Hunt froze, but Felicia stepped closer until she was practically speaking into his ear. "And I mean that literally. The Ferals are one of the Southwest's most troublesome gangs, with its members involved in everything from grand theft auto to drug sales to murder. Why'd they kick you out?"

When he turned to face her, all evidence of his infuriating disdain and smart-ass humor had disappeared. His face, weathered prematurely by the elements but in no way unattractive, was set in grim lines. His hazel eyes had darkened to a deep, dark chocolate.

"You really want to know?" he asked.

Felicia swallowed so she wouldn't say no like she suddenly wanted to. "I asked, didn't I?"

"Yeah. You asked." Hunt raised one hand, grinning when Felicia flinched. All he did was push a stray hair behind her ear.

"I got booted from the Ferals because a senior member let it slip he had a thing for werebeasts. Male ones, the younger the better. His favorite hangout was an old schoolhouse slash orphanage that catered exclusively to the troubled half-Other-born whelps of werewolves. He raved about what a classy place it was. Described the public rooms in detail, from the color of the curtains and carpet, to the design carved into the banister."

"I take it this was a place you were familiar with?"

"Only in passing," Hunt said. "I knew someone who'd been placed there."

"Is this Feral still alive?"

"No."

"No?"

"You don't believe me?"

Felicia licked her lips at the threat edging the were's voice. Just seconds ago, his eyes had gone distant, as if he'd been transported back in time and was no longer aware of where he was.

"What happened to this friend of yours?" she prodded.

"The same thing that happened to everyone who went there. Unless you were a teacher or an invited guest, that is."

"And this Feral who'd been there? You knew him?"

"I more than knew him. He was my best friend. We were as thick as thieves from the moment I first joined the gang, approximately fifteen years ago."

"So what happened?"

"What do you think happened?"

"I think you didn't like the fact that he'd been at the school, any more than you liked his attraction to kids. So you what? Fought with him and the gang kicked you out?"

Hunt smirked. "You're smarter than that, Felicia."

"You didn't fight?" she asked, although she already knew the answer. It wasn't in the files that the other team members had been given, but it was in Mahone's classified files. And she'd read those in detail.

"I killed him, but I tortured him first. Do you know a werewolf can only be killed in human form?"

"As a matter of fact, yes."

Hunt nodded, his eyes getting all hazy again. "One way to keep a were in human form is to keep him in water. So that's what I did. I hosed him down and kept him wet. I took out my buck knife and I killed him. Slowly. After that, I didn't actually wait around for the gang to ask me to leave."

Blinking rapidly to hide the sheen of tears in her eyes, Felicia nodded. "Of course. That would have been rude. It's never polite to overstay one's welcome."

Her calm words seemed to shock Hunt out of his memories. He blinked once. Twice. Then, amazingly, he chucked her chin. "The dharmire needs to watch his back. Fighting for fun is one thing. If I ever had a reason to fight him for something I wanted, I'd make sure things ended differently."

Felicia shook her head, her gaze steady. "You won't have a reason to fight him."

Hunt nodded good-naturedly. "Then enjoy the ride. And remember what I said. Anything and everything. Doggie style would be the least of your worries, believe me."

Everyone but Wraith was assembled in the conference room when Knox walked in. Thankfully, all of them, including Felicia, were dressed in street clothes. When he'd stopped by the kitchen and seen her in her thin tank top and pajama pants, her breasts loose and nipples straining against the white cotton, he'd felt a killing rage sweep over him. It had had nothing to do with her state of dress, but everything to do with the fact that Dex Hunt was standing beside her, seeing her state of *un*-dress and watching her with his dark eyes.

Knox had barely restrained himself from ripping those eyes out of their sockets and mincing them to bits with one of the chef's knives. Fortunately, he'd kept a grip on his sanity and reminded himself his foul mood probably had more to do with his frustration than any real threat he felt coming from Hunt.

He had only needed that split second of calm to realize that until she saw him, Felicia's eyes had been completely devoid of desire. Knowing that he and he alone affected her that way had threatened to shred his control yet again. That was why he'd kept his words to a minimum and gotten away from her as fast as he could.

Losing a measure of control wouldn't bother him when it was just him and Felicia, with her under him, spread wide to take him inside her. But in front of his team? In front of the werebeast? No way.

Knox deliberately pushed thoughts of Felicia and her naked, warm flesh aside. Despite his inability to read the scientists' minds, something he'd never experienced before, the trip hadn't been a total failure. Mahone had provided him with new information. The news was both helpful and devastating. The sooner the team knew about the situation, the sooner they could put aside their petty differences and concentrate on the task at hand.

"So are you going to tell us what you did today?" Felicia asked.

He returned his focus to her. She swallowed, as if she, like him, felt the same pulsing arc of electricity sizzling between them. "I went to see the scientists who worked with Barker on the antidote."

Felicia's eyes rounded. "The President authorized that? Knowing you could read their minds? What did you find out? How come you haven't—"

Knox shook his head. "I saw them. I tried to read their minds. I got nothing."

"You got nothing, or there was nothing to get?" Lucy clarified.

"Well, I . . ." Knox frowned, then tore his gaze from Felicia, wondering if lust was frying his brain. The mage's question made sense, or at least it should, but what did it matter? "I wasn't able to glean anything from reading their minds."

"Performance anxiety," Hunt whispered loudly to Felicia.

Felicia glared at him.

"Let me know when you've got the adolescent humor out of your system, Hunt," Knox said, "and then I'll continue, okay?" Knox stared at the were, keeping his face blank even though he so badly wanted to pound him into the ground. He'd decided the best way to handle the guy was to treat him like he was an annoying little brother—Lord knows he'd gotten enough practice growing up with Zeph. And, Knox knew, condescension would piss Hunt off more than any overt attempt to establish authority would.

Sure enough, when Knox crossed his arms over his chest, outwardly prepared to wait all night if he had to, Dex clenched his jaw muscles until his cheek ticked. Knox counted to five— very slowly—before continuing.

"I don't know why I couldn't read them. It's never happened before. I have reason to believe that loss of the power is associated with vamp malnourishment. Perhaps it was just a temporary block for me, perhaps not. Either way, despite the dead end with the scientists," Knox said, "Mahone's men have been busy gathering information on foreign soil. Or in this case, from above foreign soil." He picked up a stack of photos and handed them to O'Flare, indicating that he should take one set and pass them on.

"What the—" O'Flare's gaze swiftly connected with Knox's. "This is the DPRK."

"That's correct," Knox said, looking at the others. "The Democratic People's Republic of Korea. North Korea. O'Flare spent some time there before the War, providing relief inside the Demilitarized Zone to villagers in Tae Sung Dong. That zone is colored in with yellow. The red dotted line indicates the MDL, the Military Demarcation Line, where Northern and Southern troops faced off before both governments made an armistice agreement to move their troops back twenty-two hundred yards from the front line, creating a buffer zone two-and-a-half miles wide."

"Did I sign up for a geography lesson without knowing it, or is this going somewhere?" Hunt asked impatiently.

"Do you need a geography lesson, or can you tell us what the Gyeongui Line is?"

Hunt smirked. "I can help you out, sure." Hunt looked at the others. "The Gyeongui Line is a highway that's sometimes used to get from South to North Korea. Although, because the two Koreas are still technically at war, it doesn't get much use. You'd have to be insane or have a death wish to want to use it. And"—he growled, holding up his hand—"before any of you make any wisecracks about the Ferals and some of the waste-lands we've driven through, they haven't driven that particular road. I haven't, either. But I admit I'm curious. When I say no one uses this highway, am I wrong?" Hunt looked at Knox. For once, the were had seemed to abandon his attitude in favor of curiosity.

"No, you're not wrong. Still, the highway is the most obvious method of transportation between the two zones. In the mid-twentieth century, however, several underground tunnels were discovered. The consensus is that these tunnels became progressively more advanced as time went on. At some point, they were discovered and the South even used them as a marketing tool to get more tourists into the country. According to both North and South Korea, the tunnels have since been sealed on both ends and abandoned."

"If they're sealed, what do they have to do with our mission?" Lucy asked.

"As of six months ago, it looks like they were unsealed, thus enabling someone to smuggle something into North Korea from the South. In doing so, he'd avoided the traditional travel methods into North Korea by air or sea, which are extremely limited and heavily monitored."

"But six months ago, the antidote hadn't even been created, had it?" Lucy countered.

"Not that we know of. But once they began to suspect North Korea of obtaining the antidote, the FBI retrieved satellite photos that had already been taken in that region, hoping to find prior connections between North Korea and either vamps in general or the FBI scientists in particular. Instead, they found something else." Moving to a projector he'd set up toward the back of the room, Knox turned it on and brought up a slide that zoomed in on a portion of the diagram he'd handed out. "These satellite photos were taken about four months ago. This area here"—Knox pointed to an area shaded in gray— "denotes three of the incursion tunnels. You'll see the openings of this tunnel are here, on the south side, and here, on the north." Knox pressed a button on a remote, which made the next slide appear on the screen. "This shows the north end of the tunnel over a period of seventy-two hours, as recorded by these successive stills."

Knox pushed the remote button several times, switching the images on the screen. At one point, Hunt straightened in his chair. "Stop."

Knox did.

Hunt stood and walked to the screen, then pointed to several dark spots that had appeared on what should have been a slide identical to the last. "There's a change."

"Good eyes, Hunt." Knox clicked the remote again, increasing the zoom on the satellite picture until the black dots began to resemble images. Fuzzy, yes, but clearly recognizable for what they were.

Felicia gasped.

Lucy got to her feet. "They're using the tunnels to transport Others from South Korea into North Korea?"

"'Transporting' being a loose term," O'Flare agreed, his voice tight with anger, "considering they're obviously being moved against their will."

"As I said, these photos are old. We don't know if they're continuing to use the tunnels, only that they used them once four months ago. Subsequent photos fail to reveal similar activity. Chances are, if they're still smuggling Others in, they've found another way to do it."

"There are wraiths in that picture," Lucy whispered. O'Flare cursed flatly.

"Yes," Knox said as he continued to scroll through the slides.

"Oh God," Felicia whispered when she saw the picture of the vamp. Her gaze shot to Knox, who compressed his lips together. She shook her head. "Okay, okay. Hold on for a second. Let me play devil's advocate." Felicia stood and peered at the slide more closely. "How can we know these Others are entering North Korea against their will? How do we know they're not being rolled in on gurneys because they're injured?"

Hunt snorted. "Jesus, Red. That's a little naïve, don't you think?"

Narrowing her eyes, Felicia blasted Hunt with a glare. "It's naïve to question a bold assumption? These are grainy shots taken from a great distance under poor weather conditions, Hunt. Yes, given the clandestine nature of the movement, the reason for moving these individuals—who we shouldn't just assume are all Others, by the way—is probably less than altruistic, but it's best to consider all possibilities, don't you think, before we antagonize an already hostile government with assumptions?"

Glancing at Knox, Hunt grunted. "She always this mouthy? And you really want to take her to bed?" he scoffed.

Felicia and Knox reached the werebeast at the same time. He was pinned to his chair with his head pulled back, his throat vulnerably exposed, within seconds. Knox glanced at Felicia. "Go ahead. I'll hold him for you."

Disgusted, Felicia shook her head at Knox. "Let him go."

With a heavy shove, Knox released him and backed off.

"I'm getting the feeling humor is running scarce right about now," Hunt said as he adjusted his shirt and brushed back his hair.

"You're worse than the wraith," Lucy snapped. "There are werewolves in those pictures. Don't you care?"

"Of course I care," Hunt snarled. "I care that any were, wolf or beast, was weak enough to be taken down, strapped to a gurney, and transported halfway across the world. It's bad for my rep."

"You're an ass," O'Flare said. "But the less obvious issue we need to focus on is why? What do the North Koreans want with these Others? Felicia is right. We have to explore all possibilities, including the more benign. If their purpose is benign, if they obtained the antidote for humanitarian reasons, for example, we need to take that into account. It's not likely given the country's history, but—"

"Where—where did you get those photos?"

The whisper was so low it would have been easy to miss but for the raw emotion infusing it. Knox turned a split second before all the others to see the wraith standing in the open doorway of the conference room. She took several steps forward. Even as he watched, a small pack of gum fell from her loose right hand and onto the floor.

"Wraith . . ." Knox began in a low voice, instinctively reaching out for the female who naturally inspired pity even as she tried to push it away.

The wraith's expression was one he'd never seen on her—one he'd never imagined he would—but it was one he was familiar with. He'd seen it often during the War, a frozen mask of terror, usually most often seen on the faces of the young or the innocent who'd been devastated by things or images that should only have been experienced, if at all, in someone's nightmares.

"Where . . ." She turned confused eyes on Knox.

"She's shaking," Felicia murmured just behind him. Knox nodded, but held out his hand, indicating that everyone should stay back. He needn't have bothered.

The others were still, their bodies echoing the wraith's tension as they watched her carefully. Lucy flinched first when a tortured moan escaped the wraith's throat.

"Wraith," Knox said loudly, trying to get through to her. "Answer me. Do these pictures look familiar to you? Wraith?"

But she was gone, Knox realized. The moans turned into full-out groans, and those into wails, and those into shrieks so piercingly high and filled with terror that O'Flare, Felicia, and Lucy covered their ears.

Knox pushed his face in front of hers. "Wraith. Stop it. Now."

"Yeah, like that's going to help," Hunt snapped.

"What do you suggest I do?" Knox snapped right back. "If I touch her to shake her, I might push her completely over the edge."

"Well, she's already . . . there." Hunt said the last word much more softly than the first three because Wraith's screams had abruptly stopped. As she stared at the screen, Knox did as well, trying to see what she saw besides a pale vamp strapped to a gurney with restraints that went around his legs, torso, and neck.

"Wraith?" Lucy approached the wraith hesitantly. "What's wrong? What do you—"

Wraith flinched away from Lucy's outstretched hand. She took a step back. Then another. Until she once more stood in the hallway rather than in the room with everyone else. "I . . ." She shook her head as if to clear it. The movement dislodged the moisture that had filled her eyes. Feeling it, she reached up and touched the tears with her hand, then stared at the moisture on her fingertips as if it were blood. "I'm sorry," she croaked before she bolted down the hall.

"Damn it. Felicia," Knox said, turning toward her. "Can you—"

"No. I'll go."

"What? No," Knox snapped at O'Flare. "Let Felicia—"

But O'Flare was already gone.

For the longest time, none of them spoke.

Then Hunt released a deep sigh and rubbed his face. "Did you see the look on her face? Poor little wraith."

"A little late for you to grow a heart, don't you think?" Lucy asked.

Hunt smiled thinly. "Can't grow something from nothing," he agreed.

"What do you think happened to her?" Felicia asked.

Knox just shook his head and tried not to imagine the possibilities.

"Who knows?" Hunt said. "But tell me something, Red. You still think the Others in those pictures were just feeling under the weather?"

Knox looked up just in time to see Felicia, with absolutely no expression on her face, lift her hand and give Hunt the finger.

Caleb O'Flare found Wraith in the same kitchen where she'd told him to fuck off just hours earlier. She was standing with her arms braced on that metal cart, the mess Felicia and Hunt had made earlier still on the floor, staring at a wicked-looking knife lying flat on the cart's surface.

With his heart in his throat, Caleb pretended an ease he didn't feel and leaned against the doorway.

"Nice set of lungs you showed us back there. Now why don't you stop staring at the knife? You've already figured out cutting yourself isn't going to work."

A small frown formed between her brows at his words. Caleb released a silent breath, encouraged that his tactic had worked. This female wasn't going to respond to words of sympathy any more than she would a gesture of friendship. She'd be horrified by her display of weakness, and the way to get past that was to give her something to hold on to. Even if it hurt *him* to give it to her.

Sure enough, her filmy eyes seemed to clear just a little. "How do you know I was thinking of using the knife on myself and not the rest of you?"

She sounded more petulant than angry, but Caleb was careful not to show amusement. "Because I saw the scars. The ones on your wrists and your throat. That first day, when you straddled me and threatened to blow my head off."

"Ah, yes." She nodded. "I remember."

Unexpectedly, she said nothing more, just went back to staring at the knife.

"What was it about the picture that got to you?"

Again, nothing. The silence stretched on for so long that he was sure she wasn't going to answer.

"The collar," she said eventually, her voice flat.

Caleb straightened. "Collar? You mean the restraint around the vamp's throat?"

Wraith closed her eyes and huffed out a disdainful breath. "That wasn't a restraint, it was a collar. But since it's designed to accomplish the same thing—to restrain the individual wearing it—I guess we're arguing over semantics."

"How do you know what it's designed for?" He asked the question even though, in his gut, he knew he didn't want to hear the answer.

Her eyes finally moved away from the knife to lock on his. "How do you think?" she breathed.

Caleb nodded. "Personal experience."

"Bingo."

Memories assaulted him. Filled him with grief and a raw, explosive anger for the pain Wraith had suffered. "Is that what the puncture marks on your neck are from?"

Her head jerked and it was obvious that now he was the one to have surprised her. Her eyes narrowed when he took several steps toward her. He stopped a few feet away.

"The scar across your neck is from a knife, as are the ones on your wrists." His eyes dropped to her wrists, but she quickly tugged down her sleeves before clenching her hands into fists. "The one across your throat was inflicted before you died. I can tell because it's almost faded, unlike the ones on your wrists. Those you did yourself, I'm assuming in an effort to kill yourself after you came back as a wraith."

"Well, well. Seems like you're not just a pretty face. You're smart, too. Good deductions, O'Flare. Now, I think I'm—"

"I'm not done yet." He took another step closer and reached out, ignoring her swift inhalation of breath to gently move her shirt collar away from her throat. He watched her carefully, for any sign that he was hurting her, but she stared back at him, her quick breaths the only sign of her discomfort.

"These puncture wounds are even newer. I wondered what they were. They're clearly not bites since there are five holes in this little pattern here . . ." Cautiously, he slipped his finger inside her collar and, with a gentle skim of the tip, touched the mark on her neck. She jerked, her neck muscles tightening, and bit her lip. "Does that hurt you?" he whispered.

"Yes," she whispered back.

Caleb pulled his hand away and stepped back.

"Well?" Caleb finally asked. "Aren't you going to deny it?"

She actually smiled, a genuine smile resulting from confusion rather than happiness. "What is it I'm supposed to deny?"

For a second, he considered backing off. He, more than anyone, knew where this was leading and no matter what she believed, the last thing O'Flare wanted was to cause her more pain. Clearly, talking about the collar did just that, and while Caleb could physically heal a mortal wound, he didn't have the power to heal mental suffering, with or without his ancestor's help.

Torture, a voice whispered in his head, and he instinctively wanted to back away. Erase the last few minutes the same way he wanted to erase the years of war. He remembered his friend, Prince Elijah, his sister, Natia, and the feline family that had once welcomed him with open arms. Even once war had been declared, they'd loved him. Understood his need to heal others, even those who sought to kill felines in the name of patriotism. Until . . .

Now Elijah was dead. He'd been tortured to death. And Elijah's family hated Caleb. Rightfully so, since Caleb was partly to blame for Elijah's death.

But he couldn't erase any of it. Not his past and not Wraith's. He had to deal and so did she. He could help her . . . maybe . . . if she told him the truth. And if she let him.

"You have a matching mark on the other side of your throat. I'm guessing that this collar you're talking about was actually attached to you, literally, with prongs that imbedded into your skin. That tells me that the collar did more than just restrain you. What was it? Electric shock?"

"Sorry, stud. You don't win the prize. Not this time."

She moved to step around him, but he blocked her with his body. "Then what were the prongs for?"

"Move," she ordered.

He shook his head. "Not until you tell me."

Hands on her hips now, she thrust her chin out. "Why? Does the idea of me in pain turn you on, O'Flare? You need specifics for when you jerk off tonight? Need something to visualize?"

Caleb heard her words, but more than that, he heard the desperation behind them. He forced himself to give her the cruelty she needed. "Don't flatter yourself, Wraith. Visualizing you while I'm jerking off, whether you're in pain or not, would be the surest way to deflate a hard-on. I want to know for one reason and one reason only. Because it pertains to what you saw on that screen, and as such it pertains to the success of our mission. If you can't be a professional long enough to get over your own shit and tell me, then you're more fucked up than I thought you were and you don't belong on this team."

After another lingering stare, Caleb turned around and walked out of the kitchen. He was five feet down the hallway when he heard her behind him.

"A paralyzing agent."

He stopped but didn't turn around.

"The collar released a paralyzing agent, some kind of solution I haven't been able to identify even after years of research. It was used on me. On other wraiths. But I never saw it used on Others. Never expected it could be until today, when I saw that slide."

"Why wraiths?" he asked, still not turning around. "What did your captors need to paralyze you for?"

She didn't answer him right away, but he waited. When she did answer, her voice was low and fervent. "Experiments," she said.

Caleb closed his eyes, trying to erase the instant images that formed from the stories he'd heard. At one point, maybe even still today, North Korea had established Prison Camp 22, located in Haengyong, an isolated area near the border with Russia. It had been one of a network of prisons in North Korea modeled on the Soviet Gulag where hundreds of thousands of prisoners were held. Two things had stuck in his mind about what he'd heard. The first was that the prison included not just political prisoners, but because it followed the "Heredity Rule," it also housed many of the prisoners' next of kin. If a prisoner was caught trying to escape, then his family and his neighboring families were shot to death out of collective responsibility. The second thing O'Flare remembered was the prison's reputed use of torture and experimentation. A former guard there had explained that he enjoyed torturing people, and by the time the enjoyment began to wear off, he was replaced. The same guard had confirmed that prisoners were often transported to another location for chemical experiments in specially constructed gas chambers.

With his thoughts, the images he was trying to hold back formed, bright and deadly. Not of Elijah this time, but of

Wraith strapped to some table, drugged up and scared shitless while some maniacal cretin went after her with a blade in the interest of science.

He felt sick to his stomach. Suddenly wanted to kill someone for putting all that pain and hurt and fear in Wraith's eyes. All he said, though, was, "All right then."

He walked away and was so far down the hall when she spoke that she probably thought he couldn't hear her.

"I hate you now that you know. Now more than ever."

Caleb didn't betray the fact he heard her by word or gesture. He just kept on walking, whispering his reply. "I know, baby. I know."

ELEVEN

Felicia knew Knox would come to her that night. The sizzle of electricity that flared to life anytime they were in the same vicinity had to be making his balls ache as much as it was making her clit throb with sensation and yearning. Still, because she'd assumed he'd scoped out her room beforehand, she'd been expecting him to materialize, not knock on her door.

She cracked it open. "Hi," she said softly. "Is Wraith okay?"

Knox nodded, his face reflecting a weariness she'd rarely seen on him before. Frowning, she opened the door wider. Was it her imagination, or did his clothes seem a little looser on his tall frame? Did his cheeks seem to protrude just a bit more on his face? Worry began a heavy throbbing beat inside her, but he didn't seem to notice.

Nor did he make a move to enter her room. "O'Flare talked to her. Said she's okay. She told him what freaked her out about that picture."

Felicia motioned him inside. "Come in so we can talk."

When Knox hesitated, Felicia laughed. "What, after all this

time, I invite you into my room and you're going to turn me down?"

"Depends," Knox said. "Are you also inviting me into your bed?"

"I . . ." Out of habit, Felicia struggled for a response that wouldn't result in her stretched out under him, even though that was exactly where she wanted to be.

Especially now.

Staring up at him, Felicia couldn't deny something inside her had shifted. She also couldn't deny she was through fighting him.

Always before, even as she was turning him away, Felicia had the knowledge of Knox's immortality to comfort her. She might never be his, she'd reasoned, but he'd always be around. Whether she tracked him down or not, whether they were together or not, she'd know he was on the same planet, breathing the same air, as strong and vital as ever. Given the photos Knox had shown them today, she could no longer take that for granted. Seeing that vamp, restrained and helpless, had affected her so much it might as well have been Knox tied to the gurney.

Rational or not, she'd suddenly been overwhelmed by fear that if something went wrong, this mission could result in Knox's death.

That simply was not something she was willing to think about.

So, instead, she thought about their bodies coming together in passion. But then his last words registered, scaring the shit out of her.

He'd asked if she was inviting him into her bed, and only a fool would think his word choice was irrelevant. Yes, she'd been prepared for him to come to her. Yes, she was through fighting him. She was ready to surrender. To yield. To lose herself in the pleasure she knew was right in front of her.

She hadn't been prepared for him to demand the words. To demand that she take full responsibility for their coming together. Somehow, after everything they'd been through, that just seemed unfair.

So although she wanted to say yes, she, as always, forced herself to say no.

"Then I'd just as soon stay out here. Less temptation. Besides, I just came by to give you something." He held out a box.

Felicia raised a brow. "A team gift?" She smiled teasingly, hoping to get him to smile. Since the War, she'd rarely seen him smile with genuine emotion. Suddenly, she realized that more than his body, that was what she wanted from him now. "Did you have team pins made?"

"No. I had this made specifically for you."

Bemused, she opened the small box, then stared at the necklace inside. It was the vamp medallion, the same one Mara had worn. And Noella. And every female that Knox had dedicated his life to protecting. The hot sting of tears warned her how much the gesture had affected her. She shook her head. "I—I don't understand."

"I know you can't wear it. Too dangerous given what you do and the people you come in contact with."

"Then why—"

"To thank you for what you did for Mara." Raising a hand, he cupped her face. "And because you're part of us. Part of me. You always have been, Felicia. Despite the fact that it's what keeps us apart, know that whatever I would do for my clan, I would do to protect you. I—"

Felicia couldn't stop herself. She threw her arms around him and kissed him, a soft but lingering closemouthed kiss meant to express her gratitude and affection. Under hers, Knox's mouth—his entire body, in fact—was still and tense. His eyes, however, were open, staring into hers, piercing her with such intense emotion that she felt him in every pore of her body, almost as if they'd become one. His hands dropped to her hips, kneading the curves he held and pressing her into his lean, muscular body.

Shivers raced up her spine when she felt his steel-hard dick rub anxiously against her mound. "Knox . . ." she moaned, the breathy sound that of a stranger. It shocked her into pulling away.

Knox closed his eyes. For a horrifying moment, he actually swayed on his feet.

"Knox!" Pocketing the small box with the necklace, she grabbed his arm and his eyes popped open. She dragged him inside, even though the idea of her dragging the six-foot-four vamp anywhere would have been ludicrous in most situations. The fact that he docilely let her pull him anywhere made her worry transform into panic. "Sit down before you fall down," she ordered, pushing him down on her bed. He sat and she scurried into her bathroom to wet a washcloth and bring it to him. "What's wrong? Are you sick? Are you hot? Here, put this on your forehead."

She held the small towel against his head herself, peering at him closely. He stared back at her. After a minute, she asked, "How's that feel?"

"Wet. It's a word I've always associated with you, but not quite under these circumstances."

Despite his obvious attempt at humor, he sounded as if even talking had become a chore for him. "You're hungry, aren't you?" she asked.

He didn't answer. His head lolled so that his chin tucked into his chest.

Felicia threw the towel to the ground and cupped his chin in hers, lifting his face. "Knox. Knox!" When he didn't respond, she tapped his cheeks lightly, then harder.

Maybe too hard.

Suddenly, his head jerked up and a hiss escaped his lips. He captured both of her wrists in punishing grips. "What the hell?"

Felicia struggled against his hold. "That's what I was just asking. What the hell is wrong with you?"

"Nothing." He stared at his fingers wrapped around her wrists. He stood, but failed to release her. "I'm fine now. Sometimes I get tired, that's all."

His grip on her was tremulous. He was literally shaking, and sweat had beaded on his upper lip. When she stroked his hair from his face, he closed his eyes and groaned as if even that light touch was excruciatingly painful.

Abruptly, he jerked away. "I've got to go."

"You're not going anywhere—"

"Felicia, you don't understand—"

"I understand that you're sick and you are not leaving—"

"Damn it, Felicia," he yelled, grabbing her by the shoulders and shaking her with enough force to stun her. "I have to leave. Now. Otherwise I'm going to crawl on top of you, and push my dick inside you at the same time that I bite your throat. Is that what you need to hear? Fine, I said it. Now get out of my way."

She swallowed hard. He was tired and weak, but was it possible that his desire for her was the reason? Could she really affect this strong male that much? Giddy pleasure mingled with a flood of corresponding heat, as well as fury. He needed her and yet he forced her to continue denying him. Why? If he needed her so desperately, why couldn't she be enough for him?

"The female in France," she said hesitantly. "You—you weren't with her."

He slanted her a dark look. "No. I told you, I have no interest in her that way. If it weren't for my clan's needs—"

"Stop hiding behind your clan, Knox, and tell me why," she erupted, suddenly unable to take it anymore. "If you want me so much, why can't you give me what I need?"

"I told you, Felicia, I can't discuss this now. I'm going . . ." He tried to move away again.

This time it was her fingers that manacled his wrists. "No," she whispered. She said it more firmly. More loudly. "No. That's not what I needed to hear. I want to hear that you love me. I want to hear why that's not enough for you. Why you can't promise me your fidelity? I want to hear you tell me that despite all our differences, despite the fact that we don't share the same blood, that we belong together. That we'd be good together." She released his wrists as suddenly as she'd taken hold of them. Taking several steps back, she struggled to speak past her tears. "I want to hear why you haven't taken me, when it would be so easy for you to. When you know it's what I've wanted."

By the time she stopped talking, Knox's fists were clenching at his sides and he was breathing in air like a locomotive. A flush had spread across his cheeks and sparks of red were beginning to flicker in and out of his black and silver eyes, making her hold her breath in anticipation.

"I haven't taken you," he gritted, "because we both know that's the surest way for me to lose you. And of all those things you want me to say, that's the only thing I can say right now, because the rest will either scare you, be a lie, or is something I don't know."

Wearily, he sank back down to her bed, his head bent as he stared at the carpet under his feet. She breathed in raggedly as she stared at him. The desire was still there, but so was something that looked perilously close to defeat. That frightened her more than anything had up to now.

"Well, at least I can always count on you to be honest," she said, taking a seat next to him. Tentatively, she rested her hand on the bed between them. He covered it with his own. Relief was a heady thing.

"I'm right, aren't I? You need blood."

He looked at her and smiled thinly. "Yes. I need blood."

"How long?"

He rubbed a hand against his forehead. "Awhile. Mahone was supposed to have some animals brought in, but I guess there's been a delay. That, or the fucker is just getting back at me for something I said earlier."

"About him and your mother?"

He chuckled wryly. "Yeah. Sometimes I forget you know all there is to know about me."

"Not everything."

"What don't you know?"

"I don't know what it feels like to make love to you," she whispered. "I've imagined it, time and time again, but I don't know."

His hand tightened on hers until the grip was almost painful. "Why are you saying that? To tempt me? Or torture me?"

"I'm saying it because—because . . ." Tears gathered as she struggled to get the words out. Past her guilt. Past her worry. And past her own fear. "I'm saying I want to know. Now. Finally."

Although she breathed a huge sigh of relief that she'd finally said it, Knox didn't seem pleased. Neither did he move. "Why now? After all this time? When you know what I intend to do . . ."

She frowned, struggling to explain when part of her felt she'd already said enough. "That's exactly why. I've wanted you so long. Why shouldn't I have you? As to your plans, I haven't changed my mind. I won't share you, Knox. But today, no one has claim on you. No one but me. After seeing that vamp on that gurney . . ." Pulling her hand from his, she stood and paced in front of him, not liking the way that fear was once more edging out desire.

"Ah," he said. "You're worried about me? Afraid the North Koreans have figured out a way to subdue vamps? No worries, love. For all I know, that vamp was starving and didn't have enough strength to swat at a fly. There's no reason to—"

"You're starving, too," she snapped, uncertain how she'd gotten so angry so fast. "You're not feeling the full effects now, not like a full vampire would, but it's coming, isn't it?"

He stood. "Save your pity fuck for someone else, Felicia. I'm fine and I'm going to stay fine."

He turned away, stopped, then whipped back around to face her. "I don't want you because you're scared, Felicia. I don't want you because I make you come to me, either. When you open your legs for me, when you take me inside you, I want it to be because you're so hot and so desperate for my touch and the pleasure that only I can give you, that you're willing to throw away your doubts and concerns and notions of morality to have me. Until you can give me that, don't offer yourself to me again."

Her head was spinning with the pinpricks of rejection. "Or else what?" she challenged.

"Or else you just might see how much strength this old vamp has in him. And not in a good way."

She narrowed her eyes. "Then you better go find yourself something to drink, old man. Because you just might need all the help you can get."

"Don't push me, Felicia." He strode toward the door.

"How about I stop pushing you and go push someone else?" He froze at her words and she walked past him toward the door, not caring that she was once again wearing her tank top and pajama bottoms. The ease with which he was rejecting her, when she was finally, *finally* offering him what he'd been asking for, caused her to snap. "How about I go push O'Flare. He's a medic, sure to be skilled with his hands. Or better yet, Hunt. He's an asshole, but I've heard sometimes those make the best lovers. Them being so, so *nasty*," she sneered the word, stretching it out, "and all."

She didn't even see him coming. One second she was mouthing off, and the next she was flying through the air as he grabbed her, picked her up, and threw her on the bed. Still bouncing, she gasped and flipped on her stomach to crawl away from him. Instead, his heavy weight flattened her into the mattress. His dick, a hard rod that burned her even through her clothes, prodded relentlessly at the cleft of her bottom. At the same time, he stretched her arms high above her head, holding them there with one hand while the other grasped the inside of one of her knees and pulled her legs apart.

She moaned when he shifted and arched into her, thrusting his dick against the hot, moist warmth between her thighs.

He leaned over, his hot breath blasting her neck. "You just had to keep pushing and pushing, didn't you? Well, guess what? It worked. Only, I'm not going to fuck you, Felicia. I'm not going to take you so you can later blame me for taking the choice away from you. If you want me, you say so right now. Loud and clear. Do you understand?"

"Yes," she screamed. "I understand that you are a prick. A big . . ." She tried to put her knees under her so she could buck him off, but he just pressed his legs even harder against hers, laughing. "Ugly . . ." Furious, she tried to jerk her wrists loose, and he retaliated by raking his fangs against the back of her neck. She froze, but managed to pant out, "Stupid . . ." She moaned when his free hand tangled in her hair and rubbed her scalp. "Ugly . . ."

"You said that already."

"You're so ugly I have to say it twice."

"Is that it then? You've said all you need to say?"

She forced herself not to answer but couldn't stop herself from crying out when he let go of her hands and pushed himself back and off her.

She closed her eyes as the mattress bounced, and she knew unless she said something, he'd be gone.

"I want you," she whispered.

She felt him pause. "What?"

"I want you," she said louder.

"How about you say that one more time."

Her relief was overwhelming. "I want you," she yelled.

"I want you, too."

She tried to lower her arms, which were still stretched above her head, but she couldn't. An immovable force held them in place. "What . . ." Still on her stomach, she turned her head to face him.

His eyes were narrowed and heavy-lidded with desire.

"Are you . . ." she began. "You can't . . ."

Slowly, he turned her so that she lay on her back. "Of course I can use my persuasion powers to pin your arms down. As long as I have your permission. Are you going to give me permission, Felicia?"

She blinked, trying to focus on what he was saying. She moaned when he cupped one of her breasts, then the other. "Generally. . . ." She bit her lip when he tweaked one of her nipples, then moved to the other, pinching it in a firm, sustained grip. "Generally one asks for permission before taking liberties," she choked out.

"Ah, yes. Of course. I suppose I jumped the gun a bit." He leaned down and licked at her ear, his tongue thrusting into the delicate whorls at the same time his other hand slipped into her pajama bottoms. "Let me do it right. May I continue to use persuasion in order to ensure that your arms stay above your head so that I may pleasure you with both my hands?"

"No," she gasped, moaning loudly when she felt his nimble fingers circle and pluck at her clit.

"No?" Everything about him froze. His body. His mouth. His fingers. The pressure on her wrists gave and he began to straighten. "Okay . . ."

Desperately, she rushed out, "No, I didn't mean no. I meant, no, not until you say please."

"Please?" he echoed.

Slowly, she pushed up on her elbows. Knox shifted until he was on his knees, straddling her hips. She reached up, smoothing her hands over his thick, muscular biceps. "Please," she said softly. "Pretty please. Please with sugar on top. Please."

Her final please was muffled. For long, blissful moments, his mouth ate at hers. Occasionally, his head lifted and tilted to give him better access. Eventually, the frantic grind of their mouths against one another slowed, as if he was beginning to accept she was here, in his arms, and wasn't going anywhere without him.

Knox pulled back slightly. He looked at her, direct and aroused. He raised his hand and rubbed his thumb over her mouth. Firmly. Twice. She was acutely aware of every sensitive inch of her body. Her lips ached, felt swollen and needy. Her hands reveled in the feel of him, repeatedly moving from his silky hair to his muscular, broad shoulders. Her nipples tightened into painful, aching points, and she leaned into him, brushing them against his chest, wanting her thin tank top and his shirt gone so that nothing separated them.

Skin on skin. That was what she wanted. What she needed. What she craved.

She reached up and kissed him with all the pent-up passion inside her. First she nipped at his bottom lip before gently sucking it. Then she soul-kissed him, circling his tongue with her own. When he widened his mouth over hers, she drew back and playfully ran the tip of her tongue over his lips, then his fangs.

Knox growled and grabbed her hips. When he pulled her into his groin, she raised her leg, rubbing it up and down his thigh. God, he was hard. She wanted to touch him everywhere. She wanted to ease the heated ache in her body by feeling him move inside her. When she reached down to rub the front of his pants, he broke their kiss, gasping for breath. He grasped her hand, stilling her.

"No. Not now. If you touch me now, I'm going to lose it."

"I want you to lose it."

"Not before I show you everything I have to give you," he murmured, leaning down to kiss her.

Her hand snaked away from his to cup his dick. "Believe me, I know you have a whole lot to give and I've been waiting too long to stay away now."

Before she knew it, she had her arms stretched above her head just like before, his eyes staring directly into hers. "I asked you a question earlier. And then I said please. Which means . . ." Carefully, he released her. Once again, she tried to lower her arms and couldn't. He watched her, waiting for her assent.

She pouted. "Fine. But later, I get my turn."

His expression lightened and he growled. "Oh, baby. Don't you get it? Every turn is your turn." He lowered his head toward her. "Now let's try this again," he whispered.

Her eyelashes fluttered closed as his lips took hers. Once again, her body immediately responded, clenching in places she'd long since forgotten. He took his time, teasing her lips open and then retreating to kiss along her jaw and behind her ear. She moaned, wanting to feel again that hurried rush of arousal, but now afraid to ask for it.

"You're so beautiful."

Her eyes flew open as he said the words. His hand cupped her breast, and his thumb swept a perfect circle across her nipple, forcing it to harden. He kissed her again, this time using his tongue as he pulled her top up. He inhaled upon seeing her bare breasts.

"Pretty." He nudged her nipple with the back of his finger.

Felicia felt herself growing wetter and clenched her teeth.

"Your breasts are perfect. Beautiful. Full. Resilient but lush. Just like the rest of you." He cupped both of her breasts and buried his face in between them. He laved her nipples, the suctioning warmth of his mouth making little explosions go off inside her. Licking his way up her neck, he bit down gently on the vulnerable cord there, letting her feel the sharp points of his fangs.

She couldn't help herself. Her moan reverberated through the room and she tried to lift her neck higher, as if she could force those fangs of his inside her. He laughed, sliding his hands underneath her ass and lifting her groin into his. "That's not what I want to eat. Not right now."

His dark words, filled with lusty intent, had her writhing against the bed in frantic anticipation.

The hand inside her pants shifted so that his fingers ruffled her pubic hair, then slicked against her damp folds. "Goddess, you're wet." He slipped one finger into her and slowly moved it in and out, while at the same time rubbing her clitoris with his thumb. "And so tight. You're amazing."

Felicia struggled for breath as his fingers mercilessly worked her sensitive nub. "I want to see you," she begged. "Feel you. Even if I can't touch you. Please."

He paused, his eyes flashing hot. With a curt nod, he straightened, still balanced on his knees, and ripped at his slacks. When they were open, he pushed down his silk boxers so his hard shaft sprang free. It looked warm and smooth and beautiful.

"My hands," she whimpered. "Release my hands. Please."

After a brief hesitation, he did. Immediately, she sprang up and knelt down in front of him, pulled down his underwear a bit more, and took the head of his cock into her mouth.

With a long groan, he buried his hands in her hair and pushed himself deeper into her mouth. "Fuck," he hissed. "Yes. Take me inside your hot mouth. Show me how much you want me."

The words were like a sudden slap to the face.

Suddenly, Noella's words, spoken so long ago, were all she could hear.

"Knox isn't like most guys. Sure, he loves getting head, but he just doesn't love it, he needs it. It's his weakness. I'm telling you, if you ever want Knox to do something for you, just get down on your knees and suck him like there's no tomorrow."

Felicia remembered her shock at her friend's revelation, especially the way she'd used the word "you" toward the end. That had been before Knox had told her Noella had taken other lovers to her bed, but even that revelation hadn't stuck with her as much as Noella's ravings about Knox and his weakness for oral sex. Now, Knox's poor choice of words caused a blanket of ice to settle over her.

Trembling, she released him.

He pushed her hair away from her face. "You okay?"

She nodded, trying to push the image of Noella out of her head. For a minute, looking once more into Knox's face, she succeeded. Quickly, he shed them both of their remaining clothes and laid her on her back.

Kneeling above her, he kissed her shoulder and sprinkled kisses across her chest, pausing to place a firm, closemouthed kiss on each of her nipples before pulling away. Trailing one hand down her torso and back up, he touched her almost reverently, as if he suddenly realized he'd been presented with a gift too precious to rush.

"Bend your knees," he whispered.

When Felicia complied, he gently pushed one thigh to the mattress, opening her wide for his gaze and touch. She suddenly wanted to cover herself. To prevent him from seeing her. Not just her flesh, but her. Her vulnerabilities. Her flaws. Before she could move, he spread her apart and inserted a long finger into her. Felicia moaned as he circled it slowly inside her, testing the muscles that hugged him. Spasms of pleasure racked her body, threatening to obliterate all thought.

He pulled his finger out of her slowly, and then pushed it back in, even deeper than before.

Felicia's hips involuntarily lifted as her body and mind tried to absorb each new sensation shivering through her. In turn, he seemed fascinated by the sight of his finger moving in and out of her. By the contrast of his strong, tanned wrist and the soft dusting of hair covering her pale flesh. As she watched, he withdrew his hand and she was mesmerized by the slick shine on his finger. It was wet. From her.

He lifted his finger to his mouth and licked, forcing the air from her lungs in a wave of combined terror and desire. Her legs shifted restlessly and he focused on her core, pinning her in place with hot eyes. "I've got to taste more of you."

"Wait . . ."

Before she could say more, he bent down, eased her legs apart, and crowded his shoulders into the cradle of her body. He inserted his finger into her again and flicked his tongue over her clitoris. The pleasure was staggering and she moaned, a raw, desperate sound of need. He removed his finger and replaced it with his tongue, stabbing it in and out of her.

The pleasure built until she thought she was going to explode. Her body's response stunned her, making her realize that the release she sometimes sought in the darkness of her bedroom had barely touched the surface of what was possible. She closed her eyes and clasped Knox's head, sighing when the smooth strands of his hair tangled in her fingers. She almost cried out when he pulled away with one last lingering swipe of his tongue.

"I need you, Felicia. I need to be inside of you. Do you need me?"

In answer, she held out her arms.

Covering her smaller frame with his own, he gripped his shaft and rubbed it against her clit in tight dragging circles. He kissed her again as he began to enter her.

Felicia felt his heaviness invading her and widened her knees to take in more of him. When he slipped in just the slightest inch, he groaned. She couldn't look away from him. His face was contorted as if in pain. She felt a thrill at the thought that she was pleasuring him. When she felt him push a few more inches into her, the thrill was overcome by panic.

He felt huge, stretching her beyond capacity. Her muscles were tight, fighting him. "Goddess, Felicia. A little more. Take a little more of me. Yeah. Just like that."

She bucked up when he licked inside her ear and breathed his devotion. "Beautiful. You're so beautiful." Felicia's eyes teared up. She felt beautiful. She felt cherished. For the first time in years, for the first time since meeting Knox, she celebrated her sexuality.

When he began moving, she fully expected it would happen for her. She was so unbelievably turned on, there was no way she could contain the full force of her arousal for long. But as minutes passed, as Knox steadily pumped his hips into her, she realized it wasn't going to happen.

Despite the pleasure of finally being in his arms, of him finally being inside her, she knew what was wrong.

Noella. Her presence was like a ghost that, once seen, couldn't be forgotten. Felicia had let her inside this room, into the bed with them, and now her mind as well as her body was rebelling.

Knox must have sensed her frustration and/or despair. Perspiration covered his face, which had tightened into a grimace of agony. "It's okay. It'll happen, baby."

She shook her head, wanting him to understand at the same time not wanting him to. He bent her legs back farther and slowed his pace, controlling his thrusts so they were shallower. He reached down and began circling her clitoris with his finger. "Yeah, that's it," he breathed when she moaned in pleasure.

But it wasn't. The more he tried to push her over the edge, the more frantic she became. The pleasure became pain, and she began shoving at him, beating at his chest to make him stop. "No. Stop. I can't . . . It's not going to happen. Stop!"

Knox stilled and rested his forehead on her own. His arms trembled with the effort to support himself. She raised her hand and caressed his cheek. "Lie back," she whispered, giving his shoulders a push.

"Wait . . ." he began, but she pushed harder, climbing on top of him as he tumbled back. Felicia ran her mouth down his chest and swiftly covered his penis. She could taste herself on him. Knox moaned incoherently as she worked her mouth up and down him. As he got closer, she wrapped a tight fist around the base of him and used it to mimic the rhythm of her mouth. His entire body tensed, his words became more guttural as he moaned her name, each syllable vibrating through him and into her until he was shouting and shooting himself in hot pulses into her mouth. She took it all, swallowing it with a moan of heady satisfaction.

Knox sank back into the bed in a limp sprawl of arms and legs, pulling her upward. As it was in her fantasies, Felicia lay on top of him, breathing in his wonderful scent and soaking in his tremors of pleasure. He smoothed his palm against her hair and whispered her name, but it was barely audible next to the deep, rhythmic pounding of his heart.

"Well, I hope you're not going to blame that on me."

Felicia's eyes popped open at the sound of the female's voice. For a moment, she just lay there, disoriented and wondering why someone was pounding on the door so loudly. Then she realized she was still lying on Knox's chest, her ear pressed against his strong heartbeat. Across the room, Noella, dressed in a pretty white gown, sat on the ancient dresser and waggled the fingers of one hand at her.

Scrambling off Knox, Felicia pulled at the bedsheets that were pinned down underneath him, eventually managing to pull a humiliatingly small amount of material over her breasts and crotch.

Noella laughed. "If you could only see your face right now."

"You're—you're dead," Felicia whispered.

Noella narrowed her eyes, hopped off the dresser, and raised her hands, curled into claws, as if she were about to pounce. "Boo!" she shouted, then collapsed into a fit of laughter when Felicia flinched.

Wondering when exactly she'd lost her mind, Felicia glanced at Knox.

"Don't worry," Noella gasped, obviously still fighting off a fit of the giggles. "He can't hear us. No surprise there. After the way you worked him over, the poor vamp needs his rest."

"He's . . ." Felicia cleared her throat. "He's hungry. For blood."

Noella nodded solemnly. "That, too. Yes."

"Should I . . ." Felicia waved her hand feebly, glanced at Knox, then back at Noella again. "You know. I mean, my blood's not pure, but I know it'll give him something."

Noella pursed her lips. "So asking me if you can give him your blood, you're okay with. But your body is different somehow?"

Felicia glanced down at the blanket and plucked at several loose strands of yarn. "He needs blood to survive."

"He needs you to survive."

Felicia's head snapped up, a denial instinctively about to fall from her lips.

"Yes, Felicia. No matter how hard we all fought it—me and Knox in the beginning, and you all this time—you're what he needs to survive. You, not me."

Shaking her head, Felicia tried to blink back the tears in her eyes. "He married you. And at the same time he's asking to be with me, he's getting ready to marry another vamp."

"Out of duty. Not love. He won't marry for love until he's able to marry you."

"Which will never happen. He needs to marry a vampire. And he should marry one that loves him. Like you loved him."

"That's what the Council has made him believe. And yes, Felicia, I loved him. Just as I loved our children." A wistful sadness sparked in Noella's eyes. "I miss them the most. I really need to pop by and see them soon."

"Pop by," Felicia echoed on a nervous laugh. "Have you done that often? And how come you haven't popped in on me before now? I've missed you," she said plaintively.

"The term 'popping by' makes it seem far easier than it actually is. The opportunities are actually quite limited. But I miss you, too. I just wanted to make sure that when I did pop by, it would make a big difference. Now seemed like the best time."

"Why? Because you don't want me to die old before my time, a bitter, dried-up, inorgasmic old maid who can't get off because she feels like she's stolen her best friend's husband?"

Noella laughed again, a beautiful tinkling sound that seemed to make the air dance. "Something like that." With a sigh, Noella rose and approached Felicia. She sat on the edge of the mattress and looked at Knox, affection clear on her face. She reached out and stroked his hair, smiling when he sighed. Then she turned back to Felicia. "Dear, sweet Felicia. You were the sister I never had. I knew how you and Knox felt about each other the instant I saw you together. It hurt at first . . ."

Her words faltered and Felicia cried out in distress, throwing her arms around her.

Noella shook her head and pulled away, taking Felicia by the arms and shaking her. "No, you silly goose, don't feel bad. You've felt bad long enough. Yes, it hurt at first, but not the way you think. You see, I loved Knox but he wasn't the love of my life. You were."

With wide eyes, Felicia pulled back.

"Not sexually," Noella clarified, "but in every other way that counts. You were the one I could talk to, cry with, laugh with, complain with. Knox is wonderful, but because we weren't soul mates, he was more friend than lover, and it was just his bad luck that I already had the best friend in the world. He could never measure up to you, just like I couldn't, either."

"Noella . . ." Felicia choked out, then threw her arms around her once more, clinging to her friend so tightly she was sure not even death could separate them. But she was wrong.

With a final squeeze, Noella pulled away. "I must go now."

"No. Don't go!" Felicia protested.

"I must. Now remember, Felicia. A vamp can't lie. So when I say I want you and Knox to be happy together, in *every* way possible, you know I'm telling the truth, isn't that right?"

Hesitantly, Felicia nodded, which made Noella smile even more brightly. "Good." She kissed her fingers, then held them up. "I'll see you soon, Felicia. Take care of my babies for me. And take care of Knox."

"No, Noella, wait." Felicia lunged to her feet, not caring that the blankets fell away, leaving her naked. But Noella was gone, only her words touching the space she'd just occupied. Take care of Knox for me, she'd said. Take care of Knox.

Glancing down at the sleeping vamp next to her, Felicia saw his hair was still pushed away from his face, exactly where Noella had nudged it. With a sigh, she leaned down, kissed Knox on the mouth, then settled on top of him once more.

It had been a nice dream, she thought drowsily, wishing it had been real.

TWELVE

When Felicia roused again, it was to the feel of Knox's hands on her. Loving her. She stretched underneath his touch, luxuriating in it, wondering at the feeling of contentment and peace that mingled with the pleasure his hands brought her.

That was when she remembered the dream.

"Noella," she breathed.

Instantly, Knox's hands froze. He rested his forehead against her shoulder.

She heard nothing but their breathing.

He raised his head, shifted as if to move away from her.

Desperately, she wrapped a hand around his neck and pulled his lips to hers. He stiffened in surprise, then slowly kissed her back. They kissed for several moments, rubbing their hands over one another's hair and bodies, as if to confirm that they were really here, in each other's arms, where they most wanted to be.

More. More. More.

She needed more of him.

Wrenching her mouth from his, Felicia nipped at his neck.

Then his shoulder. Then his chest. She trailed a path of kisses down his ridged, hard abs, but froze when she finally noticed the necklace dangling from her neck and resting against his skin. Cupping the medallion in one hand, she jerked her gaze to his.

"I put it on you when you were asleep. I wanted to see it on you, resting against your heart." Gently, he touched her in the spot where the pendant would normally rest. "It looks good on you. It looks . . . right."

Letting the necklace drop, Felicia kissed him passionately. He responded with fervor, but then drew back, smiling at the way she clung to him. "I have one more gift for you," he said softly.

"Really?" She kissed the spot between his neck and shoulder. "I thought I was the one about to deliver a gift," she murmured.

"You've already given me the best gift possible."

Her breath hitched at the sincerity in his voice.

"My clan? We wear the medallions to symbolize our union, but also our individuality," he explained. "By wearing these medallions, made of the highest quality of gold, we can prevent another vamp from using his powers on us."

Felicia stared at him. His confession was as stunning as it was unexpected. "Why are you telling me this?" she asked.

"Because you trusted me with something precious. And I'm doing the same."

"But won't the Vamp Council—I mean, it's a secret. Something humans can use, just like . . ."

He stiffened and she immediately wanted to call back her words. "I shared something because I trust you. Telling you how to stop a vamp from using his powers on you isn't the same as telling you how to kill one. It's not the same as . . ." He started to rise, but Felicia clung to him. Frantically now, she again sprinkled kisses on his jaw, throat, and chest.

"You're right. It's not the same. Thank you for trusting me.

Thank you. Thank you." She breathed her thanks as she continued to kiss him, resuming the trail down his body that she'd started earlier. Although he resisted at first, he eventually eased back on the bed and tangled his fingers in her hair. "Thank you," she breathed.

His fingers tightened when she reached her goal.

Knox groaned incoherently as Felicia teased him with her mouth, swirling her tongue around the broad tip of his penis and then sucking it into her mouth. He shivered when she ran her tongue up and down the length of him, as if she were savoring a frozen dessert on a particularly hot day.

As she moved her mouth over him, her fingers followed, spreading the moisture left from her mouth along the length of him. With each stroke, Knox moved his hips and moaned her name.

She loved it. The taste and feel of him. His heat. The way his eyes were closed in agony as he experienced the pleasure. The pleasure that she was giving him.

Felicia started rotating her wrist so that her fingers swirled around him with each outward stroke. She followed the motion all the way to the tip of his cock before covering him with her mouth once more.

He swelled even larger.

"Wait, Felicia. Stop."

She tried to ignore him, but he grasped her hair and moved her away. Gripped her arms and lifted her up. He kissed her and smoothed away her frown of confusion. Laughed shakily. "I like a hummer as much as the next guy, Felicia. That's obvious. Believe me, I'll let you finish that way later. Right now, I don't want just your mouth. I want you. All of you."

Felicia's eyes widened as he flipped her on her back and loomed over her. She trembled with excitement.

"Do you want all of me, Felicia? Mind, body, and soul?"

Felicia's trembling magnified tenfold when Knox leaned down and bit the curve between her neck and shoulder. Swiping the small sting with his tongue, he raised his head, then kissed her roughly, plunging his tongue almost savagely into her mouth. She couldn't help but kiss him back.

The longer they kissed, the gentler he became, until he was sipping at her lips with small suctioning kisses. With one final kiss, Knox raised himself up and poised himself over her. He gripped himself with his fist, milking his cock with three quick jerks. He then guided himself into her.

He entered her slowly, invading her welcoming heat one precious inch at a time. "Fuck," he spat out between clenched teeth.

Felicia moaned as she enveloped him. She raised her hips, pushing him into her for several moments, enjoying the friction of his cock inside her. "Bite me," she gasped out.

Knox froze.

"Please," she begged. "I know you need blood. You trusted me with a secret. Trust me in this."

"You don't have to—"

"I know it'll hurt, just a little, but I also know it won't change me. I'm not scared. So even though it's not pure, even though mine's not good enough, I want to give it to you. Please . . ."

Her body bowed as his fangs sank in deep, piercing her skin with a jolt of pain that was quickly drowned by a pleasure so intense she screamed. He drank from her with deep, dragging pulls, and far from feeling drained, as if something vital were being taken from her, she felt filled up—with him, with his essence, and with the strength that was quietly surging through his body.

As he drank, his hips continued to pulse against her. Soon, the pulls of his mouth began to slow and grow luxurious. Lazy. Finally, he broke free, pulling his fangs from her skin so, so gently, but she still moaned at the feeling of loss.

"Look at me." His command brooked no resistance. Her eyes flickered open, her gaze falling on his lips first. A drop of blood, her blood, nestled there and his tongue edged out to sweep it up. "Look at me," he whispered.

She looked into his beautiful eyes and he pushed her hair away from her face. The connection between them seemed momentous, a live, undulating wire of passion unlike anything she'd felt before or would likely ever feel again. Like a cat, she stretched and preened beneath his possession, seeping herself in the pleasure of the moment and all the possibilities it brought with it.

"Tell me you're mine."

Despite the intensity of her pleasure, her resistance was instinctive and immediate. Her body stiffened. Even if she'd really received Noella's blessing last night, even though he trusted her to a certain degree, there were so many other things standing between them, least of all his duty to marry another vamp. Yet she mourned the feeling of completion that had floated through her seconds ago. Pretending she hadn't heard him, she reached up and tried to pull him down for a kiss.

He shook her off, then withdrew from her body completely, making her muscles clench with the effort to hold him inside.

Felicia whimpered. "No!"

Knox slowly pushed his way back into her, cleaving past the muscles that had just tightened to hold him in. She spread her legs wider, then closed them, hugging his hips with her thighs even as he remained motionless. She wrapped her arms around him tightly to prevent him from pulling away from her again.

"I want you to say it, Felicia."

Felicia shook her head. He thrust into her several times and reached down, playing with her clitoris. She let out a low scream. "Knox, please."

He repeated his game of retreat and penetration, moving and rearranging her limbs as it suited him.

She was close. So close.

Each oscillating thrust of his hips ended with a plea from her lips.

Please. Please. Please.

But he was ruthless.

"Not until you tell me."

She tried looking away. He cradled her face in his hands and turned it back to his. "Give it to me, Felicia. Give me everything." Bending down, he kissed the medallion that even now rested against her skin. "Tell me you're mine."

His hips were thrusting again. Still. A steady, strong rhythm that was making her catapult toward pleasure faster than she could breathe while still holding it just out of reach.

His own face contorted, and she could tell he was close to losing control.

"Please, Felicia. Tell me! Please."

Felicia bit her lip at the small tremors that started to run through her. Through him.

She was done in by the force of his response. She couldn't hold back any longer. They both knew she was his anyway. Had been almost from the beginning.

She reached up and caressed his face. She nodded. "I'm yours. I'm yours. I'm yours." She said it again. And again. Until she was screaming out her orgasm.

Knox's hips worked faster and faster, slamming against Felicia violently until he pushed down in one final thrust, grinding himself into her as if to sustain the pleasure for a lifetime. For an eternity of eternities.

But even then she knew—she was his, but he could never be hers.

THIRTEEN

As Mahone stood in front of them, each member of the Para-Ops team exhibited varying degrees of suspicion. Suspicion directed at him.

That included Knox, as well as Felicia.

Glancing at the woman who'd been a special agent under his supervision for over ten years, Mahone had to stop himself from staring. She'd always been strong, but there was something in her eyes now, a deeper strength and spark, that hadn't been there before. With her body language and placement, squarely next to Knox and the rest of the team, she confirmed not only that she and Knox had finally given in to their feelings, but that on some level the entire team had bonded. As one entity, they were now ready to take on the entire U.S. government if they had to.

Which, in a way, they were, given Knox's demand to interrogate Barker's scientists the old-fashioned way.

"Once again, I don't see why that's necessary," Mahone said. "You tried reading their minds before. Nothing came of it. The photos we gave you were taken months before Barker's death and the antidote was stolen. There's nothing to suggest that those Others have any connection to the antidote. As such, there's no reason to think the scientists will know anything about the transportation of Others into North Korea."

"That's a pretty big statement to make, Kyle, considering just how smart and well connected those scientists are," Felicia said softly, but there was steel in her words. "It also presumes the transportation of Others was isolated to that one moment in time, when it's possible the trafficking has been going on for months, maybe even years. And as far as a connection between the Others, North Korea, and the antidote? Where there's smoke, there's fire. Assuming they're unrelated would be foolish."

"Fine, but that's all in the past. Why not spend your time trying to find out where they're bringing those Others, so you can go in and find out if it's, in fact, connected to the antidote?"

"That's exactly what we intend to do," Knox said. "And the first people we're going to talk to are the scientists. Unfortunately, you're giving me the distinct impression you don't want us to do that. Why is that?"

Mahone stared back at Knox, determined not to let the dharmire intimidate him. Not today. "I don't care if you talk to the scientists. I just don't see the point."

"Then set it up. Take us to them. And in the meantime, what do you know about the use of paralysis collars against wraiths?"

Brows lifting in surprise, Mahone searched the room until his gaze found the wraith. She met his eyes steadily, saying nothing. Caleb O'Flare chose that moment to stand, effectively blocking Mahone's view of the wraith, his eyes shooting daggers.

Mahone was too tired to be amused. Even if he managed to give the Goddess the results she was looking for, there was a good chance these Others were going to be the death of him, he thought. Then he realized Knox was still waiting for an answer. "Obviously, Wraith's already told you. What do you want from me?"

"I know such a collar exists and that one was used on her. I know that reason involved experiments. I don't know why or by whom. And Wraith would rather not go into details."

Again, Mahone glanced at the wraith. O'Flare and she were now arguing in low angry tones. O'Flare shook his head and Wraith said quite loudly, "Fuck you, you nosy, self-righteous, blabbermouthed prick," before storming out of the room.

With all eyes on him, O'Flare seemed to struggle for control. When he looked up, he once again glared at Mahone, then settled back into his chair.

"Mahone. The collars. Now."

Mahone closed his eyes, fully recognizing the downside of having to bribe Others to work for you. It gave them a feeling of entitlement, he thought, oddly feeling like a parent with a brood of squalling kids.

"Fine," he said, "but you didn't hear anything from me. Wraith, like all wraiths, simply woke up one day to find herself dead. Cold. No pulse. No memory of who she was or how she'd died. She could remember what a Big Mac was, but not her name, favorite color, birthday, or anything else about who she was. Eventually, she realized memory loss was the least of her concerns. She had to adjust to experiencing the world in a whole new way. With how she experiences touch. With changes in her vision."

"What kind of changes in vision?" O'Flare asked.

"Not my place to say," Mahone said, feeling a hint of pleasure when O'Flare frowned, his annoyance obvious.

"Occasionally, a wraith has been 'birthed' in a morgue with a tag on its toe, telling it exactly who it is. Most of the time, however, it doesn't work that way. Whatever it is that causes them to come back from the dead isn't predictable, but it certainly seems to have some kind of plan."

"What about fingerprints?" Lucy spoke up for the first time. "Why can't you just print the wraiths and find out who they are that way?"

Felicia answered before Mahone could. "No prints. Whatever it is that happens to a wraith before it's born includes the elimination of any fingerprints."

"What about DNA?" O'Flare asked.

"Same thing. It's as if the wraith's body self-destructs or coats itself in order to avoid detection. It's unexplainable," Felicia continued. "Almost mystical."

Yeah. Mystical. As in, manipulated by a creature who did what she liked, when she felt like it, and to hell with how it affected others. "It—" Mahone gasped, his words catching in his throat, just as a vicious pressure grew in his head, blocking out sight and sound in less than a second. Before he could even groan, the pressure was gone. It could have been a fluke. Hell, it could have been induced by a brain tumor.

He knew instantly it had been a message from the Goddess. Apparently, she was getting tired of his mental put-downs.

The others were staring at him, Felicia's gaze just edged with concern. He shook his head and cleared his throat. "Since a wraith's properties, or lack thereof, appear to have been deliberate, certain mages are bent on solving all the riddles that are part and parcel of being a wraith."

At Mahone's words, Lucy stood, frowning. "What are you saying? That it was a mage that experimented on Wraith?"

For a moment, staring into the mage's wide, dark eyes, Mahone hesitated. Something about the way she looked at him made him uneasy, as if she could see straight into him and divine all of his secrets in a way no one else could, hopefully not even a vampire. He'd learned to protect his mind years before, in ways that were painless and painful to him, and even vampires, who were naturally gifted with telepathy, would have a difficult time breaking through his barriers. Apparently, the only being that could access his mind without his permission was the Goddess. Even so, for a crazy second, Mahone wanted to let the mage in. To share some of his burden with her. To get some kind of comfort . . . But that was impossible. He narrowed his eyes at the mage, falling back on facts to buttress his shaky emotions. "That's exactly what I'm saying. And more than that, it's far from a singular event. Before the War, a certain portion of the mage population was quite blatant about its right—no, its duty—to experiment with wraiths in order to discover the secret behind their immortality. Now they're much more discreet about it."

"Wait a minute." Lucy shook her head furiously. "If these mages were so blatant about this duty, how come I've never heard any of this before?"

"Have you ever heard of Project Life?"

From the way Lucy stiffened, it was obvious to Mahone that she had.

"What do you know about it?" Knox asked the mage.

Lucy shook her head in obvious denial, but answered anyway. "Since I was little, I was told that a group of mages had discovered the proverbial fountain of youth. That they'd traveled to a kind of Eden to find it, only to be trapped there. Project Life is a legend, a tale old mages tell the young, a way to teach them that if they just practice hard enough and stay focused, maybe they'll be the mage who'll be powerful enough to find the others and bring back the elixir. But . . ." Lucy turned back to Mahone. "But that's just a fairy tale, isn't it?"

Mahone stared at the mage. If he didn't know her secrets, he could almost buy her "more innocent than apple pie" looks and attitude. "Not to some," he said. "I've seen how obsessed some mages are with finding that 'elixir' and many of them believe it can be found inside wraiths, creatures who were once human and somehow were able to escape death and become immortal."

"So these experiments . . ." Lucy whispered.

"Resemble something closer to torture," Mahone confirmed. "I've seen the results myself, but not the collar we're talking about," he clarified. "We haven't been able to get hold of that or the chemical agent used with it. But I've seen the wraiths. I've seen what was done to them. Some of the mages? Let's just say they were fond of revisiting things. Just like a football coach watches game film, there are mages who want to record their experiments in order to watch them again and again, in case they might have missed something."

"You talk as if mages are the only ones who have experimented on wraiths. Is that a fact or are you making an assumption based on a few bad seeds?"

The hostility in Lucy's voice was one of the first cracks in her calm exterior she'd allowed Mahone to see. Her loyalty to her race was obviously one that ran deep.

"No one's going to think less of you or your race because of a few bad seeds, Lucy," Knox said.

Mahone almost winced at the dharmire's blatant, if unconscious, hypocrisy.

"Is there a recording of Wraith?" O'Flare asked.

"I don't—"

O'Flare stood, his face and his body exuding a threatening vibe that was impossible to miss. "Is there?" he repeated.

Mahone sighed. "Yes," he admitted. "I've seen digital images of Wraith detailing exactly what was done to her. But she won't thank me for telling you that, I'm sure."

O'Flare cursed, then punched his fist into his palm. Once. Then twice. "Fuck!" he shouted again, then walked out of the room.

"It seems my team needs some time to prepare before we leave to see those scientists," Knox stated, "but what you've told us is further proof that the Koreans' interest in the Others is likely connected to experiments, likely some of them involving the vamp vaccine and the antidote. How long will it take for you to get us to them?"

"You'll see them tomorrow morning. Nine a.m. I'll send a car to pick you all up."

As Mahone turned, Knox stopped him with a hand on his shoulder. The touch shocked him so much that he stared at it, his mouth hanging open.

"Thank you, Mahone," Knox said. "But do me a favor, okay?"

Mahone narrowed his eyes suspiciously. "What?"

"Leave the blindfolds and handcuffs at home this time."

* * *

While Knox didn't have to deal with the blindfold and hand-cuffs the next day, there was plenty of clandestine, superagent stuff he did have to deal with—not the least of which was Mahone's sick sense of humor.

"A limo," he sighed.

Beside him, Felicia choked back a laugh. "I have to admit, it's a first as far as I've heard. But maybe we're being harsh. Maybe Kyle's acknowledging our hard work—"

"He's calling us high-maintenance," Knox gritted.

Felicia walked toward the limo with an extra sway in her step. Over her shoulder, she winked. "High maintenance ain't bad in my book."

As the rest of the team followed her, almost all of them making a derisive snort first, Knox struggled to hold back a smile. Shaking his head, he motioned to Lucy, who was still staring at the limo with delight. "It's even cooler on the inside, I'm sure. Come on."

Four hours later, even the limo's luxurious interior wasn't a distraction.

"This is ridiculous," Wraith snapped. "We've been driving in circles half the time and I still know exactly where we are."

"Gee, thanks," O'Flare said wearily, his head tilted back on his headrest with his eyes closed. "I'm sure they've got this puppy bugged and your comment just prolonged this journey for another hour or two. Frankly, I would have rather been blindfolded and cuffed." He opened one eye to peer at Wraith. "Then again, I wouldn't want to be that helpless around you."

Wraith pressed her lips together and refrained from commenting.

"So where are we?" Lucy asked. "Because I couldn't tell you."

"We're back in D.C., about an hour from FBI Headquarters," Knox said. "And if we don't arrive soon . . ."

The limo turned and then began to slow. Everyone scattered to their perspective windows to see probably the same warehouse that Knox had visited to read the scientists' minds.

Clenching his fists and grinding his teeth, he held back a snarl of fury. Damn Mahone. Assimilating and training the team was taking long enough; they didn't need to waste more time playing Mahone's stupid games.

Knox said as much as soon as he exited the limo. Mahone simply shrugged. "You got what you wanted, didn't you? Agent Parker will escort you to the scientists now while I meet with the others."

"Wait a minute," Lucy protested. "I thought we were all going to speak with them."

Mahone glanced at Felicia with a raised brow. Felicia sighed and turned to Lucy. "I was hoping Mahone would allow that, but it doesn't make sense from a security standpoint, not when Knox can ask our questions for us. Why risk exposing the scientists to multiple people while outnumbering Mahone's security in the process?"

"Then why bring us here in the first place?" Wraith asked.

"More games," Knox concluded, but Felicia shook her head.

"No. Actually, that makes sense, too. We don't need to go in now, but that could change. Depending on what Knox finds out, one or the other of us may be needed, at the very least to consult with him about what he's found out. Or even to use one of our individual talents. We're on-site if needed. And if we're not needed . . ."

Felicia waved a hand at Mahone, who was standing with his arms crossed, a look of annoyance on his face. "So you're done explaining for me?"

Felicia just smiled sweetly, causing Mahone to sigh.

"I want to talk to each of you while Devereaux makes first contact. Felicia, you're up first."

"I didn't expect anything different."

Knox's stomach tightened when Felicia shifted her gaze to him. She didn't say anything. She didn't need to. Her expression told him all he needed to know.

She stood by him even when she couldn't physically be there.

Knox turned to the man Mahone had referred to as Agent Parker. "Let's go."

They'd taken less than three steps when two men rushed to Mahone's side, their voices hushed and urgent.

Mahone recoiled. "All of them?"

"Yes, sir."

"Kyle? What . . ." Felicia took several steps closer to Mahone even as the other agents talked over her.

"They were fine this morning. We checked on them less than a half hour ago. When the limo arrived, we went in to inform them and—"

"What's going on?" Knox asked a second before he saw Mahone's narrowed gaze shift to Felicia. Sensing the man's intent, Knox tensed and moved. Too late.

"You idiot! You don't know what you've done. What's at stake . . ." In a flash, Mahone grabbed Felicia's arm, jerking her toward him. Knox didn't see Mahone reach for his gun, but then it was in his hand, its barrel pointed directly against Felicia's temple.

Chaos erupted.

The three agents, slower to reach for their weapons, never got their fingers near them. Knox had Parker immobilized just as Hunt and Wraith grabbed the others. O'Flare shoved the limo driver back against the vehicle and pinned him there with an arm to his throat while Lucy caught Knox's eyes.

He shook his head sharply.

A mage's enchantment powers, like vamp persuasion, were, like everything else, most effective when surprise was an element. Although they could likely control Mahone within seconds, he'd be expecting it and might be able to fire his gun before the persuasion took hold.

"Stop this, Kyle," Felicia snapped, but Knox saw the hint of confusion—and yes, fear—that had darkened her eyes. Knox wanted to kill Mahone for that alone.

"Were you in on it, Felicia? Or did Devereaux have you fooled, too?"

Knox growled and, picking Parker off his feet and carrying the agent with him, stalked closer toward Mahone.

Felicia shook her head. "Knox, stop."

The command momentarily made him freeze. "I'll stop once I've killed him," he agreed.

"You're not going to kill him. No one's going to kill anyone." She glared at Mahone. "Isn't that right, Kyle?"

"Conceding that would be stupid and I've been stupid enough." Mahone narrowed his eyes at Knox. "When did you do it? Did you teleport in from the limo once you knew where you were headed? How'd you clean the blood off yourself so fast?"

In response, Knox shifted his grip until he had Parker in a choke hold. Mercilessly, he squeezed until Parker was gasping for air, his feet dangling off the ground and thrashing wildly.

"Knox, stop!" Felicia cried.

Looking at her in disbelief, Knox didn't loosen his hold. "Why are you—"

"He thinks you killed the scientists," she shouted. "He won't hurt me. He's just trying to gain an advantage, stupidly, so he can get information."

"I don't think he killed the scientists, I know he did," Mahone shot back. "There's no way anyone else could have gotten into those rooms so fast. Not without teleporting there."

Parker had stopped kicking his feet, and his gasps for air were quieting. "I didn't kill the scientists," Knox said slowly, his gaze locked on the gun at Felicia's head. If he saw Mahone's trigger finger quiver . . .

Mahone's finger didn't shift but his hand did. He snapped the gun away from Felicia, pointing the barrel upward. Immediately, Knox dropped Parker. Instead of grabbing Felicia away from Mahone, however, he grabbed Mahone and teleported into the warehouse.

As soon as his feet touched the ground again, he pushed Mahone away from him. Mahone landed on his knees with his forearms pressed into the floor. Both he and Knox cursed as the sleeves of his lightweight gray jacket darkened with blood.

Dr. Lipinski was lying on the ground, her throat sliced and blood pooling around her body. Mahone scrambled to his feet, slipping slightly before recovering his balance.

"Damn it," Knox shouted as he knelt beside the scientist's body, searching for signs of life. Of course, there were none.

Immediately, he opened his senses and tried to take in any residual thoughts or emotion that might have been trapped in the room. Just like before, he got nothing.

He heard Mahone's enraged growl, however, loud and clear, before the human plowed into him.

Mahone's strength surprised him. He'd gotten in the one punch before, but now Mahone wrapped his fingers around Knox's throat as if he truly believed he could kill him. Knox had had enough.

Picking up Mahone as easily as he had Parker, Knox pinned him against one wall. "I didn't do this," he said through clenched teeth. "Think about it, Kyle. You know I wouldn't do this. It serves no purpose for me."

"You got the info about the antidote," Mahone gasped. "You got what you needed and you killed them."

"No. I didn't kill them. Look at me and listen. I. Didn't. Kill. Them."

"You're the only one—"

"No," Knox said, emphasizing it by knocking Mahone's head back against the wall. "I wouldn't do it, Mahone. Start thinking straight or I'll snap your neck right now."

Slowly, Mahone's rough breaths eased in equal proportion to the wild look in his eyes. When he was finally calm, Knox let him go so that he slid down the wall and to his feet.

"They're all dead?" Knox asked.

"That's what I've been told."

"I want to see."

Rubbing his neck where Knox had gripped him, Mahone stared at him. "Fine."

"Mahone."

Mahone turned back to him.

"I'd advise you not to use Felicia as a shield again. Next time, I'll be expecting it. And I will kill you before I let you touch her again."

Within an hour, Knox and the rest of his team were being driven back to Quantico in the same luxurious limo. He looked around and immediately wanted to rip something—anything—apart. The contrast between their slick ride and the dejected faces surrounding him was a fucking joke.

Anger flooded his veins even harder, and Knox gritted his teeth to hold back his shouts of fury. The anger, however, was something he welcomed; it was so much better than the defeat and fear he'd felt in the isolated warehouse/prison he'd just left.

The scientists were dead. Every single one of them. Someone had gotten into Mahone's fortress of steel and had managed to slit the throats of all five.

"Something's wrong," Felicia said. "The timing of these murders is too coincidental to ignore. And you said that place was locked tighter than Fort Knox"—she didn't even smile at that—"with a platoon of agents on guard."

"It was an inside job," Knox said. "It had to be. Of course, everyone's going to deny that. They'd rather believe I had something to do with it. That I somehow materialized inside, did the deed, and then materialized out."

"That's ridiculous," Felicia sneered. "Anyone who knows anything about vamps—"

"I agree something's wrong, all right," Hunt interrupted, "and that it was an inside job. The number one suspect to look at is your pal, Mahone."

"Mahone didn't kill them," Felicia protested. "I've known him half my life and he'd never sanction something so senseless."

"Oh, come off it," Hunt snapped. "You know as well as I do he wasn't saying 'pretty please' when he was asking those scientists for information." He jerked a thumb at Knox. "I'm betting the vamp wasn't going to ask nicely, either. What does that mean? That you can believe in a government that'll use torture in order to get information, but not one who'll kill to keep the information from getting out?"

"What possible reason would Mahone have for killing those scientists?"

"Maybe Hunt is right. Maybe the scientists finally cracked and told Mahone where the antidote was," Knox said quietly. "Maybe since he didn't need us to find it anymore, he wanted to make sure the scientists didn't tell us where it was before he could get it himself." Even as he spoke, Knox wasn't buying it. He was just processing. Going through all the possibilities because nothing seemed to make any sense.

Felicia twisted around to see him. "So you think this is all an elaborate hoax? That Mahone formed the team to what? To throw you off the scent? Wave the possibility of the antidote in your face for the sole purpose of keeping it away from you? That makes no sense."

"Haven't you heard?" Wraith muttered. "Government intelligence is an oxymoron."

"Ha ha," Felicia snarled. She looked once more at Knox. "If you think Mahone is that devious, then why not me, too? I work for him after all. I'd have had the inside scoop to all of this."

Knox stared at her. What she was saying was like rubbing at an already raw wound. He didn't want to hear it, so he was harsher than he meant to be when he said, "You don't need to point that out, believe me."

She flinched and sucked in a breath. "What does that mean?"

"Nothing other than what I just said." He knew he'd hurt her, but he remained stubbornly quiet. Once again, his thoughts returned to the sight of those scientists, those *mortal* human scientists, with their lifeblood spilled around them. When he glanced up, he saw that Felicia's face had settled into a mask of stiff betrayal. Knox sighed and reached out to cover her hand with his own.

She smacked it away. "Don't touch me. Don't look at me. None of you."

"What about me?" O'Flare piped up. "I'm a human, too. Who knows, maybe I'm in on Mahone's little scheme."

"Shut up, O'Flare," Wraith snapped.

"Ah, the wraith speaks," O'Flare said with little heat. His words, in fact, sounded more obligatory than impassioned. "Although you really do need to work on your vocabulary, Wraith. They say variety is the spice of life."

"Will you all just shut your traps?"

Knox watched the amazement form on everyone's faces. He was sure his own face was just as amazed. Lucy rarely spoke with anything but a calm, rational tone. To hear her scream, in the small, crowded confines of the limo no less, was startling indeed.

"All of you have done nothing but bicker since the day this team has been formed. It's no wonder we're not getting any relevant information. You're too busy making asses of yourselves to think straight."

When Lucy looked out the window, Knox cleared his throat and motioned for her to continue. "I'd like to hear how someone who's thinking straight would proceed from this point."

When Lucy didn't acknowledge him, Knox sighed. "Please. Pretty please. Pretty please with sugar on top." As he said the words, Knox looked at Felicia, noting the blush that instantly rose to her cheeks. But he didn't miss the way she pursed her lips, either. She was clearly still pissed by his earlier comment.

Sweet and sour—that was Felicia. Suddenly, all he wanted was to kiss that mutinous expression off her face. As he pictured it, he hardened. Now, in addition to his frustration and fear, he had to deal with an aching cock that was so hard he could use it to hammer nails.

"Fine." Lucy turned to face Knox, who adjusted his jacket to cover his crotch. "Did you get a sense of anyone's identity when you saw the scientists? I don't mean reading their minds, but I know certain things just come to you, information that surrounds a person and just announces itself to those who can hear. Did you hear anything like that?"

"No," Knox answered truthfully.

The mage seemed to deflate right before his very eyes. "Oh."

"Uh, hello?" All eyes turned to O'Flare, who was waving his hand. "Human psychic here. How come no one's asking me if I know the scientists' names?"

Anticipation filled the air. "Do you?" Lucy asked.

"No."

"Prick," Wraith muttered. This time her insult was followed by a round of murmured agreements.

"I've got something better than their names."

Knox glared at the man. "Stop playing games and just tell us."

O'Flare smiled. "Okay. I've got their addresses."

"Bullshit."

O'Flare ignored Hunt. "I get these visions sometimes. Often I don't know what they are or what they mean. Sometimes my dead grandfather is able to help me out with that, but it takes a ritual or two, quite a long process really, to make contact with him."

O'Flare glanced at the wraith, who immediately looked away, but not before both Knox and O'Flare saw the spark of interest in her normally dull eyes.

"Anyway, last night, after all of the tension with Mahone, I had a vision. A series of numbers, all jumbled together. Then a list of words. Again, none of them making any sense."

"And what?" Felicia urged. "Your grandfather came and visited you and told you the addresses of five dead scientists?"

"No. He didn't have to. I didn't know it until now, but that's what the vision represents—their addresses. At least one but probably more. And the address has significance. I can't explain how I know, I just feel it. And when I get a feeling like this, I'm never wrong."

"Never?" Wraith asked hesitantly.

O'Flare locked eyes with her. "Never."

"Then what do we need to do?" Knox asked.

"I need to get back to Quantico and sit down with someone who's good at puzzles. Any chance any of you qualify?"

Knox waited for a hand to go up, but was still unprepared for the one that did.

"I'm pretty good at them," the wraith said gloomily.

O'Flare just grinned. "See? I had a feeling you were going to say that."

They arrived in Quantico within the hour. While O'Flare and Wraith holed up together, hopefully to decipher the addresses from O'Flare's vision, Felicia locked herself in her room. She was so pissed that if she didn't, she was sure she'd come unglued.

Was it true? Did Knox really think she was helping Mahone to play him? After their history? Her history with his family? After what they'd become to each other?

"And what exactly is that, Felicia?"

She shrieked and whirled to face Knox. "You—you . . ." Cocking her arm back, she punched him in the face with all her might. He didn't even try to deflect the blow, so his head snapped back. But just barely.

"Don't sneak into my room again," she ordered, "and don't sneak into my mind, damn it."

Knox touched the corner of his mouth, then wiggled his jaw. "I plead to the first but not the second," he countered. "You were muttering to yourself."

"I was not . . ." she began, but then paused. Had she . . . Okay, so maybe she had been. It didn't justify his little surprise drop-ins. She turned her back on him and rubbed her knuckles, more for something to do than because she'd hurt herself on his thick, dense skull.

"Again, I'm hearing your thoughts loud and clear with absolutely no effort on my part." As he spoke, Knox tugged her around and took her hand. After a brief game of tug-of-war, he lifted her hand to his mouth and kissed the knuckles she'd been rubbing.

She'd just started to melt before she remembered she was pissed at him. She snatched her hand away. "Don't. You might get dirty. After all, I'm a traitor, right?"

"I never said that."

"Yes, you—"

"No," Knox insisted loudly, his voice practically booming to be heard over hers. "I didn't. I said you didn't have to list all the evidence that might lead someone to jump to that conclusion."

"Someone, meaning you?"

"Of course not."

At his calm words, which she knew *had* to be the truth, she hesitated. "Then what—"

"I don't believe it, but if we don't end up finding the antidote, there are those who might latch on to that explanation out of fear. Desperation. Prejudice. Who knows?"

"Those? Those who? Your mother would never . . ." Realization formed. "Ah. You mean the Vamp Council."

His face was grim when he answered. "It's a possibility."

"And that would be pretty bad for you, right? Because it would be hard to have your piece of ass on the side—that's assuming I'd ever agree to such a position, which I wouldn't—if the Council thought she was a threat to your clan."

His brow furrowed and he shook his head. "You just love to push me, don't you?"

She scowled. "I don't have to push you. Everything that pushes you is already there. It exists just by virtue of who we are. What I am."

"I thought we settled this the other night. What you are is mine."

With a casual flick of his fingers, he undid the top button to his shirt. Then the next. Then the next. Until the broad planes of his chest peeked out from between the swiftly parting fabric.

Outrage, as well as the warm, slippery slide of desire, flowed through her. "What do you think you're doing?"

He raised a brow. "Undressing. You might want to do the same if you want those clothes to remain intact."

"You're crazy."

His fingers froze and he narrowed his eyes at her. "You're right. I am crazy. Crazy for you. Insane for you. Absolutely freaking nuts over you. Now come here."

She was looking at him as if she believed every word he'd just said.

As if she truly did believe he'd gone insane.

That was okay, Knox told himself. He didn't just feel as crazy as he'd said.

He felt crazy enough to like it.

Something about seeing those scientists, their blood staining their bodies, had disturbed him, and it wasn't because they couldn't tell them anything about the antidote.

It had everything to do with Felicia, and the reminder that just as those scientists were mortals who could be cut down with the flick of a knife, so was Felicia.

That was what was insane. That for the very first time, her mortality was a huge, looming presence between them.

And it scared the shit out of him.

He didn't know how to deal with it rationally.

All he knew was that he needed her. Right now.

Eyes on her the whole time, he finished undressing. When he straightened, he luxuriated in the way her hungry gaze swept over him, her appreciation apparent in every lingering look. She lingered particularly long on his cock, which twitched with eagerness.

"Undress for me, Felicia. Please."

He wasn't using his powers against her, but when she moved, she moved slowly. Almost as if she was drugged or hypnotized by her desire for him. That made him feel good. It made him feel so fucking powerful that he wanted to throw back his head and roar out his love for her.

Mine, he thought again. Forever.

When she was naked and standing in front of him, he bent down and kissed her. Just kissed her. Without touching her with his hands or his body, he brushed his lips against her, using the lightest of touches and the tenderest of strokes to prepare her for the storm to come.

He was going to use everything he'd ever learned about women to pleasure Felicia, but his goal was more than physical. He wanted to get so deep inside her that he would touch her soul and make her realize that, despite everything, their difficult circumstances, her mistrust, his inability to give her all she wanted, he loved her. Good, bad, it didn't matter. She was his.

Knox kissed the side of her neck and bit down gently. For a moment, he lingered, unable to tear himself away from the promise of her vein. Closing his eyes, he forced himself to move on, talking to her in the soft, crooning voice he knew she loved. "Do you know what first drew me to you? Your eyes. They show me everything you try to keep hidden. Your passion." Knox kissed her forehead and began to work his way down. "Your warmth. Your generous spirit." He kissed her shoulder. "Your fire."

Felicia arched into him. Her soft white skin was pearled with sweat, and he gently laved at the shallow valley between her breasts. He then caught a nipple in his mouth, sucking at it gently. It was already hard.

When he lifted his head, she moaned in protest.

"Shhhhh." Knox covered both breasts with his hands and continued his descent. He kissed her stomach, which quivered in delight.

He looked up at her as he moved even lower. Her legs moved restlessly. Knox bent and spread them open, then inserted a long finger into her.

She cried out his name, closing her eyes as if in pain.

"I know. It feels good, doesn't it?" He pulled his finger out slowly. Then pushed it back in. Pulled it out. In.

He nudged aside her pubic hair, rooting for her clitoris with his tongue. He laved the hard nub slowly. Her hips bucked against him.

She was so responsive, Knox thought. Amazing. He raised his head reluctantly. "I'm going to make you come like this." He bent back down again, rubbed his tongue into her heat with long, smooth strokes.

Just when he sensed her orgasm was imminent, Knox raised his head again and started to move down her body.

"No! Please!" Her voice was frantic.

"It's okay. I'll be back. I need to do this first."

Knox kissed the insides of her thighs. Her knees. Her calves and feet. He lifted one foot at a time and licked her toes. When she became so frustrated that she kicked out, he laughed, grabbed her ankles, and pulled her down. Catching her, he cradled her to the floor and kissed her sweet lips once more, sucking on her like she was candy.

He raised his head, then slowly turned her over. He worked his way up her body this time, starting with her calves. With every kiss, every touch, he worshipped her body.

When he kissed the heat of her from behind, he growled, "I love you, Felicia. Everything about you. Head to toe, there's no part of you that isn't precious to me."

He covered her with his body, kissed her shoulder, and whispered in her ear, "I'm going to spend the rest of your life proving to you how much you mean to me."

Knox pushed himself into her by slow degrees. Her body was so wet, he slid into her with ease. He felt his balls tighten but couldn't resist pumping into her for several moments.

Felicia grasped frantically at the ground, but couldn't find purchase. She thrashed beneath him and her inner muscles squeezed him mercilessly.

Knox could feel himself close to coming. He quickly withdrew from her and turned her over. He immediately kissed her sweet spot. Separated her folds with his fingers and impaled her with his tongue.

She'd started a steady series of moans, each one louder than the next. Longer than the next. Her thighs gripped either side of his face and began to shake.

"I love you. I love you." He moaned it into her. She came apart, moaning out his name as the violent waves of orgasm shook her.

Knox didn't give her time to come down. He couldn't. He was dying and the only thing that would save him was being inside her. Knox bent her legs back and pushed inside her. Felicia moaned again.

He pumped his hips into her, his rhythm increasing as the pleasure rode him, rode her. His cock felt like it was being squeezed between layers of warm velvet. Knox groaned. Slowed down his thrusting. Felt the essence of himself shoot directly into her. He shouted in pleasure.

He kissed her as she cried. He said it over and over again. "I love you."

And even as she responded and held him tight, even as she pulled him ever closer, he was mindful of one thing: She never spoke the words of love back. He tried not to dwell on it or give it any significant meaning. But when Lucy knocked on the door several minutes later, calling, "They've got an address for us," before rushing away, he was hit by the inexplicable urge to pin her down before she could get up.

Instead, he watched her bound off the bed, dressing quickly and urging him to do the same. Slowly, he got to his feet, wondering why the panic in his gut had come back twice as strong as before.

FOURTEEN

To say Wraith was "good" at puzzles had been putting it mildly. From the garbled mess of numbers and words that O'Flare had given her, the two had come up with three addresses. The first had been right on the mark. The house was in Washington, D.C., and had belonged to Dr. Neil Barker himself. It was spotless, not a single thing out of place. That meant, Felicia knew, that the FBI had already gone over it with a fine-tooth comb. They searched it again anyway. Nothing.

The second address turned out to be a coffee shop several blocks from the FBI Headquarters. Although O'Flare had wanted to take a break and get a latte, they'd all walked off, forcing him to follow or be left behind. When he'd asked what their hurry was, Knox had just shaken his head.

At the third address, they thought they'd struck gold. It belonged to Dr. Jaycee Concannon, Dr. Barker's protégée and a woman Felicia had met in person once or twice. The doctor had been quiet and unassuming. She wasn't the type of person who made a strong impression. As such, Felicia wasn't quite sure what to expect from her house, but it wasn't what they found.

Concannon had been an animal lover. Everywhere one looked, her condo was a virtual monument to four-legged creatures. She had framed pictures of animals on her walls. Her cushions were covered with animal prints. Little ceramic dogs, and glass cats, and horses carved out of wood littered every flat surface. Again, however, there wasn't a single spot of dust anywhere.

After their obligatory search, the team congregated in Concannon's cramped living room. Felicia chose to lie on the ground and stare up at the ceiling. The mood was somber. The prevailing attitude one of defeat. She struggled to say something that would rally everyone—wasn't that why Mahone had included her on the team, because of her people skills? She tried to come up with something positive to say, but all she could think of was death.

Yes, it was a morbid thought, but quite appropriate. The Para-Ops team was supposed to have been a connective force, ensuring equal protection of all creatures regardless of race or species. It was what her parents had worked and died for, and it was a shame to think it had all come down to this. They were no closer to the missing antidote, and once people learned that Others were being enslaved and that the U.S. government had failed to retrieve them, the fragile thread of hope that enabled Others and humans to at least try to live in peace would be broken, replaced by suspicion and fear. Once again, it would be every man or Otherborn for himself.

Silently, she turned her head toward Knox, who was leaning against the countertop that divided Concannon's living room from her kitchen.

He was already looking at her.

Instinctively, she raised her hand and touched her neck where he'd drunk from her. As he watched, his eyes sparked, but he didn't approach her. It was as if the cloying smell of defeat had crushed his hopes not only of a cure, but of sharing a life with her, as well.

The thought struck terror into her heart, making her realize that she really did have a reason for being here. She wasn't going to see this dharmire brought to his knees. Not here and not now.

She pulled herself into a sitting position. Raising a brow, Knox straightened. Felicia turned to the mage. "Has Mahone given us an update on whether the satellites have picked up anything else?"

Lucy, who was leaning against a wall next to a clock that had fish for numbers and cats' limbs for hands, actually snorted. "It's a little difficult—even with the help of a billion-dollar satellite orbiting the earth—to find some unknown location in North Korea that, one, might contain Others who may or may not be being held against their will and, two, might contain an antidote that may or may not actually exist."

Felicia nodded. After a brief silence, she deadpanned, "So I guess that's a no?"

Wraith, who was perched on one of the sofa's arms, laughed out loud.

Stunned, Felicia, along with everyone else, stared at the wraith.

Wraith immediately wiped her expression clean. She glowered at them, then shrugged one shoulder. "What can I say? It was actually funny." She stood and brushed past O'Flare, who was standing by a long console with a stereo system on top of it. Wraith began to flip through some albums. "Freaking LPs," she muttered. "Can you believe it?"

"If I'd wanted to sit around doing a bunch of nothing, I'd have stayed in Phoenix," Hunt sneered from his position by the living room window. He remained facing forward, staring out into the street. "At least I saw some action there."

"Sorry you're bored," Knox snapped. "Forgive me if trying to find a medical miracle with absolutely nothing to go on but a bull's-eye on an entire country is a little difficult."

"No one's blaming you, Knox," Felicia said.

"Did I say anyone was blaming me?" Abruptly straightening,

Knox strode toward the door. "I need some air." He slammed the front door behind him.

"What crawled up his vamp butt?" Hunt snorted.

Felicia surged to her feet. "Will you shut up for once? Maybe your family doesn't mean shit to you, but Knox isn't like that. He cares, not just about his immediate family, but every vamp in his clan. All hundred and thirty-seven of them. So cut him some slack, will you?"

Hunt turned away from the window to walk toward her. His expression, his every movement, radiated hostility. "I like you, Red, I really do, but maybe I gave you the wrong impression. I don't let anyone talk to me like that, not even someone with killer tits and a—"

Felicia was reaching for her weapon when O'Flare inserted himself between her and Hunt. When the werebeast kept coming, O'Flare shoved hard enough so that the werebeast took several steps back. "Back off, Hunt."

"Listen, Boy Toy, you might want to watch where you put those hands before you lose them. Then how will you satisfy the ladies?"

"The same way I always do. With both hands tied behind my back."

"Oh God," Wraith groaned from behind them. "I can't believe you just said that."

O'Flare's flinty expression could have been set in stone. He glared at Hunt, who glared right back. Then Hunt's eye twitched.

Twice.

The werebeast began to chuckle.

Felicia let out a sigh of relief.

O'Flare stepped back with a small smile.

Hunt knocked the smile off O'Flare's face with one powerful punch.

Caught off guard, O'Flare staggered back and crashed into Felicia, and they both fell to the ground. Felicia pushed O'Flare away so she'd see Hunt's next move. Instead, she saw Wraith. "Now, that was just uncalled for," Wraith said. A second later, she raised a huge marble bust of a basset hound and slammed it down on Hunt's head. Felicia winced at the sound, which reminded her of a watermelon hitting the ground.

The werebeast dropped just as Knox barreled in through the front door. "What the . . ." His expression turned deadly when he saw Felicia. "Are you okay?"

"Yes."

With a growl, Knox picked Hunt up by his leather jacket. Rushing over, Felicia placed a hand on his arm, stilling him. "Not so fast, Lancelot." She shook her head. "And don't even try flashing me those red eyes, either. He didn't touch me. He punched O'Flare, who was standing between us, and I got knocked down. Accidentally. Wraith made sure he won't be a happy boy when he wakes up. Let's leave it at that."

"He's off the team," Knox said. "He's too dangerous."

A low groan filtered up toward them. "Me? I'm a whipped dog, remember?"

Felicia briefly closed her eyes, not sure how the werebeast could even think of mouthing off when he was still hanging like a dishrag in Knox's grasp.

"Let him go, Knox."

Knox shot her a "get real" look.

"Please," she said. "For me?"

"Fine," he said, letting go. Hunt dropped back to the floor. Neither of them looked down when he moaned again. "Thank—" Felicia jumped when music blasted out of Concannon's speakers.

Knox covered his ears. "Wraith," he shouted when it became apparent she wasn't going to lower the sound. "Turn it off."

Wraith ignored him. She laughed—again—and began to swivel her hips to the tune of "Celebration." Entranced, they all watched her dance.

Wraith danced as if she'd been born to do nothing else.

Uninhibited. Unrestrained. Unabashed.

She raised her arms above her head. She pushed her butt out and bumped the air. She pulled her shoulders back and shimmied them.

She even mouthed along to the words.

When the song ended, she flipped off the stereo, still grinning and breathing hard.

Within seconds, awareness filled her eyes. Even so, her grin didn't disappear.

She held up a slim CD case. "I found something."

What Wraith "found" was a blank CD with a label that had been worn just enough on its edges that it had caught her eye. She'd peeled back the label and found that underneath, someone—most likely, Concannon—had written numbers. Wraith, who had earlier claimed to be pretty good with puzzles, took one look at them and announced, "They're coordinates." She refused to say anything else until they'd gotten back to Quantico.

Now, everyone but Hunt, who was passed out in his bedroom, gathered around Wraith as she sat at one of the dining room tables while she worked on decoding whatever it was she saw.

Knox paced impatiently. All he'd seen were several rows of numbers. How anyone could see coordinates in the mess was beyond him.

Standing behind Wraith, O'Flare leaned over her shoulder to get a better look at the disc. "Those don't look like any coordinates I've ever seen."

"Maybe that's because you were spending too much time cooped up in your bedroom. If you came up for air more often, you'd have learned a thing or two," Wraith muttered, still jotting down numbers as she stared at the CD in her hand.

Knox stopped pacing and looked straight at Felicia. She held up three fingers, then silently mouthed: one, two—

"When you get inside my bedroom, I'll be the one teaching you a thing or two."

Knox shook his head as Felicia laughed silently. Their silent connection helped loosen the knot that had twisted his insides together all day. The others? He wasn't so sure. But he and Felicia, they were truly a team. More so than he'd ever felt with Noella.

A quick glance confirmed that O'Flare had managed to render Wraith speechless. She'd turned at O'Flare's outrageous comment and now the two of them were staring at one another. "I—I—" she stuttered.

"It's okay," O'Flare said gently. "Plenty of time for that later."

Wraith recovered fast. "In your dreams," she snapped.

"Oh, yeah. There, too," O'Flare agreed.

"You—you—egotistical, stupid—"

"Wraith," Knox interrupted, correctly reading O'Flare's expression even if Wraith was too pissed off—and scared—to do so. "I wouldn't go there if I were you."

"Oh, please, like I can't handle—"

"Wraith. Listen to him," O'Flare said, his tone so silky smooth and filled with such dark sexual intent that Felicia breathed out a whoosh of air and fanned herself. Knox shot her a punishing glare but she simply shrugged.

For a fraction of a second, Wraith hesitated, then turned her attention back to the CD. "Whatever. Back off and give me some air, will you? I'm working here."

O'Flare straightened and did as Wraith commanded.

Knox had no doubts that O'Flare could see what he did—Wraith's hands were shaking.

Twenty minutes later, Wraith held out the piece of paper to Knox. "Here."

Knox took the paper and looked at it. He felt a smile split his face.

"What is it?" Felicia demanded.

"If I'm remembering my geography, Wraith's right. These are coordinates. To an area near the center of North Korea, about halfway to the Chinese border."

"What's there?" Wraith asked.

"As far as I know, hills and mountains, separated by deep narrow valleys. Most of the population lives in the low plains, not the forests."

"Forests," Felicia echoed.

"Probably close enough to a major city so that getting supplies wouldn't be so difficult. Far enough away that if you had something to hide, most people wouldn't know where to look."

"Something—or someone—to hide. Or maybe several someones. Otherborn," Felicia said.

"And maybe the vamp antidote?" asked O'Flare.

"That's what I'm hoping," Knox said. Hoping, hell. Knox was praying this was their big break. "We need to find a map. Then we'll decide whether to call Mahone—"

"You better call for a plane, too. Those aren't as easy to wrangle up as one might think."

Knox turned to face Hunt, who was standing in the doorway.

"You can get the hell out of here, Hunt. You're off the team."

Hunt crossed his arms over his chest. "I don't think so."

"It doesn't matter what you think or say or do. I lead this team and I say you're gone."

"Look," Hunt growled. "I admit I got a little carried away, but Red—"

Knox stared at the were. "What?" Knox challenged. "What could Felicia have said that pissed you off that much?"

"I implied he didn't care about his family," Felicia said quietly.

"And that upset you?" Knox asked Hunt.

"Look, it wasn't a big deal," Hunt growled.

"By the size of the bruise on O'Flare's face, he'd probably disagree."

Hunt turned to O'Flare. "I apologize."

O'Flare couldn't have looked more shocked if the werebeast had kissed him full on the mouth. "Uh. Okay. Forget about it," he said, clearly baffled.

Hunt ran a hand through his hair. "Look, I was feeling restless. Weres get bored really fast. Sometimes it makes me easily . . . riled. But from what I heard before I came in, we're ready to rock and roll. You're going to need me. And you know I can get the job done."

"Need you for what?" Mahone stepped into the room. "Knox, what's Hunt talking about?" He looked around the room. "And where's the mage?"

Felicia had heard Knox loud and clear before Hunt had interrupted him.

We'll decide whether to talk to Mahone, he'd said. Which meant he was still having doubts about both Kyle's veracity and his loyalty. She had to admit she was having doubts herself.

The notion that Wraith could so easily find a clue in Concannon's condo when the FBI hadn't been able to was a hard pill to swallow. So was the discovery of a disc with an obscure code just hours before Kyle showed up unannounced. Felicia turned to the man who'd been her boss and mentor for years.

"What are you doing here, Kyle?"

He frowned. "I got a phone message from Lucy. She said she needed me to get down here, fast. Something about a mole."

"Are you shitting me?" Knox snapped. His gaze met Felicia's. "Have you seen her?"

"Not since we came back. She headed straight to her room. I remember thinking she wasn't looking so good, but—"

Knox was already headed out of the room and down the hall, then up the flight of stairs that would take him to Lucy's room. Felicia had to run to keep up with him, and Mahone and the rest of the team weren't too far behind.

"Why would she call Mahone instead of coming to me with her concerns?" Knox growled.

Felicia shook her head. "I don't know. It doesn't make sense. Not unless she . . ."

They got to her door. Knox nodded. "Yeah. Unless she was going to identify me as the mole."

"That's impossible," Felicia said. "Lucy wouldn't do that. She has no reason to. Unless . . ." Felicia hesitated and bit her lip. She'd read Lucy's file. She knew the mage's secrets, even if no one else did. Could that rumor actually be true? But what did that have to do with Lucy's call to Mahone about a mole?

"What is it?" Knox asked impatiently.

Felicia shook her head. "Nothing. Not yet." She jerked her chin at the door. "Do it."

Knox banged on the door. "Lucy. Get your ass out here. Now."

Mahone and the others joined them. Felicia could tell Mahone was as much confused as worried.

When Lucy didn't answer, Knox banged again. He raised his fist for the third time.

A faint sound drifted through the door from inside. "Wait," Felicia said, grabbing Knox's arm. "I hear something." She strained her ears, trying to identify the sound.

The sound came again, this time slightly louder. Loud enough for Felicia to tell it was a moan of pain. Obviously hearing the same thing, Knox said, "Oh shit!" and tried the knob. It was locked.

He disappeared. Two seconds later, he opened the door from the inside.

His face was pale and awash with panic. Gripping Felicia's arm, he dragged her inside. "Something's wrong with her."

Felicia took one look at Lucy, who was writhing on the bed, and knew she'd been right. Lucy's rounded face was flushed, her wide eyes—devoid of lashes or brows—were glazed and fevered, blinking rapidly as sweat dripped down her temple. Another low moan escaped the mage just as her eyes locked with Felicia's. "I can't—it's never been this bad . . ."

Shoving Knox toward the door, Felicia ordered, "Get everyone out of here."

"What's wrong with her?"

"Knox, I need you to leave and keep everyone out, okay? She's fine."

"Fine?" Knox stared over her shoulder at Lucy, his eyes filled with disbelief. "Felicia, we need to let O'Flare look at her."

"No!" Felicia shouted, pointing her finger to order O'Flare out of the room. "I can handle this. Now leave. Everybody leave. You, too, Mahone."

Mahone didn't put up any resistance. He merely nodded and waved everyone on. "Come with me, Knox. Please."

For a second longer, Knox resisted. Then he gently gripped Felicia's chin. "You'll tell me later what the hell is going on, understood?"

Felicia nodded. "Absolutely. I'll tell you what I can."

FIFTEEN

Almost an hour later, Felicia found Knox. He and Mahone were sitting in the rec room, each nursing a strong drink and stubbornly trying to prove that he could maintain his silence longer than the other. When he saw Felicia, Knox jumped to his feet. "Well?"

Felicia nodded. "She's okay, but she's not feeling well. She fell asleep."

"Asleep? When she was in that much pain? I'm not sure that's wise. I still say we should have O'Flare look at her."

Knox frowned when he saw Felicia and Mahone exchange a glance. He wasn't a fool. Even without reading their minds, he knew they shared a secret.

No, he thought, suddenly feeling sick. Not Felicia.

To his utter shock, she reached out and punched him on the arm. "Don't look at me like that, Devereaux. It's not what you think."

Angry now, he lightly shoved her shoulder, just enough to warn her he wasn't feeling charitable. "And what is it that I think?"

"What you thought before. That Mahone and I are in cahoots."

"What?" Mahone asked. "He thinks we're playing him?"

"I never said that," Knox denied. "But obviously something's going on. Why don't you just tell me?"

"Because it's not my secret to tell."

"So you admit you're keeping a secret from me?"

"Knox, it's not like that. This is confidential information about—"

"Oh, for God's sake," Mahone interrupted. "Lucy's a half-Other."

Felicia's teeth clicked together as she shut her mouth.

Knox shook his head in confusion. "Mages aren't considered half-Others—"

"She's a half-Other," Felicia explained, "because she's part feline. Half-mage, half-werecat."

Knox let that sink in, took a deep breath, and then took his seat again. Without a word, he drained his glass, then set it down with a thud. "She's in heat."

"Yes," Felicia said.

Glaring at Mahone, Knox stood. "Why wasn't I told?"

"It's a sensitive matter—"

"No shit. A feline isn't someone who can be counted on for surveillance, intelligence, or recovery. Her nature makes her unstable."

"That's not fair," Felicia protested. "Lucy's been nothing but stable. She's having one bad night."

"With six more likely to follow," Knox gritted out. "You should have told me."

"It wasn't my place," she said simply, although her eyes begged him to understand.

"What about this mole shit? You in on that, too?"

"No!" Felicia said. "I didn't know anything about that. Not until you did."

Knox glanced at Mahone, who nodded. "It's true. I have no idea—"

"Don't lie to him," Felicia hissed.

Mahone flinched back. "Excuse me?"

"Lucy told me about O'Flare."

Mahone's facial muscles stiffened.

"I'm not going to like what you have to tell me, am I?"

"No, Knox, you aren't." Felicia glared at Mahone. "Lucy saw O'Flare plant the CD that Wraith found."

"What? But . . . That doesn't make any sense. Why would he do that?"

"The most obvious reason is to feed us information that Mahone already had."

"And the less obvious reason?"

"To enable Mahone to test us."

"Us?" Knox questioned.

"Yes, Knox. Us. Me included. Isn't that right, Mahone?"

Mahone rubbed the back of his head. "Lucy didn't tell me she thought the mole was O'Flare. If she had, I wouldn't have broken several laws to get here so fast."

"So Felicia's right? O'Flare's the one that's been playing us?"

"He hasn't been playing you. He followed orders."

"Because you didn't trust me to get the job done?" Knox said, his dark expression indicating his displeasure.

"No. Because I wasn't sure the wraith was stable enough to be part of the team or skilled enough to crack the kind of intelligence that might be thrown at her. Don't worry. She passed both tests with flying colors."

"Both . . ." Knox closed his eyes. "Son of a bitch. Both tests. O'Flare's dream being the first one. The CD being the second."

"That's right."

"So the photos of the Others being transported through the tunnels—"

"Are very real. As is our information that the antidote is most likely in the hands of the North Korean government, in a compound past Pyong-Jong, somewhere between Songnim and Sariwon. The communication I told you about—the one referring to a cure?—we have several double agents in South Korea, former North Korean civilians, screened and recruited by the Agency, who have confirmed the North Korean government has gained the support of Others—vamps who are willing to sacrifice their own kind in order to save themselves."

Felicia glanced at Knox, who struggled to keep his face impassive. He didn't like hearing there were vamps willing to sacrifice other vamps for their own agenda, but that was hardly a surprise, either. There was no proof that it involved anyone in his clan, however, and that was what he kept focused on.

"Why?" Felicia demanded. "Why didn't you give us the information if you had it? You've wasted all this time."

"A few days aren't a waste of time when forming a new team. Usually, weeks of training are involved. We don't have that kind of time, but we still needed some assurance that this team was going to be able to function, and that each of its members was going to be able to do what it needed to. If you couldn't even find the compound in North Korea, I didn't see any point in sending you there."

"Why don't you tell her the truth?" growled Knox. "That in addition to testing Wraith, you needed to test my loyalty. After all, as the leader of the largest vamp clan, who's to say the North Koreans hadn't already contacted me in order to barter services in exchange for the antidote. Isn't that right, Mahone?"

"Any thought of that was dispelled given your obvious efforts to locate the compound in question; if those fears were true, you could have easily led the team there days ago."

"And then what?" Knox demanded. "Lead them to their deaths? Thus effectively eliminating any desire for Others to work with the U.S. in the future?"

"No," Felicia protested. "He can't have believed that. Otherwise, why wouldn't he have told me . . ." Her words drifted off as she faced Mahone. "Because my loyalty was in question, as well?"

Mahone wouldn't look at her. "Nothing's changed except you've all proven yourselves worthy of this assignment and capable of completing this mission. Except perhaps Hunt. If you really think he's more trouble than help, you're free to make that decision. Personally, I wouldn't mind sending the were packing."

Mahone paused. Knox just continued to stare at him, absorbing Felicia's pain and betrayal into his system and wanting to kill Mahone for hurting her.

"Well?" Mahone breathed out. He cleared his throat. "Do you want him on the team or not?"

"Do I have all the information now, or are there going to be any more surprises?"

"You have all the information you're entitled to as it pertains to the purpose of this mission. Which, by the way, I need to make crystal clear. The purpose of this mission is to retrieve the antidote, *not* to save Others. If you can accomplish both, fine. But the antidote remains the priority. I'm assuming you can abide by those terms."

Knox smiled tightly. "I know my duty to my clan, Mahone. Nothing's changed in that regard. But if we go on this mission, its purpose will be to retrieve the antidote *and* save Others. One won't be more important than the other. Not under my leadership."

Mahone looked down and shook his head. "Fine," he murmured as he raised his head. "So what about Hunt?"

Knox glanced at Felicia, who nodded imperceptibly. After pausing briefly, he nodded as well. "Hunt stays. For now."

"I've made arrangements for the team to—"

"Were you telling the truth?"

At the female voice, Knox shut his eyes. He turned to face Wraith, wondering if his regret was obvious, a dark cloud hovering over his head.

She stood just inside the room in full regalia, but somehow despite the leather and badass bitch shoes, she looked more vulnerable than she had after seeing the slides.

"O'Flare was testing me this whole time?"

Interestingly, it was Mahone who spoke first. "I'm sorry, Wraith—"

Her expression hardened, becoming so cold that Knox half expected to see ice crystallize on her body. "Is. It. True?" she spat.

"Yes."

Knox had been waiting for it and that was the only reason he saw it. Then again, the flash of pain came and went so fast, he wasn't fully confident it had been real. Without another word, Wraith turned and walked away.

"O'Flare is going to have to watch his back," Felicia said quietly.

"Believe me," Mahone said, "that won't be a problem. I wouldn't have picked him for the job otherwise."

"Believe you?" Felicia said. "Believe you?" She ran a disgusted gaze up and down Mahone's body. "I don't think so. Not ever again."

"Felicia . . ." Mahone began, but Felicia ignored him and instead turned to Knox.

"I'll wait up for you."

He nodded, but she hadn't hung around to see it. When she was gone, Knox faced Mahone.

The man showed no sign of regret. He didn't need to.

As Knox had once told him, some things just telegraphed on their own.

"Don't play one of my team members against another again, Mahone. If you do, you'll regret it more than you do right now." With that, he left Mahone standing there.

Teleporting to Felicia's room, he arrived just in time to see her step out of her panties and unhook her bra.

"Perfect timing," she said as she walked into his arms.

Watching Knox as he slept was an opportunity too good to pass up. Perhaps Felicia should have stopped after the first hour, but she couldn't. Each time she closed her eyes and tried to sleep, she'd open them again, compelled once more to watch the way his chest moved in time with his breaths and the way his lips parted, revealing the tips of his fangs.

Unable to resist, she leaned down, slipped her tongue between his lips, and curled it around first one fang and then the other. She jerked when his fangs grew longer, pricking her.

When she looked up, Knox's eyes flashed red. "I didn't mean to wake—"

He raised himself with a smooth movement, turning at the same time so that she was lying on her back and he was above her. "If you're going to tease something with your mouth and make it grow, can I make some suggestions?"

She gave him her best come-hither stare, then rolled as suddenly as he had, reversing their positions once more. "Definitely," she said.

He grinned. "Show me what you've got," he challenged, tucking his hands behind his head.

She would, but first she wanted to kiss him again. Gently. Her tongue slipped into his mouth and took its time, savoring every taste and texture. When they were both breathing hard, she pulled away and showered kisses down his throat and over his chest. Then his abdomen. With the tips of her fingers, she caressed his quivering muscles. Then, dipping her hand lower, she cupped him in her hand.

His breath exhaled in a ragged moan of pleasure. She squeezed him tighter, moving her hand up and down the entire length of him. "That feels so good," he whispered, and she crooned, "I'm going to make it feel even better." Kneeling above him, she put her face within a hairsbreadth of his cock. When she licked just the tip of him, his hips arched up, begging for more. Her passion spiked along with his. She grasped him with both of her hands this time, running them up and down him like a favorite new toy until his hands clawed at the sheets.

"Please!" The word exploded from him.

"Please what?" His eyes narrowed at her teasing words, and she felt a jolt of sensation between her legs. She felt powerful. Undeniable. As if she and only she could give this vamp what he desperately needed. She squealed when his hands left his head and grabbed, pulling her up to kiss her passionately. Then, with his fingers tangled in her hair, he urged her down his body once more. He wasn't particularly gentle. Not with his touch and not with his next words.

"Suck me, Felicia. Now."

She didn't want gentle. Her gaze shot to his, then back down. Despite his cool command, his dick was fairly vibrating in anticipation. She licked her lips, slowly bent forward, then sucked him into her mouth.

Once again, she took her time. She became reacquainted with his size and shape, as well as what he loved about oral sex. At the same time, she discovered what she loved, too.

Knox loved it when she flattened her tongue just under the tip of his cock, but loved it even more when she swallowed him whole, squeezing as much of him as she could in her throat.

She loved hearing his groans of pleasure and used them to adjust her grip or speed.

Knox loved the slow, rhythmic slide of her mouth, which made him hum and say the sweetest things; he loved when she alternated hard sucks with the slightest hint of teeth, which made him pull her hair and talk nasty.

She loved the fact that she could make him beg and, with her hand gently cupping his balls and her tongue swirling around the length of him, drive him to such a powerful climax that his groans continued long after he'd filled her mouth with cum.

Most of all, she loved that even when he'd spent himself, he was still hard and eager for her. With the taste of him still in her throat, he maneuvered their bodies until she was beneath him. With a powerful thrust, he claimed her, drilling her with the thick stalk of his manhood until she felt full to bursting.

The whole time, he kept his gaze on hers and whispered endearments, making certain he penetrated her soul as thoroughly as he penetrated her body. When he'd wrung every last bit of pleasure he could out of her, when she was a limp, exhausted mess begging for succor, she slept. And even then, he penetrated her dreams.

Afterward, she awoke to find him watching her, a slight smile on his face as he caressed her cheek with the back of his hand. With a purr of delight, she nuzzled against him. They stayed like that for several long minutes. Eventually, he stirred.

"You know you can't go to North Korea with us, don't you?"

She froze then slowly sat up, tugging the sheet up so it covered her.

He gazed at her solemnly.

"I know," she answered softly, not surprised at his sigh of relief.

He pulled her back into his arms. "I was afraid you were going to insist on coming. You know I have faith in you, but—"

"But I'm not exactly made for jumping out of planes and crawling through wild terrain in order to infiltrate evil fortresses and rescue prisoners. Yeah, I know. I'm a good agent. Skilled at what I'm trained to do. What I want to do. I don't regret that I won't be going into that jungle with you. Except . . ." Her voice broke as she tried to communicate her feelings. She did regret leaving him. She regretted the need for him to go at all.

"I hear you," he whispered, planting a reassuring kiss on her lips. "And I'll be back before you even miss me. You'll go back to D.C.?"

"Actually," she said slowly, watching him carefully for his reaction, "I've talked with Mahone about another possibility. I'd like to go to Oregon."

Knox stiffened. "To the Dome?"

"Are you okay with that?"

"Why?"

"I'd like to see the kids," she said. "I haven't seen them in so long and I—" Felicia gasped when Knox squeezed her so tight she literally had trouble breathing. He laughed, clearly pleased with her suggestion; the sound combined with the expression on his face was startling. Tentatively, she raised her hands and tangled them in his hair, stroking him.

"They'd love that. I'll go with you. We'll teleport there and stay the day. Visit with mother and Zeph. Go on a picnic."

In direct proportion to his excitement, doubt magnified inside her. "Knox—"

"Or maybe we'll even go outside the Dome for a day. Go into the city. Not with Mother and Zeph, of course, but the children—"

"Knox, stop. I don't think that's a good idea."

He frowned even though his smile didn't completely fade. "Why?"

"I—I want to visit the children, but I don't want to make it seem like—like . . ."

Knox's frown deepened. "Like what?"

"Like we're together," Felicia blurted out.

"We are together."

"Yes, here. But . . ."

Pulling away from her, Knox jerked to a sitting position, his expression hardening. "What do you mean, we're together *here*? You think location makes a difference? Because when you said you were mine, you forgot to tell me that little qualification, didn't you?"

Felicia sat up, too. Then, still feeling vulnerable, she stood and began dressing. The expression on Knox's face while she did so—furious disbelief—confused her. She reminded herself why keeping some distance—emotional as well as physical—was going to be good for them. She'd surrendered to him physically, yes, but despite his declarations of love, nothing else had changed. They were from two different worlds and he needed to marry a vampire. It was his duty, she understood that, but she wasn't going to sacrifice her morals or desires to fit in, not even to let him populate the clan he loved. Although mating-pairs had been part of the vamp culture for centuries, she wouldn't share Knox.

Once she was dressed, she faced him. "I just don't want to confuse anyone, the children or us. Enjoying each other sexually, before you make a commitment to another, is one thing. But pretending that I'm going to be an integral part of your life is—isn't fair to anyone."

"An integral part is exactly what you're going to be. When we live together—"

"I'm not—I never agreed to come and live with you, Knox. I have my life in Washington, D.C., and I'm not going to give that up to live with you as—as . . ."

He stood as well, but he didn't bother dressing. Unconcerned with his nudity, he stood proud and powerful before her. "As what?" Knox growled.

"As your fuck buddy," she snapped, hating the fact she had to say it. Though his expression hardened even more, Felicia forced herself to continue. "Nothing's changed, Knox," she said, lowering her voice. "I don't regret what's happened . . ."

"So this is back to you expecting a commitment from me? A promise that I won't be with another female from this point on? We've tried artificial insemination, Felicia, and you know it never takes. I don't know why—"

"I have *no* expectations of you."

"You should," Knox said, grim-faced. "Because I have expectations of you."

She raised a brow. "And what would those include? Fidelity? You expect me to be faithful while you marry and impregnate someone else. While you put your dick—"

He took her arms and shook her. "Don't! It's not easy, and it's not fair, and it's not what I would want. But the vamp population is barely rising, with the birthrate having fallen sharply. What would you have me do, Felicia?"

"I'd have you love me enough to give me what I need, and leave the rest to the single males in your clan."

"What single males of any strength? If we're able to retrieve the antidote, and if we're able to obtain a sufficient amount of pure blood to get my clan healthy again, and if I can show the Vamp Council that our clan is starting to prosper and multiply, then I'll be able to give you that."

"Not once you marry. Vamps don't divorce. But even if you weren't marrying someone else, it wouldn't matter. The news is filled with reports that the Vamp Council is considering a law to prohibit vamps from marrying anyone other than another vamp." She closed her eyes, trying so hard to see things from his position, even as another part of her knew it was never going to work. Still, trying to appease him and herself, she said, "If you don't marry—and I'm not asking that of you—and what I want is to be conditioned on all those things you mentioned, then we'll deal with our options when and if the time comes. Until then, I don't want to confuse issues by having the children think I'm going to be more a part of their lives than I am. If you can't deal with that, I'll simply just go back to D.C. and—"

"No," he snapped. He released her and stepped back. "If you want to visit the children alone, then do it. I don't want to deprive them—or you—of that opportunity."

"Thank you," she murmured. She glanced around, then at the door. "You should probably—"

"Tell me something, Felicia. If all those conditions were met and I came to you to discuss our options, as you put it, do you know what your answer will be?"

Felicia stared at him, her expression solemn. She told herself to say "yes," to reassure him that of course they'd be together. Only something stopped her. Something made her hesitate to say what might not be true. It had nothing to do with her feelings for him, but everything to do with Knox's feelings for her—or more precisely, for her humanity.

"Yeah," Knox sighed. "That's what I thought."

"Knox, please—"

"I better get out there and see what's going on." With jerky movements, he dressed, then strode toward the door.

"Knox—"

Knox turned back to her. "I'm assuming you'll stick around until we leave for Korea. Or am I wrong to expect that, too?"

Biting her lip, she sank to a sitting position on the bed. "No, I'll stay. Until then," she whispered.

With a curt nod, he was gone.

SIXTEEN

Two days later, the Para-Ops team met for their final debriefing and strategy conference before embarking for North Korea. Despite his turbulent emotions where Felicia was concerned, Knox felt a great deal of satisfaction and pride as he stared at his team. Once they'd been focused on a specific target, they had, despite his expectations to the contrary, managed to put aside their differences and suspicions, and work like a well-oiled machine.

That included Hunt and Wraith.

The werebeast hadn't exactly melded into the woodwork, but he'd definitely toned down the hostility, staying in his room or leaving the building unless his presence was specifically requested, and then reverting to monosyllabic speech when addressed. However, what was most noticeable about Hunt, besides his self-imposed isolation, was the focus that had appeared in his eyes. It was as if the knock on his head by that basset hound statue, coupled with the threat of being thrown off the team, had replaced his mouthy disdain with purpose. Whether that purpose was related wholly to the mission or not,

Knox couldn't say. He wasn't about to ask or complain about the change, either. Hunt was on board and contributing what he needed to—that's all that mattered.

Wraith, on the other hand, was her regular self—bitchy, crude, irritable—with everyone except O'Flare. When O'Flare got anywhere near her, she seemed to encase herself in ice. She'd perfected the ability to look right through him even when he tried to talk to her, which he hadn't tried to do too often, probably because Wraith was rarely alone. Interestingly enough, it was Lucy who'd become the wraith's constant companion, and the two of them had even moved into the same room. Given how much time the two females had been spending together in preparation for the mission, their decision to share a room had been even more surprising.

The pair had obtained satellite photos from the coordinates that Wraith had decoded. The photos depicted a large multibuilding compound built into the side of a mountain, but provided little detail. As such, Wraith had requested aerial surveillance by Mahone's high-flying spy planes. Although he'd already been briefed in full detail, Knox had asked Wraith to present her findings to the team. That would emphasize not only her role in obtaining the information but, despite the doubts Mahone had expressed about her, her importance to the team. Knox caught Wraith's eye and she nodded, indicating they were ready to begin.

Wraith stood and walked to the front of the room. Everyone quieted and Lucy, who was operating the projector, brought the first slide up on the screen. "Based on satellite photos," Wraith began, "we already knew the target compound consists of four permanent building clusters with a perimeter area of twenty acres. These photos show us more. This one shows the deployment of armor shields along the periphery of each cluster." Wraith used a wand to point out the shields. "They're spaced several feet from the building walls, indicating they're intended to block long-distance attacks, such as those from missiles or artillery." She shifted the wand slightly. "This shows a possibly armed individual behind one of the armor shields, but other photos have shown guards on the roofs."

"What's that activity over to the right?" O'Flare asked.

Without changing expression, Wraith moved the wand to the area O'Flare was referring to. "We're not positive, but it appears this was the beginnings of construction activity that was delayed by the weather. Even though it's March, North Korea is experiencing one of its worst winters ever. It's still plagued by intermittent snowstorms, which just means our entry is going to be even more difficult."

"Is the construction for another building?" Hunt asked.

"Possibly," Wraith said. "Or if we look at the length of the area that's being cleared, an airfield."

"Makes sense," Felicia murmured. "Why continue to rely on cargo ships, which is the most likely way they're getting the Others into South Korea, when you still have to smuggle them in through the tunnels. They're also probably using commercial airplanes to enter North Korea from China. That still means they have to land in a large city, however. With an airfield, they could fly the Others to the exact spot they want."

"And now that several foreign allies besides China have instituted flights into and out of Pyong-Jong, for 'tourism' purposes," Hunt said, "that airfield would be twice as convenient."

"The biggest challenge we've had to deal with is reconciling our entry needs with our other mission needs," Wraith continued. "How do we get in undetected but still supplied with the weapons we'll need? The answer is from up high. Mahone has authorized our deployment by high-altitude transport planes, from which we'll exit wearing oxygen masks and using a fixed wing glider parachute suit. It consists of lightweight carbon fiber mono-wings, enabling us to glide a hundred and twenty miles or more before landing. We'll be virtually impossible to spot. When reaching an appropriate altitude, we'll have parachute capability. Until then, the glider can fly at approximately a hundred and thirty miles per hour. Needless to say, we won't be able to carry much equipment with us, so we're going to need to be very selective with our choice of weapons. That said, the glider suit has storage capability for weapons, including minimissiles."

Wraith clicked the remote so a rear-shot picture of a man wearing the glider gear came on.

Hunt snorted. "Batman, eat your heart out."

The corner of Wraith's mouth actually tipped up.

The were glanced at Knox, who waited for the inevitable joke about vampires turning into bats. Hunt, however, kept quiet. Figures, Knox thought. Hunt wouldn't want to be too predictable.

"Our means of entry will get us approximately twenty miles from the target location, from which we'll need to traverse through mountains and forest until we reach a rise just in front of the compound."

"What about the snow?"

"I've been reassured by the manufacturer and the FBI's parachute team that the glide suit will function in cold weather. In fact, it's naturally made to do so. In high-altitude jumping, the initial air temperature is usually twenty-five degrees below zero."

Wraith nodded at Lucy, who brought up a slide that looked a lot like the kind of map weathermen used on the daily news. "There's going to be a break in the weather in several days. We're going to be targeting that break as our entry time. After that, it's just a matter of staying warm once we're on the ground."

"Hold up," Hunt said. "Several days? We're not moving in sooner than that?"

"The glider suits are going to require a little skill," Knox said. "We'll have a few days to train, and since O'Flare has had experience with parachuting, he'll help out with that. Once we arrive at the compound, O'Flare will take care of the initial strike."

Knox gestured to O'Flare, who explained, "Initially, we need to get past the guards that are manning the exterior. The photos we have show them in the open. We can use the nerve agent sarin in a burst that will expand to an area of seventy thousand square feet in one minute, hopefully neutralizing the guards outside, as well as any other guards who respond to the attack. When they come out, we go in."

"We have several different ways to gain entry," Knox explained. "Hunt can shift into wolf form and try to get in that way. Lucy can ensure that points of entry are unlocked or kept open with her power of telekinesis. If she can get close enough, she can perform enchantments. Same thing for myself and my power of persuasion."

"And Wraith?" O'Flare asked. "What will her role be?"

"I'll be bringing along the proper explosives should we need them to gain entry," Wraith said, "along with a number of my other unique talents."

"Meaning?" O'Flare asked.

Wraith simply shrugged. "Meaning, I might want to improvise."

"All right," Knox concluded, locking eyes with Felicia. He knew the significance of this meeting's adjournment and so did she. Part of him had hoped deployment could be put off for a few more days, but Knox knew the time to move out had come. "We leave tonight for the airfield. We'll spend a few days training with HRT's Team Blue before moving on. Any questions?"

After a brief pause, Hunt raised his hand. "Just a small little detail, I'm sure, but how are we getting out?"

The others laughed nervously, as if they couldn't believe they'd forgotten means of exit.

"Teleportation," Knox said.

Hunt cocked a brow, looking a little like his old ass-were self. "Excuse me?"

At the same time, Felicia whispered, "What?"

Knox refused to look at her. She'd be angry because he hadn't discussed this part of the plan with her. She'd be angry either way. Talking would just have caused more conflict between them, which he'd wanted to avoid as much as possible given their short time left together.

"We've all agreed that this mission has two objectives, each one of equal importance. Retrieve the antidote and extricate any Others being held against their will. We're talking about an unknown quantity of Others," Knox explained. "There's no way we're going to be able to devise a traditional exit strategy given that fact."

"And that means what?" Hunt asked. "That *you're* going to teleport all of us out? As a group or singularly?"

"Teleportation is tricky enough when I'm traveling with one passenger."

"Tricky?"

"Distance does play a factor in timing. The farther away, the more time to get to point X and then back to point Y."

"You're not going to tell them what else is a factor?" Felicia hissed.

"Felicia," Knox said warningly.

"Tell us what?" Hunt asked suspiciously.

Felicia continued to stare at Knox. "Who gets to come back first? The team? The imprisoned Others? Because what happens if you're too drained to bring back the rest?"

"That's not going to happen."

"You're not strong enough to accomplish something like this, Knox. Last week, you were so fatigued, you almost passed out—"

"What?" O'Flare asked. Suddenly, Knox felt all eyes on him. "How come you didn't tell me?"

"Because it wasn't something you could do anything about. I needed to feed. I did. I'm better."

"My blood isn't enough—"

"I received pure blood since then, Felicia."

That shocked her quiet for several moments. When she spoke, her hurt was obvious. "When? From—from who?"

"From an immaculate."

"A female?" she spat.

"Yes." He could tell she didn't like the idea. Hell, neither did he. She would know that it hadn't been sexual, that it had been about survival, but given what they'd been doing when he'd taken a bite out of her, he knew it would be a difficult distinction for her to make.

"Why didn't you tell me?" she whispered.

Everyone in the room tried to look like they weren't listening.

"Felicia—"

Abruptly, she shook her head. "Never mind. I shouldn't have asked. Shouldn't care. The point is, think about what you're asking of them, Knox. You might be stronger with the pure blood now, but you've never attempted something like this, have you? Certainly not under these circumstances."

"We have no choice." Knox turned and assessed the team. "But Felicia is right. You are taking a greater risk, in some sense, by having to rely on me to get you out. It's a risk I'll be taking right along with you, but if you don't want to take it, if there's anyone here who thinks I'd leave anyone of you to die without me being right there beside you, this is your chance to back out. I won't think less of you if you do."

No one spoke.

"Final chance," Knox warned. Then, when silence continued to be the only response, he nodded. "All right. I thank you and my clan thanks you. Now let's get ready to show the world what a Para-Ops team can do."

Felicia finished packing by pretty much throwing her things into her bag; the whole time, she imagined she was throwing them at Knox's head. When he teleported in next to her, she snapped, "You should really save your strength for the mission."

He took her arms and turned her toward him, easily overcoming her stubborn resistance. "It's the only way, Felicia."

"It's not the only way."

"Then give me an alternative."

She struggled to think of something. "A stealth submarine—"

He shook his head. "Even if it's not spotted on the way there, how do we get from the compound to the water? Forget about travel time when we're all healthy, but how do we account for the condition of the Others? And then how do we escape in the sub once they're already after us?"

"Then a cargo plane," Felicia countered. "Or a Blackhawk helicopter."

"Neither of which would be allowed into North Korean airspace. Why do you think we're going in spy planes? We need to be high enough to avoid detection."

"More vamps, then," she said desperately. "You bring in other vamps to help you. You work as a team to teleport people out. Yes," she insisted when Knox shook his head. "Why should it just be you?"

"Because I'm the only one who signed up for this. There are few enough healthy male vamps as it is. I'm not going to risk them. If something happens to me, then—"

"Nothing's going to happen to you. Don't even say that."

"Felicia."

"No. Nothing. Nothing is going to happen to you, do you hear me? I won't allow it. You won't allow it!"

"No," he agreed. "You're right. I won't. Come here."

He pulled her into his arms and she went willingly, hugging him tight.

"Shhh, baby. It's okay. I'm going to be okay."

She pulled him in closer, burrowing herself into him as if that could somehow keep him with her. "The female you drank from—"

"She doesn't matter, not where you're concerned. She's someone I'm grateful to, someone who visits the Dome at times, but it's no more than a medical procedure would be, Felicia. I promise."

Of course she believed him. If he said it, it was true. Frantically, she reached up to kiss him, opening her mouth wide and rubbing her tongue sinuously against his. He tasted intoxicating, like dark chocolate mixed with mint. Moaning, she urged him on, lowering her hand to cup him through his pants and gasping when he nipped at her lips in return.

"Felicia. Wait." He tried to slow down the kiss. Gentled the touch of his mouth on hers. She wouldn't let him.

"Now," she moaned. "I need you now." Frantically, her fingers plucked at his fly, wanting to get him undressed and inside her.

With a growl, he walked her backward until her back hit the wall. Their arms tangled as he undressed her, each of them fighting for dominance—a dominance he ultimately wrested from her as soon as they were both undressed.

Knox grabbed the back of her thighs and lifted her up until her legs wound around his hips. He didn't look away as he entered her, his thick cock pushing past her plush, tight muscles with relentless intent. "Look at me," he said. "Just me."

He moved his hips in slow, shallow thrusts.

Felicia bit her lip to control her moans, but cried out when he hit a particularly sensitive spot. He spread her thighs even wider.

A faint noise drifted in from outside, causing her to flinch. Could anyone hear them? Guess what they were doing even as her heart was breaking?

"Look at me, Felicia," he said.

Even though her feelings were so intense, part of her wanted to hide. Yet she did look at him. Desire danced in his eyes, opening its arms and beckoning her to give herself over to him.

"You're so amazing, Felicia," Knox said. "I'd fuck you all day and all night if I could. But I don't want to fuck you. I want to make love to you. And that's exactly what I'm going to do."

He grasped her face and kissed her. Worshipfully. Adoringly. As he'd said, he made love to her. Despite the fact that they were leaving one another and he would be traversing into dangerous, enemy territory, with no guarantee of coming back. Despite the fact that he had her up against a wall and that part of their urgency was clearly edged by anger as well as desire.

Despite those things, he managed to make her feel as he always did: beautiful. And sexy. And loved.

Felicia felt bombarded by sensation, emotional and physical. She no longer knew where she was. The world ceased to exist. Only Knox was there. In her mind. In her heart. In her body. She felt a familiar pressure building inside her, but didn't fight it.

She embraced it.

Welcomed it.

When she came, she couldn't hold herself back any longer.

Looking into Knox's eyes, she trembled and whispered, "I love you. I love you so much. Come back to me. I love you."

SEVENTEEN

Four days later, Knox was sitting in a C-17 airplane trying to focus on the turbulence, the rattling vibrations that even his helmet and oxygen mask couldn't drown out, and the cold that made his fingers ache and his breath cloud in front of his face.

It didn't matter. Just as they often did, memories of Felicia were pressing in on him. This time, they were memories of their last time together.

Closing his eyes, he surrendered to them. After taking her against the wall, they'd dozed lazily in each other's arms. He pictured the way her hair had strewn across the sheets like a river of molten lava, heating him from the inside out, driving the beast inside him to touch every inch of her. He'd crawled on top of her again and buried his face in all that rich silk even as he'd buried his aching shaft into her hot center, pumping into her and licking the side of her neck until she'd breathed out those words again, "Bite me." And he had, this time without hesitation, piercing her with his fangs and sucking the blood from her veins, rejoicing in the feel of her entering his body even as he entered hers. Afterward, instead of feeling spent as he should have, he'd felt energized. Pumped up. Stronger than he had in years. And he knew it was because of her and what she'd brought to his life. Not just hope, but purpose.

A reason to exist that had nothing to do with duty or basic survival.

Something just for him and him alone. Something that, like the clothes he wore or the car he drove, was his simply because he wanted it to be.

Now that he'd had her, he couldn't imagine living without her.

She was already his, but he wanted her to be part of his life and part of his family. All he had to do was pledge her his fidelity during her lifetime. The fact he'd resisted doing so now amazed him.

Of course, he wanted more than that. He wanted to *marry* her, to pledge his body, heart, and soul to hers. But the Vamp Council would use such a marriage as a weapon, reminding the clan what had happened the last time a member of the royal family had married a human.

No, it would be far easier to keep the issue of Felicia's humanity, and all the suspicion that came with it, separate from Jacques Devereaux's by avoiding marriage. At least for now. As for Michelle Burgeon, perhaps a union with another male in his clan could be arranged in order to ensure the international unification of vamps over the next few years.

Be that as it may, he would always lead his clan to the best of his ability.

He would just do it with Felicia by his side. Now all he had to do was find the antidote, save his clan, and get past her fears.

Piece of cake, right?

"All right, this is it," O'Flare's voice sounded through Knox's earpiece. "I'm going to do a final assessment and then we'll be at the drop point in just about twenty minutes. Any questions?"

"Yeah," Hunt growled, obviously trying to work through the negative effects his body was encountering when flying at such a high altitude. "How come you're so damn cheery and I feel like I'm about to pass out at any second?"

"We're close to thirty thousand feet up. Most people are going to feel that way." O'Flare jerked his thumb at the masked woman at his side, who was jotting down notes on a clipboard. Melinda Murphy was a part of Team Blue, the FBI's HRT team that specialized in air missions. She'd helped O'Flare prepare the team for this very moment. "Like Murphy, I've done this before. You're uncomfortable, but you're doing fine."

Snorting, Hunt shook his head. "Tell that to my stomach. 'Cause it's not so sure. Plus my skin's tingling and I'm feeling a little too happy for my own comfort given that it's fucking freezing in here."

Knox smiled slightly, even though his own stomach was feeling a little jittery. Despite the chilling cold in the plane's interior, he was wreathed in sweat. But come on, vamp or not, he was about to throw himself out of a moving airplane with nothing but a bat suit and a few days' training to save his ass. He and Hunt would be crazy not to be feeling a few butterflies. Although he'd been feeling a bit of the euphoria and tingling that Hunt was speaking of, it had thankfully passed a few minutes before. Knox chose to think of it as an adrenaline rush rather than one of the symptoms of decompression illness O'Flare had warned them about.

"How about you, Wraith? You doing okay?" O'Flare asked.

Knox looked at Wraith, who was strapped into a jump seat with her eyes closed, looking remarkably calm. Through her mask, Knox saw her open her lids and stare at O'Flare. The "fuck you" was implicit in their cold depths before she shut her lids again. O'Flare clenched his jaw and notched it at Murphy. "Check her and Knox. I'll take care of the others."

Murphy nodded and, steady on her feet despite the jerky movements of the plane, made her way to Wraith. Almost an hour ago, while still below ten thousand feet, they'd all done their prebreathing of 100 percent oxygen in order to purge nitrogen from their bloodstream. It would, O'Flare said, eliminate 90 percent of the effects of decompression sickness. If what Knox was experiencing was 10 percent of what he normally would be otherwise, he wished he'd sucked oxygen for a whole lot longer.

It hadn't just been the jump team who'd taken the oxygen; all of the crew had, including Murphy; Leo Masterson, the aircraft commander; and Gerald Sumner, the jumpmaster. Now, as O'Flare checked over Lucy, whose pale, pinched features reflected her fear but who was managing to keep everything together, Knox yelled, "Hey, Lucy!"

The mage looked over.

"You know that telekinesis shit you pulled the first day we met?"

Lucy nodded her head.

"If something goes wrong, feel free to use it to save Hunt's ass, okay?"

Hunt glared at him. "And why wouldn't she use it to save your ass?" the were growled. Then, before Knox could answer, he grinned and nodded. "Oh, yeah. You can just teleport your ass someplace nice. Where'd you say Red was going when she left?"

Knox shook his head. "I didn't. But I'll be sure to tell her you enjoyed meeting her when I see her."

"Bullshit," Hunt said, taking Knox by surprise. "If something goes wrong, you won't teleport and leave one of us behind. And I don't know if that makes you a hero or stupid, 'cause I'd hate to see what that kind of fall would do to a creature who can't die."

Me, too, Knox thought, but he'd sure as hell spent the last few hours imagining it.

"All right, we're almost there," O'Flare said a few minutes later. "Unhook your restraints, then double-check the GPS device on your suit to make sure the coordinates are set. I'll jump first, which means I'll be in the lowest position and will telegraph the travel course for the rest of you. You ready? Sound off."

They sounded off just as O'Flare had instructed them to, lining up in front of the opening of the plane.

"Knox ready."

"Hunt ready."

"Lucy ready."

Wraith didn't answer but they could all hear her breath hitching as if she was hyperventilating, sucking oxygen in rapid, asthmatic thumps. Which made no sense, really, since she had no monitorable pulse or brain activity, and thus shouldn't even need oxygen to survive.

"Wraith!" O'Flare yelled, with no answer forthcoming.

Knox turned around. She'd unhooked her safety restraints and was standing, but she seemed to be staring at the floor.

"She seemed fine when I checked her," Murphy said.

O'Flare nodded and strode up to her. "Wraith, you need to sound off. Can you do this? Wraith?"

Wraith lifted her chin and stared at O'Flare. He reached out, checked her GPS setting himself, and triple-checked her equipment. Then he shook her by her parachute straps, causing her to face him squarely.

"You're pissed off at me, right?" he taunted loudly.

She said nothing, just narrowed her eyes at him.

"You want something else to be pissed off at me about? Mahone owed me for using me to set you up. He showed me the video files he got from that mage who put the collar on you." At Wraith's startled expression, he nodded his head and wisely backed away. "I know you don't want that to happen to others, and I know you want to kick my ass for seeing what you went through. In order to get that chance, you're gonna do whatever it takes to jump out of here and land on the ground in one unharmed piece. Or, I swear, I'll kill you myself, got it?"

With those final words, he turned and took his position at the front of the line. Wraith adjusted her helmet and mask and got into position herself, but not before glaring at O'Flare like she was imagining giving him the ass-kicking he'd mentioned.

Finally, she pulled up the gloves that would help keep her hands warm after she jumped. They all wore the gloves, but for Wraith the gloves were either unnecessary or twice as important since her body temperature was naturally so low anyway. Artificial tests had indicated she'd be fine, but there was no way to know for sure until she jumped out.

O'Flare turned and gave them all a thumbs-up. "See you down there," he yelled. Then he jumped out of the plane and disappeared.

Sumner and Masterson were shouting commands, and everything moved fast. Without hesitating, Knox followed O'Flare on cue. He swore he felt his heart stop, then explode. When his heart dropped back into his chest, he was aware of wind swooshing in his ears. For what felt like an eternity, he free-fell, his entire body rattling. Just below him, he spied the dot that was O'Flare and . . . He narrowed his eyes. The bastard was doing flips like he was some kind of air gymnast; then Knox saw him trigger the wings on his suit.

Grinning and exhilarated now, Knox waited two seconds then triggered his own wings. With a jerk, his body stalled, then started gliding forward. Adrenaline fueled by excitement rather than fear kicked in. He didn't look back, but he opened himself to the thoughts of the team members following him. He felt their terror as well as their exhilaration; he relaxed a bit when, one by one, he felt their relief. They'd all activated their wings and were anxiously hoping their parachutes opened just as smoothly.

After a few minutes, Knox had drifted low enough that he could see the Korean landscape begin to form below him. Following the trajectory programmed into his GPS, he manipulated the glider's handlebars to follow O'Flare. He had only a few seconds to experience the sheer joy of flying before it was almost time to activate his parachute.

He had ten seconds to go when his parachute suddenly activated, jerking him up and catching him around the neck, causing him to spiral uncontrollably. He struggled to free himself and keep control of the glider, at the same time trying to stave off the blackness that was blurring his vision.

He knew he was tumbling to the earth at a speed faster than normal, and although the thought of teleporting briefly flashed through his head, he pushed it away. Whatever happened to him, he couldn't abandon his team and leave with no way out.

For a split second, a combination of resolve and regret outdistanced panic.

He'd sworn an oath to save his clan and promised Felicia he'd come back to her. On each occasion, for the first time in his life, he might have failed to tell the truth.

His last thought when he landed was that it didn't hurt too bad.

Then he blacked out.

Knox jerked awake with a gasp while at the same time shoving at his face, trying to remove the slick, rubbery creature that had attached itself to him. His vision was blurred, his breaths loud and panicked, and pain radiated from his heels to the top of his head, concentrating in his neck and lower back. Voices faded in and out, and he frantically snatched at snippets of conversation, trying to orient himself.

"—emergency chute opened—" said a garbled female voice.

"—broke his back—" said a male's.

Hands helped Knox remove the mask from his face, causing biting cold air and sunlight to touch him. He sucked in loud, serrated breaths and blinked his eyes, ignoring the shadows that hovered over him and trying to determine if he was all in one piece or otherwise suffering from any gaping wounds. He panicked a little when he couldn't get his vision to focus. White dots flashed in front of his face.

"—the only body part that can regenerate after being separated from a vamp's body is a heart that hasn't been burned.

He's fucking lucky he didn't sever a limb or he'd be alive but hopping his way through the jungle."

Gritting his teeth at the pain that was shooting up his back now, Knox let himself fall back to the ground. He'd never been as happy to hear anyone's voice as he was to hear Hunt's sarcastic grumble. Not having severed any limbs was good. Very good.

"What the hell happened?" he gritted out. The last thing he remembered was seeing land and thinking he was doing pretty good for a newbie.

"Your chute opened early. Not sure why, but you're damn lucky your emergency chute activated in time to slow you down before you hit. You beat me to the ground," O'Flare said.

"The others?" Knox asked, then hissed as the bones in his back shifted, realigning themselves but making sure he felt every damn twinge of pain in the process.

"We all made it," O'Flare verified. Then he grinned. "Un-fucking-believable. I was sure two of the five of us were going to bite the big one."

"Too bad you were wrong. I know which two I would have voted for."

Knox winced at Wraith's comment, then took a closer look at O'Flare. The right side of his face was bruised and swelling. "Didn't see her coming, did you?" Knox asked softly.

O'Flare's gaze moved somewhere beyond Knox then back to him. "I was a little distracted trying to make sure you were alive." He shrugged. "At least she stopped ignoring me for a while, right?"

The pain in his back had subsided to a dull throb, so Knox held out a hand. "Help me up, would you?"

Grabbing his hand in his, O'Flare helped pull him to a standing position. Knox wobbled a little, struggling for balance given that he was still wearing the glider suit, wings extended, although half of one had broken off. Things like sensation and sound and vision were starting to align. The white dots he'd thought he'd seen were snowfall. The freezing cold, only slightly less biting than what he'd experienced when he first jumped from the plane, made him reluctant to take off the glider suit, but he sure as hell wasn't going to be able to walk in it. Peeling back the material from his sweat-soaked clothes was no easy feat.

"Don't let Hunt fool you, by the way," O'Flare said as he helped him, at the same time handing him a towel and outerwear. "He was the first one ready to give you CPR if you needed it."

Hunt growled from behind him. "You're a riot, O'Flare. Anyone tell you that?"

But when Knox turned to face the three others, Hunt jerked his chin at him. "Welcome back. Now, can we get the hell out of here and undercover before someone comes after us with one of those damn collars?"

"Here" was a low plain just north of what began hundreds of square miles of dense forest at the base of a mountain range. It had been the best spot to land but left them exposed to detection and gunfire. Whether by design or because his teammates had dragged him there, they were currently standing in an area with a frozen watering hole edged by overgrown grass and a few trees.

On a deep breath, Knox flexed his shoulders and stretched, stifling a moan. Everything was aching and sore, but working properly. He glanced at Lucy, who stood near the wraith dressed in layered camo and a ski mask, so that only her eyes were visible. "You still connected with the helo?"

She nodded. "Yes, but it's already getting spotty. We'll lose contact within a few miles. Mahone's been calling in, wanting an update, but I haven't answered yet. I didn't want to give him news about your condition until we were sure. In case it worried someone unnecessarily."

Knox grinned. "Good girl. Now you can let them know we're all fine. As soon as we bury these glider suits, we'll be on the move."

"Seems a shame to bury them," Hunt said. "You can't . . ."

Knox raised a brow. "Teleport them back? I've already expended energy having to heal myself. You wanna take the chance that I use more for the suits and don't have enough to bring you back?"

"Good point. Did anybody bring a shovel?" Hunt asked.

Lucy raised her hand. "Moving dirt and snow shouldn't be as hard as keeping two males from killing each other. How about I do that and save you guys the trouble?"

The werebeast grinned at Lucy, surprising Knox but startling Lucy so badly that she actually flushed. "I knew I liked you the best for a reason."

Lucy tried to appear unfazed by Hunt's statement, but didn't quite succeed. Blushing even harder, she turned and bumped into the person behind her. She gasped. "Sorry, Wraith—"

"Don't worry about it, Lucy," Wraith drawled. "But remember what I told you. I'm willing to give the vamp the benefit of the doubt." She stared pointedly at O'Flare. "Anyone else around here with anything remotely resembling a dick is not to be trusted."

With jerky movements, Wraith walked to where she'd shed her chute and glider. Shrugging at O'Flare, Lucy followed her. O'Flare glared at Knox. "What makes you so special that you get the benefit of the doubt?" he asked.

Knox grinned. "She can't kill me, so she's gotta live with me. You two? That's a whole other story."

EIGHTEEN

"They're all in."

Mahone heard Felicia gasp at his words. He shared her relief. Even though the mission had just begun, just knowing the whole team had made it to the ground was a considerable salve to their worries. If it wasn't a good omen, then nothing could be.

"Please continue to keep me updated," she said, and Mahone sensed she was about to hang up on him.

"Felicia, wait."

"Yes?"

"I hate that this has affected our relationship," he said. "You know I've always thought of you as—as well, one of the best agents in the Department—"

"Strange that you wouldn't have let me know, then, about your concerns about Wraith or Knox. Or that you were having O'Flare con us."

Mahone gripped the phone tighter. He'd known she'd be pissed if she found out, but at the time, there had seemed no other way. "It seemed better that way, given all the tension between you and Knox already."

"Well, that was your decision to make," she said, her voice colder than he'd ever heard it. "I just happen to disagree with it. Just like I disagree with you authorizing a mission that depends on Knox's ability to teleport the team plus any Others they can rescue back to Quantico."

Mahone gritted his teeth. "That was his decision and one he made for the good of his clan. But only once he knew you weren't going to be there," he threw out, knowing he was being manipulative but not caring. Jesus, did she think any of this was easy for him? He heard the frown in her voice immediately.

"What do you mean?"

"What do you think I mean, Felicia? Before he knew you didn't plan on going with them, he wasn't willing to take the chance on teleportation. He knew you wouldn't exit before the rest of the team, and he wasn't willing to risk you. The others? Well, I guess he views them differently."

The silence on the phone practically pulsed, making him feel even guiltier.

God, he was so sick of feeling guilty. He cataloged the pertinent events in his mind—the Goddess's visit, her ultimatum, the formation of the Para-Ops team, Felicia's suspicion and rejection. Was this his own special brand of punishment for betraying the vampire he'd loved?

Closing his eyes, he asked, "How—how is she?"

For a moment, he wasn't sure she understood that he was asking about Bianca, or whether she was going to answer.

"The same as she was the last time you asked," she finally said. "We're with the children right now and that makes her happy."

He breathed in a slow, deep breath, picturing Bianca with her cheeks flushed and her magnificent eyes sparkling with vitality. The image, however, didn't last long, and was quickly replaced by a woman with pale skin and dull, vacant eyes. "Please tell her I send my regards," he choked out.

Felicia hung up the phone without responding.

Slowly, so slowly he felt a decade older, Mahone replaced the phone in its cradle. He felt the shameful sting of tears in his eyes just before he heard movement to his right. He jerked around in his chair, stunned to see the male in front of him.

Lafleur.

"Hello, Kyle." Lafleur smiled. "Shouldn't you be preparing for Knox's arrival?"

"Please tell her I send my regards," Mahone said.

Felicia glanced at Bianca, who was currently reading Joelle and Thomas a story. The vampire Queen had ventured outside with them today, and it amazed Felicia that even while clearly ailing, she managed to recline under the shade of a large oak tree looking every inch like royalty. The Queen's eyes met hers and flashed silver before returning to the pages of the book in her lap.

Without answering him, Felicia closed the special transmitter that enabled vamps to receive calls from outside the Dome. She pocketed the small device, forcing a smile when Joelle called her over.

"Aunt Felicia, come quickly. We're getting to the good part."

She jogged over and sank to the ground, cherishing the feel of Joelle's small, sturdy body as she immediately climbed into her lap.

"Is this the good part, or the really good part?" she asked teasingly.

"It's the best part," Joelle whispered.

"'. . . and the human clutched the vampire's hand,'" Bianca continued reading, "'including her in the circle of his friends. The vampire looked at the others suspiciously, aching to read their minds and see if their smiles were genuine. But she remembered what her parents and Queen had always taught her—

that the power to read minds was a gift and a responsibility not to be wielded lightly or selfishly.'"

"I'm always reminding Thomas of that, but he says as soon as he can read minds, he's going to find out if Uncle Zeph really does have a removable thumb," Joelle whispered, making Bianca smile. "As if there's any question."

Thomas lunged for his sister, but Serena, his tutor, easily pulled him back. "None of that. Let's listen to the rest of the story."

"Yes, read on, Grandmother," Joelle drawled, eyeing her brother evilly. "I love this part."

"That's because you're a baby and still believe in nonsense," Thomas growled, reminding Felicia so much of Knox when he was annoyed that she had to bite her lip from laughing out loud.

Bianca looked up from the book. "Thomas," she said sharply. "Are you telling me you don't believe what I'm reading?"

Thomas shrugged sullenly. "Uncle Zeph says anyone who trusts humans is a fool."

"Shut up, you little toad," Joelle hissed, hugging Felicia tighter. Felicia sighed when she saw how Bianca's face had paled and her features pinched up.

Felicia patted Joelle's arm as she watched Thomas's expression shift from spiteful to stricken.

"I didn't mean you, Aunt Felicia. Honest. You're different." The boy blinked rapidly as he looked between Felicia and his grandmother, clearly trying to fight back tears.

"Of course I am, darling." She lifted one arm, and Thomas bolted from Serena's lap into her own, hugging her fiercely. She stroked his hair. "It's all right. I didn't take offense. Your Uncle Zeph is right, to a degree"—she continued to talk over Bianca's gasp—"but only because one must be cautious of anyone he or she doesn't know well, be it a human, a vamp, a werewolf, or any other living, or even once-living, thing. We all feel fear, but uncontrolled fear is what makes people do things that can hurt others."

Thomas looked up with wide eyes and sniffed. "You mean like the Vamp Council did to Grandfather? Because they feared he'd betrayed us?"

"Thomas . . ." Serena began, sounding horrified.

"Let him speak," Bianca commanded. "I won't have my grandson's questions censored for the comfort of others. Not in my presence, at least."

Serena bowed her head. "Yes, my Queen."

Bianca waved at Thomas. "Go on, Thomas."

"Cousin Bernard said Grandfather told the humans about us, including how to kill us. And that because of him, hundreds of our people were killed."

"And what do you believe?"

"I—I know you don't believe that," Thomas said to his grandmother, "but I also know you loved him."

"And do you think that would make me blind to someone's actions? That my love for one person would take precedence over my love for my entire clan? Is that what love is about?"

At Bianca's words, Felicia tensed. When she looked up, the Queen was staring not at Thomas, but at her.

"That's not fair," Felicia whispered. "He might have shared you, but you never had to share him. And you never doubted that you were the one woman he loved above all."

"One had nothing to do with the other. If I'd had to do the first, it wouldn't have changed the second."

"Then you're saying I'm a fool?"

Bianca shook her head sadly. "No. I'm saying you're human, and even if you weren't, I suspect you'd still be who you are, and who you are is exactly who Knox loves." She turned back to Thomas, who was looking miserable. "Well, Thomas. Have you thought about my question?"

"I know you love me," Thomas ventured.

Bianca nodded. "Of course."

"And I know that when I put toads in the Council's chambers, you said you still loved me, but you punished me anyway." The scowl on Thomas's face indicated he still wasn't completely happy with that fact, which was only going to prove Bianca's point, she supposed.

"That's right. And when your father did the same thing almost three hundred years ago, I punished him as well." To Felicia, whose brows had lifted into her hairline, Bianca murmured, "There are several on the Council who can't abide toads."

Felicia nodded even as Thomas and Joelle gaped. "Father did it, too?" Thomas gasped, the expression on his face clearly indicating he was proud to have followed in his father's footsteps, even if it had resulted in punishment.

"He did," Bianca confirmed. "But I punished him, just as I did you. Just like I punish Joelle when she talks back to Serena, or Zeph when he talks back to me."

"Will you . . . " Thomas looked down at the ground, jerking several strands of grass that Knox had had laid over three years ago. "Will you punish Uncle Zeph if he—if he causes harm to humans?"

Felicia barely contained her gasp.

"Well, I don't know," Bianca said slowly with a tense glance at Felicia. "It depends."

Kissing Joelle's forehead, Felicia shifted the girl off her lap, then turned fully toward Thomas. She tilted his chin up, forcing him to look at her. "Thomas, why would you ask that? Do you know some reason Uncle Zeph would try and harm a human?"

"Not you, Aunt Felicia. He'd never—"

Felicia nodded and shushed him. "It's all right. I know Zeph would never hurt me." Something inside her rebelled at the words, identifying them as a lie. "But if he's planning on hurting another human, I need to know about it."

Thomas's expression was pained, as if he knew he should give over what he knew, but was loath to betray the uncle he adored. His hesitation just made Felicia's anxiety grow even more. "Thomas, please—"

"Thomas," Bianca said in the cool, commanding voice of

the Queen she was. "You will tell me what you know immediately or you will be punished, beginning with you and Joelle spending Felicia's entire visit in the nursery."

Joelle's eyes widened and she pinned her brother with a pleading look. "Tell them, Thomas. Whatever it is, tell them."

Looking back and forth between all of them, Thomas's chin wobbled. "I—I overheard Uncle Zeph talking to Lesander and Niles." He looked at Felicia, who nodded. She recognized the names of two of Zeph's cousins, the sons of Bianca's younger brother, Lucias. "They were—they were saying how Father was a fool to sign the Treaty and that—and that the only reason he did so was because—was because . . . "

Thomas began crying uncontrollably. Knowing how Thomas loathed letting others see him cry told them all how upset he was.

"Continue," Bianca said softly, even as she stroked a hand over Thomas's hair.

"It was because he had a human's weakness in him, the same kind of weakness that—that Grandfather used to infect your insides, Grandmother, only they didn't use the word 'insides.'"

Bianca's features hardened, but she urged, "Go on."

"They said Father didn't deserve to rule the clan, not when he would stand by and let the humans do what they'd done to us. They wanted revenge for what had been done to Uncle Zeph, to Lesander and Niles, to you. They said the way to do that was to go after humans, and when the humans retaliated and Father failed to act, they—they—they could step in and take over."

Thomas threw himself in Bianca's arms, hugging her tightly.

"They said they wouldn't hurt you, but they wouldn't let you stop them, either, Grandmother."

"Did they say how they would hurt the humans, though?"

"All they said was that the cure was going to make them

stronger. I thought they meant a cure for what's made you and Uncle Zeph so sick, but later, when I asked Uncle Zeph if he thought someone could come up with the cure, he said the only thing that could cure what he had was to suck a human dry and kill it."

NINETEEN

"Funny," Wraith said from her position in the middle of the team as they trudged through snow and what was beginning to seem like miles and miles of dense vegetation. "Whenever I thought of Korea, I always thought of tropical heat and mosquitoes the size of my fist."

"And how many times have you thought of Korea in your lifetime?" O'Flare asked flatly. "I mean, in the ten or so years you've been on Earth that you can remember, that is."

With a weary sigh, Knox looked over his shoulder, already knowing what was coming next.

Wraith came to an abrupt stop, almost causing Lucy to plow into her. Although she didn't turn, Wraith glanced over her shoulder at O'Flare, who took up the rear in their single-file formation. "How about you remember that when I'm speaking, I'm specifically excluding you from the conversation?"

"You can't—"

"How about you both stop bickering like adolescents," Knox commanded, still walking in front of Hunt. "We're getting closer and we all need to focus on what we're doing here or you just may end up dying in each other's arms."

"He'll only be in my arms if I'm the one that ends up killing him."

"Listen, Wraith—" This time Hunt was the one to interrupt O'Flare. Because Hunt stopped walking, so did Knox. Leaving Wraith and O'Flare to bicker was one thing; leaving Hunt and O'Flare alone wouldn't result in hurt feelings and a few cuts and bruises, but body parts and body bags.

"Look, I don't care if we have to take five for you two to go off and fuck to get it out of your systems, but if you end up giving away our location with your goddamn yammering, I can absolutely fucking guarantee that I will rip out your throats before an enemy even thinks to pull a trigger. Do you got me?"

O'Flare scowled at Hunt, but nodded tersely.

"Fucking is the last thing—" Wraith began.

With a snarl, Hunt lunged for her. She crouched, preparing herself for the attack, but O'Flare stepped in front of her, shoving his face close to Hunt's. "Remember how this ended the last time," he warned the were.

The two males stared at each other for several tense seconds before Hunt stepped back and shrugged. "Just trying to do you a favor, Romeo."

O'Flare snorted. "Right." With that, he got back into position, not once looking at Wraith. Knox happened to be looking at her, however, when he saw shivers rack her body. Beneath her hood and scarf, her skin looked bluer than usual.

Knox cursed and walked up to her. "Pull back your scarf."

Wraith narrowed her eyes and stepped back. "Why?"

"Just how cold are you, Wraith?" he asked in response.

"I'm cold," she answered crossly. "Colder than usual. And being cold makes me grumpy."

"Pull back your scarf before I have O'Flare and Hunt pin you down and I take it off for you. That's an order, Wraith."

She stared at him mutinously, then lifted one hand—a hand that was shaking—to push her scarf aside.

Knox sucked in a sharp breath. "Fuck. Why didn't you say something?"

Her brows furrowed even as her teeth chattered together. "I don't know what you're talking about."

Knox glanced at O'Flare, who'd come back alongside them. His expression was grim as he stared at the red swelling and beginnings of blisters on her face. "It's moving into second-degree frostbite, probably accelerated because her body temp started so low anyway."

"So what?" Wraith sneered. "It's not like it's going to kill me or anything."

O'Flare continued as if she hadn't spoken. "She's not going to be able to make it to the compound."

Wraith turned on him furiously. "I can make it. You're sure as shit not going to leave me here."

"We're not leaving anyone anywhere." Knox turned to the mage. "Can you do anything?"

Lucy's eyes widened beneath her ski mask, her gaze bouncing back and forth between them. "Like what? My powers are telekinesis and enchantment. How can I—"

"There's no reason Wraith's body should be responding the way it is," O'Flare said, clearly running with Knox's suggestion. "She's dead, for God's sake. No pulse, so no blood circulating through her body, so no reason the cold should be resulting in frostbite. Maybe it's psychological."

"Bullshit," Wraith hissed.

Knox nodded. "It's worth a try. We don't know how wraiths experience physical sensation, but maybe perception is a part of how their bodies react. On some level, her brain knows it's cold so her body produces frostbite."

"Or," O'Flare said, "her body reacts with pain, based on her mind's fear of being touched."

"That's it," Wraith said. "You obviously want me to kick your ass. Both your asses."

Knox put himself between Wraith and O'Flare. "Do it," he said with a glance at Lucy.

Something very close to fear radiated from Wraith's eyes. "I don't want a mage doing anything to me."

Lucy ripped off her ski mask and raised an insulted brow. "You can room with me, but you can't let me help you?"

"That's not what I meant," Wraith snapped, obviously starting to feel ganged up on.

"Then let me try. You can trust me, Wraith."

The two females stared at each other for several long minutes before Wraith nodded. "Fine. But not in front of them."

Lucy nodded, steamrolling over Knox's and O'Flare's instinctive protests. "Let's go over there," she said, pointing to a small grove of snow-covered trees they'd just passed. Silently, Wraith turned to follow her.

"Stay in view," Knox commanded.

As they waited, their stillness made the cold sharper. The wind cut into Knox's face and he absently noted that even O'Flare's smooth good looks had transformed into that of an old man's, with a layer of frost covering it. Within minutes, the snow started to come down harder, creating a whiteout that was making it difficult for him to see Wraith and Lucy. He caught the whiff of something familiar and tensed.

Mint.

"We need to get moving," Knox called. "Now."

"I'm almost done," Lucy's voice answered.

Although it was no more than ten seconds before he saw them walking toward them, the tension inside Knox had mounted. Briefly, he conferred with Lucy, who simply said, "I invoked a spell to warm her skin and coupled it with an enchantment to make her believe she's not cold. They seem to be working. Her skin looks better. But I don't think they'll last long. She won't allow it, even subconsciously. She's too strong-willed."

Knox nodded. "Thanks for trying."

He turned and began walking, leading them forward. Hunt, however, quickened his pace to catch up with him.

"What's wrong?" he asked.

"Nothing."

Grabbing him by the arm, Hunt pulled him to a stop. "Bullshit. I can't read minds, but I can see you're freaked out. Why?"

"I don't know," Knox gritted out. "I just had a feeling, when we were waiting for Lucy and Wraith to approach, that we were being watched. And I thought I smelled mint."

Hunt's eyes widened in disbelief. "Mint? In this storm? Here?"

"Like I said, I don't know what's going on. Let's just keep moving forward."

When Knox began walking, pushing forward despite the chill that now made it hurt to breathe, Hunt fell in line behind him. Knox hadn't lied to Hunt, but hadn't told Hunt his full concerns, either. Only a few nonvamps knew that mint was a scent that was associated with the royal vamp family, one that exuded from his mother, himself, and his brother in waves usually too subtle to pinpoint. Felicia had once mentioned it to him, however, indicating that humans could in fact isolate the smell.

Because Felicia had been able to smell the mint scent shouldn't have made him afraid that he'd smelled it now. Somehow, however, the two thoughts wouldn't separate themselves in his head. Knox's feeling of trepidation was related to something he'd smelled. Somehow he knew it was related to someone on his team, but only the one who wasn't with him.

Felicia.

In Bianca's chambers, Felicia paced back and forth in front of the Queen, who sat on the chaise in her waiting room, fiddling with the bowl of caramels that Felicia had brought her on her last visit. "We need to get hold of Knox," Felicia urged. "We need to tell him what Thomas heard."

Bianca shook her head. "Thomas misunderstood. He's only ten, Felicia."

"He didn't misunderstand, Bianca. He knew too many details. Was too scared of lying to you."

"Zeph would never stand for talk of mutiny against myself or Knox."

Felicia stopped pacing to stare at Bianca. "Maybe not the Zeph you know, the one you've raised and loved, but what if Zeph isn't himself? You said yourself how weak he'd become, only to show marked improvement these past few weeks while Knox has been gone." Of course, that could be because, like Knox, Zeph had visited an immaculate, but given Thomas's revelation . . .

"Zeph's improvement doesn't mean anything. Even without feeding from an immaculate, I myself am subject to unpredictable phases of recovery."

"But what if Zeph really has come to believe that the way to save himself—the way to save the clan—is to put the clan under new leadership? Not by overthrowing Knox directly, but by creating a situation that results in the U.S. acting against the clan, therefore forcing Knox to choose—the U.S. government or his clan."

"If Knox was capable of being swayed against his clan, that would have occurred a long time ago, Felicia. Zeph knows what decision Knox would make given that scenario and so do I."

Felicia couldn't help staring. Was Knox's mother actually saying what she thought she was? "Even if he believed Zeph was killing innocent humans? I don't think so. Knox stood aside when his father was branded a traitor, not because he chose vamps over humans but because the evidence supported that conclusion. I don't believe he'd abandon humans if he were to find his own brother was having them murdered. He would not allow himself to be manipulated in such a way."

Bianca stood and drew herself up to her full height. Tiny sparks of red began to flash in her eyes, warning Felicia that she was close to losing reason and control. "This whole conversation is ridiculous given that Zeph has done nothing for me to suspect him."

Ignoring the fear that had made her pulse start to beat against her chest, Felicia tilted up her chin. "You honestly believe Thomas's reference to a cure was a misunderstanding? That it's not something you should investigate given Zeph's recent health and all the things I've told you about the team's mission?"

For a moment, Bianca seemed uncertain. She rallied back, however, clearly torn by what she viewed as disloyalty to her son. "If, as you're thinking, Zeph had accessed the antidote to purify human blood, why wouldn't he have shared it with me? Why would he have let me continue to suffer?"

"If he felt he were acting for the benefit of you and the clan, with the ultimate conclusion being enough human blood to feed you all, he could justify keeping the source from you for now."

"You really believe Zeph is in league with the North Korean government? That he's capitalizing on the torture of Others, including vamps, to persecute humans and rekindle war between the vamps and the U.S.?"

"I'm not saying I believe it. Not yet. I'm just trying to process through all the possibilities."

"Well, forgive me, but the last time someone processed through the possibility that someone in my family was a traitor, my husband was beheaded. I'm not about to let something like that happen again." Slowly, Bianca walked to the door that led to her sleeping chambers. She stood stiffly, her back to Felicia, for several long moments. Then she said, "I think it's best if you leave now."

"All right." Felicia moved to the outer door, trying to check her frustration and remember how hard it must have been for Bianca to hear what Thomas had said. "If it's all right, I'll check in with you later—"

"No, Felicia," Bianca said, turning toward her. "I meant you need to leave the Dome. Right now. I'll tell the children that an emergency came up."

A wave of emotions crashed over her, the foremost being hurt. "I'm sorry you feel that way," Felicia said stiffly. "You know how much I care for your family—"

"Apparently, caring means nothing to you humans if you can actually think my son capable of what you're suggesting."

"I'm trying to understand what Thomas heard—"

Bianca narrowed her eyes. "Thomas is an impetuous boy who doesn't realize what his stories mean. You, on the other hand, are a fool to think that Knox would ever choose humans— that he would ever choose you—over one whose blood he shares."

Backing up, Felicia opened the door to the hallway. "Knox shares my blood," Felicia said softly, nodding her head when Bianca's eyes widened. "That's right, Bianca. I fed him. He drank from me. My blood flows inside him now. It doesn't mean he'll choose me over his clan, but he's not a blind follower, either. He may think he'd do anything for his clan, but I don't. Because before he's anything, before he's vamp or human or half-Other, before he's lover, son, or father, Knox has always been two things—honest and honorable. I've always believed he got those two traits from you. Now? I'm not so sure."

Felicia stepped into the hallway and shut the door. For a moment, she leaned her forehead against it, blinking back her tears. She rubbed at her temple, trying to soothe the ache that her racing thoughts brought, but the gesture didn't help. Suspicion and doubt, fear and hurt, disbelief and betrayal—each of the emotions ricocheted through her like a bullet, making her understand Bianca's anger at the same time she cursed her inability to see beyond her loyalty to her son.

"Did you really expect differently, *Aunt* Felicia?"

Felicia gasped and jerked around at the question.

The myriad of emotions she'd been feeling vanished, leaving only one of them in its place. Fear. It expanded within her, clogging her throat, suffocating her breath, and blurring her vision as she stared at the vamp in front of her.

Zeph.

TWENTY

After Knox and the others had been walking for several hours, the snow had stopped falling and the sun had even come out, letting them cover significant ground. It was early afternoon by the time they approached the rise at the outer perimeter of the compound. "Let's stop here and take a breather," Knox ordered.

No one complained.

Knox rolled his shoulders, trying to throw off the tension that proximity had brought with it. The closer they'd gotten to their target, the grimmer they'd all become.

All of them, including the fresh-faced mage, had seen combat before. They wouldn't be here otherwise. Knox couldn't say for sure, but given the slide show of memories running through his head—of pain, of sweat mixing with blood, and of cries from both the innocent and guilty alike—Knox would bet the others were probably going through the same thing. The familiar, ever-present tension that he'd carried with him for years after the War, the one that had faded but had never completely gone away, that sharp edge of paranoia and awareness that enabled him to lead others, returned full-force and for one major purpose—survival.

As he stared at the individuals who made up his team, instinct had him assessing each of them for signs of weakness and deceit. Physically, they'd all seemed to hit their stride. Even Wraith seemed to be doing better after the mage's spell. He narrowed his eyes, watching as O'Flare attempted to check on her face, only to have the wraith turn and dismiss him. There was so much anger in her, so much mistrust, but Knox knew it had been rightfully earned. Although he saw the regret radiating from O'Flare, Knox doubted he'd ever get past the wraith's defenses again. With that thought came others, including the memory of what he'd smelled earlier and more irrational fear concerning Felicia. Knox didn't just open his mind this time—he ruthlessly probed those of the individuals around him.

Hunt was lost in distant memories, while Wraith was occupied with the pain of more recent ones. Lucy was mentally preparing for the events to come, praying she wouldn't have to kill but accepting that it was a possibility. O'Flare was thinking of his grandfather who, it turned out, really did come to him in visions. None of them emitted so much as a drop of treachery or deceit against him.

With a sigh, Knox backed off.

When he looked up, O'Flare was staring at him, his narrowed, heated gaze both accusatory and understanding. "I need a minute alone," he said abruptly. Turning, his gaze dared Wraith to say something—anything—sarcastic, but with a slight flicker of her eyes, she looked away. He stomped off and into a grove of trees, out of their sight.

Hunt shrugged. "Nature's call," he said mockingly, but sounding wearier than he ever had.

"No," Lucy said, shaking her head. "He's preparing to kill."

Wraith frowned. "How do you know that? Did he say something to you?"

"No, but I read his bio. His mother was a shamanic princess with the Sheyote tribe. It's from her he got his psychic abilities."

A faint sound, whisper soft but rhythmic and melodic, drifted from where O'Flare had disappeared. Closing her eyes, the mage smiled. "The Sheyotes use a shamanic ritual to prepare for battle, a choreographed dance where each one focuses inward even as the ensemble moves as a unified whole—circling, slicing, and turning." She opened her eyes as O'Flare's chants grew slightly louder, mixing with the sound of footsteps, lunging, and shifting snow. "It's supposed to mirror the process of being and becoming, the eternal cycle of life and death, the belief that death is not the end but just the beginning."

They were all looking toward O'Flare and the occasional blur of movement they could see through the trees. Wraith wrapped her arms around herself. "You have some weird obsession with death dances or something?"

Lucy shook her head. "No. I just research what interests me. I learn about the things I care about."

Knox stiffened, as did Wraith. The females stared at one another before Lucy shrugged. "He's done."

In under a minute, O'Flare returned, his eyes bright and his face slightly flushed. His expression, both placid and exhilarated, shifted into annoyance when he noticed the wraith staring at him. "What?" he asked irritably.

She jerked, confusion flashing on her face before she looked away and strode next to Knox to look unseeingly into the distance. O'Flare stared at her for several seconds before turning away.

Knox gave them all an extra minute, then said, "Let's move on."

A half hour later, the mage said, "We're coming up to it. It's about fifty yards in front of us."

With the mage's words, the gravity of their mission, never far from his mind anyway, settled on Knox like two tons of stones pressing on his chest. Soon, his hope for an antidote for his clan could be realized or crushed. As if his mother's and brother's continuing decline wasn't enough to make the last thought unbearable, he knew that his relationship with Felicia also hung in the balance.

It had nearly killed him to let her go, knowing that she was going home, to his home, but that he couldn't go with her. She didn't want him to be with her when she saw the children because she didn't want them getting any *ideas* about her place there.

Well, Knox had plenty of ideas, and he knew getting the antidote was going to be key to seeing them take shape.

So he would get the antidote. He would ensure that his clan began to heal. He would rescue the Others that were being held against their will.

He would share his life with Felicia.

And he would kill anything that got in the way of that goal.

It was approaching late afternoon when the team was in position and ready to move. They'd been watching the target for several hours, focusing on the ornate structure with traditional Korean architecture that, like the others, was protected by shields but seemed to be guarded the most heavily by manpower. Right now, there were approximately five guards walking the perimeter of the structure's roof, five walking the perimeter on the ground, and two standing permanent guard at the main entrance. They wore thick jackets and caps that covered their ears, and they seemed impervious to the cold that, even with gloves, was making Knox's fingers numb and difficult to bend.

Knox lifted his hand and fingered his medallion, the same kind of medallion his father had worn just before he'd been executed. He'd only been twelve then and hadn't yet received his powers. He remembered wondering if he had, if he would use them to save his father. He'd thought he would, even knowing that his father was a self-admitted traitor.

He'd asked his father for himself then—was he a traitor? His father had smiled sadly, ruffled his hair, and said no. "But

Calmet, you admitted telling him the secret to killing vamps," Knox had cried. And his father hadn't denied it. Instead, he'd said, "Not all immortals deserve that gift," before he'd been dragged away, his mother's screams echoing behind him.

"Hunt's ready," Wraith said through her headset, shaking Knox from the past. The wraith was waiting, sniper rifle ready, approximately a hundred yards away and twenty feet above them at the top of a small hill. Hunt also had a rifle with him, while Knox, Lucy, and O'Flare were armed with Uzis. In addition to her rifle, however, Wraith had an arsenal of explosives, including a grenade launcher, at the ready. O'Flare, of course, was waiting about 40 feet to Knox's left with his own special brand of laughing gas.

Knox frowned at Wraith's words. "He's shifted?"

"Yes."

"Did you see it?"

"Yes." This time, the simple word was fraught with tension. "I hope I never have to see it again, tell you the truth."

"Come on, Wraith." O'Flare's voice came on the line. "I would think you'd enjoy seeing Hunt take his most primal form. Make the exterior match the interior, right? Probably didn't hurt that you wanted him to experience some pain."

"Not that kind of pain," Wraith whispered, sending a shiver down Knox's spine.

O'Flare didn't respond.

"Where is he?" Knox asked.

"He should be coming into your sights any minute now."

Sure enough, within seconds Knox saw him. The wolf was larger than he'd expected, with a shiny coat that was the same mix of tawny colors as Hunt's hair when he was in his human form. As the wolf approached, it turned its head and seemed to look unerringly at Knox, its hazel eyes glowing with arrogance. The wolf bared its teeth. Knox swore the were was grinning at him.

Cocky bastard, Knox thought, but this time with a hint of admiration.

Hunt turned just as one of the guards manning the entrance of the building spotted him. Knox had brushed up on his Korean before they'd left, but he didn't need a translator to know the man was freaked out by the wolf's sudden appearance. He called to his fellow guard while pointing at Hunt.

Hunt sat back on his haunches and began to howl.

The guards on the roof gathered in clusters to look down at the wolf, and several men walking the grounds stumbled to a stop. When a faint, answering howl drifted from inside the walls of the compound, everyone, including Hunt, was stunned silent. Immediately, Hunt crouched down and growled menacingly.

Knox tensed and was about to give O'Flare the green light when Lucy's voice came over the line. "Abort. Abort. We need to abort."

"What?" Wraith hissed.

"Status," Knox snapped.

"O'Flare's tranced out," Lucy said. "He's out of it. He's not responding to me and I don't know how to activate the chemicals or regulate the content so I don't end up killing all of us. So abort."

Knox whispered the words. "Abort. Abort. Abort."

But he knew the chance of Hunt hearing him was slim.

"Felicia."

Knox couldn't be sure that he heard O'Flare speak the word through his earpiece or if he'd imagined it. "What—"

One of the guards lifted his gun and pointed it at Hunt.

"I'm going to shoot," Wraith said.

"Wait," Knox hissed, aware that the wolf had tensed. Sure enough, Hunt lunged and was out of range before the man fired. The wolf scampered into the trees.

"Felicia."

This time there was no mistaking O'Flare's voice or the word that he'd spoken.

"Feli—" He said the name again.

Knox was in a crouch and moving silently toward O'Flare before the final syllable faded.

TWENTY-ONE

"Move faster," Zeph hissed.

"I'm moving as fast as I can," Felicia snapped back, trying once more to wrench her arm from the vamp's grip. "How about we stop and you tell me what's going on instead?"

Glancing quickly behind them, Zeph responded by quickening his pace even more. "Don't you know? I'm whisking you away so we can be together in private." Zeph produced a facsimile of an evil leer. "What's one more dead human if it furthers the beginning of another war and the overthrowing of my brother, right?"

"I don't know what you're talking about."

Zeph shot her an annoyed look. "Don't be troublesome. Even though reading minds is tricky for me now, your suspicions would radiate from miles away. Plus, Thomas was riddled with guilt and told me about his teary-eyed confession."

As if they were blocks of cement, Felicia's feet came to an abrupt halt. "Did you hurt him?"

Eyes rounding and sparking red, Zeph growled, "Sure. I ripped his little head—"

Lightning quick, Felicia hit Zeph in the throat with the tips of her fingers. When he gagged and instinctively released her arm, she braced, whirled, and hit with a roundhouse kick that sent him stumbling back several feet before crumbling to the ground.

"Wait . . ." he gasped.

But she was enraged, drowning in the image of this vamp hurting a precious little boy. "I'm going to kill you," she vowed. "I'm going to rip your heart out and spit on it before I burn it." Swiftly, she lunged for him.

Zeph curled his legs into his chest in time to plant his feet on her chest. She went flying through the air after he kicked out, shoving her off him with a powerful push.

She grunted when she landed, then felt it—persuasion. "No," she gasped, just as her muscles froze. She tried to move, but couldn't. Furious, she fought the spell. She writhed and arched and struggled and thrashed—but only in one part of her mind. The part that controlled her movement was still held in the spell's firm grip.

Zeph half crawled toward her while clutching his stomach. He gripped her hair and yanked her forward, but her cry of pain was internalized. "You need to work on your sense of humor, Felicia. But damn, I knew there had to be a reason Knox was so crazy about you. Too bad he saw you first."

His words caused confusion to pulse through her, but it splintered under panic as she read the intent in Zeph's eyes. Was he—

He did. He leaned right in and kissed her on her frozen mouth. It wasn't a lewd kiss, but a firm, prolonged smack, a spontaneous, exuberant kiss, one a bride might get from a friend—or a brother?—on one's wedding day. He pulled back with a grin. "Knox is one lucky vamp. If I had my strength, I'd teleport you out of here, but considering I don't even have the strength to carry you, you're going to have to help me out. You going to cooperate?"

Since she couldn't nod, he must have liked something he

read in her eyes. The persuasion lifted. He cocked a brow. "I'm wondering just how much you really wanted to fight me, Felicia, because if I can persuade you to move given how weak I am—"

With a closed fist, she punched him in the face. Because she pulled it, however, his head barely knocked back. He rubbed his jaw. "Damn it, I'm not a traitor—"

"I know," she snapped, just before she grabbed his face and gave him a smacking kiss of her own. "Now tell me what the hell *is* going on."

A raspy voice came from somewhere behind her. "How about I fill you in on the details instead?"

Felicia and Zeph locked eyes. In the reflection of his gaze, she saw not one, but two vamps standing behind her.

Lesander and Niles.

As he moved, Knox continued to watch the guards outside the compound. Once Hunt ran off, they'd separated and gone back to their posts, clearly thinking they'd scared off any threat. Frustration and fury prodded him so he moved swiftly, more than twice as fast as a human could.

"What's going on?" Wraith demanded over the radio line.

"I'm going to find out. You still in position?"

"Yes."

"Good. Stay there and lock on anyone they decide to send out to investigate."

"I will, but they're looking pretty unconcerned at the moment. Stupid if they really do have a were inside that compound. How's . . ." She swallowed audibly and took a breath. "How's O'Flare?" she asked. "And why isn't that damn mage answering us?"

"I'm almost there, Wraith."

He reached O'Flare and Lucy's hiding spot in minutes.

Lucy was straddling O'Flare, who was prone on the ground and writhing like a snake. Both of her hands covered his mouth, stifling his voice until only the breathiest of sounds emerged. Her earpiece lay in the snow beside her. With wide eyes, Lucy turned to Knox. "He started to yell. I—"

O'Flare's leg thrashed out.

She closed her eyes and pressed down harder with her hands. "I used an enchantment spell but . . ." Her body lifted as O'Flare arched beneath her. "He's strong . . . hurry."

Knox rushed over, kneeled beside Lucy, and slammed O'Flare's head on the ground, not enough to knock him unconscious, but certainly hard enough to stun him. The human stopped struggling.

Lucy looked at him in horror. "Why did you—"

"Look," Knox said.

She returned her attention to O'Flare. The lingering fog in O'Flare's eyes cleared, his expression shifting briefly to annoyance, then restrained urgency. He held still, silently demanding that Lucy release him.

Knox nodded. "Let him go."

Carefully, Lucy pulled back her hands. Immediately, O'Flare grabbed Lucy's hips, shifted her back, and sat up with her still in his lap. Swiftly, he kissed the mage on the forehead, then lifted her completely off him to place her on the ground.

"I had a vision," O'Flare said, quickly getting to his feet. "About Felicia. She's in danger, Knox."

The panic was instantaneous, but Knox pushed it back, trying to remain calm. In control. Vigilant. He couldn't forget that O'Flare had been working as Mahone's stooge, manipulating Wraith, and thus manipulating them all, under the guise of helping the team.

"What exactly did you see?"

"I saw stairs. Edged with an iron banister. The iron had been forged into a repetitive design like the one on the medallion you wear. Triangles."

Knox swallowed. O'Flare was describing the stairway in the main foyer of Knox's home. "Go on," he urged.

"I saw her dancing."

"Dancing?" Wraith's breathy voice came in through Knox's earpiece. "What does that have to do with her—"

"Go on," Knox snapped louder. Wraith didn't speak again.

"She was dancing with a vamp. Only slight taller than herself. He was wearing a tuxedo and had his hair pulled back in a ponytail. Damn handsome dude but for a scar he's got running across here." O'Flare skimmed two fingers down the right side of his face, touching the flesh almost at his hairline and running it down past his jaw and into his neck.

Knox took in a shuddering breath.

Zeph.

He'd gotten the scar when he'd been fourteen and still trying to win his father's approval by proving he was a better fighter than other vamps in his class. Unfortunately, he hadn't yet learned that when it came to fighting, intelligence and planning were often more important than sheer brute strength. It had taken a school-yard ambush by a much smaller vamp wielding a hunting knife and sixty stitches for him to start. Of course, that same vamp had been brutally dealt with by Zeph's father and no one, not even Bianca Devereaux, had intervened on behalf of Zeph's attacker.

"What else do you see?"

"Two other vamps," O'Flare said, his voice sounding almost trancelike as if even now he could see them. "Much taller. Bigger. Bigger than you."

Knox frowned. Vamps that were bigger than him were few and far between, especially after the War and the distribution of the vaccine. Could O'Flare be seeing dharmires? Or vamps from outside his clan? Maybe a pair that had come in from outside the United States?

"What else can you see about them?"

O'Flare closed his eyes, concentrating.

"They're flying above them, and Felicia and her partner don't see them. They're dancing more furiously, spinning and dipping, covering the whole dance floor, but the vamps don't go away. But I see the look in their eyes. It's lust."

"What kind of lust? Desire? Blood lust?"

O'Flare's eyes popped open. "Both," he said.

Knox straightened. "I've got to—"

A blur of movement was their only warning. Hunt attacked from nowhere, knocking O'Flare down and pinning him to the ground.

"Hunt, stop," Lucy breathed, obviously keeping her voice low so she wouldn't telegraph their presence to the guards.

"You better have a damn good reason for deviating from the plan, my friend. Even though I can't die in wolf form, I can sure feel pain. I sure as shit don't relish the idea of being riddled with bullet holes."

Stepping in front of them, Knox bent and grabbed the were by the throat. He picked him up, his fear for Felicia obviously giving him the kind of strength he hadn't exhibited in years. When Hunt started to fight him, Knox tightened his grip. "Stand down, Hunt," he growled. "O'Flare had a vision that Felicia was in danger. Do not get in the way of me finding out what he saw."

Hunt's glower slowly faded. He deliberately relaxed his muscles. "Fine," he choked out.

Knox released him and turned back to O'Flare, who'd picked himself up again. Knox gripped O'Flare's arm. "What about my mother? Or children. Did you see two young children in your vision?"

O'Flare shook his head. "No. No other females. No children. But I saw something else, Knox. The three vamps with Felicia?" His eyes shifted down until they rested on Knox's chest. "They were all wearing the same medallion. They're all from your clan, and even though the vision might seem vague and benign, I know what it means. Felicia's in danger, Knox. Grave danger. And you don't have long to save her."

Knox shook himself free of O'Flare's grasp and swiftly penetrated his thoughts.

He sensed no deceit in O'Flare, no malevolence. Only truth. The truth that Felicia was in danger.

But how could he know for sure? The timing seemed ridiculously convenient. And his powers had failed him before. He hadn't been able to read those scientists' minds and then they'd ended up dead. He looked through the trees, but couldn't see the compound or the guards from his current vantage point.

"Go," Hunt said. "He's telling the truth. I can feel it."

Grimly, Knox shook his head, not denying the truth of O'Flare's words but expressing disbelief for how fucked the situation was. "We're talking about teleporting halfway across the world. If I go, even assuming I can return, I'll have depleted some of my power. I can't guarantee how much I'll have left. Whether I'd be able to transport all the Others and the rest of you as well."

"Go," Lucy said.

Knox looked at O'Flare, who nodded.

But still Knox hesitated. "Shit," he said, wanting nothing more than to teleport to the Dome and ensure the safety of his family. But he had no real proof that Felicia was in danger. He had a duty to his team, as well. And his entire clan. If he left now and couldn't return, then whether the team was able to retrieve the antidote would be irrelevant. They'd be left with no way to get out. Which meant they could very well die here in this frozen hellhole.

"Go." Wraith's voice came over the line. "Now, before it's too late."

Knox felt himself softening. He flexed his fingers, gathering the power to teleport so that it buzzed throughout his body in an electric wave.

"I'll be in charge while you're gone. We'll stay low and wait for you to return."

No one responded to the were's words. The fact that neither Wraith nor O'Flare protested his assertion of leadership told Knox how earnest they were in their urgings.

"I'll be back," Knox promised. "So long as there's a breath in my body, I swear to you I'll come back for each one of you."

Hunt nodded. "I'm going to hold you to that, vamp."

With a surge of energy, Knox left.

* * *

"I knew the bastard didn't have the guts to do what was right," Lesander taunted as he pinned Zeph against a wall. The vamp's efforts to restrain Knox's brother seemed negligible, as if he were a dinosaur pinning down a gazelle. Felicia hadn't seen him since before the War, but he looked exactly the same as he had then—tall, imposing, bulging with muscles, a vamp in full health, suffering no ill effects from the malnourishment that the rest of his kind were.

Fully pinned to the ground as she was, hands and legs locked in place by Niles, Felicia tried to focus on Lesander's words rather than the erection Niles had deliberately shoved against her. "You mean the guts to betray your leader? Does Knox know you've been feeding on pure blood and keeping it to yourself?"

Although she'd been speaking to Lesander, the clear leader of the pair, Niles lifted his hands, keeping her pinned in place with persuasion, and slapped her hard across the face. Felicia bit back any sound of pain, so he slapped her again, this time splitting her lip. Blood gathered at the side of her mouth and she swiftly lapped at it with her tongue, internally cringing when Niles followed the move with eyes that suddenly flashed red.

"I might not have shared the source with Knox, but I gave old Zeph here a little taste, didn't I, Zeph? What, it wasn't pure enough for you? Did you feel sharing blood with your less-royal cousin was beneath you? Yet you'd rather side with a half brother who has the poison of human DNA in his system?" He turned his head to look at Felicia. "No offense, of course."

Felicia glared at him. "None taken. The only poison I see are a couple of vamps who are acting like trained pets for the humans they claim to despise so much."

Lesander narrowed his eyes at her and added another layer of persuasion. He cut off her breath. Within seconds, Felicia's eyes were watering with the effort to breathe and the world started to lose focus.

"Stop," she heard Zeph yell.

Frantically, Felicia shifted her gaze between Niles and Lesander. Niles grinned evilly. Lesander had turned away to wrestle with Zeph, who'd obviously had an unexpected surge of strength.

The fingers constricting her throat were suddenly gone. Sucking in a deep breath of air, Felicia felt her arm twitch. Glancing up, she saw that Niles's attention was on Zeph and Lesander, who were still struggling. Niles's inattention had caused his persuasion over her to slip a little.

Gathering her strength, Felicia heaved herself up, trying to slam Niles in the head with either her fists or her own skull. Before her torso could lift off the ground, Niles turned back to her. This time, he hit her with a closed fist.

Felicia's head thumped back against the floor so hard she saw stars. When Lesander laughed, she saw he'd once again subdued Zeph, who was pale and breathing hard. His gaze latched on to Felicia, the apology in them as clear as the knowledge that they were going to die. She closed her eyes, calling forth memories both recent and older. Her parents. Noella. Knox and Bianca and the children. She remembered the feel of Knox's kiss and the sweetness of Joelle's hug as she'd squeezed her with her little arms. She felt a tear trail down her face; it mingled with the blood seeping from her nose and mouth.

Above her, Niles froze. He bent closer toward her, sniffing audibly. When Felicia felt the moist warmth of his tongue licking at her lips, her eyes popped open and she tried to struggle once more. She flinched in fear, at least her insides did, when she saw the demonic look that had entered Niles's ruby red eyes.

"She's got pure blood."

"What?" Lesander's full attention suddenly became focused on Felicia's mouth or, more specifically, the blood that had pooled there.

"You're crazy," she breathed. "I took the vaccine. My blood was tested—" Automatically, she choked back her words. Her blood had been tested over a month ago, by Dr. Neil Barker himself. He'd taken her blood, tested it on-site, and assured her that the vaccine was still working. He'd also told her, however, that her iron levels were low and that she was bordering on anemia. Before she knew it, he'd given her several "vitamin" shots. What if he'd actually given her the antidote instead? After all, she'd volunteered to be one of his first subjects as soon as Mahone approved human testing for the antidote. If he'd felt he needed results sooner than later, would he—

With economical movements, Lesander rapped Zeph's head against the wall behind him, effectively knocking him unconscious. Before Zeph's body hit the ground, Lesander was kneeling beside her and Niles.

He would, Felicia realized. Barker had given her the antidote. It was the only explanation and it was the reason that these two vamps were ready to rip her apart to drink her blood. Felicia's mind urged her body to move, to flee, to run, but once more, nothing happened. She simply lay there like a rock, helpless.

"Move out of the way," Lesander growled at his brother. "I want to see for myself."

Niles shoved at him with his shoulder. "Back off. I'm not an idiot. I know what pure blood smells like. What it *tastes* like." He swiped his tongue across his lips. "Hers is yummy."

Lesander shoved Niles back, hard enough to almost dislodge him from his position over Felicia. "Move, I said. I want to taste."

With an expression Felicia had rarely seen so close-up, Niles's face transformed into one of pure, primal rage. Baring his fangs and hissing, his eyes flashing like the siren on a police car, Niles wrapped his hands around Lesander's throat. Lesander's hands followed suit.

Although she felt the persuasion completely lift and the newfound freedom in her arms and limbs, she was still pinned in place by Niles's body. A quick glance at Zeph confirmed he remained prone on the ground, but a faint lifting of his eyelids revealed he was awake. Imperceptibly, he inched closer to her.

A howl of pain snapped her attention back toward Zeph's cousins. Niles had shifted almost completely off her now. Lesander had sunk his fangs into his brother's neck and Niles was frantically trying to throw him off.

Abandoning stealth for swiftness, Felicia yanked herself from under Niles and belly-crawled toward Zeph, who was moving even swifter toward her. Their arms extended to reach for one another and they managed to grab hold of one another's wrists. Zeph dragged her closer, a question in his eyes.

She nodded. "Do it," she whispered. "I don't know if it's true, but if it is . . ."

She winced when Zeph sank his fangs into her wrist and began to drink from her in strong, swift pulls. He moaned and cupped her wrist in his hands, as if to keep her from pulling her wrist away. She felt none of the pleasure that she'd felt with Knox. Instead, she felt a mounting panic. She grew slightly dizzy and feebly tried to pull her wrist away. Zeph continued to drink from her, his voracious sucks intent on draining every last drop of her blood.

She pulled harder, trying to escape him, but he growled and latched on tighter, making her moan in pain.

"Zeph . . ." she whispered, trying to get through to him. He was going to kill her, she thought. In his hunger for blood, he was going to suck her dry.

Blackness started to close in on her. She heard movement behind her. Thuds and shouts. A howl of pain.

"Zeph, no!"

Felicia's waning senses jolted to life at the sound of Knox's voice.

This time, a different pain shot through her, so sharp in its intensity that it almost drowned out everything else. Knox was in Korea. Was her mind conjuring his voice to ease her into death? Not fair, she thought. She hadn't gotten enough of him.

Then she felt Zeph's bite ease. She felt her blood circulating inside her body rather than leaving it. Forcing her eyes open, she saw the red flare of Zeph's gaze locked on something just behind her. He growled, but an answering growl—louder and much more vicious—drowned him out. Weakly, Felicia lifted her head and gasped.

I'm dreaming, she thought. Either that or I'm dead. Do the dead dream? she wondered. They must. Because standing above and slightly in front of her, his breaths billowing out of him, his muscles bulging and his eyes flaring just as they had when Hunt had challenged him, was Knox.

"Knox."

His eyes shifted to hers when she whispered his name, but almost immediately they returned to Zeph.

Knox said two words then, two words that, despite her disorientation and weakness, Felicia instantly knew were directed at his brother.

"You're dead."

TWENTY-TWO

When Knox materialized, the first thing he saw were his cousins Lesander and Niles, going at each other so viciously it was obvious their tussle was no mere spat between siblings. Their blood was flowing and spilling on the stone tiles, and by the look in their eyes they were bent on ripping out each other's hearts.

He knew immediately that they were the two vamps that O'Flare had seen in his vision.

Wildly, his gaze searched for and landed on Felicia. He spotted her feet first, which were shifting restlessly on the floor. Even as he felt a profound sense of relief that she was alive, his gaze moved swiftly up her body, inspecting her for injury, not stopping until it had no choice but to do so because the wrist extended above her head ended at his brother's mouth.

Zeph had sunk his fangs into Felicia's wrist and was sucking at her like a starving baby at a mother's breast.

The words out of his mouth were automatic, even as his brain struggled to process what he was seeing. "Zeph, stop."

Then something else registered.

Felicia's feet were shifting as she tried to get purchase on the floor so she could escape. She was trying to back away from Zeph, pulling at her wrist even as he clung to it and growled warningly. Instantaneously, Knox felt the power of his mother's ancestors flash through his veins like a bolt of electricity. He transformed, his rage and blood lust so much more powerful than what he'd felt in Quantico when Hunt had pushed Felicia.

Half growling and half roaring, he called Zeph's name. His brother detached from Felicia's wrist and Knox saw the blood—her blood—that stained his lips a macabre red. Vaguely conscious of Felicia's eyes on him as well, he stared into his brother's eyes. "You're dead," he said in a low, deadly voice before he lunged forward.

Or rather, he tried to lunge forward.

At first he thought that Zeph was using his power of persuasion to hold Knox in place, but that was impossible. Knox wore his medallion, the medallion made of such pure gold that it protected anyone who wore it from becoming susceptible to a vamp's mind reading or persuasion power. It was an ancient discovery and one Knox's clan had put into practice for the benefit of all. For a brief second, he thought of the scientists and his inability to read them. He hadn't seen them wearing jewelry, but—

The force that was holding him back suddenly pushed into him, trying to bring him to the ground. Knox resisted, throwing all his weight backward. Trembling with the effort, he turned his head and locked eyes with Lesander. Niles clung to Knox's other side, but it was Lesander who spoke.

"Hello, cousin. Fancy seeing you here. As much as I'd love to see you kill your brother, something tells me that before you did so, you'd be turning on us. Best to take advantage of the element of surprise, don't you think?"

Based on the description of O'Flare's vision, Knox had been prepared to discover betrayal. When he'd seen Lesander and Niles, their duplicity hadn't been too difficult to accept; they'd always been pricks. Zeph's betrayal, however, had stunned him. Now, he internalized Lesander's words, clinging to the hope that Zeph was victim rather than foe. Knox narrowed his eyes. "I said he was dead. You? You're going to wish I'd kill you way before I'm ready to stop hurting you."

"You forget, Knox. You might have led this clan by virtue of your mother's birth order, but I always could kick your dharmire ass even when we were kids. Now that you're suffering the effects of malnutrition and I'm not, it'll be easy as pie."

"I've always hated pie, cousin." Knox drove both his elbows back, one into each of his cousin's ribs. As both vamps instinctively retreated, Knox spun. With one elbow bent at shoulder level, he rammed it into Niles's head, shooting for the vulnerable spot where his ear had been ripped off during the War; he rubbed at the spot constantly and had often complained of its tenderness. Simultaneously, Knox grabbed Lesander's hand and ducked under his arm, twisting it to the back of his body. He then knocked the vamps' heads together, hard enough that the sound of impact echoed through the hall.

Desperately his gaze sought Felicia. She was on her feet, or at least halfway on them, as Zeph propped her up and led her to an alcove underneath the staircase. Knox cursed and teleported to them, immediately snatching Felicia away from his brother and sweeping her in his arms. "Are you with me or against me?" he snapped.

Zeph grinned and straightened to his full height. He'd already been in the process of transformation when Knox had first seen him, but it was still a shock to see him like this—his face full, his eyes bright and healthy, his body pumping up so it was nearly as tall and broad as Knox's.

"With you all the way, Brother."

"Behind you," Knox growled an instant before he transported into the nursery. Instantly, he spotted his mother urging Joelle and Thomas into a closet. Inside the closet was a trap door that accessed a secret passage, which led beneath the house to a safe location outside the Dome.

"Knox," his mother cried upon seeing him. She was trembling so badly that she could barely stand. Serena was supporting her and the vamp's eyes reflected both the horror and fear thundering through Knox's heart. Sobbing, the children hugged his knees, nearly toppling him.

He bent down, gently depositing a listless Felicia on the soft carpet, and hugged his children close. "Shush now. It will be all right."

His mother threw her arms around him. "Thank God you got to her. I couldn't—I couldn't . . ." His mother started to weep, but as badly as Knox wanted to comfort her, he knew there wasn't time.

Taking her arms, he pushed her away so he could meet her gaze. "Mother, listen to me. I have to help Zeph, but Felicia— Zeph drank from her . . ." Knox shook his head, still not understanding why Zeph had latched on to Felicia so tightly or why after drinking from her he'd recovered his full vamp strength. He knew Felicia, just like every other FBI employee, had to have taken the vamp vaccine. She wouldn't have been able to continue working there otherwise. As he spoke, her eyes flickered and she moaned his name softly, but otherwise she seemed oblivious to what was happening.

Damn Zeph. What if he'd drunk too much?

"Stay with her, Mother," Knox said, straightening. "Bring her and the children into the tunnels and get to the safe house. I'll meet you there."

"Knox!" His mother grabbed his arm. "She—she warned me, but she suspected Zeph. She was wrong, wasn't she? Zeph's not—"

"Zeph hasn't betrayed us, but our cousins have. They'll kill him if I don't go back." Torn, he pulled away. "Take care of them, Mother."

His mother nodded. Straightening and looking him in the eyes, she said, "With my life."

"One of them's coming toward me," said Wraith, who was still positioned several hundred feet away from the rest of them.

O'Flare, who was still feeling weak from the power of his vision, cursed softly. He looked at Hunt, then Lucy.

Lucy shook her head. "He's too far away for me to use enchantment."

"What about your telekinesis?"

"Even if I could affect anyone from this distance, which I can't, what do you want me to do? Hold him back? That'd be the tiniest bit suspicious, don't you think?"

"What about Wraith? Can't you—I don't know, can't you fly her over here? Above the trees, so they don't see her or something?"

"You obviously think I'm way more powerful than I am."

Fear for Wraith was blinding more than his reasoning. His vision was actually starting to blur, his limbs to shake. O'Flare stood. "I'm going to her—"

A low moan interrupted him.

O'Flare, who'd almost forgotten the were, looked over. His muscles froze in horror.

Holy fuck.

Hunt's skin was undulating in slow steady waves, not as if his blood was boiling, but as if some creature had implanted itself inside him and was slithering around, viciously eating at his insides. Agony was too weak a word to describe the expression on Hunt's face. The rippling was in his face, too, extending into his eyeballs so that they threatened to pop out of his head. Hunt's jaw was lengthening as well, and his teeth, which were sharpening and growing, were clenched with the effort to hold back his moans of pain.

Bones broke and fractured as Hunt's limbs shrank. Blood ran in long, thin rivulets, resembling ribbon that had been thrown carelessly across the were's body. Although O'Flare wasn't a hunter, he'd visited his mother's people as a child and seen how they'd dressed various animals. Hunt's body resembled the naked, veined carcass of a skinned fawn. O'Flare, who'd seen people's insides and limbs severed countless times during the War, felt his stomach roll with nausea.

But still, he couldn't look away.

In under two minutes, the transformation was complete. The wolf locked eyes with O'Flare. "Go to her," O'Flare commanded.

Hunt blinked slowly, then turned and ran toward Wraith.

Having activated the security alarm in his office, which was the room closest to the foyer, Knox bolted into the foyer in time to see Lesander toss Zeph's body through the air and toward Niles's waiting arms as if he were a football. His lacerated face spewing hatred, Zeph twisted in midair and kicked his foot out; while he couldn't stop his forward momentum into Niles, he managed to kick several of the vamp's teeth out before knocking him down and falling to the floor himself.

When Zeph got in several good punches to his cousin's face, the last one breaking his nose, Lesander leaped toward him. "Enough of this playing-around shit. Let's rip the fucker's heart out before the other one comes back."

"Too late," Knox whispered in Lesander's ear before hooking his arm around the vamp's neck and bending backward, forcing the vamp off his feet. "You and Niles never did play fair when we were kids. You never wanted to take us on when we were together. Well, we're together now, aren't we?" Lesander clawed at Knox's arm and kicked backward, but Knox squeezed tighter. "You remember how you said killing me was going to be as easy as pie earlier? I have a really good feeling you're about to choke on it. Look, your brother's already started."

Knox adjusted his hold, forcing Lesander to get a good look at his brother, whose head Zeph was repeatedly pounding into the ground. As they watched, Zeph ripped Niles's medallion off his neck. Instantly, Niles's limbs went slack and fell to the ground. He stared up at Zeph as Zeph stood and turned toward Knox.

"Good thinking," Knox said even as he ripped Lesander's

matching medallion off. Lesander, however, didn't fall under Knox's spell. Instead, he laughed. "I'm smarter than my brother, Knox. I've got gold in places you wouldn't believe." Then, using the same trick that Knox had used on him, he drove his elbow into Knox's side. Instead of relaxing his hold, however, Knox tightened it.

Lesander's growl of rage transformed into a shout of pain when Zeph punched through his chest, breaking through flesh and bone and tissue to yank the vamp's heart out of his chest. It was still beating as Zeph backed about ten feet from the vamp. Then, in a flash, Zeph transported himself to the hearth, where a fire was kept perpetually burning.

Even as Lesander gasped and heaved and growled, even as his still-pumping organ grew smoky and vibrated with the effort to return to him, Zeph clung to it tightly. "How about instead of making the bastard eat pie we make him watch his heart burn?"

"Where are you getting the pure blood?" Knox asked. "What do you know about the antidote that was stolen from the FBI's labs?"

"Fuck. You," Lesander moaned out.

Knox looked at Zeph. "Do it," Knox said.

Zeph grinned. "Anything you say, big brother."

"No," Lesander whimpered. "Please don't."

Drawing his hand back, Zeph ignored him.

"You better talk fast," Knox suggested.

"I don't know where the blood comes from," Lesander said swiftly. "Another vamp gives it to us. He just—he's recruiting. For the North Koreans."

"Why?"

"His girlfriend's family is being held against their will."

"His name, what's his name?"

"Lafleur," Lesander hissed.

Knox closed his eyes. It looked like Mahone's loyal guard wasn't so loyal after all. Knox felt absolutely no satisfaction at the knowledge.

As Zeph tauntingly moved Lesander's heart closer to the

fire, several vamps, dressed in the clan's law enforcement uniform and carrying vamp stunners, teleported in front of them. The stunners fired a laser that, when fired between a vamp's eyes, suppressed his brain activity for up to one hour—time enough to get the vamp into one of the little-used cells kept in a building at the very south of the Dome. The cell was constructed of a lethal combination of gold and lead, two of the many metals that played havoc with the electrical impulses that gave vamps their power. Once Lesander and Niles were inside it, they wouldn't be able to use any of their powers, including that of teleportation.

The security officers stood frozen until Knox snapped, "Shoot this one now." Augustus, the squad's leader, immediately fired the laser with perfect accuracy. Lesander went limp in Knox's arms. "Return the heart," he instructed Zeph.

His brother did a reasonably good facsimile of a pout. "Do I have to?"

Knox glared at him.

"Fine."

Zeph relaxed his fingers. Instantly, the heart rose and vibrated within a cloud of smoke before disappearing back into Lesander's chest. Knox knew the moment it settled there by the slight jerk he felt in Lesander's body. He immediately dropped him. "Secure both of them," he commanded, before leaving to check on his family.

TWENTY-THREE

His mother had taken everyone to the safe house just as Knox had instructed. Her gasp of relief when Knox appeared was doubled when he told her Zeph was safe. Felicia still looked dazed when she stood to wrap her arms around him, but he felt her relief as well. Even as he wrapped his arms around her, even as he kissed her passionately, part of him was someplace else. Korea.

Knox had been gone for almost thirty minutes. He turned toward her. "I need to make sure the guards have properly contained my cousins and then I have to go back."

Felicia tightened her grip on him. "Can I go with you? Please?"

Hesitating briefly, Knox nodded. After a quick farewell to his mother and children, Knox teleported to the Dome's equivalent of a jail. He was surprised to find Zeph's father, Councilman Prime, standing in the entry area. He was even more surprised to hear Prime arguing with his men, insisting that they release Lesander and Niles immediately.

Prime's argument stopped the instant he saw Knox, but he

only paused long enough to walk toward him and glare at Felicia before he started up again. "This is ridiculous, Knox. I've told your men that there must be some mistake. Whatever this woman has told you is clearly a lie. Your cousins would not attack her unless provoked."

Knox glanced at Zeph, who was negligently leaning against a wall and watching Prime with a thin smile of amusement that didn't quite mask his pain. Knox knew that his brother's casual air was for show and that the smile of amusement was the calm before the storm. "And how do you explain their attack upon Zeph and myself? How do you explain the fact my son overheard them conspiring to kill humans and to overthrow me and my mother, even as they tried to tempt my own brother to join the plot?"

For an instant, Prime looked uncertain, then blustered onward. "Frustration. Fear of the continuing weakness of the clan, a weakness that she and her associates"—Prime pointed at Felicia—"brought upon us."

Knox's hand shot out to grip Prime's wrist. "Don't point at her. Do not accuse her. Not while you defend them. They are traitors."

Prime glared at Zeph. "Talk some reason into him, Zeph. Tell him you misunderstood. Now."

Zeph straightened. His relationship with Prime had always been a distant one, with Prime having been more of a sperm donor than a real father. Before his death, Jacques Devereaux had been Zeph's primary paternal influence. Still, Zeph had been around two years old when Jacques had died and Knox knew that, deep down, Zeph had always longed for Prime's approval. Which was why, when Zeph shook his head, Knox was surprised but proud of his little brother.

"I didn't misunderstand. They tried to kill us, as well as the human."

While Prime glared at his son, Knox snapped, "They will be punished accordingly."

Prime's eyes narrowed and he tried to jerk his hand from

Knox's grasp. He succeeded, but only after Knox, who paused for a few seconds before doing so, chose to release him.

"You mean, they'll be punished if the Vamp Council finds them guilty, don't you?"

Knox heard the threat behind the vamp's words. "If the Vamp Council doesn't, the matter will be handed over to the U.S. government. In this case, the victims involved not only vampires, but a human. That puts their actions squarely within the law of the humans."

"You would dare—" Prime began.

"You have no idea what I'd dare." Knox leaned down until he could stare directly in the vamp's face. "This conversation is over. Leave."

Prime looked stunned. Truthfully, everyone did. Usually, Knox took great care to show nothing but respect for the Council's authority, Zeph's biological father included. But he didn't have the time for politeness now and he didn't have the desire to dole it out—not with what the vamp was saying about Felicia or the men who had attacked her.

As Prime transported out of the building, Knox strode up to Zeph. "I'm sorry, Zeph . . ."

Zeph shook his head. "For what? Most of the time he doesn't even remember I'm his. He always wanted me to be more like Lesander and Niles anyway. This time he just stated his preference out loud. Now, I believe you're needed elsewhere. If you need assistance . . ."

Knox shook his head, ignoring the spark of hope that had brightened Felicia's eyes. "You need to be here in my stead. What have the bastards said?"

"Nothing, but then there's nothing they can say. Thomas was telling the truth. They approached me. They solicited my participation in the murder of humans, as well as your overthrow. They tempted me with pure blood, which I willingly took." He gazed at Knox unflinchingly, but obviously still hoping that Knox believed him. "I needed to be stronger. I couldn't reach you and didn't know if you would be back. I hoped to get more information from them, to find out exactly—"

Knox shook his head. "I do not doubt you, Zeph."

Zeph's features relaxed, indicating his relief that Knox believed him.

"But if I ever catch you drinking from Felicia's wrist or throat when your life isn't on the line, I'll kill you myself."

His amused gaze darting to Felicia, who was blushing furiously, Zeph nodded. "Got it. Hands, and fangs, off your woman."

Without bothering to see how Felicia reacted to being called "his woman," Knox strode up to the cell and faced his cousins. Lesander stood straight and tall, his eyes blazing defiantly. Niles, on the other hand, sat with his face in his hands. At Knox's approach, he lifted his head slightly, only to turn away and lower his head again.

"Besides the North Koreans, who are you and Lafleur working for?" Knox asked.

Lesander smirked. "I work for no one. I act to achieve what I believe in."

"And you believe working for the North Korean government will benefit you. Giving you what? Power? Money? Validation that you're worthy despite the fact that you don't rule?"

Knox's jibe worked. Lesander lunged at him, wrapping his fingers around the bars that separated them as if he could break them in half and escape. "At least the North Koreans are Other sympathizers and honest about what they want from us. I'd rather enter into a business transaction with them than be led around by my dick like you are."

"So principle and allegiance and global benefit are irrelevant in this business transaction of yours?"

Lesander released the bars and stepped back, shaking his head mockingly. "Poor Knox. Always trying to spout the more 'enlightened' position in hopes that it will cover up the stain of your past. Tell me, why are you working for the humans?" Lesander asked in response.

"I'm working for them to benefit my clan."

"Then why is what I was doing any different? How are the North Koreans doing anything different than the federal government? They're doing the same thing—using Others, giving us what we want so they get what they want."

Knox wanted to grab the vamp by the throat again and this time let Zeph burn his damn heart. "They're imprisoning Others. Vamps. Torturing them. Using them for experiments."

"What was the War if not the sacrificing of Others for the greater good?" Lesander hissed. "We are fighting for the same thing, for the same purpose—to save our people. If the North Koreans can help us do that, why shouldn't we align with them?"

"Because saving our people isn't just about saving our physical selves. It's not about regaining our physical strength. It's about holding to the tenets our society was built on. Integrity. Strength. Constancy. Or have you forgotten already?"

"Strength without vitality is impossible. Neither is constancy. Integrity in this case is a matter of opinion. Is it honorable to let one's people—one's Queen, one's mother and brother—waste away to skin and bones while you work for the very people who caused their suffering in the first place?"

"Constancy is about more than resisting change, Lesander. It's about staying true to who we are as a people. Who I am as an individual. Who we are—who I am—is not a vamp who would betray his leader or hurt an innocent female or sell himself to a group so clearly after world power and nothing else."

"Once again, you forget your blood is tainted by a traitor's, Knox, so how can you be so sure?"

Rage filled Knox. Everything he saw became tinged by a red film.

"Let him out of that cell so he can say that to me again," Knox growled.

"Knox, no!" Felicia cried.

"There's a difference between us," Knox insisted, his gaze finding Felicia's.

"Of course there is," she snapped. "Don't you dare have a single doubt otherwise." Grabbing his arm, Felicia pulled him away until they stood outside the jail.

He breathed deeply, shaking his head. "You're right. I let the bastard get to me and I don't have the time for that. I have to go back."

"You're too weak," Felicia said softly.

"It doesn't matter," Knox said. "I have to go back." There was no other choice, Knox thought. Every second away from his team meant they were at escalated risk.

Silently, Knox cursed—they were already at escalated risk thanks to his damn cousins. Felicia was right. He had weakened. The strain on his body from his crash landing, the brutally cold walk to the compound, and then his repeated teleportation and injuries from Lesander's attack, almost made it difficult for him to keep standing. How was he going to do what he needed to do and bring the team back safe?

Felicia grabbed his hand. It was dark out, almost too dark for him to see her, but she wasted no time in cupping her hand around his neck and pulling his head toward her. Not to her lips but to her neck.

"Drink from me. Lesander and Niles believe I have pure blood. If that's true—"

Knox jerked his head back. "It's the truth. I saw what it did for Zeph myself. You've got pure blood inside you, Felicia." For a second, he felt the unwanted bite of suspicion. Had she known? Had she kept the knowledge of her purity from him all this time, knowing that while she couldn't save his mother and brother, she could help alleviate some of their suffering?

"I didn't know," she said. "I swear it. I think Dr. Barker administered the antidote to me during my last physical, when he was supposed to be giving me vitamin shots."

Knox licked his lips. "I—I—" He called himself a fool, but he believed her. And right now, it shouldn't matter whether she'd known. He was drained and he needed to be at his optimal strength if he was to complete the mission and get everyone out alive. It was the smartest thing to do.

Part of him, however, knew that even if that hadn't been true, he wouldn't have been able to resist drinking pure blood from Felicia. That would be like refusing to drink ambrosia from a chalice handed down from the Gods.

"Zeph drank a lot of your blood. I don't want to weaken you further—"

"I feel fine, Knox. I promise."

He swallowed hard. Felt his mouth watering. "I'll drink just a little. Just enough to . . ." Without another word, he gave in. The moment his fangs pierced her flesh, he wondered how he hadn't known. He should have been able to smell the purity of her blood. Should have been able to taste it the minute the drops had hit his tongue the first two times he'd drunk from her. In disbelief, he realized that the reason he hadn't noticed was because his ability to process that kind of information seemed to short out when he was with her. With her, he was always primed. It had seemed natural that drinking from her, lying with her, fucking her, would make him feel stronger and more powerful than he had in years. It had made him feel so much like himself that he hadn't thought to ask why.

The why had seemed self-evident.

It was her.

Her taste filled his mouth, then his throat, then spread to every part of him. This time, maybe because he'd been so drained or because he was waiting for it, he felt the way her blood immediately nourished him, imbibing him with an instant vitality. He felt the urge to suck her dry, to drink and drink and drink until every last drop of her was inside him.

It disturbed him even as it made him a tad bit more sympathetic of Zeph's response to her.

Still, he forced himself to slow down, to suck softer, to pull back slightly. He felt his renewed strength, even with the small amount of blood she'd given him. He didn't want to take too much—

She pushed his head down deeper, whispering for him to take as much as he wanted, and her full acquiescence was too much to fight. He might not need more of her blood, but he *wanted* it.

He gave himself over to his hunger. Planting his hands on her hips, he rubbed his body against her as he drew on her vein in long, languorous pulls. He lifted his hands to her breasts, cupping them. He felt the strong urge to leave her vein so that he could suck at her nipples.

That's when he knew he would always be drawn to Felicia for who she was and not what she could give him.

He would always want her more than he wanted her blood.

After several minutes, he withdrew his fangs and licked at the puncture wounds on Felicia's throat until they closed. He kissed her ear, and then her lips. "Thank you," he breathed.

She nodded her head, stroked his hair, then said something that struck him with terror. "I want to go back with you."

Lucy was panting by the time she and O'Flare made it to Wraith's side. She knew instantly O'Flare wasn't going to like what he'd be seeing. Wraith was sitting on the ground, the wolf's—Hunt's—snout resting on her thigh while she stroked his coat. She didn't appear to be in pain. Was it because Hunt was in animal form that she could touch him?

The guard that had been sent to search the area sat gagged and tied in front of them, the yellow stain around him indicating just how afraid he'd been of the wraith and the wolf he'd encountered.

"Shit," O'Flare gasped. "You couldn't have told us you were okay? We've been hauling ass to get over here."

Not looking up from Hunt, whom Wraith was now scratching behind the ears, Wraith shrugged. "The exercise is good for you."

Lucy saw O'Flare clench his hands into fists and take a step toward the wraith. She didn't believe he was going to actually reach for her, but she wasn't taking any chances, either. The last thing she needed was to have the three of them going for each other's throats and attracting the attention of the rest of the guards.

"We need to send him back," she said.

O'Flare turned around and looked at her. Even his incredulous expression was enough to send shivers down her spine. Closing her eyes, she cursed herself for her stupidity. The one time she was attracted to a man of worth and it was someone who had the hots for a ghost with big tits and the gift of immortality.

Kind of hard to compete with.

As soon as the thought formed, Lucy was overcome with guilt.

Get over it, Lucy. None of it—not her condition, which Lucy knew damn well wasn't a gift, and not the fact that O'Flare was attracted to her—was Wraith's fault. Besides, being attracted to a man was the last thing Lucy wanted or needed. Sure, she could use one when the heat was upon her, but she'd been dealing with that on her own for years and she'd continue to do so.

She wasn't weak, she reminded herself. She wasn't her mother. She didn't need to have a man in her bed or between her legs to be of value.

"The other guards are going to be suspicious if he doesn't return soon," she said firmly. "They'll come looking for him. Even if they don't find us, they'll lock down even tighter. Move the Others. Move the antidote. Who knows?"

Gently nudging Hunt to the side, Wraith stood. Noticeably, Hunt stayed close to her. "But you can use enchantment on him, right?"

Lucy nodded. "I'll make him forget he saw us. He'll think he got lost in the snow, that he peed his pants in his panic, and he'll be too embarrassed to say anything to the others."

"That's good," O'Flare said even as he continued to scowl at Hunt.

Lucy swore she saw a taunt in Hunt's eye. The wolf wagged his tail and very deliberately rubbed himself against the wraith's legs. Lucy grabbed O'Flare's arm and tried not to imagine his thickly muscled arms wrapped around her, easing her pain when she most needed it. "Come on, O'Flare, I need your help."

O'Flare resisted her for a moment, but then blew out a breath and followed her. "What do you need?"

She reached up, put a hand around O'Flare's neck, and went up on tiptoes, speaking to O'Flare privately in case the guard understood English. Although she knew it would do absolutely nothing for O'Flare, something devilish compelled her to press her breasts, meager as they were, against his arm.

Wraith was in denial, but O'Flare wasn't going to leave her there for long. Lucy might as well give the wraith a reminder that she had feelings for O'Flare and that she was going to have to deal with them sometime. The fact that making Wraith jealous was mean really did make Lucy feel bad. She liked Wraith, she really did. But she was going to get a little satisfaction from the wraith's discomfort, too.

Lucy was mostly sweet, but she was also part cat.

And she tried to always be completely honest, especially with herself.

"I'm going to enchant him," she breathed into O'Flare's ear, "and then I want you to remove his gag. If he's truly enchanted, he won't cry out. But I need you to be ready in case it doesn't work. You'll have to muffle him fast, so the others don't hear. Okay?"

With her last word, Lucy went down on her heels and deliberately dragged the palm on O'Flare's neck down his shoulder and arm.

When she peeked, O'Flare was looking at her, slightly puzzled. The wraith, on the other hand, looked like she wanted to rip Lucy apart limb by limb.

Lucy internally shrugged. Sorry, Wraith. Gotta help out my boy.

Knox pulled away from Felicia with enough forcefulness to make his displeasure clear. She wanted to go back with him. Absolutely fucking not. "You admitted you didn't have any place there, Felicia."

"I admitted I wasn't trained to jump from planes or crawl up mountains. But I don't need to do that. Not anymore. You've already been there. When you teleport back, it's just a matter of getting into and out of the compound. I'm trained in entry and exiting. I'm trained with weapons. I can help you now."

"No."

Felicia glared at him. "No? That's all you have to say?"

"That's all I need to say. You're not getting there without me, and I'm sure as hell not taking you."

"What if the team is gone?"

Knox jerked back as if she'd slapped him. "What? I've been gone thirty minutes. Why would the team be gone?"

"Who knows? Maybe they were forced to move without you. Maybe they were discovered. Maybe they're even dead."

"For Goddess's sake, Felicia—"

"I'm not saying I want that to be the case, but what *if*, Knox? You can't do what needs to be done by yourself."

"If that's the case, which it won't be, then I'll come back for help."

"For who?"

"Zeph," he said automatically.

"Zeph? Zeph who is certainly stronger than me, especially now, but can't hit the side of a barn with a bazooka? Zeph knows nothing about entry or human response to stress."

"Then one of the guards here," Knox said, knowing she

was sucking him into an argument he should never have engaged in.

"One of the guards? When you can't be sure of their loyalty? Or what they would do if they got their hands on the antidote?"

"Damn it, Felicia," he growled, pushing her away when she tried to take his arms. "I don't have time for this. I'm not taking you."

"I'll let you take me back first," she bargained desperately.

That startled him enough that he dropped his hands. She wrapped her arms around his neck, giving every indication that he'd have to pry her fingers loose to leave her. Automatically, his hands rubbed her back. "What?"

"I know that's your biggest concern. That you won't have enough power to transport me. But I'll let you bring me back first, so that won't be a concern."

He pondered her words, trying to give her the benefit of the doubt, then said, "Nice try, Felicia. You wouldn't do that, not in a million years."

She scowled, clearly unrepentant for her lie. "Okay, fine. But what if you do run out of power to teleport, Knox? Your biggest fear is leaving one of the team there. If I'm with you, I can give you the energy you need. All you'd have to do is drink from me again."

"If I drink any more from you today, you'll be the one that'll be depleted."

"Not enough to kill me," she said flatly.

He took a deep breath, wanting so badly to deny what she was saying. Unfortunately, he couldn't.

He'd fallen in love with Felicia knowing full well that she wasn't a lady afraid of getting her hands bloody. She was a warrior. A trained special agent who put her life on the line constantly. What she was asking was that he recognize that fact. Her presence would make the chances of success greater, but if anything happened to her . . .

"Nothing will happen to me as long as nothing happens to

you," she said quietly. "And if something happens to you, I might as well be dead anyway."

Knox cupped the sides of her face. "Don't even say that," he gritted out.

"It's true. I can't stay here just waiting for you to come back. Not when I know I can help. Please, Knox."

Knox stared down at her and thought about what she'd said.

She meant it. She loved him, whether she'd said it or not. And in many ways, his death would be hers. She was also correct on another point—as long as he was alive, nothing and no one was going to harm her.

Without saying a word, he removed his sweater, leaving himself wearing only a long-sleeve thermal undershirt. He pulled the sweater over her head and adjusted it to make sure most of her was covered. Then he took her with him.

TWENTY-FOUR

Felicia was wobbly and disoriented when she realized she was standing in the snow. Sucking in a breath, she clutched Knox to her as he inserted his earpiece and said, "This is Knox. I need your location." Even as he spoke, however, Knox held Felicia closer to him, whether to shield her from the cold or give her comfort after the trauma of teleportation, she wasn't sure.

It had hurt and she hadn't been expecting it to hurt. It hadn't during the quick trip to the Dome's jail. But this time?

One minute they'd been standing in the underground tunnel and the next they were standing here. She couldn't consciously say she'd been aware of time passing, yet she'd been aware of pain, a pain that had faded within seconds of their arrival. Of course, it had been immediately replaced by the jolting shock of cold, but Knox's sweater, still warm from his body heat, was enough to make the cold bearable.

So was the joy that he'd given in and brought her with him.

"I'll be right there. I've got Felicia with me." He paused. "I'll explain later, but have the females shed any extra clothes they don't need. She'll also need a gun." He looked at Felicia. "Can you shoot an Uzi?"

She rolled her eyes. "Does a vamp like blood?"

He smirked. "Yeah. An Uzi's fine. The guards?"

Knox listened for at least a minute now. He grinned, the expression as well as the squeeze he gave her waist making her breath catch.

Oh, Noella, she thought. How could you have slept with anyone else but Knox? If I had my choice, I'd never miss a single night with him.

He couldn't have heard her thoughts—he wouldn't—but his eyes darkened and he squeezed her again. This time, however, he shifted his hand down and squeezed her ass.

Then he winked at her before patting the same cheek he'd squeezed.

Given the seriousness of their predicament, his flirtatious gesture seemed both ridiculous and endearing.

He laughed. "Gives meaning to the phrase 'scared pissless,'" he said. "Is Hunt still in wolf form? Well, get him out of it. We're going for a direct attack this time. O'Flare, get the gas ready. Then . . ." Knox frowned when the sound of an engine drifted toward them. "Yeah, I hear it. Get under cover and in position."

Knox dropped to the ground a second after Felicia did. Together, they crawled toward the trees screening them. With a hand barring Felicia from moving too far forward, they looked through the cover and down into the valley. A convoy of trucks approached steadily from the east. The guards manning the main building didn't seem the slightest bit surprised.

They waited silently, until Felicia turned toward him. "There's something I don't understand about what I saw in the Vamp Dome. When a vamp is losing a fight, why doesn't he just teleport away?"

"First, because it's considered very cowardly. Second . . ." Knox hesitated. Telling her about the medallion had been one thing—even if a vamp couldn't read a human mind or use persuasion, his ability to teleport was always a fallback defense. It could mean the difference between life and death. But this was Felicia, he reminded himself. Felicia, who'd given her blood to him so freely and who was risking her life in order to save those that Knox—that she—loved. Reaching out, he rubbed her back, then cupped his hand at the base of her neck. "It's a blip in vamp powers. It has to do with the electromagnetic pulses that run through a vamp's brain. Being in close proximity to another vamp affects those pulses, canceling out the brain waves necessary to teleport. It's similar to the reason why wearing gold prevents a vamp from reading your mind or using persuasion on you."

She nodded, her expression placid. When she leaned in and kissed him, he knew she'd correctly interpreted his openness as trust. Feeling closer to her than he'd ever felt to anyone, he kissed her back—slow, gentle, sipping kisses that reminded her that, for him at least, love and trust went hand in hand.

The sound of engines ceased as the trucks arrived at the front of the main building. When Knox pulled away, Felicia's eyes were cloudy, almost dazed. Then she shook her head and her eyes cleared. They watched as the guards hailed the men inside the truck.

"This could be good," Felicia said excitedly. "They're bringing something or someone in, which either means they're going to unload here and open the gates to bring stuff in, or they're going to open the gates completely and drive the trucks in. Once they open the doors, Lucy can hold them open."

"We'll still have to immobilize the guards."

"Maybe Hunt can run through the doors. Get inside that way."

"Maybe," Knox said, "but they've already seen him as a wolf once. Chances are they'd suspect something at that point."

Knox frowned and held up a finger, obviously listening to someone through his earpiece. "Wraith's on her way with your weapon," he told Felicia. Then he shook his head. "It's not your fault you can't enchant all of them, Lucy, any more than it's my fault I can't persuade all of them. Between us all, we'll get in and get out. Right now, let's just wait and see what's on those trucks."

The answer came within minutes. They were Others.

Others on gurneys. Others strapped down with collars around their necks. Others that looked dying or ill. A vamp. Three werewolves. A—

"Is that a shape-shifter?" Felicia asked.

Knox nodded.

"I've never seen one before. I've heard of them, of course, but I've never seen one in its natural form."

It looked a little like Hollywood's version of an alien. Smooth, translucent skin, so pale it was as white as the snow, maybe even whiter. Large, dark eyes with no white to them. A nose and mouth that were humanlike but so flat they almost seemed to disappear. No hair. No ears. Felicia couldn't tell whether the one on the gurney was male or female.

"I've got your—oh fuck."

Both Knox and Felicia jerked at the unexpected sound. Wraith had snuck up on them. Crouched low, she scrambled up to them, passing Felicia an Uzi and earpiece in the process. Her eyes, however, were locked on the next gurney being unloaded from the truck.

It was a wraith, one that looked so much like their Wraith, but so much unlike her. Same shocking white hair, although this one's hair was longer. Same bluish skin, although hers was bluer, probably a result of the cold and her thin clothing.

The sight of the earphones gave Felicia pause. She knew wraiths were soothed by music, but the earphones suggested that someone cared enough about the wraith to put them on her. Was it a caring born from compassion or self-interest? Rumor had it that wraiths were particularly susceptible to madness, and maybe whatever experiments these people were doing wouldn't be served with a wraith in that particular state of mind.

Helplessly, they watched as the guards lined up the gurneys, eight all in a row, clearly not wanting to open the compound's large wooden gates until the last possible moment. The trucks started their motors and were driven off.

Felicia slipped on her earpiece and checked her weapon.

"O'Flare, are you ready?" Knox asked.

"I can't shoot the chemicals now," he said. "Not with those Others down there. Not when I don't know their medical condition—"

"We don't have a choice. We—"

"Where's Wraith?"

Felicia heard the sudden tension in O'Flare's voice. So did Wraith because she immediately looked at Felicia. Knox, however, didn't appear to notice. "If they're brought inside, it'll only be that much harder to get them out. We've got to get them now. If that means they'll be a little worse for wear, that's a risk we have to take. We'll have our gas masks and we can—"

Felicia saw the instant Knox realized he didn't have a gas mask for her. A split second after his eyes widened, he cursed. "Hunt? How long will it take you to shift?"

"Knox, is Wraith with you?" O'Flare interrupted again. "Is she okay?"

Knox's gaze bounced to Wraith, then back to the compound. "She's fine, O'Flare. Now, if Hunt can distract them enough, the rest of us will shoot from here."

"Don't give yourselves away too soon," Wraith said suddenly.

Felicia's unease crystallized into outright fear. "Wraith—"

"Wraith, whatever you're thinking, don't," O'Flare growled.

With Knox between them, Wraith straightened and moved forward.

Felicia grabbed Knox's arm. "Knox!" What was she doing? Had Wraith already lost her mind?

"As soon as we've—Wraith, where the hell are you going?" Knox pushed himself up and made a grab for Wraith. Wraith evaded him easily, slipped out of their cover, and walked calmly toward the front entrance of the building manned by guards.

"Get the fuck back here now, Wraith," Knox gritted, obviously aware she could still hear them on her earpiece. "That's an order."

O'Flare, Lucy, and Hunt were talking all at once.

"Shit, is she crazy?"

"Prepare to fire on the bastards."

"The Others—"

"We have no choice."

"Everyone calm down. Calm down," Knox snapped. "Stand down. Stand down, damn it!"

"But Wraith—" Felicia said.

Knox looked at her. "It's out of our hands now. I don't know what she's doing, but we're about to find out."

All of them grew quiet except for their combined breaths heaving in and out over their communication line.

Felicia flinched as the guards shouted at Wraith, pointing their guns at her and gesturing for her to put her hands up. They seemed clearly thrown by the fact that she kept walking toward them. Felicia flinched when a shot rang out from the roof. Wraith's body jerked as she was hit in the shoulder. Somehow, she stayed on her feet even as her jacket, which she must have had draped over her shoulders, fell to the ground.

Knox was half shouting. "Don't shoot. Don't you move, O'Flare, or I'll kill you myself. You, too, Hunt. If we give ourselves away now, we lose the element of surprise. You will listen to me—"

"She's got explosives strapped to her," Felicia whispered.

Knox's words stopped mid-sentence. His eyes met hers. "She's going to blow the gate."

"No, she wouldn't . . ." O'Flare whispered.

"She has missiles. Why . . ." Tears filled Felicia's eyes. "Oh God. She can't die, but she can feel pain. She can feel pain, Knox."

No more shots rang out. Clearly, the guards were afraid shooting Wraith would result in triggering the explosives. The ones on the ground fled. One brave guard on the roof decided to take his chances. He fired his weapon, then fired it again.

Wraith's body jerked several times, but she was close enough to the gate now that it didn't matter.

"Remember what Wraith told you," O'Flare commanded in a near whisper.

Knox said, "We will," just as the explosion shook the earth and blasted open the compound's large wooden doors. Felicia saw sparks and smoke, as well as what appeared to be bits of debris flying into the air. She screamed. She heard the others scream. But clearest of all, she heard O'Flare scream.

"We're moving," Knox yelled. "Now. We're moving."

With Felicia beside him, he leapt out of their cover at the same time the rest of the team did. They all came out firing.

Felicia shot two of the guards on the roof and they both came toppling down. Knox got another on the roof, and then one that had been hiding around the corner of the building. One by one, the team took the guards down. In seconds, no more remained.

O'Flare and Hunt, still in human form, covered one another with their weapons as Knox and Felicia scrambled toward them. O'Flare ran to the spot where Wraith had stood, screaming her name.

Knox shouted to him, "O'Flare, help Lucy. We need to get these Others off these gurneys and under cover. Bring them into the trees."

Lucy rolled one gurney toward the trees even as she used telekinesis to roll another alongside her. Felicia was right behind her with one of the Others. O'Flare, however, didn't appear to have heard Knox.

"Where is she? Where the fuck is she?" he yelled, turning in a circle in search of Wraith.

Knox strode up to him, grabbed him by his shirtfront, and shook him. "Listen to me. We have a short amount of time to get these Others out of here before more guards come out. Help us, damn it!"

O'Flare shook his head, which seemed to clear some of the daze from his mind. He nodded. "Okay, okay." He ran toward the captured Others, but instead of rolling them as Lucy and Felicia were, he unstrapped one, flung him over his shoulder in a fireman's lift, and ran with him into the trees. Almost immediately, he was back for another.

In the meantime, Knox moved to the remaining Others, running between them as he unsnapped their collars and fired questions at them, hoping to get some information as to what they would find inside. "We're here to get you out. There are others inside. Did the men who took you say anything? Did they say why they were taking you? What they wanted to do with you?"

Most of the Others seemed too weak, almost catatonic, to answer.

Then a deep voice, low but steady, came from the werewolf that O'Flare was currently releasing from his restraints. "The guards who took me . . . One seemed to be filling the other one in, like he was new or something. He said we were the next installment of Others. That there were only one or two left. He said . . ." The werewolf paused and gritted his teeth, obviously fighting off some kind of disorientation or pain. He shook his head. "The younger one asked whether any vamps had survived. That it didn't seem safe to work with them, even to test the effects of a cure to the vamp vaccine. He didn't sign up for that."

Adrenaline rushed through Knox at receiving yet more confirmation that the antidote existed. "Did he say where? Where the Others were? Where the labs were?"

The werewolf shook his head and seemed to collapse. O'Flare swung him over his shoulder and began carrying him away.

"He said—he told the young guard to stay away from the green door," the werewolf gasped out as O'Flare carried him away. "The green door's where the dangerous stuff is kept."

The green door. Knox looked at Hunt, who had just returned from carrying the last Other into the bush. Then he looked at the rest of the team. "You three will stay with the Others."

Felicia shook her head, but Knox kept his voice firm.

"You'll do as I order, damn it. You need to stay with these Others. You need to be with them in case more armed guards come out and you need to be with them in case something happens to me. We'll be back to get you out of here."

The wildness in O'Flare's eyes hadn't disappeared, but it seemed to clear enough for him to hear. He glared at Knox. "You two get in and then get out. You heard Wraith's last words. Make all this worth it."

Knox nodded. "We will."

With a final glance at Felicia, he and Hunt ran into the compound.

TWENTY-FIVE

A s Knox entered the compound, he immediately noticed that for all the traditional architecture of its façade, the inside was all simple lines and polished metal. It was clean to the point of sterility.

It was also empty.

They walked through a loading area that dead-ended and split into a T. Hunt and Knox stood back-to-back, pivoting 360 degrees and holding their guns at the ready.

"Guards guarding nothing? Seems silly," Hunt said.

"More unbelievable than silly," Knox replied. "Maybe they're waiting in an interior room. Waiting until we go for the antidote or the captured Others to show themselves. Maybe the werewolf who told us about the green door was setting a trap."

"So we gonna dance a little more or you gotta plan?"

"Howl," Knox retorted.

The were shot him an "eat shit" glare. "Excuse me?"

"When you shifted that first time," Knox explained, "a were howled from inside. Maybe if you—"

Nodding abruptly, Hunt threw back his head and howled. It

was the same howl he'd given in wolf form, and the sound caused the hair on the back of Knox's neck to stand on end. Almost immediately, the howl of another were sounded from the hallway to the right.

"Bingo," Knox said.

Hunt moved to follow the sound, but Knox placed a hand on his arm, stopping him. "Despite what the werewolf told us, we don't know how many Otherborn are in there. We don't know why no one's shown up yet or if there's anyone waiting for us in this cavernous building. If we really are alone, we need to get out of here as soon as possible before anyone returns. It makes sense for me to check on the Otherborn prisoners. I can start teleporting them to Quantico, then return for the others."

Hunt looked uncertain, then downright shocked. "You want me to get the antidote?"

Unbelievably, Knox felt himself smile. "Is this my ideal situation? No. But I know if it's here, you'll find it. And I know you'll find a way to get it outside."

Solemnly, Hunt stared at Knox, then notched his chin at him. "I'll get it. For you. For Wraith. For all of us." A huge grin split Hunt's face. "Mainly, though, so you can tell Mahone that I'm the one that saved the day; seeing the guy's face when you tell him will be all the thanks I need."

Knox turned and started down the hallway where the howl had come from. Over his shoulder, he called, "If I pass a green door on my way, I'll call out to you. Otherwise, you assume it's down there."

"Good luck." Hunt turned and ran down the other hallway.

Knox moved swiftly, checking each room he passed to make sure it was empty. He knew he'd made the right choice— the only choice—and the irony of it struck him hard. He'd hated Hunt on sight and now the were could hold the fate of Knox's entire clan in his hands.

Interestingly, Knox wasn't as bothered by the thought as he should have been.

He checked a total of five rooms before he reached the end of the hallway. There, he found another door. Inside the room, there were three Others, each locked in tall cages, naked and beaten like fucking animals. A werebeast, a werecat, and a shape-shifter. Knox ripped the lock off the first cage and approached the werebeast huddled in the corner. He wasn't wearing a collar, so Knox tapped the Other's mind. He was met with nothing but weariness and defeat. Knox picked him up, cradling him in his arms like an infant, and teleported him to Quantico.

Several suited agents and med techs jumped when Knox appeared beside them. The agents started talking on their phones and the med techs rushed toward him, taking the were, putting him on their own gurney, and checking him over.

Knox immediately teleported back to the compound. By the time he'd transported the werecat and shape-shifter, as well as searched the rest of the wing for other signs of life or the antidote, he was feeling only slightly weaker than when he'd started. That sent a rush of hope through his system. Maybe the team's first mission was going to be a success, after all.

His hope waned a little when he finally teleported outside to join the others. Felicia ran to his side. "Did you find them? Find it?"

"I sent Hunt for the antidote while I teleported three Others. You haven't seen him?"

She shook her head. "We didn't hear shots or signs of trouble from out here. Weren't there reinforcements inside?"

Knox shook his head grimly. "That's the strange part. There was no one inside. At least no one I encountered. But Hunt—"

"Hunt can handle himself, but I'll check it out."

Knox's protest was automatic. "No, I don't want you going in there. Not without me."

Felicia arched a brow. "Excuse me?"

Knox grimaced. Vamp females weren't the kind to hide while their males did the dirty work; Felicia certainly shared the same characteristic. "Uh—O'Flare and Lucy will need you?"

"Nice try," she said after the moue left her lips, "but between the three of you, you'll be fine. Which way did Hunt go?"

Knox took a deep breath, then gave in gracefully. "Down the hallway to the left. Looking in particular for a green door."

Felicia nodded. "I heard the were. Don't worry. If Hunt hasn't reported in, chances are there's nothing to report. Now get to work, soldier. I'm freezing here."

Reaching out to rub her arms, Knox couldn't believe it when he grinned. All this, and this woman still had the ability to make him smile. "We'll see about warming you up when we're out of here." He gave her a swift kiss on the lips.

"You bet your sweet vamp ass we will. Now go," she urged.

"Be careful," he shouted as she readied her weapon and ran toward the compound.

He called for O'Flare to start bringing him the remaining Otherborn. At one point, Lucy used her power to float a shapeshifter into Knox's arms. One by one, he teleported each of the Others to the designated room in Quantico.

By the time Knox had teleported his tenth Other, Mahone had arrived. He stood silently toward the back of the small room where the medics had situated themselves.

After handing the werewolf to a medic, Knox turned toward Mahone. "Lafleur's a traitor."

Mahone just shrugged. "Old news, Knox. We found that out for ourselves when he showed up dead. How much longer do you have?"

"One more Other and then the team," Knox said, hating the sudden weariness he heard in his voice. His strength was starting to wane and his limbs felt alarmingly heavy. That's when it hit him. He hadn't even thought of it before, even though he should have. The last Other that needed to be teleported was a vamp, but he hadn't even considered the fact that being that close to another vamp would render teleportation impossible.

He stared at the thin, worn gray carpet beneath Mahone's feet. Knox was going to have to leave one of his own—maybe not one of his clan, but one of his people nonetheless—behind.

Could he do it?

Later, he told himself. Think of that later. Right now you need to go back for Felicia. For the rest of the team.

"What about the antidote?" Mahone asked.

"I sent Hunt for it. He hasn't returned. Yet."

Staring at him, Mahone shook his head. "Risky move, Knox. And it appears the risk didn't pay off. Perfect for us really."

Knox stared at him, certain he'd misheard. "Excuse me?" He shook his head, but the fog that had formed in his mind was just getting worse. What was going on here? He was so weak, and the weakness had hit him so suddenly.

Too suddenly, he realized. Right around the time Mahone had shown up.

Swiftly, he tried to teleport. When he remained exactly where he was, he was literally stunned silent by shock. Just like the time he'd tried to read the scientists' minds, he could barely fathom his inability to do something that was normally as easy as breathing.

Knox's gaze swept the room, searching for any sign of foul play. Metal was a vamp's weakness. If someone had brought the right metal into the room, it could explain the downward turn in his energy.

Before Knox even realized the man had moved closer, Mahone punched him in the face hard enough to rock him back on his heels. "It's obvious you don't have the strength to teleport and bring them back. Give up gracefully and we might let you keep your heart." Mahone turned to the two muscle-bound agents who'd been standing behind him. Vaguely, Knox noted that the medics had cleared out with the Others sometime while he and Mahone had been talking. "Restrain him," Mahone snapped.

He'd suspected it back in Quantico, Knox reminded himself. It was his own fault for trusting a man just because he'd seemed to genuinely love his mother.

Knox moved back, somehow managing to keep himself out of reach. Again, he tried to teleport. Again, he couldn't. His mind was racing, trying to understand what could be motivating Mahone's actions. "Why would you want North Korea to have the antidote? They've threatened the U.S. with nuclear destruction."

Mahone smiled tightly. "Still haven't caught on, have you? Lafleur stole the antidote and killed Barker to do it. He injected the other scientists with the antidote so they could serve as test subjects, then he used persuasion to wipe their memories clean. We suspected Lafleur but couldn't prove it, so we let him stay on, pretending we trusted him while we monitored him."

"But the scientists, I tried to read their minds—"

"You might have thought you were keeping your secrets, Knox, but before he turned, Lafleur gave us a great deal of information. Metal? It's so cliché. Like Superman being unable to see through lead."

"Sorry we couldn't be more creative," Knox gritted.

"We wanted to give you a sign of good faith, but the truth is those scientists were wearing gold underneath their clothes and we were quite pleased when you couldn't read their minds."

His suspicion was swift but unwarranted. He hadn't given Felicia the medallion or revealed its secret purpose until after he'd tried to read the scientists' minds. Still, the way he automatically thought of her made him wonder why. But there were other questions in his head he needed answers to right now.

"I don't understand. Why send us for the antidote in the first place then?"

"Because at that point, we wanted the antidote. We just didn't trust you enough to let you read the scientists' minds. Plus, if Lafleur turned out to be a traitor, what's to say you weren't in on it, too?"

Grasping his head to keep it from rolling off, Knox struggled to understand. "So who murdered the scientists?"

"They weren't murdered, Knox. They died. Died from taking that fucking antidote. When we finally realized that, we made it look like murder so we wouldn't cause a nationwide panic . . ."

The rest of Mahone's words faded as a loud buzzing sound flooded through Knox's brain. The scientists had died because they'd taken the antidote? The same antidote Felicia suspected Barker had given to her?

No, not Felicia. Felicia couldn't die. Please—

Mahone, oblivious to Knox's thoughts, kept talking. ". . . delay? Using O'Flare to set up Wraith so they'd turn on each other? It's all been part of the plan because the FBI no longer wants you to bring back the antidote. Only we couldn't just tell you that, now could we? We leave the antidote in the North Korean's hands and they'll eventually take it. Especially once we leak false information that the vamp vaccine, and not the antidote, turns on its host in five years, destroying its immune system."

Stumbling back, Knox suddenly straightened, blinking when he felt something surge inside him. He focused on the fury and the swelling of his muscles. He imagined a few stuttering sparks of red lighting his eyes and was careful to keep them lowered to the ground.

With every word Mahone spoke, Knox felt an influx of strength as his royal blood strained to transform him. Although it went against everything he was, Knox heeded his instincts and took several more steps back. With some amazement, he felt his muscles bulge even tighter. Flexing his fingers, he quickened the steps taking him away from Mahone.

"Going somewhere, Knox? You won't be able to stop it. The country's as good as dead."

"What about the Others I just delivered?" Knox forced out. He needed to keep Mahone talking. Distracted. Whatever it took to get to Felicia and make sure she was okay. "Are you going to return them or simply kill them?"

Mahone waved his hand and the two agents came around to the side, the three men clearly intending to box him in as Knox's back came up against a wall. "Do you know how difficult it is to get agents in North Korea? Do you know the simmering threat that country's posed to the U.S. for years given their expanding nuclear program? Most people believe the danger is in the Middle East, and while that's true, people tend to forget that North Korea is just a bomb waiting to explode."

"So you're just going to wipe them out?" Knox asked. "Women, children, innocents alike?"

Mahone shrugged. "They'd do the same to us."

Knox wasn't at full strength, but he felt better. Good enough that he could transport if he needed to.

It wasn't their proximity, Knox realized, but something about his position in the room that had been weakening him. Careful to appear more weakened than he felt, Knox slumped against the wall. "And that makes what you're doing okay? So what now? Let the team, including Felicia, die?"

"Felicia? You brought Felicia into this mess? No matter. As an agent she knew the risks going in."

Knox's mouth twisted bitterly. So much for company loyalty. "Just like my mother did, right?"

Mahone's brows lifted. "Your mother?"

Knox felt a jolt of surprise at the blank expression on Mahone's face. Mahone had no clue what he was talking about.

Knox didn't betray his thoughts by so much as a flicker.

Swiftly, knowing it would probably deplete the last of his powers, Knox entered Mahone's mind.

That's when he realized the creature in front of him wasn't Mahone.

It could only be one of the infamous shape-shifters, one who'd taken on Mahone's form and was clearly being fed information by another—someone who was knowledgeable enough to know a lot of what Mahone knew, but not knowledgeable enough to know about Bianca Devereaux.

Knox locked eyes with Kyle Mahone's imposter. "You're not wearing gold. Why? There's something in the room suppressing my powers, isn't there?"

Mahone's face smiled tightly. "In the walls."

Knox nodded. "But only in one wall, right? That wall over there?" Knox said, pointing to the wall farthest from him.

Mahone frowned. "How—"

"Guess they thought it was good enough for government work, huh?" Knox lunged and gripped the shape-shifter and wrapped his arms around it in a bear hug, squeezing tight. In a matter of seconds, he teleported the thousands of miles back to North Korea.

Once there, he shoved the shape-shifter to the ground. "Restrain this bastard, O'Flare."

TWENTY-SIX

Felicia hadn't found any signs of Hunt or anyone else inside the compound. She had, however, found the lab and had filled a box with all the vials and containers she'd discovered inside it. She'd brought out anything that could possibly be the antidote, planning to take it with her when she transported back with Knox.

But where was Hunt? She couldn't help but wonder if he'd grabbed the antidote and run. A were with that kind of prize could virtually name his price and sit back to watch the vamps fall at his feet.

Once she'd returned, Felicia had almost gotten used to Knox popping in and out as he'd been transporting the Others. After a while, he'd started to look tired. When she'd pointed that out, however, he'd brushed her off.

And she'd allowed herself to be brushed off. After all, this was Knox. He wouldn't risk their lives or the antidote for his clan by being foolhardy.

He still wasn't back after his last teleportation. Felicia told herself he was probably just waiting for Mahone's scrambling staff to find space for the newest Other arrival. When five more minutes passed, she reminded herself how much stronger he'd been after she'd fed him and that he was going to be fine. And when another ten minutes had passed, she'd seen the concerned looks on O'Flare's and Lucy's faces and she'd begun to panic. For all of two seconds.

Then O'Flare's eyes widened as they settled on something behind her. The relief that swept over his face was so contagious that Felicia's knees almost buckled. "I knew you wouldn't . . ."

Turning, Felicia's words slowly died.

Wraith. She was walking slowly toward them, her steps almost robotic, her face paler than usual with dark grooves under her eyes.

Felicia was happy to see her, of course. But O'Flare? He brushed by Felicia at a dead run. He threw his arms around the wraith then, stepping back, did the unthinkable.

He planted his hands on Wraith's chest and shoved, toppling her to the ground. "What were you thinking!" he shouted.

Felicia gasped and ran. Before she could get to them, O'Flare had straddled her and pinned Wraith's wrists to the ground next to her head. Distantly, Felicia noted that despite his aggression, his hands gripped Wraith's wrists over the sleeves of her jersey rather than her bare flesh.

Wraith immediately tried to buck him off her, but O'Flare rode the undulation of her body with the ease of a seasoned bull rider. Leaning down, he pressed his upper body into hers. "How the fuck could you do something so fucking stupid?"

At O'Flare's double F-bombs, Felicia stumbled to a stop and looked back at Lucy, sure that her uncertainty was reflected on her face. Hesitantly, Lucy moved from the side of the sole Other left to their care and took a step forward. "O'Flare, why don't you—"

O'Flare and Wraith rolled in the snow, leaving a visible indentation in their path. Then Wraith managed to gain the top position. She planted her feet in the snow and leaned back, trying to yank her wrists from O'Flare's grasp. O'Flare refused to release her. *"Let. Go!"* she screamed.

She screeched with rage when O'Flare flipped her on her back again.

"Don't you ever do something that stupid again, do you understand me?"

"Get off me, you idiot. You asshole. You pig-sucking, big-headed, lily-livered—umph."

O'Flare lowered his head and took Wraith's mouth with his. The wraith completely froze as O'Flare's mouth rocked on hers, lifting and then immediately going back for more, retreating then invading, kissing her with long, deep penetrations of his tongue and pulling back to sprinkle hard, brief kisses on her lips before repeating the process all over again.

Although she hardly considered herself a voyeur, Felicia couldn't take her eyes off them. O'Flare looked like a man who'd starve if he couldn't kiss Wraith, and that immediately brought to Felicia's mind an image of Knox drinking at her neck, his hands gripping her with the same desperation that he sucked her blood.

Feeling herself flush, Felicia glanced at Lucy again. The mage had turned away.

A breathy whimper floated through the air. Felicia turned back just in time to see Wraith's lips move against O'Flare's. It was only for a heartbeat, and then she pulled back and kneed O'Flare in the nuts so hard that he whimpered and crumpled on top of her.

Wraith shoved him off her and stood. That she immediately walked past Felicia instead of kicking O'Flare in the face spoke volumes about her priorities. Her main objective? Get as far from O'Flare as possible.

"Thanks for your help, ladies," she snapped. "So much for loyalty within the sisterhood." She reached Lucy and turned around, tracking O'Flare, who'd gotten shakily to his feet.

Walking toward her, Felicia shook her head in wonder. "Wraith . . ." She ran her gaze up and down the wraith's body.

She looked exactly as she had before, except for a few pink lines on her face that were still fading. "You look wonderful," Felicia said, throwing her arms around her much like O'Flare had done.

Wraith immediately stiffened and pushed her away. "Okay, everyone's obviously shaken by my reappearance so I'll cut you some slack, but let's remember the reason for the 'don't touch the wraith' rule—it hurts me. You don't want to hurt me, do you?" She sounded almost desperate.

"You didn't look like you were hurting too bad when O'Flare was kissing you," Lucy said archly. Felicia thought she did a commendable job disguising her true feelings for O'Flare. No one but a woman who'd pined for love for almost a decade would guess her feelings for her teammate.

"I—I—" Wraith shot a wary glance at O'Flare, who had almost reached them. His eyes threatened retribution, but he stopped by Felicia's side.

"It did hurt her," O'Flare said gruffly. "And I'm sorry about that. By the time I was thinking straight and I realized that, I pulled back, but then you kissed me—"

"I did not kiss you back," Wraith countered. "I—I was just setting the stage for my attack. And your apology isn't accepted."

"Neither is your bullshit," O'Flare said.

"Whatever—"

Wraith's succinct comeback was interrupted by a sudden groan. The last ailing Other had regained consciousness and was thrashing weakly at the blankets that covered him. Lucy ran to him and whispered, "It's all right. You're going to be okay." As the emaciated vamp writhed in pain, Lucy knelt beside him and went into what Felicia had termed her "magic mode." Soon, the vamp's body stilled and he was breathing peacefully again. Lucy readjusted his blankets, looked up, and nodded. "He's okay. I blocked the pain and he'll sleep for a while longer. What do you think is keeping Knox?"

Felicia shuddered. How had she allowed O'Flare and

Wraith to distract her so completely from thoughts of Knox? Guilt was a bitter taste in her mouth. "I don't know. He should have been back by now. He should have—"

Before she could finish her thought, Knox suddenly appeared in front of her. He wasn't happy and he wasn't alone. Felicia flinched back when she saw the rage on Knox's face as he shoved Kyle Mahone to the ground next to O'Flare. "Restrain him," he ordered O'Flare.

Felicia's nausea was immediate. No, she thought. Not Kyle.

O'Flare moved quickly and without hesitation, pinning the man down while Wraith and Lucy ran to wrap his hands and feet with rope.

"Knox, where have you been?" Felicia grabbed his arm and he immediately swept her into his arms.

"How are you feeling? Are you feeling okay?" He shook her slightly when she didn't answer. "Talk to me, Felicia."

"I—I'm fine. I'm okay. Why have you brought back Mahone?"

Slowly, Knox released her and looked at her searchingly. Something like confusion, then suspicion, flashed across his face. He took several steps back. "This isn't Mahone," he said slowly. "It's a shape-shifter in disguise."

"What?" Lucy narrowed her eyes and mumbled something about roses.

The scent on the chilled air instantly registered.

Lucy waved her hands in front of Mahone's twin. In one blurred rippling motion, Mahone's face disappeared and was replaced by the bug-eyed exterior of a shape-shifter.

"This is the third shape-shifter we've encountered today," O'Flare said. "Before today, I'd never seen one in person."

"Few people have," Lucy said. "They're more accepted by the mage community, although that's changed recently. Their population has been plagued by rebellion. So many shape-shifters are unhappy with the way they've been treated since the War."

"Yes, well, they need to get in line," Wraith snapped.

Lucy shrugged. "Instead, a large number of them are choosing to separate from their leaders in order to take action. Whatever action's needed to further their own agenda."

"This one's agenda has to be monetary," Knox growled. "Whoever he's working for wants to use the vamp antidote to wipe out this entire country."

"But how can the antidote do that?" Felicia whispered. Knox hadn't looked at her again. Why wouldn't he look at her?

"It purifies human blood but also poisons it and eventually kills its host. That's how the scientists died." Pacing, Knox tunneled his fingers through his hair. "So the FBI decided to change the terms of our agreement. This shifter was supposed to keep the antidote in North Korean hands and stop me from bringing the rest of you back." Knox turned and punched his fist into a tree, sending splinters flying.

Fear seized her instantly but she managed to stay calm. Of course he wouldn't look at her. Since she'd probably been given the antidote, that meant she was going to die just like those scientists had. Or was she? "But if that's not Mahone," Felicia said, "you can't know the FBI has betrayed us. You even implied you don't know who hired him. Maybe one of these rogue shape-shifters kidnapped Mahone. Or maybe it was a vamp, someone like your cousins who wants to force change."

Knox shook his head. He circled the shape-shifter now, flexing his hands as if he was imagining strangling it. He knows things only Mahone would know, but not everything. "Not *everyone*."

"Okay," Felicia said slowly, guessing that Knox was talking about Mahone's relationship with Bianca. She certainly couldn't know for sure. Yet Knox had proven he'd trusted her. He'd revealed more than one vamp secret to her. So why was he ignoring her? Why was he being so cold when he must know how worried she'd been at his delay? How scared she'd be by what he was telling her? "But this shape-shifter hasn't said it was Mahone who betrayed us, has he? Because—"

"Your girlfriend is smarter than you give her credit for, dharmire," the shape-shifter said, looking calm as it sat bound hand and foot on the ground. The way he said "dharmire" sounded remarkably similar to the way Lesander had said the word.

Knox froze behind the shape-shifter. "I'd ask what you mean, but why don't I just read your mind instead?"

Seconds ticked by as they all held their breath. Watching Knox's face, Felicia knew immediately something was wrong.

"You can't do it?" she asked.

"I can, but it's all jumbled," Knox said. "It's like I'm reading fifty different answers to the same question, but they're all in the same voice."

The rage in Knox's voice was overshadowed only by his confusion. To Felicia's disbelief, the shape-shifter laughed. "Want me to add one more?" With a soft ripple of movement, the shape-shifter changed its appearance to look like Knox. "How's this?"

"Let's see if you can duplicate something else. Wraith?" Knox commanded, "Gun."

Wraith immediately tossed Knox her pistol.

Leaning down, Knox ran the barrel down the shape-shifter's cheek. "I'll give you a choice. I can either shoot you in the head and silence those voices or I can rip out your throat and let you bleed dry. Either way, you're going to die if you don't tell me who hired you. Was it a vamp?"

"I don't know."

"Knox . . ." Felicia tried to interrupt, but Knox ignored her.

"Male or female?"

"Male."

"Knox . . ." she tried again.

Again, he ignored her.

"What's his name? Was it Lafleur?"

"No, but I don't know his name."

Knox cocked the trigger on the gun. "Then how do you know it wasn't Lafleur?"

"He—he—" The shape-shifter was whimpering now, the high-pitched sounds of his fear sounding a staccato beat. "Because Lafleur's the one who took Mahone and fed me the information. Right before Lafleur was killed."

"What about the Others we brought back? Where were they taken?"

"The medics and most of the agents you saw when you teleported the Others were really with the FBI, so I assume they were taken to get medical care. Cloning Mahone just ensured that I and the other agents could get inside."

"One last chance," Knox crooned and held up Wraith's gun. "Who was he?"

Knox's image disappeared as the shape-shifter frowned and regained his own form. "I'm telling you, I don't know. He contacted me only by phone. I was supposed to keep you from returning the antidote, that's all. He said the antidote would serve two purposes—saving vamps and killing humans, but only the humans he chose to kill."

Knox glanced at Felicia, but she couldn't figure out why.

"What do you mean?" Knox asked.

"I don't—"

Knox shoved the barrel against the shape-shifter's face. "What else did he say?"

"Nothing, nothing. He just mentioned some doctors who'd died and that he was the reason."

"Him? Not the antidote?" Knox clarified.

"Right."

Once more, Knox looked at her. This time, the look on his face was clear—suspicion.

That look snapped something loose inside Felicia. Maybe it was the image of a vamp bleeding Mahone dry for information. Or maybe it was the image of Knox holding a gun to someone with *his* face while he ignored her. Whatever the reason, Felicia felt rage spark inside her, as sudden and intense as if someone had suddenly doused a dying fire with gasoline. "How did this person get in touch with you in the first place?"

Felicia snapped. "Do you guys have a service or something? Need to impersonate someone, call 1-800-NOT-REAL?"

"Felicia," Knox began, his voice wary.

Now he was wary? Now he chose to acknowledge her? Before he could guess what she intended, Felicia wrested the gun from Knox. He grasped for it, but was too late. She shoved it between the shape-shifter's eyes. "Where's Mahone? Is he alive?"

"I—I don't know."

"Who has him?"

The shape-shifter's mouth worked up and down as if he was trying to talk but was too scared to get the words out.

"Tell me who it was that hired you."

Eyes rolling back crazily, the shape-shifter's gaze skipped from Knox back to her. "I don't—"

Felicia lowered the gun and fired it into the shape-shifter's leg.

He screamed in pain.

Tears filled her eyes and she raised the gun once more. "You tell me—"

"Felicia," Knox said. "Felicia, love, give me the gun."

"Don't you dare call me your love," she snapped, her voice trembling. "He needs to tell us. Tell us," she screamed, part of her thinking Knox's refusal to acknowledge her had been based on transferred betrayal. He'd agreed to work for Mahone, Felicia's boss, to save his clan. Over and over again, they were confronted with evidence the FBI had been playing them.

Did he blame her?

Yes, she realized, he did. He might not realize it, but he'd been blaming her for what he'd seen as Mahone's disloyalty. Biting her lip, she finally shifted her gaze to his. She saw the newfound knowledge in his eyes, as well as the regret. She shook her head and turned back to the shape-shifter, who cringed back, whimpering.

"Tell me or I'm going to blow your head off, I swear."

"Pri—"

Felicia jerked as someone spoke from behind her.

"What?" Knox leaned forward, obviously thinking the word had come from the shape-shifter.

Felicia, on the other hand, turned toward the forgotten vamp, lying underneath a tree where they'd left him.

Hand trembling, she dropped the gun and ran toward the gurney. She knelt down beside the vamp. It took everything Felicia had not to flinch back from the sight of the male's skeletal features. The grooves under his eyes were so deep that his eye sockets practically dropped into them. Starving, she thought, and I can feed him. I can give him strength. But right now, she needed—Knox needed—information. "Who? Who was it?"

"Pri—" he gasped again.

"Prime," Knox said from behind her, his voice tight with fury. "Dante Prime? Is that what you're trying to say?"

The vamp closed his eyes and nodded. Shifted. He coughed and his features tightened as if he was in great pain.

"How—How do you know that?" Knox asked, but the vamp was obviously unable to answer more questions.

Felicia looked at Knox, expecting to see anger, pain, confusion—something—but he'd closed himself off. There was no hurt there. No betrayal. No nothing. Despite what had just gone on between them, she placed her hand on his arm, knowing that he had to be hurting, wanting to offer him some comfort.

Once more, he moved away from her. Her hand fell. At the same time, her heart shattered completely.

The pain was sharper than any set of fangs could ever be, piercing not just her exterior but her very being. She'd always known that deep down inside, Knox hated his human half and feared one day she'd betray him. Yet even when she hadn't, even when it was Kyle or another vamp who hurt him, he rejected her.

He's just surprised. Hurt, she told herself once more. He didn't mean anything by it.

But it meant something to her. Something significant.

She glanced over her shoulder and saw O'Flare tending to the shape-shifter's leg wound. Felicia swallowed at the chastising look O'Flare shot her. Even Wraith looked a little critical. Felicia knew she deserved it. She, who was trained to read a person's expression, intonation, and syntax—she, who'd rather not use force but would if necessary—had shot the shape-shifter when everything pointed to the fact that he'd been telling the truth. She'd lost control of herself, and her desperation to learn the truth about the antidote—not just for Knox, but for herself, she realized—had made her willingly hurt another with no good cause.

She turned away and once more stared down at the ailing vamp. Perhaps it was only another attempt to make amends to the friend whose husband she'd desired and taken into her bed—or perhaps it was to make amends for shooting the shape-shifter. Whatever the reason, Felicia rolled up her sleeve. "I'm going—I'm going to feed him." When Knox whipped around, his eyes flashing, she shook her head. "Not at my throat, but with my wrist. Like I fed Zeph. I can't—I can't bear to see another vamp hurting. Not when he might actually accept the help I offer."

Her meaning was obviously clear to him. It seemed to penetrate the defenses he'd once more built around himself. Frowning, he said, "I didn't mean . . ."

She pushed down the blanket that had been pulled up to the vamp's chin, intending to prop him up and hold her wrist to his mouth. Instead, when the lowered blanket revealed the same medallion that Knox wore, she reached for it.

Knox, who'd already been bending down toward her, cupped his hand beneath her elbow, stopping her. With his other hand, he lifted the medallion. "My clan," he whispered. "But I don't recognize . . ." He turned the medallion over.

Knox's eyes widened as his hand froze. He shook his head. The hand cupping her elbow began to tremble. His gaze sought out Felicia's.

"What is it?" she asked.

"My father. He wore a medallion like this, with three D's inscribed on the back. Three D's for the three Devereauxs. He had it on him the day he was executed."

Knox turned the medallion over so that Felicia could see the back.

She saw the three D's immediately.

Viciously, Knox ripped the chain from the vamp's throat. Instantly, the vamp opened his eyes and for a moment they flashed with rage. A growl, weak but distinct, escaped the vamp's mouth.

"Where did you get this?" Knox asked. "Where . . ." Gritting his teeth, Knox grabbed the vamp by the throat.

"Knox, stop," Felicia yelled, grabbing at the arm holding the vamp's throat. With a snarl, he pushed her back. Hard.

Stunned, she lay on the ground, staring up at him.

The regret in his eyes was instantaneous, but when he reached for her, she flinched back. His expression going blank, he turned back to the vamp. "My father wore this when he was executed. Were you there? Did you steal it from his body? You bastard, you had no right. It belonged to him. It was all he—"

O'Flare grabbed the same arm Felicia had. "Knox, you have to stop. You're going to snap his neck."

"If I do, his neck will fuse back together. My father'll still be dead—"

"Knox." The vamp's voice was barely half a whisper. "My—my son."

Felicia's gasp was drowned out by Knox's.

O'Flare slowly withdrew his hold on Knox, and Knox removed his hand.

Felicia couldn't see the vamp's face, but she saw the bunching of Knox's shoulder muscles and the way they seemed to ripple with tension. She heard the hope that edged his voice when he said, "Father?"

Felicia clamped her hand over her mouth to stifle her moan. The word had been spoken in Knox's voice, but at the same time in the voice of a very young boy who was afraid to believe that something special had just been given to him.

"What? How?"

Suddenly, Knox stood, fists clenched, and stared down at the vamp he believed to be his father. "Who turned you?" Knox spat out. "What vamp gave up his life to turn a traitor?"

"Not . . ." the vamp whispered, shaking his head.

"Damn you!" Knox turned on his heel and walked past Felicia, who was still on the ground where he'd pushed her, without a backward glance. When he was about thirty feet away, he stopped and braced his hand against a tree. Slowly, Felicia got to her feet and walked to the pile of their supplies. She searched through it until she found a knife.

"Felicia . . ." O'Flare said gently, but she ignored him.

Swiftly, she cut her wrist.

Stumbling back to the vamp, she paused and looked at O'Flare, then Lucy and Wraith. "Will you—will you hold him?" Implicit in her plea was her certainty that once the vamp tasted her blood, it would likely want more. A hell of a lot more.

They scrambled to obey her. While O'Flare restrained the vamp's head, Lucy and Wraith each grabbed one of his arms. Felicia knelt beside the vamp, nudged his chin to open his mouth, and turned her wrist so that a stream of blood dropped into his mouth.

The vamp choked initially, but then he swallowed. Almost instantly, his eyes popped open, wild with thirst. He moaned and immediately tried to sit up. To reach for her. He couldn't. The others, with obvious effort, held him away from her.

She gave him as much as she could spare, knowing that Knox would need the rest to get them out of here. Unable to help herself, she looked at him. His face was still turned away, but he was hitting the tree, over and over again, with both fists as if it were a punching bag. Even with the distance between them, Felicia could see the dark blood that smeared his knuckles.

"Keep him down," Felicia said soundlessly. She saw O'Flare flinch and wondered at it, but it was a vague thought, coming to her through what felt like layers of ice. Funny, she wasn't cold anymore. But neither was she warm.

She was nothing. Numb. It was as if the pain had finally become too much for her and she'd escaped to another time. Another place.

Oh, how she wished she'd found it sooner.

With slow, determined strides, she approached Knox. Sensing her, his arms dropped to his sides. She stared at them and the way his blood dripped into the snow, staining the stark white with spots that quickly blended into abstract patterns. The wounds closed within seconds.

"You need to feed so you can teleport the team out," she said, proud that her voice was clear and steady.

When he didn't answer, she looked up, wondering if she would see distaste on his face. Disgust. She wasn't sure if she could take that, she thought. She just didn't know.

Instead of disgust, his face was twisted into lines of grief and regret. "Felicia, I'm sorry."

"Me, too," she said. She lifted her arm, holding it straight out and offering him the wrist she'd just used to feed his enemy. "Drink. Please. So we can all go home." Suddenly, she frowned. "Hunt?"

Knox shook his head. "He's obviously dead or he's run off with the antidote."

She didn't argue with him. She simply held her wrist up farther. "Drink."

Reaching out, Knox gently took her wrist. He stared down at the wound. Shook his head again. "Felicia, love, I—I—"

"Please," she choked out, her voice and body beginning to shake. "Please just drink. I know you hate me. I've always known it. You hate that I'm human. You hate that part of you and you hate yourself for wanting me. That's why I fought you. Not because of Noella. Not because you wouldn't marry me. But please spare me any more. Please just drink."

"I'm so sorry," he said again.

"Drink," she screamed.

Closing his eyes, Knox took a deep breath. When he opened them, she saw his determination. Slowly, he pulled her forward, ignoring her wrist. Willingly, she tilted her head. One more time, she thought. She'd let him have her vein one more time.

And when his fangs pierced through her skin and began to draw out her blood, she kept her arms by her side rather than pull him closer. She compressed her lips together rather than release the moan of pleasure fighting to escape. And she held back her tears, her love, her regret, her pain.

She held back everything of herself even as she gave him everything inside her.

Knox was panicking. With almost fanatical speed, he teleported the team back to the same tunnel beneath the Vamp Dome where he'd found his mother, Felicia, and the children. Of course there was no one there now, but he swiftly set Lucy down. Then Wraith. Then O'Flare.

When he was back in North Korea, Knox strode toward Felicia, who was once more kneeling next to the vamp—his father. "Let's go."

She shook her head. "Search inside first. For Hunt—"

"You already checked. He's gone. So is the antidote." His eyes shifted to the basket of vials she'd brought out. "Or maybe—"

"You don't believe that and neither do I. But I might have missed something. Maybe Hunt's hurt. Maybe he was killed. Maybe the antidote is still inside. I need you to double-check, and you can't take me back first. You might—you might need to feed again before you can bring your father—I mean, the vamp—back."

When Knox scowled, Felicia lifted her chin. "I know what you're thinking, but you can wrap him in a blanket. That way, you don't touch his skin. You'll be able to transport him."

Knox remained quiet. Fabric didn't affect vamps the way it

obviously affected Wraith. It was the proximity of one vamp to another that prevented teleportation, not the actual touching of their skin. But he knew she'd fight him if he tried to teleport with her now. Plus, she was right. He needed to confirm whether Hunt or the antidote was inside. "Stay here," he commanded, then teleported swiftly back into the compound.

He ran down the hall where he'd last seen Hunt. Opening and closing doors, he searched every room, every possible hiding space. He pulled open the green door that the werewolf had told him about. It led into a lab but Felicia had already swept it clean. Shouting Hunt's name, Knox searched the rest of the wing.

There was no sign of him.

No sign of foul play.

No blood on the floor suggesting he'd been wounded.

Bastard, Knox thought. Filthy traitor. Just like—

Knox shook his head. No, he wouldn't think of his father or how he'd escaped. Or who'd turned him. There was nothing he could do about it now, just as he couldn't know whether Jacques Devereaux had been lying about Prime. Granted, his father was now a vamp, but maybe he'd figured out a way to lie. Or maybe turned vampires *could* lie . . . But no, he told himself. Knox's gut told him his father hadn't been lying. It told him Prime *had* betrayed him. Betrayed them all. For that, he would suffer.

But there'd be time for that soon enough when he had Felicia back in the Dome. Then he'd come back and get the truth from his father, once and for all.

Knox froze. Then what was he going to do? Kill the man his mother obviously still loved? And then what? He knew what he *wanted* to do. Get down on his knees for pushing Felicia. Or worse yet, rejecting her because he'd been so damn thrown by what he'd thought was Mahone's betrayal and by the shocking reappearance of his father.

He'd seen the look in her eyes. She'd seen his doubt and suspicion. The suspicion that Prime had planted.

Prime, who'd taken the antidote—the thing that could save

their race—and perverted it. He'd probably contaminated it, maybe even before Barker's death, so that humans would think it was poisonous. Why? So he could control it. So he could dole it out to who he wanted and when, like with the North Koreans, manipulating his clan's salvation like a chess piece.

Ultimately that kind of power and control was what Prime savored, and he'd been willing to kill anyone—vamps or humans—who got in his way.

The fact that he might have placed one particular human in danger would ensure his death. Only, Knox had probably hurt Felicia the most.

He wondered, for the very first time, whether he deserved to have someone like Felicia. Whether being with him would be a burden rather than a blessing.

Her life had already been so hard. What could he bring to it besides more pain? Even if he swore his fidelity and married her exactly as he'd dreamed of, she'd always be the outsider in his clan. She'd also be marked as a vamp's wife by her own people, many of whom would see that pejoratively.

Could he really do that to her?

Would she even give him the chance now?

He didn't know, but that had nothing to do with the fact that he'd die to protect her.

Swiftly, Knox ran outside and grabbed the box Felicia had filled with vials from the lab. He then teleported to the Dome, not back to the tunnel where the others waited, but to the Dome's own lab. Several of his scientists jerked at his sudden appearance, but recovered quickly. "Store these and begin classifying them immediately," he ordered swiftly, not waiting for their assent before he transported back to Felicia.

Only, she wasn't there. And neither was his father.

Disoriented, he turned, searching the grounds and calling her name. He was in the right place. The pile of supplies was right beside him. He popped inside the compound once more and searched there.

Nothing.

He searched the entire perimeter outside.

He searched each of the smaller buildings that were, as expected, empty but for numerous crates and vehicles.

He called her name until he was hoarse.

Finally, he fell to his knees in the snow.

There was only one explanation. She'd left him. She'd fed his father, giving him the strength to teleport them away. Who knew where they could be? Likely somewhere as far away from him as she could get. Some place where he'd never find her.

"Felicia," he roared.

No, he thought. He wasn't going to let her go. He wasn't going to give her up. He'd find—

Knox heard the footsteps behind him a second too late. "Sorry about this," Hunt said, just as something solid slammed into the back of Knox's head. Pain exploded behind his eyes and he felt himself falling forward.

Ice pushed against his face and he blacked out.

TWENTY-SEVEN

Teleporting with Knox's father turned out to be quite a bit more painful than traveling with Knox. Whether it was because of her weakened state from feeding Knox and his father, or Jacques Devereaux's weakened state, or simply that he hadn't had as much practice as his son when it came to teleporting, Felicia screamed in pain when they landed. Her limbs tangled with Jacques's and they both tumbled to the ground. Felicia barely missed hitting her head on a pile of rubble. Stunned, she lay on the ground, aware that her face was scratched up and that various sharp rocks were poking through her clothing. Breath hitching in and out of her, Felicia raised herself on one arm. "Jacques?"

He lay a few feet in front of her, flat on his back, staring up into the dark sky. He turned his head toward her. "I'm—I'm okay." Painfully, he got to his feet despite the fact he nearly fell twice.

Felicia stood as well. "Where—where are we?"

"France. In the garden of the home I shared with Bianca, Knox, and later Zeph."

Felicia's confusion had to be self-evident. Nothing about the rocky terrain, overgrown by weed and debris, resembled any garden Bianca would ever have. A few yards in the distance stood a castle made of stone, marble, and tile. While it had probably been glorious at some point in the past, it was now in disrepair, with the top of the front tower completely gone, a few winding stairs still visible. "You lived here with them?"

"During the French Revolution."

"Before you betrayed your family by giving away vamp secrets, you mean?"

Jacques didn't bend his head in his shame. To the contrary, he threw back his shoulders, standing tall and lifting his chin arrogantly. Absently, she noted that his resemblance to Knox was remarkable, right down to his silver hair. "Who turned you?"

"Who do you think?"

"Bianca?" she gasped, knowing how much the vamp Queen had mourned the loss of her husband, but not understanding how it was possible that husband was still alive.

"Bianca," he confirmed, his eyes softening as he spoke his wife's name.

"But how? Everyone knows a vamp can't turn a human without sacrificing herself."

Jacques smiled tightly. "Everyone but the head of the royal family, who's sworn to keep the knowledge a secret, even from her own heirs, in order to prevent the turning of unwilling humans."

"But what if something happened to Bianca? If she died without passing on the information . . ."

"Arrangements have been made. The information would have passed to her successor, but privately." The vamp walked across the field, dodging several boulders and clumps of weed, only to stop where the castle's wrought-iron fence barred the way. He wrapped his fingers around the bars and stared at his former home.

"What happened to you?"

Jacques's mouth twisted. "An unfortunate series of events."

Felicia joined him. "So you didn't tell Calmet how to kill vamps?"

Jacques rested his forehead against the wrought-iron bars. "I didn't say that."

"So Knox was remembering correctly. You did confess to that?"

"Yes."

"And Bianca knew? And she still turned you?"

"She didn't know until after the fact. And she turned me because she knew I wasn't a traitor."

Angered by the vamp's riddles and nonanswers, Felicia propped her hands on her hips. "I don't understand. Did you tell Calmet how to kill vamps? Were you a traitor or not?"

"Yes. And no."

"Dear God!" She shook her head in amazement. "I can't believe it. You're even more infuriating than your son."

"Yet you love him."

She pressed her lips together, refusing to answer.

Jacques sighed. "Okay, listen. I told Calmet the secret to killing vamps but only because there were vamps killing humans, in a deliberate and methodical manner, and I couldn't let that continue without at least giving the humans a chance to fight back."

"But Bianca—"

Jacques whipped his head toward her and his eyes flashed red before he visibly controlled himself. "Bianca didn't know what I knew. What I was planning. I wanted to protect her. I realize now that was unwise, but . . ."

"Unwise?" The lunacy of a human male keeping a secret from his immortal vampire wife—the vampire Queen no less— to *protect her* from danger—was infinite. Yet, as a human who loved the vampire Queen's son, she could roll with it. At least, she might be able to if Jacques would stop being so damn vague. Felicia clenched her fists and almost jumped up and down in frustration. "Protect her from who?" she shouted.

"I don't know," Jacques roared back. "Or at least, I didn't know. Not then. All I knew was there was someone within her clan encouraging vamps to kill humans. Mind you, this was before the war between your people and ours. Humans didn't even know about us, so any mass murders that were being committed by vamps weren't being committed in self-defense or out of fear. They were being committed out of pure hatred. Greed. Blood lust. And I didn't know who was involved."

Staring at Jacques, Felicia finally understood. "That's why you confessed. So they wouldn't try to read your mind and find out your suspicions. It's the same reason you didn't tell Bianca so she would publicly intervene and plead for your life. If you did, there'd be a reason for this murderer to seek her out and find out just how much she knew. But once you were accused, why didn't she just read your mind, with or without your permission?"

"Because that would be as good as admitting she really did think I was a traitor."

Stunned silent, Felicia sank to the ground. Within minutes, she began laughing, a harsh, hysterical sound. "So she let you almost die instead?"

"She risked her life to turn me, giving me a chance to live."

"Risked her life? But you said . . . I thought . . ."

"While the death of the turner isn't a foregone conclusion from turning a human, it's a high possibility. Knowing that, I refused when she offered, but on the night Prime had me detained, she teleported inside my room. She told me her secret. I—I couldn't resist her. I allowed her to do it, of my own free will. When she was done, we both passed out. By the time I awoke, she was gone. I went crazy, not knowing whether she was alive or dead. Then Prime came into the room."

Felicia grabbed the fence bars and pulled herself to standing again. "Prime? He knew?"

Jacques nodded. "But not until after."

"After?"

"After he tried to kill me. You see, he was supposed to deliver me to the executioner. A nice, civilized death. But he wanted to kill me himself. To make it hurt. We fought. I escaped. Afterward, Prime told everyone I'd been beheaded or more likely that's what everyone assumed. Prime knew, however, I'd been turned. It's the only way I could've bested him."

"So he didn't admit you'd escaped." Felicia nodded in understanding. "Of course not. He wouldn't want to admit you'd gotten away from him. He's too proud for that. And you're right, he must have maneuvered around telling a lie."

"It's a skill some vamps have perfected."

"But wouldn't Bianca have known that, as a turned vampire, you couldn't die by behead . . ." But then she remembered. "No, wait. That's not right . . ."

Jacques nodded. "That's right. A vampire's body can heal itself provided there's no severing. The heart is the only organ that, once severed from a vamp's body, can regenerate itself, and only if it hasn't been burned. And since I never came back to her . . ."

"Why was that? After you turned, after you escaped, why didn't you come back? Smoke out the rogue vamps yourself?" Felicia's voice got louder as she spoke, automatically expressing the frustration and anger she knew Knox would be feeling if he'd been here. "Why did you let your family continue to believe you were dead? Why did you let your son continue to believe you were a traitor? Don't you understand how much he's suffered for that? How much he's had to prove himself because of his sin of carrying human DNA?"

Grabbing her shoulders, Jacques shook her. "I was changed, but I'd used all the strength I had to escape Prime. I was weak afterward, Felicia. I had to find blood. Assimilate to drinking it. Then I—I—" He shook his head. "I went to a friend for help. It was a mistake."

"Calmet," she guessed.

"Yes," he whispered. "And he betrayed me. He didn't kill me, but he used what I'd told him about vamps to imprison me. By the time I was free and managed to make my way back here, my family was gone. And when I tracked them to the United States, Prime was ready for me. I've been his prisoner all this time. Recently, Prime decided to turn me over to the North Koreans so they could inject me with who knows what and dice me up. Killing me would be too merciful, you see."

"But why didn't Prime call out Bianca long ago?"

"He couldn't know for sure it was Bianca who'd turned me. I never admitted it. Besides, what could he do? Accuse the vamp Queen of treason when he'd already told her people that I'd been beheaded?" Jacques snorted. "Besides, direct confrontation isn't exactly Prime's style. He knew he wouldn't be able to turn the clan against Bianca or Knox. He had power and respect. The rest he could continue to do on his own."

"The rest," Felicia echoed. "Like turning Knox's cousins against him. Like encouraging vamps to kill humans instead of trying to work toward peace." She shook her head. "Why are you telling me all this? A human . . ."

"Not just any human, Felicia. The human who gave me her blood. The human who loves my son. The human my son loves."

Felicia wasn't sure she believed that, not anymore. She didn't know what to believe. Thinking about Knox and his rejection hurt so much, but she managed to form one thought related to him. "I hope—I hope Knox rips his heart out and burns it twice over."

Jacques smiled. "From what I saw of my son, something tells me you just might get your wish."

"I'm not certain I like the were, Knox, but since you trusted him enough to send him after the antidote, you should probably give him the benefit of the doubt, don't you think?"

Despite the pile driver operating in the back of his head, Knox heard Noella's voice loud and clear. He forced his eyes halfway open, blinking to clear the film that coated them. He wondered suddenly if this was how Wraith saw the world on a regular basis; with that thought, he told himself he should really try to be more tolerant of her inner bitch.

"Come on now, Knox. We don't have much time. Open those spectacular eyes for me."

Knox finally got his eyes all the way open, but then they widened even farther.

Noella.

She sat on a raised table beside him. He wasn't even sure if he said her name, but she smiled and caressed his cheek with her palm. It felt smooth and cool. It felt real. And she looked real, far healthier than she had in the years before her death. She looked like the bright-eyed, fun-natured vamp she'd been on their wedding day. He'd been a proud vamp when she'd walked down the aisle toward him.

But remembering the pride he'd felt for her on that day and every day afterward didn't erase the fact that he hadn't loved her. Not the way he loved Felicia. "I'm so sorry, Noella," Knox whispered.

She pursed her lips and shook her head, then laughed, a light, tinkling sound. "Don't be, darling. We both knew it wasn't a love match. It was fun, though, and you never failed to make me happy. Just as Felicia did."

"I know you consented to us being together, but—"

"No buts. Whether I'd consented or not, whether I'd died or not, it would have happened. Yes," she insisted when Knox shook his head, "it would have. Not even you could have fought it, Knox."

"I'm not sure the same can be said for Felicia."

Sighing, Noella placed an arm around Knox and helped him sit up. He looked around, absently noting he was back in the lab inside the compound. "Why are we . . ." Then he remembered hearing Hunt's voice right before he passed out. "Hunt. That—"

"Careful. You don't want to curse him just yet. Wait and see what he has to say first. I'm certainly waiting on pins and needles. Now, about Felicia . . ." Noella said.

Swallowing with difficulty, Knox rubbed his hands across his face. "When I teleported here with the shape-shifter, when I saw my father . . ." Knox's eyes widened and he grasped Noella's arms, still stunned when they didn't slip right through his fingers. "My father! He took Felicia—"

"No, she went with him willingly. You hurt her terribly, Knox. Least of all when you pushed her. Most of all when you rejected her. Her touch."

With the barest of shoves, Noella managed to push him away and break his hold on her. "I—I was in shock," Knox explained. "I didn't know what to think. What to say."

"You were angry with her because you were angry with Mahone and your father. You were also angry with yourself. Lumping all of you together because of your human DNA."

Was that really what he'd done? Knox wondered. Unable to categorically deny it, Knox bowed his head. "You're right. That's exactly what I did. And she didn't deserve it. My mother tried to warn me. She said I'd hurt Felicia someday when I chose the clan over her, and she was right. I didn't mean to, but I did."

"So what are you going to do about it?"

"What can I do now?" He swung his feet off the lab table and jumped to the floor to start pacing. "She's gone. Who knows where my father has taken her." Once again, he froze. "My father is a vamp. Humans can't be turned into vamps without killing the turner. Who . . ."

Noella shook her head. "Sorry, but that's not why I'm here. You're going to have to deal with the issue of your father on your own, I'm afraid."

Standing in front of her now, Knox gently took her by the waist and lowered her until her feet touched the floor. He looked down at her, seeing both Thomas and Joelle in her pretty features. "Why are you here, Noella?"

"To tell you not to waste any more time fighting your feelings for Felicia. She's never going to accept sharing you with anyone else. That's just not how she's built, Knox, and she shouldn't have to change. Besides, you don't want anyone else. You never have." For a split second, hurt flashed in her eyes.

Knox groaned. "Noella . . ." he breathed.

Her face split into a wide smile and she patted his arm. "Don't worry about me. I miss you all, especially the children, but I'm happy. It's better than you can ever imagine, Knox. No sickness, no pain, no suffering."

"What happens when we die? What happens to someone like Wraith? Why is she here?"

Noella threw back her head and laughed. "That's just like you, Knox. Your dead wife appears to bless the union between you and your future wife, and you still have the fortitude to ask questions you feel will benefit one of your friends. But I can't answer any of those questions, darling. Please don't ask me to."

"Felicia? My future wife?"

"Can you really say you're surprised?"

Before parachuting into North Korea, he'd vowed to be with her, but he hadn't allowed himself the fantasy of marriage. "The Vamp Council—even once Dante Prime is removed," Knox said with a scowl, "is lobbying to pass a law forbidding unions between vamps and nonvamps."

Noella quirked a brow. "And you're going to let a little thing like that stop you? To be honest, I'm surprised you've let them sway you this far. To even consider marrying another vamp out of duty? What were you thinking, Knox? What happened to the little boy that snuck a hundred toads into the Vamp Council's chambers?"

"His father was beheaded, or so he thought, and the fate of the clan put on his shoulders. That tends to sap the fun out of a guy, you know."

Pulling him close, Noella hugged him. Knox buried his face in her neck but could smell none of her clean, musky scent. He thought of the children and how they'd never get a chance to hold her like this.

"I'll hold them again someday," Noella said.

Knox started and pulled back. Had she—

She smiled sadly. "I didn't have to read your mind, Knox. Even now, some things are just obvious. But until I can hold Thomas and Joelle again, they'll have Bianca to hold. And Felicia as well."

"How can you let her take your place so easily?"

Again, Noella smiled. This time, however, she backed away from him. "She's not taking my place, Knox. She's taking her rightful place. I know you don't believe, even now. So ask the were."

Almost choking, Knox scowled. "The were?"

"He knows much about regret and opportunities lost. Now I have to go." Her lips twisted ruefully, although the joy in her eyes still sparkled. "I'm afraid I've used up all the visits I'm allotted. But I'll be watching over all of you and sharing all the joy you find together. It's time to wake up now, Knox."

Knox lunged forward and reached for her. "Noella, no—"

With a final wave of her hand, she disappeared.

"Noella! Noella, wait."

Knox bolted awake and sat up. He was still in the compound's lab, but contrary to his dream, he wasn't lying on one of its long tables. Instead, he was stretched out on the floor. His head still throbbed, reminding him that Hunt had attacked him from behind. Why, then, hadn't he tied him down? He had to know Knox would—

"Dreaming of your dead wife? Bad sign for Red."

Knox stiffened at the sound of Hunt's voice.

"Still, you really went ape shit when you found Felicia missing. Next time, keep your cool and I won't be able to sneak up on you so easily."

Turning his head, Knox stared at the were, who was leaning casually against a wall. Knox got to his feet and gingerly touched the back of his head. The wound had already closed, so his fingers, when he withdrew them, didn't come back bloody. His head was still tender enough, however, that he had to suppress his first instinct to throw himself at Hunt.

Only Noella's words stopped him.

Since you trusted him enough to send him after the anti-dote, you should probably give him the benefit of the doubt, don't you think?

"Where've you been, Hunt?" Knox asked in a deceptively light tone.

Hunt smiled. "Yeah. Like that. Restraint. It throws most people every time." He straightened to face Knox squarely.

"Answer my question."

"Why? Were you worried about me?"

"Worried that you took the antidote with every intention of pawning it to make a few million bucks, yes."

The werebeast nodded. "Of course. I'd have thought the same thing."

"You're saying that's not what you did?"

Hunt lifted his arms and swept them down his body. "You see any cold hard cash around? 'Cause I certainly don't."

"Maybe you had a change of heart. Knew I'd track you down and kill you eventually, so you decided to bring the antidote back and beg for mercy?"

"Yeah," Hunt sneered. "I begged the way I always do—by bashing you in the head. Did it work? You feeling merciful right now?"

"Where's the antidote?" Knox asked.

"Where's your fucking squad of vamp goons?"

Knox stopped circling Hunt and frowned. "What goons?"

The werebeast just stared at him.

"Are you telling me there were vamps here?"

"I'm telling you that when you sent me down that hallway, graciously allowing me to retrieve the antidote for you, there was a gang of vamps waiting for me. They weren't exactly pleased to see me, either. More like lying in wait to tear out my throat. One of them almost succeeded, too." Hunt turned his

head to show Knox the deep, bleeding scratches on his throat.
There were several puncture wounds, too.

"He bit you?"

"Right as I was shifting into wolf form. But you tell anyone
and I'll kill you."

"That'll be hard for you, considering you're going to be
dead soon."

Hunt smiled tightly. "Yeah, I figured you wouldn't believe
me. That's why I kept hold of this." Hunt held up a small vial
containing a bluish liquid.

Knox kept his body relaxed, fighting the urge to snatch the
liquid from Hunt's fingers. "What do you have there? Looks a
little like mouthwash."

Hunt sighed. "Look, I transformed into a wolf in order to
save my ass. Escaped into the woods with this thing in my
mouth. You ever try to run with glass in your mouth, knowing
if it broke you might be dead a million times over? If this shit
didn't kill me first, I knew you'd get the job done."

"You haven't convinced me yet."

Hunt casually tossed the vial in the air and caught it in his
hand while Knox followed the movement and held his breath.
"Okay, then how about this? I was injured. Dazed."

"I didn't see any blood."

"Doesn't mean there wasn't any." Hunt shrugged. "Ask the
vamps when you see them. Maybe they took the time to clean
up. You are a fastidious lot, aren't you?"

Knox scowled. "Go on."

"I made it into the forest. Had to go long distance because
they were after me. I lost them. I passed out for a while. By the
time I came to and came out to find you all, I see a vamp popping in and out with the team. It looked like you, so I figured
it *was* you."

"So why didn't you come forward?"

"Because then I saw Red and another vamp that looked a
hell of a lot like you. I was, to put it mildly, a little stunned."

Knox took a deep breath. Hunt was right. By the time he'd

teleported O'Flare out, his father had ingested enough of Felicia's blood that his malnourishment had already begun to reverse itself. He had looked startlingly like Knox, which had only confused Knox more. As he'd told Noella, he knew there was no way to turn a human into a vamp without resulting in the turner's death. What vamp had sacrificed himself for his father?

"Anyway, I saw the dude teleport away with Red. That normally wouldn't be enough to convince me it was you, except for the fact she went willingly. She wrapped her arms around his neck and rested her head on his chest, oh so close. Mighty strange if the vamp wasn't you, I figured. But then you showed up, freaking out and running around like you'd just had your heart ripped from your chest. Needless to say, I was a bit confused. I waited until you were distracted and knocked you out, figuring I'd find out whether you were the real Knox Devereaux or not. Turns out you are."

With those words, he extended the vial toward Knox.

Slowly, Knox reached for it, half expecting Hunt to snatch it back and laugh. Instead, Hunt's palm didn't move. Knox picked up the vial and stared at it. He smiled and nearly rolled his eyes. It was labeled, VAMP ANTIDOTE. "It's probably labeled this way to make us think it's the real thing when it's not."

Hunt stretched his back, wincing slightly. "Oh, it's the real thing."

"How do you know that?"

"Because I lifted it from the head vamp that was giving the orders to rip my throat out."

"Head vamp?" Knox said, carefully closing his fingers around the vial before slipping it into his pocket.

"Yeah." Hunt turned to Knox. "Some guy the others called Prime."

Closing his eyes, Knox pictured Felicia cutting open her vein to feed his father and his father transforming as a result of that. "So my father was telling the truth."

And maybe he'd been telling the truth about not being a traitor, too.

"So, we going to go track down this Prime dude?"

Hesitating, Knox fingered the tube of antidote in his pocket. Again, Noella's voice echoed in his head.

She's not taking my place, Knox. She's taking her rightful place. I know you don't believe, even now. So ask the were.

"We're definitely going to track Prime down. But first, I need to ask you something."

Hunt planted his hands on his hips. "Ask then, but ask fast. 'Cause I'm really burning to show Prime what happens when he messes with this were."

"I love Felicia, but I have two problems. First, whether or not the antidote killed the scientists, we have to test it. If it really is dangerous, I can't in good conscience let it be used yet. That means my clan isn't going to get better. Not for a while. Even without considering that, I still have a duty to make sure it grows in numbers. Second, if by some miracle Felicia survives all this and still wants to be with me"—Knox winced as he remembered how he'd rejected her and, worse, how he'd pushed her down—"I don't know if making her part of my life would be in her best interest. Not anymore. I can't believe I'm asking this, but someone I trust seems to think you can give me some guidance. So what do you think?"

"You're serious?"

"Damn it, don't make me ask again, Hunt."

"Okay, okay." Hunt held out his hand. "Easy with the red eyes. I'm just surprised. It's not like I've had much luck with commitment, either."

Something in Hunt's voice suggested the were was downplaying his experience in that arena. Before Knox could ask him to explain, Hunt spoke.

"Okay, look, the whole reason we've been brought together is because there's always going to be someone willing to hurt someone else to get what they want, right?"

"Right," Knox said slowly, confused by Hunt's sudden topic change.

"You know that old saw about nurture and nature? Who's born bad and who's taught to be that way?"

Knox nodded.

"I believe everyone is capable of turning evil. Maybe it's a case of good to bad, or bad to badder, but it's in all of us. A lot of these humans and Others who are stirring shit up weren't born bad, they're just responding to a need that isn't being met."

"What kind of need?"

"Whatever. In a vamp's case, maybe it's hunger. In a shape-shifter's, acceptance. Or in a were's case, maybe it's"—Hunt looked away and shrugged—"maybe it's revenge. Unmet needs can make a person crazy. Make him do things he'd never thought possible."

"So how does this help me with Felicia?"

"Felicia's your need, man."

Stunned, Knox stared at the were, who smiled tightly.

"Yeah, sorry to get all woo-woo on your ass, but it's true. Sure, you have lots of needs. You need to love and take care of your family. Same with your clan. You need to lead by example and serve society and do your duty and all that shit." Hunt rubbed his hand against the back of his neck. "Heck, I think you've even needed to be a pain in my side ever since we met. But your true weakness? The one thing that you'll always need, the one thing that'll drive you over the edge someday if you don't have her, is Felicia. And you're her weakness, too. So what does that tell you?"

"It tells me I'm fucked," Knox said.

Hunt grinned widely. "Yeah, but if you play your cards right, it's gonna be in the best way possible."

TWENTY-EIGHT

Knox and the other Para-Ops team members, minus Felicia, strode into the Vamp Council's morning session. They were followed by a group of Knox's royal guard, stunners at the ready.

There were nine elders in all. All of them stood at their entrance. Knox instantly saw the confusion and fear in Prime's eyes and smiled grimly.

When he'd returned with Hunt to the Dome, there'd been no sign of Felicia or his father. Knox had sworn the other team members to secrecy, not wanting to upset his mother or get her hopes up until they were able to locate them. Then he'd gathered the guards and filled them in on what was going to happen.

Zachariah Commons, a vamp who'd served on the Council a hundred years before Prime, glowered at him. "What is the meaning of this, Knox? We're in session, about to sign the law prohibiting nonvamp marriages."

Knox looked down at Commons. "Good thing I came in time to stop you. Because frankly, such a move would be foolhardy, as well as a complete waste of time, considering I'll be marrying a human shortly."

Commons gasped and clutched at his heart as if he could really be struck down by a heart attack. "How dare you? You know your duty demands you mate with a vamp. Or are you saying you'll marry the human but agree to the mating-pairs?"

"No mating-pairs for old Knox here," Hunt said, slapping a hand on Knox's shoulder. "This vamp is taking the plunge dreaded by all bachelors since the beginning of time, which includes the vow of monogamy. Granted, Red's worth it but—"

Knocking Hunt's hand off him, Knox growled, "Hunt . . ."

Prime stood but paled and fell back in his seat when Knox moved toward him. He raised his chin, quivering though it was, and struggled to speak. "This—this man found out his father, Jacques Devereaux, is alive. Someone turned him into a vamp and for all we know, it could have been him. He—"

The rest of the Council stared at Prime as if he'd gone mad. Knox, however, just stared at him in amazement. By his own words, Prime had just admitted he knew Jacques Devereaux was alive *and* a vamp. He'd confirmed what his father had accused him of.

Realizing his mistake, Prime shook his head. "I mean—I mean—"

"What's this about Jacques Devereaux?" Commons asked. "You told us long ago he'd been executed, Prime. And we all know it's impossible to turn a human into a vamp without dying yourself. Yet here Knox stands before me."

Knox frowned. *Had* Prime told them his father had been executed, or had they all just assumed the execution had been carried out as planned? Since Vamps couldn't lie, Prime couldn't have actually *said* he'd seen Jacques Devereaux beheaded. After all, he couldn't lie outright. Even now he'd said the turning *could've been* done by Knox, which suggested Prime didn't even know who'd turned his father. Ignorance and evasion, but not outright deception.

Prime cowered back when Knox slammed his palms on the table in front of him and leaned down until his face was just inches away.

"I'm going to enjoy ripping your heart out, Prime. But first, I need information. Where is Kyle Mahone?"

Prime puffed out his chest and raised his brows imperiously.

Reaching out, Knox grabbed Prime's medallion and ripped it off him.

"Knox! Have you gone mad?" Commons moved to grab him, as did several others on the Council. Before he could, Hunt, O'Flare, Wraith, and Lucy restrained them. Growls erupted from the vamps' throats until Knox ordered his guards, "Shoot any vamp who tries to stop me."

The growls stopped and all the Council members stood still, watching Knox carefully. Knox ripped off Prime's shirt, then stripped him of the rest of his clothes to make sure, like Lesander, the vamp wasn't hiding gold anywhere else on him. When Prime was wearing nothing but his shorts, Knox taunted, "Although I don't doubt for a moment you'd shove gold up your ass and enjoy it, I'm sure no one wants to see anything more." Knox tapped Prime's mind not just for Mahone's secrets, but for everything in it. He delved deeper than he'd ever delved before, making no allowances for the vamp's privacy or for his mental well-being, either.

What Knox read was horrifying and it was enough to shame him.

His mother had been right. Jacques Devereaux hadn't been a traitor. He'd simply been a human torn between two races—his own and that of the vampire he loved. Moreover, because Prime had convinced other vamps to turn humans and a few of the turners had survived the process, Prime suspected it was actually Bianca who'd turned her human husband into a moite. The possibility stunned Knox but not as much as the knowledge that Prime had been using the newly turned vamps for his own purposes. There were now leagues of vampires, original and turned, that posed a growing danger to humans, particularly if the vamp antidote worked.

With a growl of disgust, Knox disengaged. As soon as he did, Prime stared at him vacantly, obviously shaken by the depth to which Knox had probed his mind. Mercilessly, Knox pierced the vamp with persuasion—forcing him to feel fear and, yes, the type of shame he'd never otherwise feel on his own.

"The shape-shifter was telling the truth about Lafleur being dead," Knox told the team, "but he was alive when he helped kill the scientists. They didn't die from taking the damn antidote; that was just a line of bullshit Prime planted. In addition, what he didn't tell us was that Mahone killed Lafleur. Of course, Prime punished Mahone for that, but they've kept him alive—barely—in case they need him in the future. Plus, Mahone has more secrets in him, which they've slowly been trying to extract. Somehow, however, no matter how many vamps have tried, they haven't been able to access Malone's mind completely." Not even Prime knew about Bianca's relationship with Mahone. However he was doing it, Mahone was continuing to protect Knox's mother.

Knox looked at O'Flare. "He left Mahone in the same warehouse where those scientists died."

O'Flare nodded. "I'll contact Team Blue immediately." Releasing the vamp he'd been holding and shoving him into a chair, O'Flare strode outside.

Knox took in the rest of the Council. "Now, gentlemen, I apologize for any embarrassment this is going to cause you, but I'm going to need each of you to take off your medallions and allow me to probe your minds. If anyone objects, they'll be stripped down just like Prime. I hope we can avoid that."

As one, the Council's gazes moved to Prime, whose soundless whimpers and frantic tics outwardly revealed the emotions he was still experiencing. Commons stood and slipped his medallion off, then tossed it to Knox. "I'll go first."

Knox dipped his head. "Thank you, Councilmember Com—"

The door to the chambers swung open once more. Knox blinked.

In the doorway stood a vamp looking as powerful as any he'd ever seen. Next to him stood Bianca. Knox inhaled sharply at the vision of his mother, radiating all the things that had been taken from her not just in the past ten years, but in the past three hundred, ever since his father had been taken from them. Health. Vitality. Beauty. Joy.

Knox grinned. "Hello, Mother." Knox turned to the man he'd thought he would never see again. "Hello, Father. You're just in time to take over, but first I need you to answer one question for me."

His father lifted a brow, but the small smile on his face told Knox he already knew what he was going to ask. Knox didn't bother to account for technicalities. Felicia was his and she'd always been his. That was why, when he asked his question, he referred to her the way he'd always thought of her.

"Where the fuck is my wife?"

The world had turned red. Everything he saw, which was very little given how swollen his eyes were, was tinged in varying degrees of scarlet and brick and, yes, even pink. Mahone bit back a groan when he felt the damn vamp prodding at his brain again, trying to suck out the information that Mahone was stubbornly clinging to.

National secrets.

Personal secrets.

Secrets that, if revealed, would result in the deaths of so many.

Maybe even the death of Bianca and her clan.

They'd gotten the information about the Para-Ops team, Barker, and the scientists because Mahone hadn't had enough time to train his brain to suppress those memories. Not surprisingly, they had no knowledge of his bargain with the Goddess and he assumed that was through her own doing, not his. But they obviously wanted more. More than the vamp antidote. More than a preliminary alliance with the vamps that would ultimately be used to infiltrate them.

Otherwise, they would have killed him hours ago.

Clenching his jaw against a sudden spike in pain, Mahone sensed the blessed darkness closing in on him again. Once again, he fought it off. He couldn't pass out. He couldn't sleep. He wouldn't be able to block his thoughts if he did.

Bianca had taught him to do it for a reason. He couldn't betray her. Not again.

"And what of me, Mahone? You give no thought to our bargain? To how your brethren will surely perish once you're dead, dead because you wanted to protect one vampire?"

Mahone's head jerked to the right, his blind eyes trying fruitlessly to focus on the soft, feminine voice, even though he knew it was in his own head or coming from a transparent visage that he wouldn't want to look upon anyway.

Once had been quite enough.

Light flashed behind his lids, dispersing red in favor of white. Instantly, his pain was gone, his consciousness separated from his body as if he'd been given a high-octane painkiller.

Damn it, go away, he tried to yell. He didn't want her here, cajoling him to let the bastards rape his mind so he could continue doing her bidding.

She made a sound that, oddly enough, sounded like an indulgent chuckle. "Very well. But your shields won't last for long, Mahone. Not without more." He flinched when he felt her breath against his face, fire and ice, burning his skin as sensation returned.

"Who . . . Why . . . ?" he managed to choke out, even though he didn't really believe she'd tell him who she was or why she'd really come to him. However, he didn't need her to give him answers. He had a pretty good idea who she was. He had from the very beginning.

She was the Earth Goddess Essenia.

The deity most of the Others worshipped but few had claimed to meet.

The Goddess who, despite her threats, must have sought Mahone out in order to save her creatures, not kill them. But the fact that she needed to prove a prophesy true to save them, the fact she'd needed to come to Mahone at all, made him wonder if it was really *her* they needed to fear, or someone else.

Someone higher up on the totem pole, so to speak.

Someone or something . . .

The pain he felt ratcheted up several notches, making him gasp.

"You're smart, Mahone, but you need to save your strength for your current situation rather than figuring out the meaning of life. Just don't put me in the role of savior. Not yet. My anger is real. My vengeance unimaginable. But I want you to have your year. So reach for the pain, Mahone. Focus on it. On me. On how much you hate me and what I'm making you do. Reach for it."

When the light faded, he automatically mourned it. Was tempted to follow. But he didn't. Instead, he did what she'd told him to do.

He reached for the pain. Focused on it. Bit his tongue. Immersed himself in sensation until it became his entire world. Until he could hear his own crazed shouts echoing around him. Until even the vamp trying to read his mind had to back off or risk that the pain radiating from Mahone would enter his own body.

And when the pain eased slightly and he heard the muddled sounds of voices, Mahone marveled at the fact that he could actually open his eyes and see the two males in front of him.

"It's no use. The bastard's too strong."

The vamp he'd never seen before turned to the man dressed in "Caribbean Joe" casual, the one the vamp called Smith. With balding hair and wire-rimmed spectacles, the man looked harmless despite the great power he wielded. He was the beginning and ending of pain. He was the bigger motive behind all of this.

"I have a plane to catch," Smith said with obvious disgust. "Before I do, I want word that he's dead. Do we understand each other?"

"Yes, sir. But what about Prime? He wanted to interrogate Mahone—"

"Dante Prime thinks he's in charge here, but we both know that's not true, now don't we? Do you have a problem with that?"

The vamp didn't answer and the reason was obvious. He didn't want to admit he had a problem and risk pissing off the boss, but he couldn't lie either.

Smith obviously came to the same conclusions. "You'll be well compensated for obeying me, I assure you. If not with money, then with more blood. *Pure* blood. Remember?"

"Yes," the vamp answered, obviously properly swayed.

Leaning against an intricately carved wooden cane, Smith pivoted and slowly began to walk away. Gasping and gurgling past the blood in his mouth, Mahone had to try several times before he could be heard. "Who?" It came out as barely a whisper. The next word came out only slightly louder. "Why?"

The man with the cane stopped. He didn't turn to face Mahone, but his voice drifted back to him, clear and concise. "We're a quorum, Mahone. A unified front. We're here and we're everywhere. And we want things back to the way they were. If the FBI won't give it to us, we'll get there ourselves, one painful step at a time."

He finally turned and smiled, and it was the kind of smile one gave a friend. "You're spoken well of, Mahone. I regret things had to end this way for you."

Mahone didn't even bother looking at the vamp who was surely sharpening his fangs in anticipation of ripping Mahone's throat out. At least the pain would end now. But not yet. He couldn't let it go yet.

He'd hang on to it until the breath left his body. That way, no stray memories would sneak out to endanger those Mahone loved.

Hanging his head, Mahone sighed. This time, however, when the blackness called out to him, he almost couldn't fight it back. Just when he thought he was going to lose, he heard shouts and a commotion.

Hands touched him. His binds loosened. Voices called out.

One voice Mahone recognized.

He couldn't move. He couldn't open his eyes. He could barely gather the energy to breathe. But he heard O'Flare's voice just the same.

"We're here, Mahone. We made it back. And we got the antidote."

TWENTY-NINE

After feeding Bianca, Felicia had gone to the nursery to rest. Twenty minutes later, she still felt weak, even though Bianca had been careful to drink only a few sips from her vein. Apparently, it didn't require a huge amount of pure blood to strengthen a vamp, but Felicia had given her blood to quite a few of them in the past twenty-four hours. Even so, her body didn't feel half as weak as her soul did at the moment.

She'd at least hoped to see Thomas and Joelle one last time before she left, but they weren't there. Serena had probably taken them out into the garden to enjoy some fresh air and sun. It was a beautiful day, after all, poetically reflecting the fact that Knox's father had reunited with his wife just as he should have long ago.

Seeing Jacques and Bianca together and in full health had been almost more than she could bear. The sheer love and happiness that had radiated from them had served only to remind her why a union between her and Knox could never be. Sure, Jacques had been human. Once. But look how that had turned out. Now that he was a vamp, he would help Bianca lead her clan. Just because Knox would be relieved of that duty didn't mean he could abandon all the other responsibilities he had to the clan.

The antidote wasn't going to save his people, at least not yet. Although Felicia had pure blood, she wasn't stupid. It might not last. Or she could be dead tomorrow because of the antidote. Besides, even if the antidote turned out to be completely safe, she couldn't give vamps blood at enough volume or enough frequency to save the entire clan. And it wasn't like the vamp clan was going to suddenly suffer from a population explosion just because they got healthy. That meant Knox would still be duty-bound to produce children with another vamp.

Throwing herself on Joelle's bed and burying her face in the girl's pillow, Felicia sobbed. She told herself to be honest for once. If it was just the issue of his fidelity, Felicia knew she'd no longer fight it. She loved Knox so much that she'd rather share him than lose him.

But the truth was, Knox no longer wanted her.

He couldn't. Not when he'd looked at her with such disdain and pushed her away from him.

She had to accept that. She needed to learn to live without Knox, just as she should have learned to long ago.

"I probably shouldn't be thinking what I'm thinking, not given where we are, but that's the thing about you. I see you and reason flies out the window."

Felicia froze and slowly lifted her head. Knox was sitting on Thomas's bed, which was no more than five feet from Joelle's bed. She inhaled his wonderful mint smell and had to blink back the fresh wave of tears that filled her eyes. Pressing her lips together, she swiped at her face and stood. "Your father didn't betray your clan. He and your mother will explain everything, but I'm leaving—"

Knox pulled her into his arms and kissed her. His lips, his tongue, his fangs—each fully participated, urging—no, *begging*—for her to respond. To reciprocate. Automatically, she did.

While she was still reeling from shock, he gave her another one. Her muscles tightened as they teleported, then her body sank into something soft and luxurious. Knox was on top of her, covering her with his warm, sheltering presence even as he continued to kiss her greedily. Desperately.

Wanting only to keep kissing him, Felicia nonetheless pulled her mouth from Knox's and pushed against his shoulders. Finally, he backed off and rested his forehead against hers, breathing harshly. Felicia realized he'd teleported them into his bedroom.

Of course, she assumed it was his bedroom. She'd never actually been in it. Fearfully, her eyes took in everything, dreading the moment when she'd see Noella's things or her picture. She'd loved her friend totally, but to see her now, here—

"I didn't share this room with Noella."

Her gaze snapped guiltily to Knox's. She tried so hard to appear unconcerned. "It wouldn't matter if you had. She was your wife, after all. I'm nothing to you. Less than nothing. You proved that in North Korea."

Although his expression hardened, Knox eased himself off her. When she scrambled away from him and tried to stand, however, he took her arm. "Nope. You're not getting away that easy."

She wrenched her arm away and, in two seconds flat, she had him on his back on the bed, straddling him. Too late she realized he wasn't exactly displeased. He grabbed her wrists before she could move off him.

"You have to know how sorry I am for what I did. For how I hurt you. I never wanted to hurt you, Felicia. I was just so confused by what was happening. By what I saw as Mahone's betrayal. By being reminded of my father's—"

"Yes, well, those are humans for you. Completely untrustworthy. Which is why I forgive you. You can't help how you feel about me, right?" Angrily, she fought him harder, trying to get away so she could scream out her grief in private. When she almost succeeded in freeing her wrists, Knox rolled so that she was once again under him.

"Do you want to know how I feel about you? I feel like you're the only thing that's keeping me from ripping out my own heart and killing myself, that's how I feel about you."

Stunned, she stopped struggling to stare up at him.

"Don't get me wrong, Felicia. I love my children. I love my family and my clan. But sometimes the responsibility of being everything to them has made me want to just end it all. Want to hear how else I'm fucked up? Sometimes I was almost jealous of my mother's and my brother's weakness, because it relieved them of the responsibility that I was beginning to resent. Hell, that I already resented. Because that responsibility was what was keeping me from you and I couldn't take that. That's why I tried to include you in my deal with Mahone. That's why I kept pursuing you when I knew you just wanted me to leave you alone. Because I knew, whether by my own hand or someone else's, I was going to die without you. The fact that you're human has absolutely nothing to do with any of that."

Felicia felt his words soften her heart. She felt the hope that sprang to life inside her like a flower pushing through its bulb, reaching out for the sunshine that beckoned it. "How can I believe that now?"

"I don't know. But I'm hoping it'll help that I've already informed the Council that I'm going to marry you. With both my parents' blessing, by the way."

Stunned, Felicia was sure she'd misheard him. "You told them—what? You told them we were going to be married?"

He smoothed back her hair and kissed her lips, a gentle butterfly kiss that had her lips automatically pursing in return. "I know I should have waited until you accepted my proposal, but at the time there were so many things I had to attend to first."

"What do you expect me to . . ."

Knox slipped away from her, and despite herself, Felicia grabbed at him, tightening her hold on his shirt desperately.

"Shhh," he soothed. "It's okay. I'm not going anywhere. Just let me do this. I've wanted to do it for so long."

Hesitantly, she released him and let him slip off the bed. She pushed herself to a sitting position and swung her legs to the side, freezing when Knox bent down on one knee. He held out a ring, one she'd never seen before, that sparkled with the fire of several diamonds.

"Felicia Locke, will you do me the honor of being my wife and the only female I'll ever love throughout all eternity?"

Felicia couldn't take her eyes off the ring he held out. It almost seemed to blind her, when in truth she knew her tears were what made her vision blurry. Finally, she met his gaze.

"I'm going to die before you . . ." she whispered.

Smiling, Knox shook his head. "By only a few seconds at the most, I'm sure. I won't be able to live without you, immortal or not."

"I—I—won't give up my job. I'm a good agent—"

"The best. That's why you'll continue to serve under me."

She cocked a brow at that. "Under you?"

Knox shrugged and stood. "Of course. I know perfectly well that's your favorite position anyway."

Her hand trembled as he took it and held the ring just at the tip of her finger.

"I want babies," she choked out. "Lots of dharmires who can play in the sun and laugh at the stories that Thomas and Joelle will tell them. Not stories of past betrayals or regrets, but of trust and hope for the future."

"I'll give you lots of babies and it'll be my absolute pleasure to do so. Now, all you have to do is say yes."

Felicia hesitated, not because she doubted what her answer would be in any way. She hesitated because her thoughts turned once again to Noella and the conversation they'd shared in her dream.

Now, remember, Felicia. A vamp can't lie. So when I say I want you and Knox to be happy together, in every way possi-

ble, you know I'm telling the truth, isn't that right? Then Noella had left, but not before saying, *Take care of my babies for me. And take care of Knox.*

I do believe you, Noella, Felicia thought. I promise I'll take care of them. And thank you.

With a whisper of what could only be Noella's laughter tinkling in her ear, Felicia said, "Yes," and slipped her finger into Knox's ring.

"Mahone has been rescued and Dante Prime has been taken into custody," Isaac Smith confirmed. "But as we planned, Prime knows nothing about any of you, my true identity, or that of my main source of information."

"And what about your source of information?" a man, his face displayed on one of Smith's twelve video screens, asked. "How can you be sure he wasn't compromised? That he hasn't given the FBI the details that might have them knocking on all our doors within the hour?"

Murmurs of agreement and concern drifted from the screens depicting the other Quorum members. Although they didn't know each other's identities, Isaac did. That was what made Isaac's life so valuable and his job so dangerous. His continued vitality depended on his ability to give the Quorum what it needed. Anonymity. Maneuverability.

Immunity.

Unfortunately, Isaac was one man. A human. A smart one, yes, but one who needed allies he could, if not trust, at least use until their usefulness wore out.

"My source left well before the Para-Ops team arrived. I left one vamp behind. He, unlike my main informant, is dispensable."

"But was he captured? He might be dispensable, but how do you know he won't talk? Or be forced to reveal his thoughts?"

"Again, he doesn't know enough to implicate us. In any event, after Prime was detained, my main informant reported to me immediately. He has proven himself loyal to our cause. Nothing in that regard has changed."

"What of the North Koreans?" The question came from the Quorum's sole female member. "Do they suspect anything?"

"No. As far as they're concerned, the Bureau infiltrated the compound and took back the antidote as well as the imprisoned Others, end of story. I've assured them that while they no longer have proprietary possession of the vamp antidote, we will continue to finance their experiments with the Others. Of course, they will continue to forward us their results."

"This is a major setback, Smith." This time, the statement came from a man with a distinct Texan accent.   .

"But only that. A setback," Smith assured him. "The Bureau knows nothing about us or our contact within the Devereaux clan." Even as he said it, Smith cursed his parting statements to Mahone. He'd been vague, but Mahone was smart. Plus, Mahone had seen his face. That did complicate things, even though he would never admit it. And of course, he'd changed his appearance in the past. He could do so again, especially given the amount of money the Quorum was paying him.

"I think we should let things lie with the vamps for now," Quorum's female said. "Focus on other things."

"But we're making progress . . ." Smith began, even as he knew protesting would be futile. The Quorum was rattled, and when rattled, its instinct was to lie low.

"The felines perhaps," she said. Her suggestion was followed by murmurs of agreement.

Smith sighed and, not wanting to push too hard, gave in gracefully. "Perhaps you're right. We'll put our focus elsewhere and see what comes of the vamp antidote. Who knows, maybe there will be a disastrous side effect, after all."

Smith pressed the button that made all the video screens go blank.

Instantly, the male behind him tsked. "Let things lie with the vamps, did she say? I'm not sure I agree, Smith. And leaving disaster to chance has never been my cup of tea."

Turning, Smith countered, "Prime's detainment is going to mean increased scrutiny for many months—maybe even years—to come. We need to be patient. Take time to assess. Especially now that the vamp clan's leadership is shifting. You've regained your full strength, so perhaps your own skills will be recognized . . ." Smith's voice trailed off at the vamp's snort.

"I maintain my anonymity, yes. Neither Prime nor Mahone ever saw me in a situation that would implicate me or connect us. They have no idea I'm working with you. But I'll be dealing with the fallout of my father's actions, which will place unwanted scrutiny upon me. Something tells me I'm going to learn firsthand exactly what my brother has had to deal with all these years. Lucky for me," Zeph Prime said as he stood, "I've always known what a bastard my father was." The vamp nodded at Smith. "Fine. Focus on the felines. But I'll expect the Quorum to deposit funds into my account every month as always."

"Of course," Smith replied. "Tell me, though. Why didn't you kill Felicia when your cousins had her? Why not your brother?"

"Because if I'd tried to kill either one of them, my cover would be blown. And I wasn't about to rely on my dumb-ass cousins to do the job. Certainly not when they don't even know of my connection to the Quorum. I want separatism between Others and humans, but I want to maintain my status in my world, not destroy it."

Smith nodded. "Don't worry, Zeph. As I said, this is only a slight setback. Otherborn unity is continuing to fracture. In time, the Quorum's mission will be accomplished and things will be back the way they should be—with humans and Others living separately."

"Yes," Zeph agreed. "Separately. As it should be. Every human and Otherborn for himself."

EPILOGUE

E ven as she arched her neck to give Knox easier access, Felicia said, "Are you sure you want to risk being accused of rudeness? I know how vamps feel about decorum, especially on special occasions. What will our guests think when the bride and the groom don't show up for their own wedding reception?"

"Fuck what the guests think," Knox growled before sinking his teeth into Felicia's throat and drawing on her deeply. She hissed at the pleasure and pushed his face deeper into her throat, just as she tightened her legs around his waist and pulled him deeper inside her.

Knox groaned when she clenched her muscles around his shaft, clearly overcome by the feel of the wet, heated pressure gripping him like a glove that was two sizes too small. Her repeated gasps, which kept time with the heavy thrusts of his hips, answered his desire with her own, assuring him that she was getting closer and closer to peaking.

Devilishly, he gripped her face and plunged his tongue into her mouth, plumbing every inch of it even as he slowed down.

She whimpered, reluctant to let the promise of such intense pleasure diminish, but he raised his head and sprinkled kisses on her face. "Soon," he whispered. "But not now. Not yet. I don't want this to end."

She took in several deep breaths, then nodded. Raising a hand, she caressed his brow, which was covered in sweat, just like the rest of him. Her own sweaty limbs trembled even as they clasped him tighter, refusing to let go in spite of the exhaustion that tinged the pleasure he was giving her. He'd been pushing them both for hours, refusing to withdraw from her body for even a moment.

"My wife," he said with the same awed reverence he'd been using all evening. "My wife. You're my wife. Always, Felicia. From the first time I saw you. From the first time we kissed and I entered your body. You've always been mine. Today we just confirmed it in front of everyone else."

"Yes," Felicia wailed out as the tip of his cock hit her cervix, sparking inside her the same intense sensation that was filling her heart. She was his. She'd always be his, just as he would always be hers.

She wanted all the pleasure he could give her, as well.

Straining closer to him, she bit his throat, certain that the feel of her blunt teeth nipping at his skin would send him hurtling out of control. Sure enough, his eyes flashed red and his muscles pumped up, something he allowed now but had obviously held back when they'd been together in Quantico. The first time he'd let it happen, she'd been furious at the realization that he'd held back from her, that even when they'd made love in the past, he'd had the control to hold back a part of himself.

As soon as their orgasms had waned and she'd regained her strength, she'd fought him like a tiger. Biting and scratching him until he'd subdued her with his body and the hard thrust of his dick inside her, pinning her to the bed. He'd driven her to another screaming orgasm. Afterward, he'd held her in his arms, whispering his apology and swearing he'd never hold back from her again.

Not now. Not now that they were finally together.

Sure enough, he wasn't holding back, at least in that sense. But even as his body transformed, even as he grew heavier and thicker and harder inside her, he still maintained control over his slow thrusts. With his teeth clenched and his expression tightened into one of pain, he withdrew from her completely only to push slowly inside her again.

"Why? Why are you waiting?" she moaned.

He opened his eyes, blinking against the sweat that dripped into them, and smiled faintly. "Because I love how you fight me for it. And how good it feels when you stop fighting."

She narrowed her eyes at him and tried to push him away. His dark laugh shivered through her even as he clenched her hips tighter, forcing her to take all of him. She held her breath and moaned at the feel of his cock tunneling into her. But she gave him what he wanted.

Every time he withdrew, dragging against the walls of her channel and shooting pleasure through every part of her, she squeezed her muscles tighter, not just in an attempt to keep his thick cock inside her swollen, fluttering flesh, but because, as he'd said, it would heighten their pleasure when he returned. As her body initially rejected him, he responded by pushing even harder to get inside her. And as his thrusts got harder, they got quicker, too.

Soon, he was out of control, fucking her with frantic, pounding thrusts of his hips that she answered with her own. "I love you," she moaned out even as she opened her arms to an orgasm so powerful she saw her tremors shimmer through his own body.

"My wife," he chanted as he continued to thrust. "Love you. My wife." With one last thrust, he froze and arched his head back, the muscles in his throat straining as he groaned and emptied himself inside her.

They held one another for what seemed like hours. Felicia relished every second, just as she always would. She'd never take a moment of her life with Knox for granted because, in her heart, she knew someday death would take her from him. That is, it would separate them until he joined her in the Otherworld, which, given he was immortal, could be a very long time.

Despite what he'd said about her death preceding his by only seconds, despite the fact he'd begged her to let him, she'd refused to let him turn her. She'd done so despite the fact they both *believed* Knox's death was only a possibility rather than a foregone conclusion. First, no matter what anyone speculated, Bianca never had and never would confirm she'd actually turned Knox's father. According to Jacques, she'd take that secret to the grave, passing it on to her eventual successor the way she was supposed to, in a ritualistic ceremony complete with sealed, confidential documents. Second, a vampire who turned another might not automatically die, but the risk was still there; Felicia wouldn't risk Knox's life, *ever*, even if failing to do so deprived her of an eternity with him.

Knox would, however, always be part of her, whether she existed in this world or the Other one.

Tightening her arms around him, she pressed her lips to his temple. "My husband," Felicia sighed. "My love for all eternity."

Lucy was sipping at her Shirley Temple, watching the wedding guests, Others and humans alike, boogey on the dance floor to the classic wedding tune, "YMCA." Wraith, of course, was in the middle of it all, her face wreathed in smiles until she happened to lock eyes with O'Flare, who was dancing in the corner of the dance floor with a petite feline with long chestnut hair streaked with caramel and blond highlights. Sighing, Lucy shook her head fondly. O'Flare was such a bonehead sometimes.

And speaking of boneheads? Lucy scanned the room, decorated in the frills and flowers that Felicia had insisted on, for Hunt. She hadn't seen him at the ceremony, but she'd hoped he'd at least attend the reception. Even though she should accept he hadn't come, for some reason she didn't want to. Accepting that left her with the image of Hunt sitting at some bar, alone, knocking back a beer. While there was nothing wrong with that, Lucy couldn't help thinking this was a time for all of them to be together. Excluding Knox and Felicia, of course, who could be forgiven for their absence.

Giving up the search for Hunt, Lucy stood and joined everyone on the dance floor. She was just beginning to enjoy herself when the band switched to a slow song. Wraith immediately left the floor, not sticking around to see the feline slip out of O'Flare's arms or, a minute later, see O'Flare walk across the room, as far from Wraith as he could get. Shaking her head, Lucy moved back to the bar and watched Knox's father hold Bianca Devereaux close. If all eyes weren't on the couple, they should have been, Lucy thought.

Their love was a beautiful sight. A true miracle.

About thirty minutes later, a movement at the edge of the dance floor caught her eye. It was Mahone. She thought he'd left a long time ago, but— Lucy flinched at the raw agony that was on the man's face. Before she could stop herself, before she could weigh the rightness of her actions, she reached out and enchanted him. Just enough so the pain raging inside him wouldn't hurt quite so bad. Mahone turned and looked at her. For a second, his gaze pinned her in place, his expression grim. She assumed he'd felt her magic and was angry with her. But then he smiled thinly, tipped his head, and mouthed a thank-you. He strode swiftly toward Wraith, who was looking a little shell-shocked. Lucy wondered why. She'd seen her dancing with a handsome vamp, then Wraith and O'Flare had talked for a bit. Predictably, it was only a short time later that they'd separated, O'Flare going in one direction while Wraith had gone in the other. Lucy had thought Wraith had gone outside for some fresh air, but maybe . . . Had she and O'Flare snuck away together?

Lucy felt a spurt of jealousy as she remembered the way O'Flare had kissed Wraith in Korea. She hated her pettiness, but she couldn't help how she felt, could she?

She watched as Mahone and Wraith spoke. The longer they spoke, the louder Wraith's voice became. Lucy walked quickly toward them. In her periphery, she saw O'Flare heading that way, as well. As she reached them, Wraith said, "Don't you tell me this takes precedence over my wants, Mahone. We had a deal, and the deal was the team would get the information I need."

Mahone nodded, clearly trying to appease the wraith. "And this doesn't change that, Wraith. You've earned the information, no one's saying otherwise. But whoever's drugging and raping the werecats has escalated things so that the whole feline community is out for blood. If we don't give it to them, they're going to turn on us. I need the Para-Ops team to settle the situation and then it can focus on your needs."

"Maybe that's not good enough," Wraith hissed with a scowl. "Maybe I want someone to acknowledge that my needs are the most important thing for fucking once."

Shaking his head, Mahone said, "I'm sorry."

O'Flare reached them. "What's going on?" he asked.

Wraith turned toward him. "Nothing. Mahone here was just telling me the details of your next mission."

"*Our* next mission?" Lucy asked.

"That's right," Wraith said. "*Yours*. Because *I'm* done."

"Wraith . . ." Mahone and O'Flare said almost simultaneously.

The wraith ignored them and stomped away. O'Flare was right behind her.

Lucy looked at Mahone. "What . . ."

Mahone shook his head. "The bride and groom have arrived. I'll fill you in later. In the meantime, I need to talk some sense into Wraith. Tell Knox . . ." Mahone's gaze homed in on

Knox's mother like a heat-seeking missile. This time, his face remained expressionless, his eyes devoid of a single spark of emotion. "Tell Knox and Felicia I said congratulations." With that, Mahone strode outside.

Sighing, Lucy stared at Knox and Felicia. In addition to their matching medallions, each now wore matching rings, a simple band of gold symbolizing their never-ending love and engraved with a single word: "recognition." Felicia had shown Lucy the matching bands, but she hadn't explained the inscription.

She hadn't needed to.

Lucy pasted a smile on her face and moved toward the newly married couple to obey Mahone's orders.

Keep reading for a preview of the next novel
in Virna DePaul's Para-Ops series

CHOSEN BY FATE

Available Fall 2011 from Berkley Sensation!

SIX MONTHS LATER
AN ABANDONED WAREHOUSE
WASHINGTON, D.C.

Caleb's hands moved swiftly and efficiently as he set up the mobile radar equipment he'd spread out on the roof. The building below his feet had been swept and a perimeter established. Now all Caleb had to do was determine who was in the room with Mahone and whether Mahone was still alive.

Briefly, he glanced at Ethan Riley, leader of Hope Restored Team Blue and the four men, skilled in entry and perimeter surveillance, who'd accompanied them here. "Did you get in touch with the Para-Ops team?"

Riley looked up from checking his rifle. "They've detained the vampire Dante Prime. Devereaux said he tried to teleport here, but he'd depleted his powers in Korea . . ."

Caleb snorted. "No shit." Although vamps could teleport to and from anywhere in the world, provided they'd been there before, that kind of travel drained them. Before he and the rest of the team had interrupted the Vamp Council to question Dante Prime for treason and conspiracy to commit murder, Knox had spent several hours teleporting between North Korea and the United States. Each time, he'd carried a wounded Other or one of his team members back with him. It was a wonder the vamp was even capable of talking at this point. Add everything else that had happened to him—

"Is it true you found his father? And that he'd been turned into a vampire?"

Caleb didn't even look up. The Para-Ops team had trained with Team Blue's aerial experts before dropping into North Korea. At the time, Knox's father hadn't even been on their radar and for good reason—everyone believed he was dead. How the hell news of Jacques Devereaux's return had spread so fast, Caleb didn't know. Still, Riley had to know how fruitless his question was. "No comment."

He sensed Riley wince. "Sorry."

Caleb shrugged. Just because a person expected a particular result didn't mean he shouldn't try to get around it. Caleb was always trying to get a different reaction from his teammate Wraith, regardless of how unlikely that was. "No worries. I'm as human as you, remember?"

Now it was Riley who snorted, prompting Caleb to smile tightly.

Okay, so maybe he wasn't quite as human as Riley. They shared the same DNA but being able to communicate with his ancestors, hear the Great Song, and occasionally walk the Otherworld made him a little different.

Different didn't always mean better.

His fingers moved faster. Almost there. Glancing at his watch, Caleb clenched his teeth and felt a bead of sweat trickle down his temple. He knew they couldn't go in blind but—

"What about your wraith? Was she what you expected her to be?"

Caleb paused for only a fraction of a second before continuing his task. "She's not my wraith. She's a wraith who decided to keep the name Wraith, just to be ornery. And she's exactly what I expected her to be." What he didn't say was that she was also far more than he'd expected. A heinous bitch, yes, but one whose attitude and mouth was designed to hide something textured and complex and . . .

Disgusted with himself, Caleb pressed his lips together and pushed thoughts of Wraith out of his head.

Get Mahone out. That's all he could think about right now.

"Finally!" Snapping the last wire in place, Caleb flipped on the power and adjusted the radar settings, then scanned the building's interior until the radar picked up body heat. "Bingo."

Caleb immediately zoomed the camera in and got a good look at Mahone.

Dear Essenia, he thought, automatically invoking the name of the Earth Goddess to give him strength—strength he was clearly going to need to help Mahone. Although humans believed Essenia was an Otherborn deity, few knew Earth People—like the Native American tribe to which Caleb belonged—had prayed to the same deity for centuries.

With his wrists shackled to chains hanging from the ceiling, Mahone looked like he'd gotten into a fight with a chipper machine and lost. His face and body were covered in blood, and what was left of his clothes hung on his battered body in shreds. From his position on the rooftop above, Caleb once again adjusted the settings on the mobile radar equipment. The image on the screen zoomed out, losing detail and focus until it shaped the entire room, and provided grainy outlines of Mahone, a desk, a table, and one other individual, whose silver hair, height, and slim build proclaimed him to be a vampire.

When Caleb and the five members of Hope Restored Team Blue had arrived at the isolated warehouse twenty minutes earlier, Caleb had figured Knox, leader of the Para-Ops team, had made a mistake by not sending any Others with him. That, or Knox simply had faith in Caleb's ability to take down anything that got in their way, human or not. Either way, Caleb was getting Mahone out and he planned on both of them to be breathing when he did it.

Caleb thought of the first time he'd met Mahone and the

vision he'd had. He'd had the same vision several times since and the moment he'd met Wraith, he'd become convinced that the black-and-white aura that hovered near his own had to be hers. Upon their meeting, he'd felt a sizzling arc of connection that had only intensified with time. Apparently she hadn't. In fact, she seemed to have no use for him and spent most of her time pushing him away. Maybe the aura belonged to Mahone, instead, and the vision had been a premonition of this very moment, Mahone straddling the line between life and death, waiting to see whether Caleb could save him.

Luckily for both of them, Caleb had come prepared.

He looked at Riley. The man might be a little more chatty than Caleb liked, but he'd had no problem taking Caleb's lead on the current mission. He was smart and he was a clean shot. That's all that mattered right now. "Mahone's in bad shape. We need to get in there fast. I'm hoping the vamp will teleport as soon as he knows he has company, but I need you and your team to cover me in case he decides to stick around. Are your shooters set up around the perimeter of the room?"

"They've all checked in and are in the crawl space, with their weapons ready."

"Obviously your bullets won't kill him but, along with the Hyperion gas, they may buy me enough time to get to Mahone and extract him."

"How long does it take for the Hyperion to immobilize a vampire?"

The Hyperion was something Caleb had developed toward the end of the War. The government hadn't known about it and he'd only used it a few times before peace had been declared. The testing he'd conducted had been limited, but he felt fairly confident it would work.

At this point, he figured his odds of getting out with Mahone were only slightly below average. "Usually about sixty seconds, but that's with a vamp who's been weakened by the effects of the vampire vaccine. From the looks of this one, he's had pure blood recently. Still, he might not be at full strength."

"If the vamp's immobilized by the Hyperion, how do we keep him contained while we take him in?"

"We don't. That's not what we're here for. Our sole objective is to rescue Mahone."

Riley nodded, but looked troubled. "You said he's doing bad . . ."

Caleb tried to keep his expression blank. "Doing bad" was an understatement. Mahone probably had less than five minutes of life left in his broken body. "Just get me to him. I'll take care of it from there. You ready?"

Riley communicated with his men, then nodded. "It's a go."

Slipping the small gas pellet from his pocket, Caleb held it up. "Remember, you have to stay back. Help me hold back the vamp, then get your men out. You're maintaining the perimeter, not going in. This gas immobilizes vamps and weres, but it does far worse to humans once enough of it is absorbed in your bloodstream."

"What about you?"

"I've built up a resistance. It's not extensive, but it'll give me the five minutes I need. If we don't make it out, it'll take two hours for the gas to dissipate. Don't come into the room until that much time has passed. Understood?"

Riley nodded and held out his hand. O'Flare shook it, then strode to the door that would lead him from the roof to the room below. He moved quietly, his breathing low and shallow, his gun held at the ready with the gas pellet in his other hand. He'd activate it as soon as he got close enough and it could work its magic on the vampire.

When he entered the room, he immediately saw Mahone. Even the radar's enhanced imaging hadn't prepared him. The vampire wasn't touching him, but Mahone's facial features were contorted in agony, his body writhing and jerking even as he remained silent. Fuck, Caleb thought when he saw the blood seeping out of Mahone's eyes and ears.

"Hey vamp," he shouted at the same time he threw the pellet, which would emit a toxic but invisible gas. The vampire whirled around, his eyes flashing red the instant he saw Caleb. He bared his fangs and came at him, his feet gliding above the ground. Caleb fired a round directly at his chest, causing him to fall back. At the same time, Riley and his men fired as well. As the vamp jerked with the impact of the bullets, O'Flare ran for Mahone. He reached up and felt his pulse.

It was barely there. He literally felt the man's life bleeding out of him.

Laying his hands on Mahone's bloody chest, Caleb closed his eyes. Bullets still fired around him, some coming too damn close. Damn it, Riley's men had to get out before the gas reached them in the crawl space. "Get out!" he yelled.

"The vampire teleported," Riley shouted. "We're clear."

With a sigh of relief, Caleb willed his consciousness into a trance and called to his ancestors for their healing help. He saw them in the colors that swirled behind his eyelids and felt their presence in the heat that immediately suffused his body. Their voices chanted low and soothing, directing him to keep one hand directly over Mahone's heart but place the other over his eyes. Caleb willed the healing heat building within his body to transfer to Mahone. As it did, he took some of Mahone's pain into himself.

He felt his own heartbeat slow.

His limbs weakened.

His body began to shake with the effort of remaining upright and he clenched his teeth, sensing he needed to maintain contact far longer than he ever had.

Come on, come on, he urged himself. Hang in there.

The dizziness came next. Then the nausea. He could feel his lungs filling with the gas that swirled around them and knew his time was running out.

His body jerked as he coughed and the movement threatened to pull his hands away from Mahone.

They had to get out of there, but if he disconnected too soon it would all be for nothing. Mahone would die. Hell, Caleb would probably die, as well, too weak from the healing to get out on his own.

But then he felt Mahone's chest rising strongly and his pulse beating regularly and he knew it had worked. The heat slowly left his body and the voices of his ancestors faded. Caleb whispered his thanks, then opened his eyes. Swiftly, he reached up and unhooked Mahone's chains from the manacles around his wrists. Mahone groaned and slumped over just as O'Flare caught him and threw him fireman-style over his shoulder.

Caleb staggered a few steps before he turned, intending to carry Mahone to the doorway. Halfway there, his knees buckled. Caleb lost his grip on Mahone, and the man slipped and rolled a couple of feet away. Grunting, Caleb fell on all fours, his head hanging, his lungs seizing up.

He'd waited too long. They were both going to die in this warehouse just like those scientists. He looked up, eyes watering, searching the room, thankful that Team Blue had obeyed his orders even as he regretted the fact no one was going to be able to help him.

But then he saw her. Wraith. Running toward him. He tried to open his mouth. To yell at her to stop. He didn't know how the gas would affect a wraith. Since it worked so well on vamps, immortality had nothing to do with it. But he couldn't make a sound and Wraith kept coming. She knelt beside him and pulled him up. She was yelling something and he tried to make it out.

"—have to walk! I need to get Mahone. Can you walk, O'Flare?"

She was looking frantically between him and Mahone, the indecision on her face readily apparent. She couldn't carry them both out of there before the gas ended them.

"Leave me—" he tried to say, but again no sound came out. It didn't matter. Wraith understood.

She grabbed him by his shirt and shook him, hanging on when he began to slide, practically keeping him on his feet. "No fucking way, O'Flare. I didn't survive Korea just to come back and lose you in the States. Stay on your feet and move. You're walking out of here. Got it?"

The vehemence in her voice roused him enough to nod. She released him and, although he swayed on his feet, he didn't fall. Quickly, she grabbed Mahone, carrying him in the same lift O'Flare had used. Then amazingly, she positioned herself next to him and ordered, "Lean against me if you need to. Start walking. Now."

Caleb walked. He didn't know how he did it, but he managed to put one foot in front of the other. At one point, he did have to lean on her and he sensed how it slowed her down, but she didn't move away. She stayed with him.

Until they made it out into the open air. He heard shouts and the sound of stomping feet just as he collapsed.

When he came to, he was being loaded into an ambulance. Riley's face hovered above him. "Mahone?" Caleb rasped out.

"Still alive," Riley said. "But I don't know if he's going to stay that way."

From the worried expression on the man's face, Caleb knew his own chance of survival was also in question.

"Wraith?" he asked, grabbing on to the man's shirt when he didn't answer. "What about the wraith?"

Riley shook his head. "I don't know. She passed out, same as you. No pulse, remember? No breath. No way to tell if she's alive or dead. They took her in another cab. Your guess is as good as mine."